INHERITANCE ACCEPTED

A Vampire Hunter Novel

Book II
INHERITANCE SERIES

CHERYL A. HUNTER

INHERITANCE ACCEPTED

A Vampire Hunter Novel

Book II
INHERITANCE SERIES

GRAND OWL PUBLISHING
CHERYL A. HUNTER
©2022

Artwork by Cheryl A. Hunter

ISBN: 979-8-9865743-2-5
PUBLISHED BY Grand Owl Publishing
www.grandowlpublishing.com

Printed in the United States of America

Table of Contents

Chapter I
Home in Salem

James

When I opened the door, a young man in jeans, a white shirt, and a maroon apron stood before me. "Delivery for Mr. Merden."

"Yes, please bring them in." I stepped back and let him inside. "You can put them all on the dining room table."

He set the two vases he carried down. "I'll get the rest." He went back out to the delivery van and made several more trips to bring in all the flowers. "That is all of them, sir."

"Thank you." I gave him a tip and closed the door. I wanted the house to look and smell beautiful when Arianna arrived. She was only about an hour away, so I set about arranging the bouquets of roses around the house. I placed the vase with a dozen of pink roses and a congratulations decoration on her desk, and I laid a small gift next to it. I positioned a vase with a dozen red roses on the dresser in the bedroom and put a budvase with a single red rose in the bathroom.

The doorbell rang again. "The door is open. Come in, Marie," I called as I headed back downstairs.

She glided through the door. Marie St. Claire looked to be in her mid-forties, but she was much older having lived in Salem since its founding.

"The house smells like roses, James." She took my hands as I reached her. "It's lovely." Marie wore her usual attire, a long multilayered skirt, a cotton blouse, a shawl tied around her waist, and because it was summer, sandals on her feet.

"Thank you. Arianna has been in Connecticut for almost a week visiting her friend and picking up her dissertation copies." I led Marie into the front sitting room, and we sat in the two wing back chairs near the hearth.

"How was your conference?" she asked.

"It went well. A number of people attended my presentation. My paper is being considered for publication in the conference anthology."

"Congratulations. You work hard. And how was New Orleans?"

"We had an exceptionally good time. We walked along Bourbon Street and listened to Jazz. We went on a steamboat ride. It was Arianna's first trip to New Orleans." Arianna was only twenty-six, and until just a few months ago, she was in school working to complete her PhD., so she did little traveling. It was something I hoped to change. "Oh, and she won three hundred dollars at the casino playing the slot machines. It was her first time at a casino," I added.

Marie laughed. "I guess she has good luck." She looked at me and smiled. "Oh, I am going to enjoy having you in Salem again, James. It has been far too long since you lived here. I've missed you."

I smiled at her. "I am incredibly happy to be back, Marie. Would you like a glass of wine?"

"No, no, I just stopped by for a quick visit to say hello and tell you I am home. When do you expect Arianna to arrive?"

I looked at my watch. "In about 30 minutes. Tell me, how was your visit with your sister?"

"We had a very pleasant visit. Aster now lives in the outskirts of Savannah. She's active in her community working on Historical records." It was not wise to ask Marie too many questions, so I nodded and waited to see if she offered more. She didn't. "Well, we will catch up soon, James."

"You don't plan to stay and greet Arianna?"

"I am sure you want to be alone with her tonight." Marie smiled and headed to the door. "You hunted today I presume?"

"During the night."

"Shall we hunt together soon?"

"Yes. It will give us an opportunity to catch up. Thursday?"

"Good. I'll stop by in the evening and visit with you and Arianna before we go."

"Thank you. I know you will like Arianna when you get to know her."

I opened the door for Marie, and she took my hands. "Be well, James."

"You too, Marie."

I closed the door and looked at my watch. Arianna was due momentarily. I adjusted a vase of red roses on the foyer table and took another vase into the kitchen. While there, I checked on the casserole I made for her dinner. I enjoyed cooking before I was turned, and I often cooked for my aging parents in this kitchen. Of course, the kitchen had been remodeled since that time with modern appliances, flooring, and cabinets, but being in the room brought back many, many, fond memories of Mom sitting at the table crocheting while Dad read the newspaper. He read every word of the paper every day. I stared at the chairs, and I pictured them in my mind. I missed them. The downside of immortality was watching so many people you love age and die. The truth was, I sometimes envied them. Mortality defines one's life. People know they will die, and that creates a sense of urgency to accomplish goals, travel, and love someone.

Love. I now had Arianna in my life. I had someone to live for, someone with whom to share experiences, and someone I wanted to make happy. Someone who made me happier than I have ever been in my life.

The rattling of Arianna's old blue car in the driveway brought me out of my thoughts. I knew she would never let me buy her a new car, but she needed one. I adjusted the hall flowers, and I opened the door to greet her.

"Hi" she called cheerfully. I went out and took the boxes she carried. She kissed me, and then kissed me again. "I missed you." She kissed me again.

"I missed you too." I leaned forward and kissed her.

"I'll get my suitcase; be right back." Arianna pulled away and went back to the car. I watched her as she leaned into the vehicle to retrieve the suitcase. Her waist length, light brown hair was in a ponytail, and the hair fell over her right shoulder as she reached into the car. She wore a white silky blouse tucked into a short, black skirt that showed off her long, shapely legs. I could not wait for her to wrap those legs around me. I brought the boxes inside and set them down. She came inside, and I kicked the door closed.

I set down the suitcase then pulled her close to give her a proper greeting. "I really missed you." I kissed her mouth, her chin, and down her slender neck. She wrapped her arms around me. I picked her up and walked to the stairs.

"The roses are beautiful, and the house smells wonderful." She kissed me as she unbuttoned my shirt.

I carried her up the stairs to our bedroom. I set her down on the bed, and she slid her hands inside my shirt and pulled me down to her. She ran her delicate hands up and down my back, and I felt her nails travel over my back. I shuddered with need.

"I want you," she whispered very softly in my ear.

I stood up and quickly undressed. Arianna sat up, lifted her arms, and I removed her shirt and bra. She leaned back, and I pulled off her skirt and panties in one swoop. She looked at me seductively as she scooted further back up on the bed, but I had other plans. I knelt on the bed, reached out and grabbed her leg, and then pulled her back toward me. I pulled her up onto my lap, and she closed her eyes and gasped as she settled on me. I slid the ponytail elastic out of her hair, and her hair fell down and wrapped around the two of us tying us together. Then we began to move as one in a slow but powerful rhythm.

It took me so long to find Arianna and to find love. I breathed in her scent and imprinted it on my mind. I touched her everywhere. I caressed her smooth skin, and I memorized every curve. She molded to me, and we became one.

Arianna gathered her mass of silky hair and pulled it to one side. It fell in a long sheet over her left shoulder leaving her right shoulder bare. I caressed that shoulder then kissed and nibbled on it as the force of our love making increased.

"James." Her voice was a raspy whisper. She threw her head back, and I buried my head in her hair which carried the scent of her strawberry shampoo. I kissed my way down her neck, to her shoulder, and to her chest. Arianna closed her eyes. I kissed my way back up and put my hand behind her neck. I took in another breath, and her scent filled me. I had to have all of her. I closed my eyes and bit her. A gasp, a sigh, and then a soft sensual moan escaped her lips.

When I leaned back, she opened her eyes. "I love you," I whispered. She responded by lowering her mouth to mine.

I lost myself in her. Her tongue tickled my neck, and I shivered with pleasure. Her lips barely touched me, but they ignited a fire in my skin everywhere she touched. "Arianna, join with me." I felt her breath, the light pressure of her mouth, and then she bit me.

I held her tight. I wrapped my arms around her back. I felt her imminent release, and her fingernails dug into me as we shuddered in mutual pleasure.

Slowly and carefully, I eased her back down onto the bed. "Welcome home, my love." I breathed between kisses.

She smiled. "It is good to be home. To be with you."
I rolled over and laid by her side. "This is your home. I meant it when I said you can change anything. We can paint, redecorate, buy new furniture, anything you want." So far, Arianna changed the bedroom curtains to white drapes on a traverse rod, she put a new comforter in a seashell design on the bed, and purchased several sets of new towels, but she had not changed much else in the house.

"I'm not in a rush. We have time to make changes." Her fingers lazily floated over my chest.

We certainly had time. When I first met Arianna last year at Weymouth University in upstate New York, I never imagined that one year later we would be living together at my home in Salem, Massachusetts. Our home.

Arianna took a deep breath. "Dinner smells good, and I'm starving."
"Let's go eat." I pulled her up and held her robe for her. I slipped on a pair of shorts, and we headed downstairs. [overprinted: "It smells delicious."] Arianna sat down, and I opened the wine. [overprinted: "I hope you like it."] I poured the wine for us. Yes, white wine is typically served with chicken, but we both prefer a full-bodied red wine. "To happy days in Salem."

"To happy days." She clinked her glass to mine, and we drank.

Arianna set down her glass and took a bite of casserole. "Oh," she sighed, "this is amazing."

"I'm glad you like it."

She ate most of the casserole. Her eating habits had improved since her transformation from a first level vampire hunter to a super hunter. However, I tended to side with the old hunter Giovanni that she needed to hunt occasionally. When a person with the hunter gene is bitten by a vampire, the person transforms into a vampire hunter. Normally, the new hunter is trained and learns how to eat to sustain his, or in very rare cases, her body. However, Arianna did not know she was a hunter. Last year, when she was attacked and bitten, she underwent the second transformation into a super hunter. Her body was now very similar to a vampire, and she required blood to sustain her new physiology. Unfortunately, that was a problem because eating meat was not a regular part of Arianna's diet.

Vampires mostly feed on animals now, and Arianna has the ability to hunt like a vampire, but unfortunately, she does not like ingesting blood either. However, this was not the time to mention hunting or Giovanni, both of which might upset her, and I desperately wanted her to be happy. So, I smiled at her. "Dessert?"

"There's dessert?" She looked around and spotted the covered plate on the far countertop. "Chocolate cake?"

"I know it's your favorite." As I stood up to get the cake, she pulled me to her and kissed me. "You spoil me."

"That is my plan." I kissed her. "I hope you like it. I haven't baked in years." I brought the cake over to the table and took off the glass cover.

"Well, it looks and smells delicious."

I cut a large piece of cake and set it on a plate. I watched as Arianna cut the cake with her fork and sensuously put a piece in her mouth. She rolled her eyes. "Oh, this is chocolatey and delicious." She took another bite. "Oh, James, you have to try this." She held out a piece of cake on the fork for me, and I took a tiny bite.

Normally, human food has little appeal to me. I derive little nourishment from it, and most of it does not taste good. However, the flavor of the chocolate cake exploded on my tongue. "Wow. It really is delicious."

Arianna sliced another piece. "More?"

"Yes."

She fed me another piece. We sat side by side feeding one another, and together, we finished half of the cake.

Arianna stood up and put the dishes in the dish washer. She washed her hands and then turned around. "Ready for more dessert?" She opened her robe and let it fall to the floor revealing her slender, naked body. Her skin was creamy white and flawless.

"Absolutely." I moved swiftly to her and began kissing her and moving my hands all over her magnificent body. It was good to have Arianna here, and I knew we were going to be incredibly happy living in Salem.

*****

Over the next two days, we spent much of the time in bed. Arianna also spent considerable time unpacking more of her clothes. She needed closet organizing systems for the walk-in closets, so we went to the local home store for supplies. Everywhere we went, people smiled and were friendly. Most people in town did not know me or my family. I built the home for my parents in 1885. As far as the town was concerned, I was the latest James Merden to inherit the house. I did live at the home occasionally, but in the past ten years, I was a rare visitor. Therefore, most people accepted that Arianna and I were new to town.

On Thursday morning, I reminded Arianna that Marie was visiting in the evening before she and I went hunting.

"Does she eat anything?" Arianna asked while she made out a grocery list.

"Sometimes, but I think tonight we will just have wine while we talk."

Arianna and Marie got off to a rather stilted start last Halloween when they met at the annual Salem Halloween Ball. Marie knew Arianna was different because Arianna could block her when she was trying to compel my realtor, Mrs. Ballard. Marie was not accustomed to someone stopping her from doing what she wanted to do. Of course, at that time, no one knew that Arianna was a vampire hunter. Not even Arianna knew. Well, Marie suspected because she sought out Giovanni and sent him to New York to meet Arianna.

Both Arianna and Marie were strong willed and opinionated women, and I wanted this evening to go smoothly. They were the two most important women in my life, and I hoped they might be friends. Well, maybe friends was asking too much, but at least friendly.

After dinner, Arianna went upstairs to freshen up while I straightened the kitchen. I opened a bottle of wine and put it in an ice bucket. I set it and three glasses on the small table in the front sitting room. When the doorbell rang, Arianna came downstairs. I straightened my shirt and checked my hair in the hall mirror then opened the door.

"Good evening, Marie."

"James, good to see you. You look well."

I ushered her in, and Arianna was right by my side. "Hello Marie, welcome."

Marie took Arianna's hand in hers. "Thank you, dear. I am so glad that you have come to Salem. I haven't seen James this happy in years, and his happiness is so very important to me."

"To me as well, Marie. Come in, and let's have a glass or two of wine."

"Thank you."

The two women led the way into the sitting area and took seats side by side. I poured us each a glass of wine. "To Arianna and Marie. Joy and happiness."

"Cheers," they said almost in unison.

"It truly is good to have you and James here in Salem, Arianna, but you may find it a little too quiet."

"I don't mind quiet, and I have always loved Salem." Arianna took a drink of wine. "Can I ask you how you managed to stay in Salem so long? Others must move after a number of years because people begin to notice their lack of aging."

Marie smiled and leaned back. She took a long drink. "Well, it is well known that I am a witch. People avoid me, and I do go for prolonged periods of time without being seen often in town." She paused. "And sometimes a little compelling is necessary."

Arianna laughed. "Not according to Giovanni."

"But you don't see a problem using it."

"Well, I don't think it should be used frequently or without just cause, but I think it's necessary in some circumstances."

"That is very wise." Marie took another drink and turned to me. "So, James how is your novel coming along?"

"Progressing very well, thank you. I am nearly finished with the first draft."

"Already?"

"I have been inspired since Arianna and I decided to move to Salem."

"And you, Arianna, are you working on anything?"

I winced because I was not sure how Arianna would react to that question. So many of her friends and family were upset with her decision to move to Salem with me and not seek a teaching position after receiving her PhD.

Arianna sipped her wine. "I am reading up on vampire mythology and lore. It's fascinating because some of it is true, and some of it is way off the mark."

"That is interesting." Marie leaned toward Arianna.

"I am thinking about what I want to do. I'm writing and also keeping a journal to record the changes I am undergoing and my feelings about those changes." She let out a deep breath. "I never had any time off, and I'm finding that the creative side of my mind has really been starved. There are so many things I have been interested in doing but did not have the time."

"Well, now you have lots of time," Marie said kindly. "Relish your freedom and the time you now have. Be creative and enjoy every day. There will be time for work."

"Thank you, Marie." Arianna sounded relieved. "That is the nicest advice I have received."

I smiled. This was going better than I ever imagined. I refilled the glasses.

Marie and I left a short while later to hunt. We had to go further away because in the Summer many people were outside even late at night. I drove to the state park, and Marie and I went deep in the forest.

"Arianna seems to be very comfortable here in Salem," Marie remarked after we fed and were returning to the car.

"She is much better," I replied. "If only her family would stop pressuring her. She loves living in Salem, and it is far enough away from everyone that she can relax a little."

"Her family means well."

"I know. Arianna's parents, well mostly her father, were extremely upset with her decision. In fact, her father tried more than once to convince her to move to California and live with them."

"It will pass," Marie said gently. "Her parents want what they think is best for her, but I think Arianna is a strong woman and will do what she believes is best for her."

"Thanks, Marie. That makes me feel better. I'm happy that you like Arianna."

"She makes you happy, so I am happy." Marie thought for a moment. "That's not entirely it. I like her. She is strong and unapologetic. Most people are nice to me because they fear me, but Arianna does not fear me. She is simply a kind and generous person. She is special."

"She is special." I repeated. A few minutes later, I dropped Marie off at her home. When I arrived at my home, I saw a light on upstairs. No doubt Arianna was sitting in the chaise in the area behind the stairway, also known as a crying room, on the second floor. I rarely sat in that chaise, but Arianna loved it. Sure enough, when I went upstairs, she was stretched out writing in her journal.

"Hello, my love." I leaned over and kissed her.

"How was hunting?"

"Good. I am beyond happy that you and Marie are getting along."

"I like her. We just got off to a rocky start, but I think we can be friends. She really loves you." Arianna smiled at me and closed her journal. I offered her my hand, and she stood up.

I kissed her again. "Still, I am happy you two are friendly with one another." I followed her into the bedroom. "What did you do tonight?"

"I talked to Caroline." Arianna stopped undressing. "James," she paused, "would you mind if Jack came to visit for a few days? Caroline is overwhelmed."

I started to undress. I really did not relish the idea of Arianna's godson staying with us, but I knew she wanted to help her friend. Jack was almost five years old and very possessive of Arianna, and she adored him. I smiled at her. "No, I do not mind at all." I continued to undress.

"Are you sure?"

"Yes, he's your godson, this is your home, so he is welcome."

"Thank you, James. He really is a nice kid when you get to know him." She finished undressing and got into bed. "Jack Sr. is going to be away in a couple of weeks for work. I thought if we took Jack for a few days, it would give Caroline a break."

I nodded my agreement. "Whatever you want is fine with me." I got into bed and turned off the bedside light. Although I do not need sleep, I do rest for a while most nights. Mostly, I make love to Arianna and hold her in my arms until she falls asleep. I pulled her close.

"We can take Jack to Odiorne Point in New Hampshire. He will love the Science Center and then a walk on the beach exploring the tidal pools." Arianna cuddled up next to me. "I'll call Caroline tomorrow, and I can pick Jack up in two weeks." She sighed as I traced my hand down her back and over her hip.

"I'll take a ride with you to pick him up."

"You will? Thanks." She slid on top of me. Her hair fell in front and tickled my body. "I love you." She lowered herself down and kissed me.

I wrapped my arms around her back. "Anything for you, my love."

*****

The next morning, Arianna dressed and went into the small bedroom across the hall from our room. I heard her moving furniture around as I finished dressing. "James," she called.

I poked my head out of our bedroom door. "Yes?"

"I think we will put Jack in this room. This is the smallest bed, and the room is closest to us."

Jack clung to Arianna most of the time, and he always managed to sleep in bed with her. He did not like me at all. He thought of me as a rival for Arianna's attention.

"James? Are you listening?"

"Oh yes, sorry. I think it's a good room for him. You should get new bed linens."

"Yes, none of the other linens fit this bed. I thought about getting something neutral. Maybe a nautical print." She picked up a corner of the floral quilt that was currently on the bed. "I think we should put the bed against the wall too. I'll borrow the bed rail from Caroline, so he doesn't fall out of bed."

I smiled and nodded my agreement. Arianna was making this her home and that made me happy. "I'm going to write. Let me know if you need any help."

"I will." She went back to rearranging the furniture.

I went into my study and turned on my computer. I heard Arianna singing along to a song on the radio while she rearranged things to her liking. I smiled as I sat down to write, but I continued to listen to Arianna sing. It was music to my ears.

Chapter II
Jack's Visit

Arianna

Jack sat at the kitchen table and ate his breakfast. "Auntie, can I have more milk please?"

I walked out of the pantry with a cooler. "Absolutely, you need milk to grow big and strong." I refilled his glass and took several ice packs out of the freezer and added them to the cooler. "Would you like a muffin?" Jack nodded yes, so I cut a blueberry muffin in half and set the piece on his plate.

Just before seven o'clock James returned. "Good morning."

"Good morning, honey. How was your run?" I smiled at him. James' curly, jet black hair was damp and tousled from hunting. His tee shirt and running shorts clung tightly to his tall muscular body.

"Very good. It is a good day for our trip to New Hampshire." He walked over to me, put his arm around my shoulder, and kissed me very delicately on the lips. He turned, walked over to the table, and sat down opposite Jack. "How is your breakfast, Jack?"

"Good." Jack did not look up, and I distinctly heard a "Humph" from him.

James leaned back in his chair and eyed him. Jack was dressed in the pair of green shorts, dinosaur tee-shirt, and sandals that I bought him when we went shopping yesterday. "Are you ready to go to the beach and the Science Center?" Jack nodded yes. James turned to me. "I'll go upstairs, shower, and get ready while you two finish breakfast."

He left the kitchen, and I sat down and took a drink of tea. The muffin looked good, so I buttered it and took a bite.

"Does he have to come too?" Jack asked.

"Why wouldn't he come with us?"

Jack just shrugged his shoulders.

I stood up to wash out my tea mug and kissed him on the head. "You are both my boys." I rumbled his curly, blonde hair and then started to pack up the cooler with drinks and snacks for the trip.

It was a warm and sunny day. Perfect beach weather. I went out to the car and put the cooler on the back seat. James brought out the beach bags of towels, water shoes, sunscreen, and other necessities. I took the bags from him and put them in the trunk.

"We need to get a family car," James grumbled as he looked at my rusty, blue car. He preferred his sporty little car, but driving it was not practical with a young child.

Once the car was packed and Jack was secure in his car seat, I sat down in the passenger's seat. James got in behind the wheel and paused a moment before starting the car. He looked over at me. "We need a family car." He quietly but firmly emphasized each word.

Fortunately, the Science Center was not busy when we arrived. James parked the car, and the three of us walked inside. There were displays that talked about animal rescues, marine life, and migration. There was a humpback whale skeleton and several skeletons of pilot whales. Although many of the exhibits were hands on exhibits for children, some of them were too advanced for Jack.

When we entered the Discovery Dock area for younger children, Jack ran over and climbed aboard a small, wooden boat. He pretended to haul in fish, and then he steered the play boat.

When we went into the adjacent room, Jack ran over to the touch tanks. An energetic, young Science Center worker put a star fish in his hand, and he squealed with delight. He also held a green sea urchin and a hermit crab. I took pictures to send to Caroline.

"That whale was big wasn't it, Jack? Did you have fun?"

Jack vigorously nodded his head, yes. I washed his hands and toweled off his wet shirt. "I'm hungry, Auntie."

I looked at my watch. It was almost noon. "Me too."

James and I decided to leave the park and go to a restaurant for lunch instead of eating at one of the food trucks. At the Seafood Shack, I ordered fried scallops, my favorite, and I ordered Jack a kid's fish burger meal. We sat outside at a table with an umbrella and ate. A light breeze off the water stirred the air. Caribbean music set the mood, and I found myself moving and humming to the music. Several sea gulls flew overhead looking for scraps of food, and one sat on the fence nearby and intently watched Jack eat his french fries.

When I finished eating, I leaned back into James, and he wrapped his arm around my waist. "I want to stop at a store for a few supplies."

James looked at his watch. "The tide is going out. It will be low tide in a couple of hours." He looked at Jack. "Would you like to nap before we go in the water, Jack?"

"No!" Jack snapped his reply.

I knew better, and he was fast asleep before we drove the short distance to the store.

James parked the car on the shady side of the building. "I'll wait in the car with him."

"Thanks. I won't be long." I went inside and purchased a pail and shovel. I also purchased more snacks and drinks for later. When I returned to the car, I put everything in the back seat. "James, should we go back to the state park?" I whispered so as not to wake up Jack.

"How long do you think he will sleep?"

"I think at least an hour."

James drove back and parked the car under the trees right alongside a small grassy area. We opened the doors and windows to keep the car cool, and we sat in beach chairs next to the car and read. James stayed in the shadows of the trees. He was much more sensitive than I to the sun, so he had on light khaki pants, a long-sleeved white shirt, sandals, and a hat.

I wore a tank top and shorts over my two piece swimsuit, so I took off the tank top. I stretched out my bare feet. The warmth of the sun felt good. I sighed. Now that I was a vampire hunter, extended periods of time in the sun made me tired. I wasn't as sensitive as James, but it was one of the changes I least enjoyed about the transformation that nearly killed me last year.

"What is wrong, love?" James put down his book.

"I used to love to lay out in the sun and tan."

He moved his chair closer to me and gave my hand a squeeze. "I know. And I am sorry."

"No reason to be sorry," I replied. "If it wasn't for you, I might have died." I reached in my tote bag and took out a plastic bag.

"What's that?" James asked.

I held up the clear pouch. "It's a waterproof bag for my phone." I put the phone inside, snapped the two rows of zipper closures, rolled the top down, and snapped the flap over. "I can still use the phone and even take pictures, but the phone is protected from water."

"I have a waterproof phone case for my phone."

"Well with this pouch if I swim or drop the phone in the water, it's protected. Plus, I can hang the phone around my neck by the lanyard, and when I put it in my pail, the phone won't get scratched or covered in sand."

Jack started to stir. "Auntie?"

"I'm here, Jack." I stood up and gave him a cup of water then I lifted him out of his car seat and sat with him in the chair. I ran my fingers through his hair and hummed to him. James watched me for a few minutes then went back to his book.

When Jack was fully awake, I took him to the bathroom to change into his swimsuit. I put on his water shoes, and I put sunscreen on him. I took off my shorts, put on my water shoes, and picked up my pail. I handed Jack a pail and shovel. "Are you ready to explore the tidal pools and find sea creatures, Jack?"

"Yay!" He took my hand, and we walked back to the car. I tossed my shorts and Jack's clothes inside. James had exchanged his pants for a pair of swim trunks, and he put on water shoes as well. I took James' hand, and the three of us made our way down to the tidal pools. It was low tide, and although Jack was small, we were able to walk out on the rocks quite a distance from shore. I stayed right at Jack's side, and James stood a few steps further away just in case Jack fell in or a wave caught him.

While we were exploring, I saw something move under the water. "Jack look." He peered into the water.

James came closer and looked down too. "What do you see?"

"I'm not sure." I looked down into the water. "I saw something move." I reasoned that in New England there wasn't anything poisonous in the water, not that it would harm me anyway. I let out a steading breath and plunged my hand down into the water. I felt around, pulled my hand out, and gasped. I held a lobster.

"Wow!" Jack screamed.

James looked at me with wide eyes.

"Hand me the tub please, James." He filled our clear plastic tub with sea water, and I gently placed the lobster in the tub so we could observe the creature and keep it safe. Jack tentatively put his hand on the edge of the tub. "Be careful, Jack. Lobsters can pinch. Touch the back away from his claws." Jack touched the back of the lobster and quickly withdrew his hand.

I looked up at James. He shook his head. "I have never seen anyone reach in the water and pull out a lobster before." He put his arm around my waist. "You are amazing, my love." He kissed my cheek.

After we took many pictures of the lobster, we returned him to the ocean. He scampered away quickly. We continued to search the tidal pools. We found a couple of starfish, and we saw several crabs. As we explored, we started to move closer to shore. Even though James wore a very wide brimmed hat to keep the sun off him, he could not stay out in the sun long, so he retreated to the dense shade under the trees. Jack and I stayed in the shallow tide pools and picked up seashells, driftwood, and sea glass. I found a few crab shells that were mostly intact, and Jack found a tiny star fish on a rock.

"Can I keep him, Auntie?"

I looked at the star fish. It was dry and dead. "Yes, you can keep that one."

We sat at the water's edge, and Jack played in the sand. He laughed and giggled as he built a tower of sand and then a wave washed it away. He did it over and over again.

After playing, Jack was covered in sand, so I took him to the outdoor shower and washed off as much sand as possible. We sat on a bench to dry off, and I wrapped him in a big beach towel imprinted with colorful cartoon fish. When we returned to the car, our feet were once again covered in sand. I pulled a bottle of baby powder out of my bag and sprinkled it on Jack's feet to remove the sand then did the same for my feet.

"That really works." James dusted his feet with the powder. "I didn't think it would work."

I put our pails full of sea treasures on the floor in back. "James, it's a good thing we took my car. You would not want sand in your car," I said very seriously.

He laughed. "Very true." Then his expression turned serious. "We need a family car."

Once we were on the road heading back to Salem, I texted Caroline pictures of Jack playing at the Science Center and in the tidal pool including one of him with the lobster.

OMG!!! Caroline texted back.

Jack quickly fell asleep in the back seat. I reached back and took the toy shark I bought him at the Science Center from his hand and tucked it next to him. "He had so much fun today," I whispered quietly to James.

"We all had fun." He smiled. "I haven't spent the day at the beach in a long time."

"Thank you." I leaned over and kissed him. He took my hand, brought it to his lips, and kissed it.

*****

Jack stayed with us a couple more days, and we took him to several attractions in Salem including the pirate museum. I worried it might be scary for him, but he wasn't scared at all as we walked through the exhibit. As always, we exited into the gift shop. "Would you like a pirate hat, Jack?"

"Yeah! I can play pirates at home."

I picked up a pirate hat and placed it on his head. "Let's get Bobby something."

"Can we get him a sword?" Jack asked hopefully.

I shook my head no. "He's too young for a sword."

"Oh," Jack sulked.

"Do you want a sword?"

His whole face lit up in a smile. "Yes!"

"Ok. Go pick one out." I directed Jack to the basket of plastic swords while I looked around for something for the baby.

"Maybe a pirate PJ set?" James laughed and held up the outfit complete with a tiny pirate's hat.

I shook my head no. "Maybe a stuffed animal." I walked over to a whiskey barrel full of stuffed animals and sorted through them. "Do you think Bobby would like a parrot stuffie or a dolphin stuffie, Jack?"

"Parrot," Jack replied, but he was so engrossed in selecting the right sword he did not look up.

Sadly, we packed everything into my car the next morning and drove Jack home to Connecticut.

Caroline greeted us at the door. "Thanks for taking Jack for a few days." She looked more relaxed than when we picked Jack up. Her red hair was pulled back in a bun, and she wore a cute sun dress and slip-on sneakers. Caroline and I have been friends since we were kids. She knew everything about me but the most important thing: that I was a vampire hunter. I often wished I could tell her. There were times when I wanted her opinion and support.

"We had a lot of fun," I told Caroline.

"You spoil him so." Caroline shook her head as she unpacked the tote bag of toys and clothes that I bought Jack during his stay. I shrugged my shoulders.

James sat down at the table with us. Caroline turned to him. "And thank you, James, for putting up with him."

"He was no problem at all," James replied. "Arianna did all the work."

"Are you sure you can't stay for dinner?" Caroline stood up and poured her and I each a cup of tea.

"Actually, James and I are going to an exhibit at the Fine Art Museum tonight," I reminder her.

"That sounds like fun. Have you found a job yet?"

I sighed. "Not yet. I'm not in a rush."

"How is your father taking it?"

"Not well." I let out another deep sigh and shrugged my shoulders.

Caroline leaned back in her chair, studied us, and drank her tea. "You two look comfortable and happy together." She drank more tea. "I wasn't sure it was a good idea at first, but Arianna, obviously, you made the right decision, and I am happy for you."

"Thanks, Caroline."

*****

James took me to a restaurant on the wharf to celebrate the anniversary of our first date. The day he helped me unpack. After dinner, I hooked my arm through his as we strolled home. I looked up. The sky was a swirl of dark clouds. Thunderstorms were in the forecast.

"So much as happened in a year."

"The best year of my life." James leaned over and kissed me.

"For me too."

We approached the Hawthorne Hotel where we attended the Halloween ball the year before. "Would you like to attend the ball again this year, Arianna?"

"Yes. Could we get two extra tickets? I think Trina would love to attend."

James laughed. "Marcus might not be thrilled to go to a ball, but I will get four tickets."

We turned and walked past the visitor's center and the museum then we saw Marie coming out of a side street.

"Marie," James called.

She turned toward us and smiled. "James. Arianna." She suddenly stopped and stared at me. We quickly walked to her.

"Marie? What is wrong?" James asked.

Marie reached up to touch my locket, but she pulled her hand away quickly. "Arianna, where did you get this?"

Instinctively, I reached up and grasped my locket. "My great grandfather gave it to me. Why?"

She looked around to make certain no one could hear her. "That locket is enchanted."

"Enchanted?" James and I said a little too loudly.

"Let's get back to your house."

Marie led the way, and we quickly walked home. Once inside, Marie looked at my locket again. She did not attempt to touch it. "I can see a red aura around it."

I took off the locket and looked at it. James leaned close and looked at it too. We did not see the glow.

"It has been enchanted by a witch," Marie explained.

"Why?" I asked.

Marie shook her head. "There are many reasons for enchanting an object, but why this particular locket is enchanted I don't know." She reached out again but did not touch it. "You say your great grandfather gave it to you?"

"Yes. When I was a child. He said his grandmother gave it to him and told him to give it to his daughter or granddaughter. His grandmother was Giovanni's wife. The locket is how we figured out that Giovanni and I are related."

"Have you ever felt any power when wearing it, Arianna?"

I shook my head no.

"Only a witch can see the enchantment. Do you have other gifts from your great grandfather?"

"A few yes. This locket, a jewelry box, and other pieces of jewelry."

"The locket is incredibly old. It is possible it was enchanted when it was passed to your great grandfather, so he may never have known."

I sighed. "Or he knew, and the enchantment is for a reason I have yet to discover."

Marie thought for a few moments. "Can I see the other pieces and the jewelry box?"

"Absolutely." I led her upstairs to the bedroom.

She looked at the gold hoop earrings and the necklace with a cross, a solid gold heart, and an Italian horn. She looked at the jewelry box carefully opening each drawer. She sighed. "Nothing else is enchanted."

"Is it ok to wear the locket here in Salem? Can other witches see it is enchanted?" I asked.

"Yes, they will see it glowing red, but I doubt anyone will ask you about it. In Salem, many people own enchanted items. Protection spells are the most common."

"Thank you, Marie." I trusted what she said, but I decided to be very selective where and when I wore the locket in town.

Chapter III
Fall in Salem

James

The weather turned cooler, and Arianna began decorating for Fall and for Halloween. Salem was a Halloween town, so most people went all out with decorations, and Arianna embraced the tradition. I parked in the driveway and looked at my white, two-story, Federal style home, which was decorated for Halloween for the first time, ever. The narrow walkway up to the black front door was lined with pots of yellow, orange, purple, and white mums. Three hay bales were stacked to the right side of the door and on top were more mums, ornamental cabbage, and several pumpkins. There were also two large black spiders crawling up the hay bales. A witch's hat adorned the front door and a garland of fall leaves wound around the doorway.

As I stood staring at the door, it opened. "Hi" Arianna called as she stepped out onto the small landing. A large black spider perched over the doorway looked like it was ready to attack her.

"Hi. The decorations look nice."

"Thanks. I love the fall." Arianna looked over at the neighbor's house then pulled me inside the door. "Have you noticed the neighbors peek out of their windows when we are outside?"

"Yes, they are wary of me. Some of them believe I am the same James Merden who built this house." I laughed. "Of course, it's the truth, but my story is I am a relative who inherited it, and I am sticking to the story." I knew I needed to call a landscape company and have trees and shrubs planted to entirely block the neighbor's view.

Arianna smirked. "Well, I'll see if I can change their minds about you. Did you have a good hunt?"

"I did." I took off my boots.

"I was just going to have a snack."

In the kitchen, there were artificial garlands of colorful fall leaves and strands of white lights along the tops of the cabinets. On the center island, there was a floral arrangement in a pumpkin vase, and the placemats were now fall themed. A bottle of red wine and two glasses were also on the table. "Open the wine please, James."

Arianna walked over to the stove, lifted the lid of the pot, and stirred the contents. I looked over her shoulder, macaroni and cheese again. "You could hunt with me occasionally. Giovanni thinks you should," I said as casually as possible. She did not respond immediately. Anytime hunting was mentioned, Arianna got a little annoyed, but she obviously needed the extra nourishment. Her physiology was now similar to a vampires' physiology, and she needed blood to strengthen her.

She continued to stare at me, but then to my surprise she said, "Maybe I will one time."

I held my emotions in check. "You can hunt with me anytime." I popped the cork on the bottle of wine. Arianna turned off the gas and spooned some of the gloppy yellow mixture into a bowl. I wrinkled my nose. "What is in that macaroni and cheese?"

"Sliced up hotdogs. Giovanni is always telling me to eat more meat. They are beef franks." She sat down and started to eat.

I knew hotdogs were not what Giovanni meant when he said to eat more meat, but I didn't say a word and poured the wine.

"Oh, I went to the Historical Society today." She took another bite. "They said I can have access to any materials in their possession for my research."

"Did you find anything interesting?"

"A few historical facts, but nothing on the legends surrounding Salem." She ate another spoonful of macaroni and cheese. "I decided to volunteer there a few hours a week. They received a large donation from a lifelong Salem resident who recently passed away. His family has been here for generations."

"Who passed?"

"Mr. Tanner. Did you know him?"

"Not him, but I knew some of his relatives."

"Some of the material dates back to the early 1800s."

"Really?"

She nodded and ate more of the macaroni and cheese. "The Historical Society needs help going through the boxes, processing, and cataloging the materials, so I thought I might lend a hand."

"That sounds like something you will enjoy."

She got up and spooned the rest of the mixture into her bowl. I watched her closely. Her silky hair was in a high ponytail that bounced as she moved. Her jeans fit her snuggly, and the grey sweater she wore was a little big and exposed the top of her bare right shoulder. I leaned back and admired her as I sipped my wine. I hoped she didn't have any plans for tonight. Her glass was empty, so I refilled it.

"Are you trying to ply me with alcohol?" she laughed when she returned to the table.

"Do you mind?"

"Not at all." Arianna finished eating, drank down the wine, and then went to the sink to clean the bowl before putting it in the dish washer. I quickly refilled her glass again. "The full Harvest Moon is tomorrow night."

"Ok." I really was not paying attention to what she was saying. I watched her stretch and stand on her tip toes as she craned her neck to look out the window at the moon.

"We are going to the Harvest Moon celebration tomorrow night." She turned to look at me. "James? Did you hear me?"

I straightened up in my chair and cleared my throat. "Oh. Yes, I remember. Harvest Moon celebration."

She rolled her eyes as she so often did. "So, what should we do tonight?" she asked in a very sweet but seductive voice.

"I have no plans." I gave her a wry smile.

"Really?" She sauntered up to me, swung her right leg over my legs, and sat down on my lap facing me. "No plans at all? Nothing you want to do?"

I pulled her head down and kissed her lips and then kissed down her neck and nibbled on her bare shoulder. I slipped my hands up inside her shirt. She did not wear a bra. She raised her arms, and I removed the sweater and then started kissing her breasts. "Well, I have some ideas."

She let out a soft moan as I continued kissing her. "I thought you might."

*****

Marie hosted the Harvest Moon Celebration this year, and she selected a meadow near a stream quite a distance from town. Arianna and I held hands as we walked to the celebration. The sky was clear, and the stars were out. A perfect night for a party.

"James, Arianna, welcome." Marie greeted us with a large glass of wine in her hand. "We have a nice sized gathering tonight."

I surveyed the crowd and took note of the people present. Several vampires stood together near the bonfire. One of them nodded to me. "You need to acknowledge the vampires," I whispered to Arianna. She turned to face them, and we both acknowledged them with a nod.

"I will get glasses of wine."

Arianna looked around in wide eyed wonder. Marie went off to greet more guests, and I walked to the refreshment table. I poured two plastic glasses of wine and returned to Arianna.

"James, this is Penelope. She is part of the local coven."

I handed Arianna a glass of wine. "Nice to meet you." I shook Penelope's hand. "You work at the bank, right?"

She took a sip of wine. "Yes, I do. How are you two enjoying Salem."

"It's wonderful." Arianna took my hand. "Everyone is welcoming."

"It's the best place to live," Penelope agreed.

We mingled, and once everyone arrived, Marie stood in front of the gathered crowd. "Welcome and thank you all for coming tonight as we celebrate the Harvest Moon. As you know, this is a time for gathering with friends and reflecting on the year and on life. First, let's all raise our glasses in a toast. To dear friends who give us love and support and to the promise of a new year."

We raised our glasses and drank.

"Now, who wants to speak first?" Marie asked the crowd.

"I would like to," Arianna replied.

Marie beckoned her forward. "May I present Arianna Sabini, a new resident of Salem."

There was a chorus of welcome from the crowd. "Thank you, Marie, and thank you all for the warm welcome. This year has been life changing for me. Not only did I complete my PhD.," she paused and acknowledged the clapping of congratulations, "but I underwent a transformation. There were happy times, difficult times, and scary times, but most importantly, I met my soul mate. The person who I know will always be by my side." She held out her hand, and I walked to her and took it in mine. She faced me and smiled. "This year has been eventful, but I would not change anything because I found you. I love you, James Merden."

"We are soul mates, Arianna. I will always be by your side, and I know you will always stand by me. I love you." I leaned in and kissed her to loud applause.

"Well, that will be difficult to top." Marie hugged me and Arianna. "Of course, James and Arianna moving to Salem is something for which I am thankful." She smiled at us then addressed the crowd. "And who is next?"

Not everyone spoke. Some people preferred to reflect in private, but the atmosphere was lively and warm, and it was truly a night of celebration.

When the party broke up, Arianna and I started our walk home. We were not far from the meadow when Arianna stopped. She pulled arm guards out of the waist band of her jeans and put them on. A bared owl glided in silently and landed on her arm.

Arianna pet the grey bird, and I saw myself as Arianna transmitted what she saw through the bird's eyes to me. The bird took flight again, and it flew above us as we walked toward the road and then home. In the front yard, Arianna called the bird to her, and it again landed on her arm. She stroked its head, and the owl hooted contentedly before taking flight. It was always fascinating to watch Arianna communicate with birds. So far, she could communicate with hawks and with owls. Her ability was unique, and the fact that she could transmit what she saw to me and to Giovanni when we were nearby was remarkable which was why Giovanni insisted that only a few people know about her ability.

*****

A week later, I worked in my study. I had an appointment with an agent soon, so I worked well into the evening. When I went downstairs, Arianna sat at the desk in her office typing on her laptop.

"Sorry, I didn't come downstairs all day. I was on a roll," I apologized as I entered the room. The walls in her office were painted a very pale shade of blue/green and the trim was painted white. She purchased an L-shaped glass desk and set it to face the window overlooking the side yard. There were new white bookshelves on two of the walls. She draped a lighted pumpkin garland over the tops of the bookshelves, and on one shelf, sat a lighted jack o lantern decoration.

Arianna looked up from typing and smiled at me. "No problem. I have been keeping busy."

"What are you working on," I asked.

I found this book at the library book sale today." She handed me a small book with a white cover. "It is essentially a textbook of non-fiction readings, prompts, and writing exercises. I am doing one of the memory exercises."

I sat down in the white wicker chair beside her desk, picked up the book, and looked through it. "It looks interesting."

"Yes, it is. Earlier, I wrote about watching my grandmother bake a three-layer cherry nut birthday cake for me when I was little."

"What are you working on now?" I asked.

"I'm writing about the time when I was in the hospital having my tonsils out." She paused. "I don't remember much, but I do remember my great grandfather sat by my side the whole time. I thought writing about him might make me remember more about him."

I nodded, and she began typing again.

"How old were you?"

"I was four. I remember a few months later, I was extremely sick again. It's weird, but I never was sick again after that year."

I looked at her. "Never? Not a cold, the flu, chicken pox?"

"No, nothing."

"That is odd."

As I read the memory exercise, I thought about Arianna's great grandfather. Giuseppe was a mystery. In June, Giovanni recognized the locket Giuseppe gave her in her graduation photos. The locket belonged to his wife, Gianna, and she gave it to her grandson as she lay dying after a vampire attack. Giovanni thought his grandson perished in a battle, but obviously he survived. We were pretty certain that Arianna's great grandfather and Giovanni's grandson were one in the same making Arianna and Giovanni related. Not that being related helped Arianna and Giovanni get along, and they continued to be at odds with one another. Now we know that same locket was enchanted by a witch. The mystery surrounding Arianna's great grandfather continued to deepen.

"Oh, James. I saw Marie at the farmer's market earlier today. She was buying herbs."

I was incredibly happy they were getting along so well.

"She told me to tell you a pack of wolves moved in the area."

I looked up at her. "What!"

"A pack of wolves moved in the area," she repeated. "I didn't know there were wolves this far south. I thought they all lived at the Canadian border. Anyway, Marie is stopping by about midnight." Arianna looked up from typing. "James what is wrong?"

"Nothing." I looked at my watch. It was 11:25 pm. "I think I'll go change. I'm sure Marie wants to hunt together tonight."

"Ok. I am finishing up." Arianna resumed typing.

I got up and went upstairs to change. Wolves. Here. In Salem. Not what I needed.

The grandfather clock in the foyer started to chime out twelve times as Marie arrived. "She certainly is punctual," Arianna commented.

"Good evening, Marie." I opened the kitchen door to let her in.

"Hi, Marie. Would you like a glass of wine?" Arianna asked.

Marie looked at Arianna eating a bowl of cereal and shook her head. "No thank you, dear," she said softly. "James and I should be going. Would you like to hunt with us? It would ease your hunger."

I think my heart stopped. Asking Arianna if she wanted to hunt usually ended in an argument when Giovanni asked. "Not tonight, thanks," she said cheerfully as she poured another bowl of cereal. "You two have a good hunt."

I leaned down and kissed her. "We won't be long. Lock the door behind us." Arianna's eyes widen in surprise at my request, but she shrugged her shoulders. She stood up, kissed me, and locked the door when Marie and I left the house. We were hunting locally tonight, so we walked down the street. Very few houses had lights on, and we walked in silence until we were under the cover of the trees.

"Arianna told me about the wolves. When did they move in?" I asked as we started to run.

"The werewolf pack leader came to visit me last night. Several of them purchased homes in the new subdivision at the edge of town."

"Did you tell them about Arianna?"

"No. I am under no obligation to tell them anything about hunters or vampires for that matter living in my clan area. It is protocol for them to inform the clan leader that they have moved into the area. As you know, the treaty restricts their actions. They can only detain a vampire if a human's life is in imminent danger, and since there is very little human feeding, I don't expect a problem."

"Arianna thinks they are real wolves."

Marie stopped, so I did as well. She looked at me.

I shrugged my shoulders. "Arianna has refused most training. She has no idea there are humans that can shift into wolves," I explained.

Marie sighed. "James, that girl needs to be aware of the dangers that are in the world."

"Wolves will not harm a hunter especially a super hunter like Arianna."

"True, wolves have traditionally been the companions of hunters," Marie paused, "but there are many other dangers. She cannot ignore what she is. She needs at least some training."

"I know." I ran my hand through my hair. Arianna's determination to stay out of the supernatural world was frustrating. We were part of that world no matter how hard she tried to ignore it.

"And she needs better nourishment. Cereal is not food for a hunter. Honestly, where is Giovanni? He needs to have a talk with her."

"He has tried. At least now she eats some meat. When she first transformed, she pushed me away and refused to talk to Giovanni. She was in deep denial about her transformation, and finally, her body was starved for blood and nourishment." I stopped and shuddered thinking of that day.

36

"She found me feeding in the forest, and she was crazed by a lack of blood. I watched in shock and terror as she dropped to the ground and fed from the doe I killed. I did not know what to say or do. Then she realized what she did, and she was horrified that she drank blood. She ran off. I thought she would never speak to me again, Marie. She was repulsed by it." I shook my head. "Finally, fear of it happening again made her accept some training and start to eat better food."

Marie was quiet for a moment. "I did not realize she had that adverse a reaction to her transformation. Has she ever hunted?"

I nodded. "After the battle with Darius, she did come out with me and Marcus. I took down the doe and she fed."

"She has never done it alone?"

I shook my head no.

"Either you or Giovanni need to speak to Arianna. She must learn to hunt, and she must eat better."

"I will speak to her again about eating more meat."

We continued to look for game.

"You should tell her about the wolves tonight, James," Marie said sternly. "She needs to know."

We smelled a herd of deer up ahead, and we stopped again. "Giovanni is coming to visit soon. I will tell him about the wolves. I think it's best if Arianna learns about them from him."

Marie stared at me with squinted eyes.

"After all, we have some prejudice against the wolves," I nervously added.

Marie put her hands on her hips and gave me a sideways look. "Really? What are you afraid of?"

"I don't want to upset her, and I think Giovanni is better suited to explain them to her." I took a deep breath. "Besides, Arianna is unlikely to run into the wolves. She doesn't come into the forest alone."

"You know best, James," Marie said sarcastically. She turned and looked over the herd of deer. "Those two older ones." She pointed to the two deer that were off to the side.

I nodded, and she and I prepared to leap, but I knew this was not the end of the discussion.

Chapter IV
Mom's Visit

Arianna

I spent the last few days cleaning and organizing the house. My mother was coming for a visit, or I should say an inspection, and I wanted everything to look good. I decided to put her in the bedroom farthest from our room. I put hangers in the closet and pouches of rose potpourri in the drawers. Since my mother lives in California, I put a blanket and a heavy comforter on the bed. I also put an extra blanket on the quilt rack in the room.

It was late at night, and James and I lay in bed cuddling and talking. "Arianna, Marie and I are going to hunt before it gets light. We plan to go deep into the state forest since we will be finishing when the sun comes up. We won't have cell service, but I will text you when we are heading back."

"Ok. When you leave, I will sleep." I wrapped my arms around him and kissed him. "What time is Marie stopping by?" I laid a line of kisses across his chest and then back to his mouth.

"Not for a couple of hours." He pulled me up on top of him and let out a moan.

"Oh good," I breathed into his ear. I got up on my knees and placed my hands on his chest. James traced his fingers ever so lightly up and down my inner thigh. I closed my eyes and relished in the sensations. He sat up quickly and kissed me, and as he did, he slid his hands underneath me and lifted my body onto his.

"Oh, James," I breathed into his mouth. Waves of pleasure rocked our bodies. "I love you." I lost myself in our coupling, and I gave myself entirely to him. He wanted to get married, but I did not feel the need for a legal document. Afterall, we were bonded to one another and did not need anything more.

The next morning, I was eating breakfast when James and Marie returned. "Good morning," they said as they walked into the kitchen.

"Good morning. Did you see anyone while hunting?'

"It was uneventful despite the number of deer hunters," James informed me.

Marie looked down at my plate. "May I suggest a piece of meat with those eggs, dear?"

I looked down. "Oh, I had some." I stood up and went to the microwave and removed a plate with two breakfast sausages.

Marie looked at the two small patties and sighed. "Well, I need to be going," she said. "Your mother arrives tomorrow, Arianna?"

I nodded. "You should stop by to meet her, Marie."

Marie smiled nervously. "Perhaps. We will see." She took James' hands. "Be well." She looked over at me. "Both of you."

"We will," we replied in unison.

Marie left and James sat down. "What do you have planned today?"

"I want to purchase a half dozen of pumpkin muffins and get a bouquet of flowers for the guest room. I also want to make certain everything is set for my mother's visit."

"The house has never looked better," James replied.

I got up and rinsed my plate. I turned back to face him. "I waited for you to come home to shower." I slid my cotton night shirt off and stepped out of my panties then quickly left the room and headed up the stairs. James came up behind me, picked me up, and carried me to our bedroom.

He set me down near the bed, and I helped him undress. "In the shower?" he asked as he slid his hand up and down my back.

"I love that big, beautiful shower."

James grinned. He insisted on remodeling the master bathroom and enlarging the shower before we moved in. He picked me up and carried me in the bathroom. He continued to hold me while he turned on the water and stepped inside the shower enclosure. We kissed as he laid me down on the oversized shower bench. I looked up at him as he stared down at me. I saw the hunger in his eyes.

"You are so beautiful, Arianna. I love you."

"Show me how much you love me." I reached up for him. He slid on top of me, and I wrapped my legs around his back while the water fell like rain over us, and the room filled with steam.

Later that afternoon, I went downtown. It was a chilly and cloudy October afternoon, yet the city was full of tourists in town for Halloween Haunted Happenings. I bought a bouquet of flowers at the florist and then picked up my pumpkin muffin order. I put everything into my tote bag. I decided to cut through the park on my way home. A group of children played football. A couple of mothers sat at a picnic table and talked, drank coffee, and watched their children play on the swings and slide. At the edge of the park, three teenaged boys pulled a dog along by a rope. I looked closer and realized it was not a dog. It was a wolf pup. I quickly walked over to the boys. "What are you doing with that wolf?" I asked them.

"None of your business, lady," the older of the three said to me.

"Wolves are protected animals. Where did you get it?"

"We found him on the street where those new houses are," the blonde-haired boy replied.

"Anyway, he's not a wild wolf," the oldest said. "He's a wolf hybrid."

I did not like the look in his eyes. I stood my ground and stared the boys down. I pulled the rope out of the third boy's hand. "Well then, he belongs to someone. It is stealing. I should call the police."

"No, no, don't call the cops," the blonde boy begged. "You take him. Let's get out of here." Two of the boys ran off immediately. The oldest stared at me and refused to move, but I glared at him, and finally, he turned and ran off.

Once they were gone, I bent down and pet the puppy. "I am going to take you home," I said. As if he understood, he immediately started to pull me along. I was so annoyed with those boys. The subdivision was at the very edge of town. There were only five houses, and they were up a small hill and surrounded by woods. As I walked up the road, a man in his mid-twenties suddenly came out from the trees right in front of me. He had brown hair that was a bit shaggy. He stood about six feet tall, and he was very muscular. He took a deep breath. He stared at me.

"Hello," I said loudly.

He looked down at the puppy on the rope. "What are you doing with him?"

"Is he yours? Three boys had him in the park. They said they found him in this area, so I brought him home." Two more people appeared so quickly I jumped. The man was tall and also very wide and muscular. The woman stood about my height, but she was heavier than me. They also took a deep breath and stared at me. The three of them looked at each other. "I didn't take him, I assure you." Surely, they didn't think I took the puppy.

Finally, the older man stepped forward. "I am John, this is my wife Adrian, and my son Jason." He reached out his hand.

I handed him the rope. "I am Arianna. Please be careful with him. The three boys that took him looked like trouble."

Jason stared intently at me which made me uncomfortable. He approached me. "Thank you for bringing back my little brother."

I smiled uneasily. "Little brother?"

"Yes," John replied. "Tommy here is like a brother to Jason." He gave Jason a stern look.

"Well, I need to be getting home," I said. "Watch that puppy."

Jason stepped in front of me. "Can I walk you back?"

"No, thank you. I am fine."

"Are you sure? Those boys might be waiting for you."

"I can take care of myself. I will be fine." I nodded, turned, and headed back down the road.

*****

James and I arrived at the airport just before Mom's plane landed. He looked relaxed, but I felt nervous. Mom came out of the gate. She carried a tote bag, pulled a rolling bag, and looked perfectly put together. She wore a pair of black slacks and a matching jacket over a V neck white silk blouse. Her hair was almost to her shoulders and neatly styled. She wore black pumps and over her arm was a lined leather jacket. "Hi" she called.

We walked quickly to her, and James took her bags. I gave her a hug. "How was your flight, Mom?"

"It was smooth. Oh, it is good to see you." She hugged me tight.

"It's great to see you too." It really was nice to see my mother. I knew she was here checking up on me, and I was anxious to show her how happy I was living in Salem with James. We left the terminal and walked to the car.

"We need a family car," James said quietly as I squeezed in the back seat of his little sports car for the ride home. Mom and I talked the whole way back, and James stared ahead pretending to concentrate on driving.

"Oh, the house is beautiful," Mom said as we pulled in the driveway. "It's Historic, right?"

"Yes," James replied. "It was built in 1885."

"And your family has owned it all this time?"

"Yes."

I noticed the neighbor looking out the window again. I understood the neighbors were more than a little curious. The house was empty for years, and now, we were living there, and we had a steady stream of visitors.

"What a cozy room," Mom commented when we went in the front sitting room with the large fireplace. "And I love the eagle over the mantle." We took her upstairs to her room. "This is very nice."

James put her large suitcase on the bed. Mom opened it and took out a box. "Arianna, I brought the jewelry from your dresser as you asked." She handed me the box.

"Thanks, Mom." I wanted Marie to look at the jewelry and see if any pieces were enchanted,

Next, she took a large bag out of the suitcase and handed it to me.

I opened it. Inside was the red and white hand crocheted afghan that my grandmother made me when I was in high school. "Thank you." I hugged the blanket.

She smiled and took out another small box. "You only had a few items on the dresser, so I brought them as well."

"Thanks." I took the box from her.

"The house is big for just the two of you," she commented.

James took that as his cue to leave. He excused himself and left the room so we could talk.

He wasn't even down the stairs when Mom asked, "Are you sure this is what you want, Arianna?"

"Mom!" I looked at her. "You just said the house is beautiful."

"Oh, and it is. But are you sure you want to take time off? You are only twenty-six and just beginning your career. Dad thinks he can get you a post doc in the Classics Department at the university."

I took a deep breath. "Mom, I am sure this is what I want to do. I went from high school to college at sixteen, finished my bachelor's degree in three years, and then went right on for the master's degree and PhD. I need time to discover what I really want to do in my life. Can you understand that?"

Mom thought for a moment and then smiled at me. "Of course, honey. I can see that you need some time." She patted my hand. "And I see that you are very happy with James."

I relaxed a little, but I also knew she did not give up that easily. "You get settled and then come downstairs for a nice cup of tea." I kissed her and left the room.

"How is she doing?" James asked when I walked in the kitchen.

I rolled my eyes, sat in a chair, and dropped my head to the table. I looked up. "She says she understands, but."

James bent down and kissed my head. "It will get better."

The first night Mom was in Salem, we took her to a restaurant down on the wharf for sea food, and then we stopped at a pub for a drink.

"Your brother is settled in Montana. He likes his new position with the university."

"I am glad to hear it." Albert rarely called me. Of course, I rarely called him. Mom kept us informed on what the other was doing.

"He has been making friends."

"Good for him."

Mom turned her attention to James and asked him questions about Salem, about the house, and about his plans for work.

"Actually, 1 will be meeting with an agent soon," he informed my mother.

"But is that enough to live on?" she asked.

"Mother, we have enough money," I said sternly. I didn't think it was appropriate for her to ask James so many personal financial questions.

"It's ok," James replied, but I gave my mother a pleading look, and she did not ask more questions.

The next day, I took Mom around the town, we went shopping, and then we walked the beach. Mom picked seashells as we walked along and talked. It was a warm October day, but she wore a sweater and a jacket. I grew up in Connecticut, but she and my dad moved to California right after I finished my freshman year in college, so now she was accustomed to the warmer climate.

As I watched her, I realized that I haven't lived with my parents since I left high school. I only went to California for short visits between semesters. I did not even go there for summer break because I always took classes, did research, or worked. Maybe, Mom hoped I would live with them after I finished my PhD. It was something to think about, but for now, I just wanted to enjoy her company.

I woke up when I felt James stir.

"Good morning." He kissed me.

"Good morning. Going hunting after Boston?" I asked.

"Yes. I should be back home by midafternoon."

I watched James as he dressed. I liked watching him. He was graceful and yet strong. He buttoned his shirt and tucked it into his slacks then he put the tie around his neck and started to tie it.

"Arianna?" I looked at him, and he smiled. "Are you ok?"

Was I ok? Mom had been here two days. She obviously came to Salem to see James' house and to make certain living here with him was what I wanted. I guess I understood my parent's concern. Dad was teaching, so he could not come. I tried to get them to visit for Thanksgiving, but Mom and Dad were obviously anxious to see where I lived and what I was doing. I loved my mother, and I was enjoying her visit, but I overheard her giving a reconnaissance report to Dad from the guest room several times already. "I'm ok."

"Giovanni is due early this afternoon. I will try to be back soon after he arrives."

"Ok. Don't rush. I told my mother you had to go into Boston for the day."

"Giovanni is hoping to learn more about Giuseppe from your mother; although, your father probably knows more."

"Yes, probably, but he is reluctant to talk about my great grandfather."

"I wonder why?"

"I don't know." For some reason, Dad avoided talking about him. However, when I thought about it, Dad did not talk about anyone in the family. "They will be here the whole weekend. We need to plan some activities."

James kissed me again. "We will plan a typical October weekend in Salem for your mother and Giovanni. It will be fun." He finished dressing and put on his shoes. He put his suit jacket on and picked up his bag of clothes for when he hunted later. I got out of bed, slid on my bathrobe, and went downstairs with him. "Have a good day." James kissed me and ran his fingers through my hair.

"You too." I stretched up and kissed him. He went outside to his car, and I closed the door as he drove away. My mother was still sleeping, so I went in the kitchen and poured myself a bowl of cereal. I turned on my laptop, read the news, and checked email while I ate. I had an email from Caroline. Her life was a combination of taking care of the kids and running the house. I needed to visit her again soon. I sent her an email asking when Jack Sr. was going to be away again.

I got up and put water on for tea. I took out two mugs and small plates. Before the water boiled, my mom joined me in the kitchen. "Good morning, dear. How are you this morning?"

"Good morning, Mom. Did you sleep well?"

"Yes. Yes, I did. Has James left already?"

"He wanted to catch an early train and avoid the morning rush."

She sat down and opened the paper. The tea pot whistled, so I poured water in the mugs. "Would you like apple tea?"

"Does it have caffeine?"

"No."

"Then I'll have English Breakfast tea, thanks."

I put out a plate of muffins, a small basket of assorted jams, and warm, soft, spreadable butter.

Mom picked up a pumpkin muffin. "These are incredible. I have to take some home to your father." She spread warm butter on the muffin.

"I'm glad you like them." I took a pumpkin muffin, sliced it, and put a pad of butter on each side. "I'll order some, and we can pick them up before we take you to the airport."

Mom took a bite of a muffin. "Delicious." She took another bite. "Really good."

"And the bakery makes them all year."

She savored another bite, drank her tea, and then leaned back in her chair. "This is a beautiful home, and you two seem so happy here." Mom reached for the second half of her muffin and took a bite. She chewed slowly intentionally. No doubt she was carefully framing her words. "You and James are wonderfully comfortable together. It's like you've been together for years."

"That's good, isn't it?"

"Oh yes. Yes, it is good." I knew she had more to say, but instead she smiled. "I'll have another cup of tea, please."

Later in the morning, we took a walk around the neighborhood and went to a restaurant on the wharf for an early lunch. It was warm for October, and the sun was shining, so we sat at a table on the deck overlooking the water. "Do you remember when we went to Gloucester that summer for vacation, Arianna?"

"Yes, I remember seeing the fisherman statue."

"We never came to Salem."

"You should definitely come back with Dad. I think he will enjoy it here."

The waiter brought our food to the table. The platters were piled high with fish, scallops, clams, and shrimp. I ordered onion rings and Mom ordered fries, so we could share and have both.

"This is a lot of food," Mom commented as she squeezed lemon on her fish.

"Anything we don't eat, we will take home for lunch tomorrow." I dipped a tender fried scallop in tartar sauce and put it in my mouth.

"The fish is perfect," Mom commented.

As we ate, the sea gulls flew around us looking for food. The sun glistened off the water, and several sail boats passed by. Mom and I chatted about the family and the upcoming holidays. She suggested either James and I visit California for Christmas, or we all meet in Florida and visit Grandma. I was tempted by the prospect of going to Florida. I missed my grandmother, and I wanted to introduce her to James.

After lunch, we made a few stops at shops on the wharf. All the shops were decorated for Halloween. Assorted sized pumpkins, a black feather wreath, and several black ravens decorated one shop window. We went inside to look around, and Mom purchased a pumpkin spoon rest. We stopped at the café, and I purchased more pumpkin muffins, and then we strolled back home.

Giovanni arrived just before two o'clock. He put his bags in the bedroom upstairs and then came in the dining room. I expected James at any time, yet he had not texted since lunchtime before he headed into the forest.

"My mom brought photos of my great grandfather, Giovanni." I only had one picture of my great grandfather, and Giovanni wanted to be certain he was actually his grandson. Of course, I could not tell my mother everything, and I was glad she did not ask too many questions. I motioned for Giovanni to sit down, and I placed a cup of coffee in front of him. Giovanni nodded his thanks.

"It's interesting that your family and John's family were from the same small village in Italy. I wonder if the families knew one another?" Mom handed four photos to Giovanni. "We only have a few photos of Joseph, and Arianna, you are in every picture we have of him," my mother added with a laugh.

Giovanni tentatively took the pictures as if he was afraid to look at them. He flipped one over. I heard him suck in air.

I looked at the picture over his shoulder. "Great Grandpa had thick black hair."

Mom laughed. "She always thought he looked so young and had jet black hair."

"What do you mean?" Giovanni asked.

"Well, look at the picture." She pointed to the photo. "His hair is mostly grey, yet she always said he had all black hair. I guess it was because she idolized him."

Giovanni smiled at my mom and then looked at me. I gave the very slightest of shrugs. The picture clearly showed a man with black hair, but neither Giovanni nor I said anything. I was the only one in the family who saw him with black hair, and for many years, I thought that I imagined him that way.

"I'm sure I have more pictures in my cedar chest. I have to go through it, but I know I have more."

Mom's cedar chest was bottomless, and she thought everything was in there. She also always said she had to go through the cedar chest, but of course she never did.

Mom took the pictures back and looked at them again. "Do you think it's possible the families knew each other?"

Giovanni shifted in his seat. He pulled down the front of his tan shirt and tugged on the piece of rawhide that held back his long white hair. He wasn't good at conversations especially those that might require him to stretch the truth. "It's possible. Do you have Joseph's birth certificate?"

"No, we don't. We only have documentation from when he arrived in the U.S. from Italy." She reached into the tote bag beside her chair and pulled out several pieces of paper. "This shows he arrived at Ellis Island with a baby girl." She handed him the photocopies, and Giovanni examined each carefully.

"Mom, where did you get this?"

"The Ellis Island website. They have the records of the people who came through Ellis Island online. I printed this, but we can send for a better copy."

"And neither Luisa nor your husband ever returned to Italy?" Giovanni was all business.

Mom shook her head. "No, we've never been to Italy. We do plan to go some time." She stood up. "More tea or coffee?"

"No, thank you," Giovanni mumbled.

"Yes, please," I said hoping for a chance to talk to Giovanni alone.

"I'll put water on." Mom took our cups and headed into the kitchen.

"Are you certain my great grandfather is Giuseppe your grandson?" I asked quietly as soon as Mom was out of ear shot.

Giovanni nodded, "It is definitely him."

"You see he has jet black hair, right?" I asked Giovanni.

"Yes"

"So, Great Grandpa must have compelled them to hide the fact that he wasn't aging?"

"It appears so." Giovanni grunted. He did that when he did not like something. "He never did follow the rules."

"Well, he had a good reason in this case," I responded coming to my great grandfather's defense. Giovanni just grunted again. "He didn't compel me though. I guess he figured he didn't have to because I was a little kid. No one would believe me."

Giovanni remained quiet for a few moments. I heard the tea pot whistle. "Maybe he was unable to compel you."

Giovanni's statement took me by surprise. "What?"

"Maybe you could not be compelled. Darius said he knew what you were when you were a child."

"I just thought he knew I had the gene." I wanted to say more, but mom walked in the room. "Here's your tea, Arianna."

"Thanks." I steeped my tea bag thinking about what Giovanni just said. Why didn't my great grandfather compel me? Was I already a hunter at that young age, and therefore, I could not be compelled? But I was so young. No, I could not have been turned at four years old. We did not yet know how or when I was turned, or if the gene spontaneously activated as Montgomery Hale, a vampire from New York, believed, but it was unfathomable that I was turned so young. Who would turn a child? There were still so many unanswered questions.

Giovanni asked my mother a variety of questions about the family. She answered his questions, and he looked troubled.

My mother looked at her watch. "James is late, isn't he?"

"The trains are probably behind schedule. He should be here shortly." I already thought James should have returned by this time, and I was worried.

54

Chapter V
Intruder

James

I was able to find the information I needed in the Boston library quickly. I had a few other errands to do while I was in town, but I was able to catch the train back to Salem as I planned. I changed my clothes at the station and then drove to the state park to hunt. I looked at my watch. I was on schedule. Hopefully, Arianna and Giovanni would not have time to argue before I returned.

I stepped out of the car, locked it, and pocketed my keys. I was in luck, there was only one pickup truck parked in the pull off. There was always a chance of running into hikers or hunters at this time of year during the day, so I walked slowly into the forest until I was sure there was no one around.

I caught the scent of a person and quietly moved in closer. It was a hiker moving at a moderate pace up one of the trails that led to the West. I headed East. I knew the area well, and I quickly went up and over a small rise through a dense part of the forest where humans rarely traveled. There was a small stream nearby, and I made my way to it looking for game. I followed the stream only for a short distance when I came upon a herd of deer. Fortunately, deer were in abundance, so I selected an animal and moved in for the kill.

By the time I drained the animal, I sensed a couple of coyotes who were drawn to the scent of blood. I leaned back to see how close they would come. One of the animals eyed me but moved closer. I took out my knife and cut back the skin, and then I slowly stood up and stepped back. The two coyotes cautiously moved closer to the downed deer, and I slowly moved away so as not to scare them.

I went back to the stream and stopped to wash my hands. As I shook off the water, I caught another scent. This time it was a vampire. I did not want to alert the vampire that I caught the scent, so I bent down again and washed my hands while trying to determine the best course of action. A vampire out in the day hunting this deep in the forest was not that unusual because the dense trees protected us from the sun. Vampires came to Salem as tourists just as humans did, but this scent was somewhat familiar, and the vampire stayed far enough away that I was lucky I caught the scent at all.

I stood up and looked around. I turned and casually moved toward the scent. Normally, a vampire would either move along or make contact, but this one did not. I concentrated and heard the vampire move quietly, but whoever it was stayed away. Finally, I called out. "Hello. My name is James. I mean you no harm."

No response.

Vampires are not always a social group, so I was not too concerned, but I was cautious. I decided to head back to the car. I moved quickly away from the stream thinking the vampire would continue in the other direction. I heard movement to my right and realized the vampire was shadowing me. That was concerning. I tried to intercept, but the vampire moved away whenever I got close. The vampire was playing games and did not want to be seen. The question was, why?

I pretended I was not interested and moved away. Then I picked up speed, jumped the stream, and made a sharp turn back. I hoped my skills were better than the opposing vampire's skills. If they were, I would get right behind the vampire undetected, and sure enough, it worked. I heard the vampire moving up ahead. It was searching for me. Then I caught a strong whiff of the vampire's scent and stopped dead. It was Tony from New York City.

I crouched down and remained far enough away so he would not catch my scent. Why was he here? Was he looking for Arianna? Whatever he was doing, it was not sightseeing. He stopped and listened, and I stopped too. He had not been a vampire for long, and I had no doubt my skills were superior. When he started to move again, I crept closer and then jumped him. I had him locked in my arms before he realized I was even there.

"What are you doing here?" I growled.

"I have a right to be here," he struggled, but I held on.

"Why are you here? Are you alone?"

"Let me go," he grunted. He struggled to get free, but I held on. .

"Why are you here." I emphasized each word.

He would not answer. Then he managed to get a hold of his knife, and I had to let go or be stabbed. He turned to run, and I grabbed his shirt to stop him. We struggled, and he yanked the shirt out of my hands, and a piece tore off. He ran. I tossed the material aside and followed.

I finally caught him, and I tackled him to the ground. We fought and rolled. We clawed and tore at each other. I knew if I could bite him, I could subdue him. I grabbed his arm, and he turned sharply. I saw what was in his other hand just in time. I shut my eyes tight as he sprayed me with silver. I screamed and wiped as much as I could away with my shirt.

Then I smelled something else. I froze. Wolf. I could not open my eyes yet. I stood there waiting. Then I felt it speed by me. There was nothing I could do. I tuned in to the sound of the stream and staggered to it. The pain was fierce. I fell to my knees, and feeling with my hands, I crawled toward the sound of rushing water. As soon as I felt water, I plunged my head in and slid in deeper until my head was fully under water. I used my hands and scrubbed my face to wash off the silver, but I kept my eyes clamped shut. Finally, I leaned back, pushed my wet hair off my face, and wiped my eyes with my shirt. The pain was subsiding, so I slowly opened my eyes. I could see. I rolled onto my back and laid there on the bank. I closed my eyes again and waited for the pain to be gone.

Chapter VI
Werewolves

Arianna

Giovanni looked at his watch then looked at me.

"I think I will text James just to be certain everything is ok. Excuse me." I went into the kitchen. It was not like James to be late. I waited a couple minutes, but there was no reply. I went back in the dining room. "I texted him, but he probably doesn't have service right now." I locked eyes with Giovanni to convey my nervousness.

He got the hint. "Well, I think while we wait for James, I will unpack and take a short rest." Giovanni stood up.

"That's a good idea." I tried to keep the nervousness out of my voice. "Let me know if you need anything, Giovanni."

My mother helped me carry the cups and plates into the kitchen. She yawned, and I looked into her eyes and caught her gaze. "Mom, why don't you go lay down for a while? You aren't used to the time change yet."

She yawned again. "I think I will. I am tired."

As soon as she went upstairs, I texted Giovanni. *Something is wrong.*

Let's not panic, he texted back.

I'm going to go see if I can find him. Mom is going to nap. I don't want her to know I'm out looking for James.

Don't worry. I will handle things here. Keep in touch often and be careful.

I rolled my eyes. I put on my shoes and jacket and headed out the door. I should have taken my car, but I did not want to arouse suspicions with my mother should she hear or see my car leave. As soon as I was able, I went into the woods and quickly ran to the state forest where I knew James hunted. I stopped and listened hard. I texted Giovanni, *His car is here, but no sign of him yet. I may lose cell service.*

I headed up the trail. And then I smelled a vampire. I stopped instantly. It wasn't James, but I knew the scent.

"Arianna?"

"Yes, Marie. Over here." I came out from behind a tree. "What are you doing here?"

She wrapped her shawl tighter around her body even though I knew she was not cold. "I come here often to gather herbs and bark. I have been out in the forest for a couple of days." She looked at me, and her eyes widened. "Why are you here? Isn't your mother still visiting?" There was an edge to her voice I never heard before. She looked around quickly. "Where's James?"

"I don't know. That's why I am here. He's late and hasn't called or answered my texts."

She took off her shawl and tied it around her waist. "Let's go."

"Do you know where he might have gone to hunt?"

"We often come here. He will have gone to the stream." She ran, and I followed her. Suddenly, she stopped and held up her hand. There in the bushes, close to the stream, was a fresh kill. The coyotes tore at the meat then stopped and raised their head in alarm. They ran into the trees as Marie approached. "They didn't make this kill. There isn't enough blood."

I looked around and searched with my mind. There had to be a hawk here somewhere, but I could not find one. It was noticeably quiet. Too quiet. "There's nothing here, Marie. Nothing."

"Something is definitely not right. Stay close." We ran silently. I kept my mind open hoping to find a hawk. I stopped. Something caught my eye, and I turned. Marie stopped and followed my gaze. There was a piece of clothing caught on a tree.

"Does it belong to James?"

"No." I smelled the cloth and wrinkled my nose. "It does belong to a vampire. The scent is strong, and it is somewhat familiar."

"That means it is fresh. It rained last night." She did not have to say more. I thought the same thing, did James run into another vampire and was he ok? Marie examined the area. "There was a struggle here. Look two sets of prints. This way."

We ran on, and finally, my mind touched a hawk. It was quite far from us, but I was able to transmit an image of James to it. I slowed slightly because I was seeing through the hawk's eyes and also trying to watch where I was going.

"What's wrong, Arianna?"

"Nothing. I am in contact with a hawk. It is searching for James."

She did not reply but kept even with me. I knew James told her about my ability. It took a few minutes, but finally, I saw him. I looked over at Marie. We still were not entirely sure who could see my transmissions. So far, I only successfully transmitted images to James and Giovanni, so Giovanni believed it was because of a blood connection. Marie's face did not change, and it would if she saw James, so I knew she did not see what I saw. "I see him, Marie."

"Where? Is he ok?"

"He looks ok, but his clothes are dirty and wet and torn."

"Which way?"

I stopped and closed my eyes for a few seconds. I saw James look up at the hawk; he knew I saw him. The hawk turned and flew to me. "Follow the hawk. He will bring us to James."

We came to the edge of a small clearing and James appeared. The hawk screeched down, and I held up my arm. I forgot my guards in my haste to find James. I winched when the hawk landed on my arm, and its talons cut through my light jacket and deep into my skin. I stroked the bird and transmitted my happiness and thanks. James and Marie stayed back until the hawk took flight once again, and then they rushed over to me.

"You don't have your guards." James looked at my arm.

"I was in a hurry. I'll be ok."

Marie took my arm and looked at it. "We need to wash this."

The three of us walked toward the stream, and I took off my jacket and washed the cuts. I dipped my arm into the chilly water. The cuts would heal fairly quickly, but my jacket needed to be repaired.

"James what happened?" Marie asked.

"I saw a vampire in the forest."

"Yes, we saw his ripped clothing. Who was it?" Marie asked.

"Our friend Tony," James said to me.

"What? Here? I knew that scent was familiar."

"Who is Tony?" Marie asked.

"He was turned by an old vampire who was part of Darius' clan," James explained.

"The old vampire said he knew I was a hunter when I was a child," I added.

Marie looked hard at me. "Clearly, there is more to this story."

"There is." I shook the water off my arm.

"What are you two doing here?" James asked.

"I was worried. You were late and not responding to my texts. I came to look for you and ran into Marie."

"I'm sorry to worry you, Arianna."

"I think we should get back to the house," Marie suggested. "What is your mother doing, Arianna?"

"She's taking a nap. Giovanni is there with her."

We walked quickly toward James' car, and I texted Giovanni as soon as I had cell service. He was at the door waiting for us when we arrived home. He motioned us to the kitchen, and I heard my mother sleeping upstairs.

"What happened?" he asked.

"I was hunting when I felt the presence of another vampire. I knew I smelled this vampire before. I was able to get behind him and grab him. It was Tony from New York City. We struggled, and I asked him what he was doing here, but he wasn't talking. He broke away, and when I caught him again, he sprayed colloidal silver in my face."

"Silver? Then he was prepared in case he ran into you or someone else." Giovanni looked disturbed. Marie looked carefully at James making sure that he was ok.

James continued, "before I recovered, a wolf ran past me chasing after Tony. I'm sure he is long gone by now."

"A wolf?" I asked.

Giovanni sighed. "I hoped to tell you this later when we have more time. A wolf pack has moved to the area."

"Wolves don't like vampires?" I was confused.

"Arianna, these wolves are not ordinary wolves," Giovanni explained. "They are werewolves. They are humans who have the ability to shift into wolf form."

"What?" I looked at James and then at Marie. They both nodded yes. "Werewolves are not mythological?"

"They are real. Several families purchased homes in the new subdivision," Marie added.

I turned to James. "Why didn't you tell me they weren't animals? I assumed the wolves were the regular four-legged kind, not someone who can shift into wolf form." My tone was sharp. I knew James wanted to protect me, but not having all the facts was more likely to harm me than help me.

He placed his hands on my arms and looked into my eyes. "I'm sorry, Arianna. You are right. I should have told you. I just thought it was better for Giovanni to explain it to you. Vampires and wolves have not always been friendly toward one another."

"Still, you should have told me, James."

He nodded his head.

"Wolves and hunters have always had a close relationship," Giovanni began. "It was common for a first level hunter and a werewolf to marry and have children. Of course, that was at a time when there were many hunters and werewolves. I will tell you more about them later."

"Wait a minute," I said suddenly. "Marie, you said they moved into homes in the new subdivision?"

"Yes, why?"

"Oh my god. That puppy was not a puppy at all."

The three of them stared at me. "What?" James asked.

I quickly explained that I took what I thought was a wolf hybrid puppy away from three boys in the park and returned the puppy to the family that lived in the new subdivision. "I thought it was strange that Jason referred to the pup as his brother. The father explained that the puppy was like a brother to his older son."

"Who did you meet?" Marie asked.

"I met John, his wife Adrian, and their son Jason."

We heard a noise, and the four of us looked up at once. "Your mother is waking up, Arianna," Giovanni said.

"You two better get upstairs and get cleaned up," Marie said.

We both nodded. "Are you staying Marie?" James asked.

"No, I don't think this is the time to meet Arianna's mother. I will search the area and make sure this Tony is gone."

"Be careful, Marie." James was clearly concerned, but there was no point in telling her not to go search for Tony. She would not listen.

"I will. And I need to know more about this Tony and the old vampire. I'll be back later tonight."

"Hurry, James." I pulled his arm. "My mother is awake, and we can't let her see us like this." We quickly went upstairs to our bedroom and closed the door.

Chapter VII
Midnight Meeting

James

After Arianna's mother fell asleep, Marie came to the house. We sat in the kitchen, and we told her everything we knew about the two vampires. "We first saw the old vampire on a trip to the Metropolitan Museum in New York City," I explained to Marie.

"Yes, he was very creepy. He just stared at me and seemed to growl," Arianna added. "At Christmas time, when we were back in the city, I saw a vampire talking to a group of young girls at the café in Macy's. I foolishly confronted him. The old vampire came out of the kitchen, and he said he was training Tony, who was a newly turned vampire."

"We were lucky to get out of the situation without a confrontation," I told Marie.

"He said he knew I was a hunter when I was a child," Arianna told Marie.

"So, he knows about your past, but you do not?" Marie thought for a few minutes.

"Darius also said he knew me when I was a child."

"And this old vampire was not with Darius when you defeated him?" Marie looked at the three of us, and we shook our heads no. "I don't think it is a coincidence that this vampire is here at the same time as Giovanni," she stoically commented.

"I agree," Giovanni replied. "I called Marena, and no strange vampires are in the area. Marcus, Trina, Simon, and several others searched for signs. It rained yesterday, so we can't be certain no one was there."

"Giovanni, have you ever met the old vampire?" Marie asked.

"I have been thinking about him, Marie. I never met him, but when I looked at the picture James took in December, his face looked familiar. He looks like a man from my village in Italy, but that man was not a vampire, and I thought he was dead."

"Is it possible he was turned?" Marie asked.

"I thought he died, but then I thought my grandson was dead too."

"When I first met you, Giovanni, you told me everyone in your family was dead."

"And so, I thought." Giovanni shook his head. "The night I nearly died, Giuseppe told me that he fell in love and had much to tell me, but we had to respond to a vampire attack on Lord Benenati's estate. When we arrived at the castle, it was on fire. It was chaos, and we were overtaken by vampires. Lord Donati sent his son and a company of men to help, but the fight did not go well. The old one resembles one of several men I saw fall from one of the towers. Then I was wounded and thrown into a fire. As I lay there, I saw Giuseppe. He too burned, and he looked at me then collapsed. I called out then collapsed myself. I woke up weeks later. A group of villagers rescued me. I asked about Giuseppe. They said no one else survived. When I recovered, I went back and searched the area. I found the remains of a broach my grandson always wore on his tunic. I knew then, or thought I knew, he was truly dead." Giovanni took a deep breath, "From the photograph Arianna's mother showed me, he looks basically the same as when I last saw him."

"Hunters age slowly," Marie commented.

"True, but not that slowly." Giovanni looked exasperated. "He must have been turned again not long after that battle." He shook his head. "I don't know. He was always difficult. After his grandmother was killed, he was so angry. As the years passed, he gained many followers. Finally, I left the area. I was gone for many years. I returned only because I heard the war intensified in the area."

"Of course, he was difficult and angry," Arianna replied. "His parents were dead, and his beloved grandmother died protecting him."

"He was a hot head. He angered quickly, and he never followed the rules," Giovanni said angrily.

"Did you ever talk to him? Try to help?" Arianna was also getting angry.

"No one could ever talk to him," Giovanni fired back. "He never listened."

"Well," Marie said loudly interrupting their escalating argument. "There are a number of unanswered questions."

Arianna got up. "Would anyone like a drink?"

"Yes, I think we can all use a drink." Marie replied.

We went in the front sitting room. Marie and I sat on the love seat, and Arianna and Giovanni sat across from one another in the chairs on either side of the love seat. The tension in the room rose. Arianna and Giovanni were at odds yet again. Arianna had nothing but praise for her great grandfather, and Giovanni obviously had difficulties with him. I didn't want to add to the problem, but I wondered if Giuseppe was truly dead. Vampires often faked their own death, so why not a hunter? I took a deep breath, "It is possible Giuseppe is still alive."

"Yes, I have considered that possibility," Giovanni replied.

"What?!" Arianna yelled a little too loudly, and we all looked up hoping she did not wake her mother.

"It is likely he faked his own death." Marie said almost to herself.

Arianna looked shocked. "No, he wouldn't leave me," she said softly.

"At the time, he may not have had a choice," Marie said soothingly. "But if he is alive, where has he been for twenty plus years, and if Darius was the reason he left, why hasn't he returned now that Darius is gone? He must have heard about Arianna by now."

"Unless he is out of the country," I added.

Arianna stood up, walked to the buffet, and picked up a tray with glasses and a decanter of Cognac. She set it on the table, and I rose and poured each of us a glass. We raised our glasses but did not toast and drank.

I refilled the glasses. "So, what is our next move?" I asked.

"Watch for Tony and try to capture him if we see him." Giovanni said gruffly.

"I will sweep the area several times a day while Arianna's mother is here." Marie smiled at us. "We don't want her wondering where you three are off to every day."

"I'll do it during the night. I will hunt every day to keep my strength up just in case there is trouble," I said.

Giovanni nodded his approval. Arianna said nothing.

"I assume Tony was here watching, but he was not supposed to be seen." I shook my head. "But why was he watching?" I could not help thinking the old vampire was planning an attack.

"At least now he knows there are wolves protecting the area and Arianna," Giovanni added.

Arianna raised her head. "They are protecting me?"

"Yes, wolves work with hunters to keep the peace, deal with rogues, and," he paused, "keep vampires in line." He gave me and Marie a pained look. "We should meet the families as soon as possible."

"I will arrange it," Marie said. "I will call John tomorrow and arrange a meeting in the field near their homes tomorrow night at midnight. And since he has already met Arianna, he must have questions."

"Yes, and the sooner we explain the situation to them the better prepared they will be in case Tony or someone else returns." Giovanni was obviously happy there was a werewolf pack in the area.

"Well, I will be leaving now." Marie stood up, and I walked her to the door. She took my hands in hers. "Be well."

"You too, Marie," I squeezed her hands. "Be careful."

"Good night." She opened the door and slipped out into the night.

Giovanni went upstairs to bed, and I went in the kitchen. Arianna stood at the counter. She poured a bowl of cereal and sat down at the table. "I don't think my great grandfather would leave me."

"He may not have had a choice." I stood behind her and kneaded her shoulders. She sighed and leaned her head against my arm.

*****

The next night, after Arianna's mother went to bed, we walked to the field to meet the werewolf families. Arianna took my hand as we walked. "This is exactly what I don't want to do," she whispered.

I did not know what to say. Arianna knew nothing about vampires, hunters, or wolves a year ago. I put my arm around her and pulled her close. I knew she wanted nothing to do with the workings of our world, but I also knew she could not entirely remove herself from it.

We arrived at the field and waited. "I will introduce the pack leader," Marie said.

"Let me do the talking, Arianna," Giovanni said.

"Gladly," she replied. "I don't know why I'm even here. I refuse to get involved in these matters."

I heard Giovanni draw in a deep breath and slowly let it out. He tried to be patient with Arianna, but he was a stubborn and impatient man.

The moon peeked out from behind high thin clouds and illuminated the field on the edge of the subdivision where the families lived. We did not have to wait long. We smelled them before we saw them, and we watched them emerge from the trees and head toward us. There were twelve of them, seven men and five women.

"Hello," one of the men said to Marie.

"Hello, John. Let me introduce Giovanni, Arianna, and James."

John looked from Arianna to me and back to Arianna. "I knew you were a hunter when you came here with Tommy. Why did you ignore our status? Marie said you would explain." He spoke directly to Arianna.

"I'm sorry," she said taking a step toward him. "I did not know what you were or anything about werewolf and hunter relationships."

"Let me explain," Giovanni interrupted. John looked at him. "I am Giovanni, a hunter. Arianna has been a hunter less than a year and has never met a werewolf."

John relaxed and let out the breath he seemed to hold since he arrived. "I see."

"No disrespect was intended," Giovanni informed him.

"I absolutely meant no disrespect," Arianna quickly added. "I just had no idea."

Now John smiled. "I understand. I guess I jumped to conclusions. To be honest, I wasn't exactly sure you were a hunter. I have never met a female hunter before, and I should not be surprised that you never met one of us." He extended his hand and Arianna took it. "Let me introduce you to the others." He pulled Arianna forward a couple of steps then let go of her hand. "You already met my wife Adrian, and my eldest son Jason."

Adrian waved, but Jason strode right up to Arianna and extended his hand. She shook his hand and quickly pulled it back. "I am very happy to officially meet you, Arianna." Jason smiled at her.

"This is Malcolm, my second, his wife Emma and their son Maxwell; Jeffrey and his wife Tanya, their sons Trey and Ty and their daughters Susan and Katherine; and this is Sam." They all exchanged nods and said hello, but only Malcolm and Sam approached her and shook her hand. "The younger children including Tommy are asleep."

Arianna turned to us. Her eyes were wide, and I saw she was uncomfortable. Giovanni saw the look in her eyes and stepped forward. "It is a pleasure to meet all of you," he said.

"Do you live in the area?" John asked.

"No," Giovanni said slowly. "But I am here often training Arianna." Giovanni did not disclose that he and Arianna were related.

I saw Arianna stiffen, but she said nothing.

"I believe one of you chased a vampire out of the area last night," Giovanni said.

"Yes, I was on patrol and saw him sneaking around, so I followed him from a distance. Then that one came along and chased him." Jason pointed to me.

"Did you see any others?" Giovanni asked.

"No, but I didn't like the smell of him. Why did the other one chase him?'

Everyone was tense. I knew Marie was annoyed with Jason's tone and was doing her best to keep quiet, but I was surprised when Arianna spoke up. "Excuse me," she said quite loudly. "He has a name, and you know it, so use it."

The others remained quiet, and John glared at his son. "Show respect," he said through gritted teeth.

Jason continued to stare at me. He turned to Arianna. "I assure you; I meant no disrespect to you." His emphasis on the "to you" did not go unnoticed. "Why did James chase him?" Jason asked Arianna directly.

She glanced toward Giovanni who gave the slightest nod. "That vampire is not friendly. He is part of a group of vampires who have tried to kill me." That caught the wolves' attention, and they gathered closer to Arianna. "James," she emphasized my name, "Giovanni, and Marcus, a vampire friend, fought with me to defeat some of these vampires, who were also using rogues, back in March. The vampire who was here last night is named Tony. Although he was not part of the battle in March, we know he is part of the group."

"Jason, get that material you brought back. I want everyone to smell it and remember it." Jason took off for his home and returned quickly with the ripped garment. They all breathed the scent in deeply. "We will kill him if he returns," John said.

"We prefer him alive," Giovanni said sternly. "We need to question him. He is a minion in the group, but I am sure he knows something."

"As you wish," John replied.

"You should report to Marie," Giovanni informed John.

"Why?" John stammered.

"She is the clan leader."

"Yes, but there is a hunter here, and we should report to her," John said sternly.

Giovanni looked at Arianna. She sighed. "I request you report to Marie," Arianna said to John. "She is clan leader and more knowledgeable than me."

John nodded. "If that is all, I will dismiss everyone." Arianna looked to Giovanni who nodded, so she nodded her agreement. Everyone but John and Jason returned home.

"May I ask what is going on?" John asked.

"Giovanni will explain everything," Arianna said. "But now, if you will excuse me, I need to return home in case my mother wakes up." Arianna turned to me. "Please don't be too late," she said softly. "Good night," she said to John, and she started to walk back.

"Wait," Jason called to her. "I will accompany you back to ensure your safety. I have patrol duty tonight."

Arianna looked annoyed. "That won't be necessary."

"I am going that way anyway."

"How do you know where I live?" she asked defensively.

Jason shuffled around. "I followed you the other day." Arianna glared at him. "I was worried those boys might go after you," he added quickly. "I was just doing my job." He looked at Giovanni for help.

"Arianna, it is best not to go back alone," Giovanni said.

"Fine," she said with a sigh. "Let's go." The two of them started to walk down the street.

"Arianna is having difficulty with her transformation," Giovanni explained to John. "She does not wish to involve herself in our world."

"Why? There are so few super hunters. She must take responsibility."

Giovanni shook his head no. "Unfortunately, Arianna did not know she was a hunter until she was bitten a second time."

"How is that possible?"

"We don't know. She was unmarked. She was never trained. She had no idea what she was or that vampires even existed. Marie came to find me last year after she met Arianna here in Salem. When I arrived in New York, where Arianna lived at the time, the vampires there had just been informed that she was a hunter. She was away at the time, and before anything could be explained to her, she was attacked and bitten. James, his friend Marcus, and I were able to save her. After she transformed, we told her she was a vampire hunter and explained our world."

John shook his head. "No wonder she wants nothing to do with us."

"When she awoke after the attack and transformation, she was quite angry. She denied what she was and tried to go on with her normal life. But instinct and hunger overwhelmed her, and she had no choice but to accept her transformation. She began to accept some training only after an encounter with Tony and another vampire. Then in March, Darius attacked her again, but this time he was killed."

"You killed him?" John said to me.

"No. I was there, but I did not kill him."

"As you can see, she will not embrace this world or accept the role she plays in it. She will do only what is absolutely necessary." Giovanni looked at John. "I think it is best this information stay between us alone."

"Yes, I agree." John shook his head in disbelief. "And she lives here with you?" John asked me.

"Yes, she does."

"You should contact Marie with any information you discover. I will also talk to Arianna and tell her I told you the situation, but no one else in the pack knows," Giovanni told John.

"You may also contact, James," Marie said to John. "Especially if Tony returns. It is imperative that he and Arianna know immediately."

John hesitated but then nodded. "As you wish."

The three of us said good night to John, and we walked back. Marie left us before we reached my home. We were about a block away when we saw Jason. He sauntered up to us and looked extremely happy. "Arianna is safely inside. Her mother was up and wondering where everyone was when we returned, but Arianna took care of it."

Giovanni grunted. He did not like when Arianna compelled humans.

"Good night, Jason," I said.

"Night." He continued walking away.

I quietly opened the front door. "Good night," Giovanni said as he went upstairs to bed without saying a word to Arianna.

Arianna wore a night gown and robe, and she sat on the sofa in the living room in front of the fireplace. I walked in the room and sat down next to her. Her eyes were wet. "I'm sorry, James," she said softly.

"There is nothing to be sorry about, love."

"I know Giovanni is annoyed with me." She sat up straighter. "I wish you and I could just go away together. Disappear somewhere where we can be alone."

I felt the same way, but it was not possible. Not now. I stood up and reached out to her. She took my hand and stood up. We slowly and quietly walked upstairs to our bedroom. I flicked the lock closed on the door and undressed then we got into bed. I smoothed her hair back from her face and softly kissed her. "I love you."

She responded by raising her head and deepening the kiss. She nibbled on my bottom lip then laid back down. She ran delicate hands up my bare chest. "James, make love to me," she whispered. "Let it be just you and me for a while, so we can forget about everyone else."

I looked into her dark brown almost black eyes. She was all I needed in life. "Just us," I whispered, and I kissed her again. We lost ourselves in one another, and for that time, it was just the two of us, and then she fell asleep in my arms.

I kissed her softly when she began to stir. Arianna opened her eyes and smiled up at me. She looked refreshed. She slept well, even if it was just for a few hours. We showered together but didn't talk much. I did not want to talk about Tony or the wolves, and I was glad she didn't either. Right now, I just wanted quiet time with her. I shampooed her hair and then conditioned it. She massaged my back and shoulders as she soaped me up, and I trailed soft kisses all over her as I gently soaped her body. When she reached for the shower door, I took her hand and brought it to my lips. "I love you."

She turned and put her arms around my neck. "I love you."

We stepped out and dried off.

"What time is our trolley tour?" Arianna asked as she towel dried her hair.

"11:30."

"I don't hear Giovanni yet."

"We were up late. He'll get up soon," I assured her. Arianna's mother was already awake and showering, so we dressed, went downstairs, and started breakfast.

"I'm starving." Arianna said as she went to the cabinet and took out a box of cereal. I put on coffee and water for tea while Arianna ate. "I think I will make scrambled eggs this morning."

"I can cook bacon," I suggested.

"Maybe breakfast sausage. I think Giovanni will like sausage."

"Giovanni will probably want rare steak."

"We can put steaks on the grill for dinner," she laughed.

Felicia waked in the kitchen. "Good morning, dears."

"Morning, Mom." Arianna gave her mother a kiss.

"Good morning, Felicia. Would you like coffee or tea?"

"Tea, thank you, James."

I set a mug of hot water in front of her and slid over the basket of teas. Arianna set a small creamer of half and half on the table and moved the sugar bowl next to it.

"Mom would you like breakfast sausage and scrambled eggs?"

"No sausage, but scrambled eggs sound nice."

I put breakfast sausage patties into a fry pan, and soon the aroma of sausage filled the kitchen. Arianna mixed up a large batch of scrambled eggs.

"Good morning," Giovanni said as he came through the doorway. "It smells good in here."

"Scrambled eggs and sausage, Giovanni?" Arianna asked cheerfully as she poured him a cup of coffee.

"Yes, thank you." He smiled at her.

"Would anyone like toast?" Arianna asked.

"No thank you," Felicia and Giovanni said together.

"Giovanni, you have to try one of these pumpkin muffins," Felicia pointed to the basket. "They are amazing." She reached for a muffin, cut it open, and put on a pad of warm butter.

I set a plate of sausages on the table, and Arianna set down a large bowl of scrambled eggs. I drank coffee but did not eat anything, and fortunately, Felicia did not seem to notice.

"We have a fun filled weekend planned," Arianna informed her mother. "We are all going on the trolley tour and to the Salem Witch Museum today."

"I am excited to see the sights," Felicia replied.

"And Mom, you and I are going to go to the Witch Trial candlelight tour tonight."

"Oh, that sounds fun." She looked from me to Giovanni. "Aren't the men going?"

"Oh no, you ladies have an enjoyable time together," I said. "Giovanni and I will meet you after the tour, and we will all go out for a drink."

"Tomorrow, you and I are going to the House of Seven Gables." Arianna explained to Felicia.

"It sounds like we are going to have a great weekend." Felicia rose and put her plate in the dishwasher. "Well, that was delicious. I think I will get dressed." She took a second cup of tea and headed upstairs.

"Maybe tonight after your mother is asleep you should hunt with James," Giovanni suggested.

"I will go with him, but I will not feed." Giovanni gave her an angry look and started to say something, but she interrupted him. "We are having steaks for dinner tonight."

"Hum," Giovanni grunted. "Steaks are a good idea."

It was a beautiful Fall day, and Giovanni and Felicia enjoyed the sights of Salem. We took the trolley ride all around the town, and then got off at Friendship Park when we passed by again.

"We are in luck. We can get on board the Friendship today." I led the way to the replica ship, and we walked up the gang plank. A tour guide answered questions as people made their way around the ship. We went below deck and looked at the crew areas and the cargo hold. Although this was a replica, the ship was accurate, and it was magnificent.

As we exited the ship and walked back to the main street, I smelled a wolf. Jason stood by the visitor building and watched. I made eye contact with him but neither of us acknowledged one another. He did acknowledge Giovanni. I was glad Arianna was engrossed in conversation with her mother and did not see him. We left Derby Wharf and walked down the street to the café for refreshments.

"The Pumpkin Chai tea is fabulous here, Mom. Thick, rich, and foamy," Arianna explained.

"I'll have one."

"Giovanni, would you like a Pumpkin Chai tea too?" Arianna asked.

"No, Thank you. Just black coffee."

"Should we sit outside?" Arianna asked her mother and Giovanni.

"Fine with me," Giovanni replied.

"Mom?"

"It's a little chilly, but yes, sitting outside sounds nice."

"Are you sure, Mom? You aren't accustomed to the cold."

"I'm ok. The tea will warm me."

"Two black coffees and two Pumpkin Chai teas," I confirmed. "Anything else?" They all shook their head no, so I placed our drink orders.

The sun was low in the sky. The leaves were in full color, and the air was clean and clear as it often was in the Fall in New England. We sat at a small table outside and watched the people go by.

"The colors are beautiful," Felicia commented, "I miss the changing seasons and the Fall colors."

"Then I am glad you came to visit, Mom," Arianna said with a smile.

We were almost finished when I spotted a large group of tourists walking toward us. "Looks like a cruise ship is in town."

"A cruise ship?" Felicia asked.

Arianna nodded her head yes. "A couple cruise lines now have New England tours that stop in Boston, Salem, and several other ports up the coast."

After spending the day downtown, Arianna and Felicia stopped in several of the shops while Giovanni and I went home for the car and drove to the grocery store for the steaks. As we pulled into the driveway, we saw Marie. "Is everything ok?"

"Yes, everything is fine. Arianna and her mother are on their way home. I kept an eye on them. And I was not the only one."

"Jason."

"Yes."

Giovanni grunted. "Why shouldn't he watch over her? He is a wolf, and it is his responsibility to look after her even if she does not appreciate the protection."

"Arianna will not be happy if she sees him," I said.

"He kept his distance," Marie informed us. "Giovanni, are you leaving early tomorrow?"

"I plan to leave by ten o'clock. Marena and I have dinner plans tomorrow night." He picked up two bags of groceries. "I will start preparing the steaks." He took the bags inside.

"Can you stay for dinner?" I asked Marie.

"Thank you, but not tonight. I have plans." She waited until Giovanni closed the door. "James, I don't like Jason hanging around Arianna."

"I don't either. I saw him earlier today. But, if it keeps Arianna safe, I really can't complain."

Marie nodded. "I guess. There are so many vampires and people in town for the celebrations. Be careful."

"I've sensed quite a few vampires in town. They are blending in well. They just are having a fun time."

"I will do a quick look around and then stop by tonight after Felicia has gone to bed." She let out an annoyed grunt. "At least with the wolves on patrol, we can be fairly sure no one is hiding in the forest."

"Arianna said she will go with me when I hunt tonight. Why don't the three of us go after you say goodbye to Giovanni?"

"Yes. I like that idea." She started to walk down the driveway and waved. "Maybe we can get her to feed. Until later."

I looked at my watch and went inside. "I will start the grill, Giovanni."

By the time Arianna and her mother returned, the grill was ready, and we had the steaks rubbed with spices and ready for grilling. The two of them carried several bags in each hand. I took Arianna's bags, and she gave me a little kiss.

"Felicia, shall I carry your purchases upstairs too?"

"Thank you, James." She handed me the bags. "I think I will make a salad." She walked into the kitchen.

Arianna wrapped her arms around my waist, pulled me close, and kissed me passionately. With my arms full of bags, I was unable to hug her, but I enthusiastically kissed her back. "I should probably help with dinner," she said sadly as she pulled away.

"Probably should." I started up the stairs. "Oh, Marie is coming by later to say goodbye to Giovanni, and she will come out with us tonight." Arianna nodded and went in the kitchen.

In under thirty minutes, we were sitting around the table eating.

"Salem is fascinating. So much History," Felicia commented. She took a sip of wine. "Have you been to Salem before, Giovanni?"

"Oh yes. I visited here many years ago. It has changed much since that time."

"I will have to bring your father here, Arianna. He will love the history."

The tour started at seven o'clock, so I drove Arianna and Felicia to the back side of the cemetery where the tour began. Arianna leaned over and kissed me rather more passionately than I thought she would with her mother present. "See you soon," she whispered.

"Giovanni and I will meet you in front of the museum entrance when the tour ends." I kissed her back. "Have fun."

I watched as they joined the group and were handed candles by the tour guide. I scanned the crowd carefully because I sensed a number of vampires were present waiting for the tour to start. None were familiar. I also smelled, wolves. I scanned the crowd again. I didn't see Jason, but I did see the two sisters Susan and Katherine. I turned the car around and sped back to get Giovanni. He wanted to look around the area and talk to John again.

Arianna and Felicia spent the next couple of days talking, shopping, and walking around town. Arianna took her mother over to the Historical Society to show her the work she was doing.

I was upstairs writing when I heard Arianna's car in the driveway. I saved my document, then went downstairs and opened the door to let them in. "Did you enjoy visiting the Historical Society?" I asked Felicia.

"It is an interesting place. I can't say enough about how rich this town is in history. No wonder you two love it here."

I took her coat and hung it in the hall closet then we all went in the kitchen.

"Arianna, the work you are doing there is fascinating."

"I am enjoying it, Mom."

"Your dad was worried that you were not doing anything and wasting time but going through those newspapers and magazines is really interesting."

"And it is important work. Cataloging is a necessary skill in my field."

Felicia nodded but looked worried.

"You don't need to worry about me, Mom," Arianna gave her mother a hug "I am writing, working, and rediscovering my creative side. That is as important as teaching. I can't teach if I'm burned out."

"Your father just worries, dear. We both want the best for you."

"I know, and right now this is best for me. I am happier than I have been in a long time." Arianna smiled at me.

"Felicia, I want to assure you that Arianna's happiness means everything to me."

Arianna set a plate of muffins on the kitchen table and poured two cups of tea.

Felicia smiled at me, and I believed she understood the depth of my love for Arianna. "These muffins really are delicious," she said as she reached for one.

*****

The morning of Felicia's flight back to California was busy. "Felicia is that all your luggage?" I called up to her. She purchased so many things she needed to check an extra bag.

"Yes, James. Thank you." She came down the stairs carrying a large floral bag that was bursting at the seams.

Arianna came out of the kitchen. "Mom, I packaged up muffins for you to take to Dad."

"Oh good. He is going to love them."

I took the bag from Felicia. "Are you two ready?"

They nodded yes, and we walked outside.

"Thank you both so much for a wonderful visit," Felicia said to us.

"Thanks for visiting, Mom."

Felicia turned around and took another look at the house. "You have done a wonderful job decorating too, Arianna."

Arianna continued to add to her holiday display. Besides the three hay bales, colorful mums, and the ornamental cabbage there were now corn stalks, a very large pumpkin flanked each side of the door, and the top of the door was capped by a spray of dried husks and natural materials. The three big spiders now had a few smaller spiders for company. Arianna hoped for trick or treaters this year, but I was not as optimistic. While we were looking at the house, I noticed Mrs. Grady on the sidewalk across the street. Arianna turned and saw her too.

"Hello, Mrs. Grady. How are you?" Arianna waved.

The frail old woman lifted her arm and gave a little wave.

"Your neighbors are not that friendly though," Felicia remarked.

"I'm sure they will be friendlier once they get to know us, Mom. Remember the house has been empty for years."

It was mid-morning, so the traffic was light. I concentrated on driving, and Arianna and her mother chatted on the way to the airport.

I parked in short term parking and unloaded the bags. "James, do you need a cart?" Felicia asked. "Those bags are heavy."

"I have them." I replied with a smile.

Check in went smoothly. Fortunately, they did not weigh the carry - on baggage. We walked Felicia over to the security check point entrance. "Felicia it was a pleasure having you visit. Please come again."

"Thank you, James. You make my daughter incredibly happy." She hugged me.

"Bye, Mom." Arianna hugged her mother. "I'll miss you."

"Oh, I will miss you too, honey." There were tears in both their eyes.

"Give Dad a hug."

"I will. You take care. I love you."

"I love you too." They hugged again. Arianna wiped her eyes. I handed the bags to Felicia, and she got in the security line. I put my arm around Arianna's waist, and she leaned into me as we watched Felicia go through the security screening. She picked up her bags, waved, and headed for the gate.

Arianna breathed a sigh of relief. "Well, that went well." We sat down to wait until Felicia's flight took off. Arianna hooked her arm in mine and rested her head on my shoulder.

"It was nice having your mother visit."

Arianna lifted her head and whispered in my ear. "We have the whole house to ourselves again."

"What did you have in mind?"

"You will see," she said mischievously.

Chapter VIII
Albert's Call

Arianna

Now that my mother's visit was over, I spent more time in the archives at the Historical Society pouring through Mr. Tanner's donation. I wanted to help the Historical Society, but I also wanted to see if I could find out more about James' family and about the incident leading up to James being turned by Marie. Of course, James told me when and why he was turned, but his account lacked the details he normally included in a story. Unfortunately, Mr. Tanner did not keep the items in chronological order. I read quickly, but there were many boxes of materials to go through.

On my way home from the Historical Society, I stopped at the grocery store for cheese to make a seafood casserole. The cool weather made me want to cook and bake. Of course, I ran into Jason.

"Hi Arianna." He reached me with a few long effortless steps.

I concluded that although I was not going to get involved in the politics of the clan, I could not avoid everyone especially since we lived in a fairly small town. "Hi Jason. How are you?"

"Doing good and you?"

"I'm well, thanks." I put the cheese into my cart. I noticed he had beer, chips, and a jar of dip in his cart. "Having a party?"

Jason laughed. "No, just an ordinary night. Some of the guys and a few of their girlfriends are coming over later."

I nodded and selected another package of cheese. I started to walk to the wine section. He followed me. I selected a couple bottles of red wine that James and I liked and put them in the cart.

"Arianna, would you like to come over tonight and have a beer." He touched my shoulder as he looked down at the wine in my cart. "I can get a bottle of wine if you prefer."

"Oh, thank you, Jason, but tonight I plan to spend a quiet evening home with James."

"I was wondering," he paused, "how long you have lived with James?" I looked at him but did not answer immediately. "I was just curious," he added.

It was not a secret. "We moved in together over the Summer."

"Have you two been together long?"

"Over a year."

Jason nodded. "Well, it was nice to see you, Arianna."

"Nice to see you too, Jason."

I went home and started cooking dinner. I put on a Caribbean music playlist, and then put a pot of water on the stove to boil for the pasta. As I made the casserole, I danced around the kitchen.

"Umm. That smells good even to me. What are you cooking?" James asked when he came in from hunting later that evening.

"Seafood casserole."

James leaned over to kiss me and stopped. He smelled my shoulder then wrinkled his nose.

"What's wrong?" I asked.

"You saw Jason today?"

"Yes, how did you know?"

"I can smell him. He touched you on your shoulder." James scowled. "What did he want?"

I put my hands on my hips and looked at him. "Really, James? You aren't jealous, are you?"

He shrugged. "Sorry. I'm not fond of wolves." He leaned in and kissed me.

I relaxed. "I saw Jason at the grocery store when I bought cheese for this casserole. You can smell where he touched my shoulder?" I reached over and turned off the oven, opened the door, and removed the casserole dish. The cheese bubbled and popped.

"He probably touched you intentionally knowing I would smell him."

"Well, you have nothing to worry about." I kissed him. "No one can compare to you."

James pulled me against his body and kissed me passionately. "There's no one like you, Arianna."

I returned the kiss then reached in the drawer for a serving spoon.

"The casserole smells good."

"Thanks, would you like some or are you just going to enjoy the aroma?" I laughed.

"I think I will try a little."

I reached into the cabinet and took out a dinner plate. I spooned a dollop of casserole onto the center and grated on fresh black pepper. I placed the plate in front of him. I took out another plate and piled on casserole for me. I grated on pepper and set it down. I brought over a plate of pineapple and gelatin salad and then I set a bowl of steaming broccoli on the table.

James wrinkled his nose, and he pushed the bowl of broccoli closer to my side. "That doesn't smell good at all," he shuddered.

I grabbed a bottle of wine out of the chiller. "We should have white because we are having fish."

"True, but red is so much better." He opened the wine while I took glasses out of the cabinet.

"Cheers, my dear Arianna."

"Cheers." We clinked glasses and drank.

James poked a bit at the casserole and then took a small bite. "Yum. This is good."

"I'm glad you like it." He ate the food on his plate and then got up and served himself a tiny bit more. I had another large serving, most of the pineapple, and I ate all the broccoli.

After dinner, James and I took our laptops and lounged in front of the fireplace on our new, soft, brown, leather sectional sofa. Since moving in, we started updating some of the furniture because many of the old pieces were just not comfortable. Although our bodies adjusted to the temperature, so we were never too hot or too cold, James and I both enjoyed the ambiance of a fire.

"Oh James, I received an email from Dean Branson."

"How is the dean?"

"He's doing well. He invited us to a party after the Weymouth football game on Thanksgiving Day."

"Would you like to go? It would be nice to visit with our friends."

"Yes, it would be fun."

"I'll make hotel reservations."

I sent an RSVP to the dean and continued to scroll through more email. I looked over at James. His fingers flew over the keyboard. He was almost finished with his novel and had a meeting with his agent just after Thanksgiving.

My phone rang.

"It's probably Giovanni," James said without glancing at the phone.

"Probably," I mumbled. Even though Marie sent him regular reports, Giovanni called us often for updates. Fortunately, there were no further signs of Tony, the old vampire, or the few others we knew to be associates of Darius. Now that Halloween was over, there were very few vampires in the area, and Marie knew each of them. The wolves were doing daily patrols which made Giovanni happy.

I reached over, picked up my phone, and looked at the caller ID. "It's Albert?" My heart sank. "Albert never calls." James stopped typing and sat up as if bracing for bad news. Hesitantly, I pushed the green button. "Hello?"

"Hi, Baby Sis." I cringed at his words, Baby Sis. Yes, I was his younger sister, but why did Albert need to call me, Baby Sis? I took in a deep calming breath. Albert sounded pleasant, but I could not help thinking something was wrong. Albert was seven years older than me, and he never called unless my parents were visiting me, or it was a holiday.

"Is everything ok? Are Mom and Dad, ok?" I quickly asked.

"Yes. Yes, everything is fine," he laughed, "can't I just call for no reason?"

"Oh, ok." I wasn't sure what to say. I hadn't spoken to Albert since my graduation in May, and I suspected that my mother called him, so he could say congratulations.

"So, how are you?" He sounded very cheerful.

"Good thanks. And you?" I slid closer to James on the sofa.

"I'm good. Yes, really good. In fact, I have some incredibly good news."

"Oh?"

"I'm getting married!" he blurted out.

"Oh," I stuttered, "that's wonderful."

"The date is set for New Year's Eve here in Montana."

"New Year's Eve?"

"We thought it was an easy date to remember."

I looked at the phone and rolled my eyes. "You mean you thought it was an easy date to remember."

He laughed.

"Albert, New Year's Eve is less than two months away. Can a wedding be put together that quickly?"

"Patty thinks so."

"Her name is Patty?"

"Yep, her name is Patty. She's an undergrad." I heard someone in the background, but even with my sensitive hearing, I could not make out the words. "Oh wait. She wants to talk to you."

I heard rustling and giggling then, "Hi Arianna!" Her voice was loud and high pitched. "This is Patty."

"Hi, Patty. Congratulations on your engagement."

"Thanks so much." She giggled, and I heard her take a deep breath. "Albert said to send you an email, but then he decided to call. So, I know we haven't met or anything, but you are Albert's sister, and well, I don't have any sisters, three much older brothers, anyway, will you be one of my bridesmaids?" She said it all without taking another breath.

I was stunned. I looked at James. He smiled. "Umm, yes, Patty. Thank you. I'm honored."

"I'm so glad," she squealed "Well, I'll be in touch. Albert has your email, and Arianna?"

"Yes?"

"I promise not to pick out a hideous bridesmaid dress. Thanks."

I heard her squealing with delight to someone, and Albert came back on the phone. "Thanks," he sounded relieved.

"Of course, I'd love to be in your wedding! You are my brother." I paused to gather my thoughts. "Have you told Mom and Dad yet?"

"Called them last night. They seemed happy."

"Well, why wouldn't they be happy?"

"Did you hear me say Patty was an undergrad?"

"An undergrad can be any age." I suddenly felt nervous. "How old is she?"

"Relax, she'll be twenty-one in a couple weeks." There was a brief silence. "So, Dad is still upset you took a semester off." His tone indicated that I was the subject of much of the conversation last night despite his good news.

I let out a deep sigh. "Well, he's really going to flip when he finds out I'm planning to take next semester off too."

"Wow! Do me a favor. Tell him now so he gets over it before the wedding."

"Dad would never make a scene at your wedding."

"I'm not so sure. He is pretty upset. He says you are wasting valuable time."

"I know what he thinks, Albert, but I want a break."

"Hey, I understand. After grad school, I needed a break too. It's a lot of work, and you did it faster than most people." Now I heard him sigh. "Let me give you some advice, Baby Sis. Get affiliated with a school. Get a post doc. Do research."

"I am doing research."

"I know, Mom told me, and it sounds interesting, but get affiliated with a university. It'll get Dad off your back."

"I shouldn't have to get him off my back," I grunted.

"Oh, I know, but trust me, it's easier than arguing with him."

It all made sense now that I thought about it. That is why Albert went to Alaska years ago. He did whatever he wanted there. He talked up his research, but I now suspected he really was just coasting. Taking a break. Enjoying life.

"Fight the battles you can win," he advised.

"So, I should lie?"

"No! Never lie. They'll catch you in a lie." He paused. "Look, if you want to take time off to do some independent research ask for an affiliation. Most schools will take you on as long as they don't have to pay you. Get library privileges and an email address. Heck, go to your alma mater, you might even get desk space there. And don't forget grant money. You need an affiliation for grants."

"True," I mused. "A grant can make things easier. So that's what you did?"

He laughed. "I did. I went to Alaska for some time off. I did independent research for over a year then they asked me if I wanted a job in the lab. Well, money was running out fast, so I took it. Once I had experience, it was easy to get another position. I started my job search last year, and now I am on staff full time at Montana University, I have a comprehensive benefits package, a retirement plan, and I'm getting married."

I never had a conversation like this with Albert before. I learned a lot. Our father was very demanding, and he expected Albert and me to be successful. Taking a break was not acceptable in his opinion. "I can call around and see if there are any opportunities available."

"That's exactly what you need to do. Although Dad probably will not think it's enough," Albert laughed, "he should ease up a little."

"Thanks, Albert."

"Believe me. It will be better for you and for Dad."

That was the most conversation Albert and I had in years. In fact, it may well be the most we talked to each other. Ever.

"Mom said you are very happy in Salem."

I was certain that was not all Mom said. "Yes, I am. She seemed to have a good time when she visited."

"She really did. And I heard something about pumpkin muffins."

I laughed. "Yes, Mom loved them."

"Dad did too. Any chance you might bring muffins when you visit?"

"Absolutely."

"James will be coming with you, won't he? I want to meet him."

I did not have to ask because James nodded his head yes. "Of course, he will come with me."

"Gram is making the trip too. Said she had to see me get married."

"Really? Grandma is going to Montana? Wow! But it will be nice to have the whole family together."

"Mom and Dad are going to fly to Florida and get her, and then they will all come here. Dad doesn't want Gram flying alone."

"That makes sense."

"Well, Baby Sis, it was nice talking to you. Thanks for being in the wedding. I'm sure Patty will be in touch soon."

"I'm looking forward to the wedding, and thanks for the advice. Bye."

I hung up the phone and sat dazed for a few moments. "That was weird."

James nodded. "Albert is getting married. Good for him."

"Yes, that is weird too."

James stopped typing and looked at me.

"Albert never talks to me. In fact, I'm surprised he called me directly. Usually, he calls Mom, and she calls me."

"Well, a wedding is a major event. I'm sure he wanted to tell you himself."

"No. No, that was totally out of character for him. Patty said he was going to email, but then he decided to call. I don't know what is going on, but that was definitely not like Albert."

"What did Patty mean by she wouldn't pick out a hideous bridesmaid dress?"

I laughed. "Well, usually bridesmaid dresses are hideous. I think it's a plot, so no one looks better than the bride on her wedding day," I explained.

James chuckled and went back to typing.

I sat there thinking for a few minutes. "We have to get Giovanni invited to the wedding," I said abruptly.

James stopped typing again. "Excuse me. You want to get Giovanni invited to Albert's wedding? He's supposed to be my uncle. How do you intend to get him invited?"

"I'm not sure. But, well, he should see his great, great, great grandson get married." I thought for a few moments. "Does compelling work over video calls?"

James shook his head. "I don't think so, but maybe. I've never tried it. And you can't be serious about compelling them to invite Giovanni. He would be terribly upset."

"True, but it's for him. And what he doesn't know won't bother him."

James gave me a sideways look. "You can be devious sometimes, Arianna. It's scary." He thought for a moment. "Maybe if we just ask, they will invite him."

96

"Maybe. After all, it is the holidays. I'll tell my mother Giovanni will be with us for the holidays and ask her if Giovanni can be put on the guest list."

"I think that might work."

"If not, want to take a weekend get a way?"

My mother called the next day, and we discussed Giovanni, the rehearsal dinner, and travel. Since my grandmother was going to make the trip from Florida, Mom said it would be nice to have Giovanni. She thought he and Grandma would get along well. Things were falling into place.

However, as the days passed, the wedding consumed a great deal of my time. There were many things on which the groom's family had to decide including the rehearsal dinner. I received several calls a day from my mother about the arrangements. Albert helped Mom because we had no way of selecting a rehearsal dinner venue without his help. Patty sent a great many texts and pictures of dresses, shoes, and accessories. The only consistency in the dresses was every single one of them was a shade of pink. It was exhausting.

On my way home from the Historical Society, I stopped at the grocery store, and while standing in the check-out line, I flipped through a bridal magazine. I decided to purchase it.

When I pulled in the driveway, James came out to help me with the groceries. It was raining hard, so I darted into the house with my purse and a couple of bags. I went into the kitchen and started to put the groceries away.

James saw the magazine on top in one of the bags, pulled it out, and started flipping through it. "I didn't realize there was so much to planning a wedding?"

"Tell me about it. Whatever happened to a simple ceremony and a reception with close family and friends?"

"Oh, that reminds me, your mother called while you were out. She said she tried your cell phone, but it went right to voice mail."

"I had to turn it off so I could get some work done."

"She said to tell you she had shopping to do and would call back later."

I made a turkey sandwich and poured a glass of iced tea. I knew she wanted to talk about the wedding events. Apparently, even though the wedding was less than two months away, it was going to be an elaborate affair, so the rush was on.

"My paper and power point are completed, but I need a few run throughs to polish my presentation for the conference this weekend." I finished my sandwich then started to clean up. "James, the Providence Mall is close to the conference. It is a big mall with a wide variety of shops. I want to get a few outfits for the trip."

"That's a good idea," James replied. "I should get a new suit for the wedding and for interviews with agents. I haven't needed a suit in a while, and mine are getting old."

"I just checked on snow fall rates in Missoula, Montana. We will be just North of there. The area is surrounded by forest. All my boots are more stylish than sturdy, and I want to go with you when you hunt at least some of the time."

James looked up at me. "What's wrong, Arianna? Are you nervous about going to Montana?"

I hated to admit it, but part of me was not looking forward to the trip. The wedding stress was only part of the reason. I had never been to the wilderness, and I was a little scared. I nodded yes. I stood near the sink, and James came over and wrapped his arms around me.

"I will not let anything happen to you. We will be fine. Besides, as you said, Missoula is close by, and it is a moderate sized city."

I nodded and gave him a kiss.

"You are right though; you will need a good pair of boots."

"I present in the round of panels right before lunch on Saturday. We can leave right after the luncheon for the mall."

James laughed, "Arianna, I have noticed that you do more shopping than attending panels when you attend conferences."

Now, I laughed too. "I know. I see attending a conference as a way to build my vitae and as a chance to shop someplace new."

Chapter IX
Thanksgiving at Weymouth

James

It was unseasonably warm for November, so I had the top down on the convertible as we drove to Weymouth University in upstate New York the day before Thanksgiving. Arianna stretched out in the passenger's seat, and her hair fluttered in the breeze. Her conference was a success as was our shopping trip. She was right, the Providence Mall had a variety of shops, and the merchandise was trendy and stylish. Now that the pressure of presenting was behind her, she spent a great deal of time flipping through bridal magazines and searching online for bridal ideas. Patty sent pictures of several more bridesmaid dresses, and although she promised not to pick something hideous, the dresses were, well, hideous. Arianna's eyes went wide when she saw the bright pink gown that Patty said was her first choice. So now Arianna looked for dresses too and hoped to tone down the pink, at least for her dress. She closed the magazine and sat up.

"Did you find anything interesting?"

"Not really." Arianna had a mischievous look on her face. She reached over and ran her hand over my chest and then down into my lap. She moved closer and kissed my neck. "What time are we meeting everyone?"

"Eight." I kept my concentration on the road, but she unbuttoned my shirt and ran her hands across and down my chest.

"How much longer before we are at the hotel?"

"About an hour." I closed my eyes for a second and then snapped them open.

Arianna moved closer to me, but the space between my body and the steering wheel was small even though the seat was as far back as possible. She leaned over and bumped the steering wheel a little. "Sorry. This car is really small." She leaned back in her seat but placed her hand on my thigh.

I glanced over at her. Her smile told me exactly what she had in mind. I accelerated.

Less than an hour later, the tires squealed as I turned the corner and pulled into the valet area. I jumped out, went around, and opened Arianna's door.

"You go ahead. I'll be right there." She leaned in the car and gathered up her purse and tote bag.

I nodded, gave the attendant the car key, and went to the front desk. I was signing the register when Arianna joined me and put her arm around my waist.

"Do you have luggage, sir?" the front desk clerk asked.

"We'll get it later, thank you," I replied.

He smiled at Arianna and nodded. "Room 342. There is coffee, tea, and cookies in the lobby. Enjoy your stay." He handed me a small folder with our keys.

"Thank you."

We took the elevator to the third floor, and we walked down the hallway to our room. Once inside, I kicked the door closed, flipped the lock, and feverishly began kissing Arianna. My hands roamed over her body as I removed her clothes and tossed them aside.

"James, I want you." She slid my shirt off then unfastened my jeans and skimmed them down my hips. I kicked them off and pulled her close. She locked her arms around my neck as I lifted her up and fell with her on the bed.

I ran my hands up and down her glorious naked body. Her nails ran up my back as she arched her back with pleasure. "Now," she demanded. She closed her eyes and threw her head back when I entered her in one thrust.

"Yes." Her eyes popped open, and she rolled us over. She straddled me, and I cupped her breasts. She slid her hands up my chest and down my sides. My skin tingled everywhere she touched. I closed my eyes and let her take me where she willed as she rode up and down on me driving us higher and higher. I gripped her hips tightly and we moved together at a feverish pace.

She leaned forward and her mouth sought mine. She consumed me. Our bodies continued to move together at a fevered pace, but perfectly in sync. We were made for each other. I needed her. My body ached for her. For every part of her.

I sat up and wrapped my arms around her pulling her into my body. Her breathing was fast and hard. She was at the edge of release. I increased the pace. She wrapped her legs tightly around my waist as I flipped her onto her back and slid my hands underneath her.

"James." Her voice was horse and ragged with passion.

"Look at me."

She struggled to open her eyes, and I watched them cloud over with passion as I drove her to the edge. She was all there was for me. Nothing else mattered. I shifted our position just slightly, and the climax burst out of her with such force it took me under as well.

I held Arianna close for a long time. Her body pressed hard against mine. I buried my face in her hair and just breathed in her scent as we very slowly resurfaced.

"That was nice." Arianna let out a contented sigh and ran her fingernails teasingly up my back.

I eased off her and lay by her side. She pushed me onto my back and crawled on top of me. She tangled her fingers in my hair and looked down at me. A wicked smile curled her lips. "And it is not over yet."

I growled, pulled her down, and devoured her mouth.

*****

We arrived at the bar just before eight o'clock. Marcus and Trina were already there, and they waved as we entered. Marcus and I met at the university many years ago. We were about the same height and had similar features, so people often thought we were related.

"Hi," we greeted each other enthusiastically.

Arianna and I sat down, and a few minutes later, Giovanni and Marena arrived and joined us at the table. They were an odd couple and not because he was a vampire hunter and she a vampire. Giovanni had a very blunt and rough personality, whereas Marena was soft spoken and sophisticated. She gathered up her layered flowing dress as she sat down. She placed her hand on Giovanni's, and her golden eyes sparkled when she looked at him.

Marena turned toward me. "How was the drive here?"

"Good. It was a beautiful day for a drive."

The waitress brought two bowls of popcorn and set them down then she took our drink order. Arianna and Trina each took a handful of popcorn. "I love popcorn." Trina took more. She was a very perky young woman. She was short, and she had blonde spiky hair with purple ends that matched her purple shirt.

Arianna took another handful of popcorn. "Really? James doesn't like it." She motioned to Giovanni and Marena who both shook their heads no.

Marcus made a face as Trina tried to get him to try a small piece. He kept his mouth clamped shut and vigorously shook his head no, again and again.

"Looks like the popcorn is ours, Trina."

"Nice of them to bring a bowl for each of us."

They both laughed.

The waitress returned with our drinks. She set down two more bowls of popcorn then left the table.

Giovanni cleared his throat and sat up straighter. He was not one for frivolity. "I have been getting regular reports from Marie. John and the pack have not seen or smelled any strange vampires."

"I have never met a werewolf," Trina said excitedly.

"You are not missing much," Marcus remarked. "I'm glad we don't have any around here." He looked over at Giovanni. "Sorry, Giovanni, no offense."

Giovanni grunted. "Wolves have always been a hunter's ally." He felt their presence would help keep Arianna safe, and although I was not thrilled to have them around, anything that kept her safe was fine with me as long as they kept their distance.

"Well, I hope I can meet one when we visit Salem next month." Trina raised her eyebrows and smiled.

"Oh, I'm sure you will, Trina," Arianna assured her. "I run into Jason all the time. Sometimes, I think he follows me."

I could not help the sigh of annoyance that escaped me. Marcus looked at me, and I caught his eye. He got the message that we would talk about it when we were alone. Marcus was the one person whose counsel I sought when I was troubled.

"Arianna, typically a hunter welcomes their help and protection," Giovanni grumbled.

"Good thing I'm not typical," she replied sarcastically. "I wanted to ask you if we have any wolves in our family tree."

"As far as I know, we do not."

"Good."

"Well," Marena interrupted and changed the subject before Arianna and Giovanni started arguing, "I suggested to Giovanni that maybe Tony was just in the area for Halloween, but Giovanni said no."

"I don't think so either." I shook my head. "He was scared. I don't think he was meant to be seen. Did Giovanni tell you that he sprayed me with colloidal silver?"

"Yes." She paused. "Not that it will help with someone like Tony, but at the regional meeting in February, I plan to propose a ban on using colloidal silver on a vampire except in self-defense."

"There's a meeting in February?" I asked.

Marena nodded. "Yes. It seems Darius was the one stopping meetings. Apparently, he did not want us collaborating with one another. Now that he is gone, there has been some maneuvering among the groups in New York, but it is confined to the area." Marena sipped her drink. "Several other clan leaders in the region contacted me, and we agreed we need to have regular meetings." She smiled at Giovanni. "And Giovanni will preside over the meetings."

"Congratulations, I think, Giovanni," I said with a laugh.

"I am the only active hunter in the area," he grumbled. Arianna narrowed her eyes at him, but she did not say anything.

"I've spoken to a number of vampires in the city," Marcus began. "Marena is right; several people are positioning themselves to take over, but no one from another district is trying to move in." He leaned in and whispered, "it seems most of them were not sad to see Darius gone. Many wanted to oust him for years, but no one had the power to do it." Marcus leaned back and let his words sink in.

"He's right. Darius was a bully that no one liked."

We all jumped and looked up. Hale stood right beside us. He came up so silently, and we were so involved with the conversation, we did not notice him. This worried me. Were we getting complacent? How was it possible that none of us sensed him approaching until he spoke?

Montgomery Hale was a professor at Weymouth University. Fifty years ago, when I was first at the university, I worked with Hale. There was a multi-state murder spree at the time, and Hale was convinced that someone was killing people with the hunter gene. We tested many bodies and determined that a substantial number did have the gene. Of course, we now knew Darius was behind those killings and the killings years later.

Hale took a chair from the next table and joined us. The waitress came over to take his order. "Cognac, please." He waited until she left, and then he lowered his voice and leaned toward us. "I have been doing research and talking to other vampires in the area. Darius' blood lust was not popular. It appears, Arianna was not the first person Darius targeted. Although, his vendetta against her seems to have been more intense than others. I was told by one vampire that Darius' obsession with killing Arianna was so great they feared the national leaders would take notice. Now that he and his thugs are gone, people are no longer afraid to speak out." He stopped and leaned back in his chair as the waitress brought his drink. "Thank you." He handed her a bill. "Keep the change."

"Thank you, sir. Can I get something for anyone else?"

"No thank you," I replied. She smiled and turned away. "So, Darius did not have the backing of his clan?"

"It appears he had his followers, but he acted primarily alone, but no one dared oppose him." Hale paused and took a drink.

"What about that old vampire and Tony?" Arianna asked.

"If they are still in New York, neither seems interested in taking over," Hale replied. "With Darius' death, his followers just seemed to disappear. There is a problem though." We all looked at him. "Darius used rogues to attack those who opposed him, and no one knows what happened to his rogues."

Arianna gave a visible shudder. I put my arm around her. Rogues attacked her twice last year. Darius kept them on the verge of starvation and that made them extra mean.

"Is it possible the ones he used in March were the last ones he had?" Arianna's voice cracked as she spoke. "Rogues are vampires that cannot adjust and go crazy. How many can there possibly be?"

"That's the problem," Hale replied. "We don't know if there are any more, or if they were all killed."

"We saw Tony in Salem," she added.

"Yes, and why is a mystery, but I think it is safe to say they are still after you, Arianna." Hale looked at her. "The good news is I think they do not have widespread support."

"That's good news?" Arianna questioned.

"Yes, it is good news because they are acting alone. However, it is bad news because I believe there is a reason they are still after you. I believe Darius acted on a personal vendetta." Hale paused and drank.

"What are you holding back, Hale?" Arianna looked anxious.

He sighed and looked her in the eye. "It is my opinion that Darius and the old vampire are seeking revenge for something either in your past, or more likely, in your family's past."

Giovanni sat up straighter. Arianna stiffened.

Hale turned to Giovanni. "You said the old vampire looks familiar?" Giovanni nodded. "It is my belief that the vendetta must have something to do with Arianna's great grandfather."

"No." Arianna looked at Giovanni.

Giovanni's eyes narrowed. His face was stern. "Giuseppe was a hot head and always caused conflicts."

"No. That is crazy. What could he possibly have done that would warrant vengeance on me?"

"Arianna, you only saw the loving grandfather. The truth is Giuseppe had many enemies. He was power hungry and never listened to anyone. He acted first and thought about his actions second." Giovanni shook his head. "And he likely made some enemies here as well. I agree with Hale. Giuseppe's actions have put you in danger."

"That is the only explanation. How else might a vampire know Arianna unless he saw her with Giuseppe." Hale paused and looked directly at Arianna. "They both wanted to kill you as a child. It must be because of your great grandfather."

Giovanni showed no emotion. "And I believe James is right. Giuseppe is still alive."

Arianna looked around the table and shook her head. "No that is not possible. If he were still alive, he would have come back to me, especially now. Darius is dead."

"He may not be in this country." I laid my hand over Arianna's. "If he was trying to protect you and faked his death, he would not take the chance of being seen alive."

"I will have the opportunity to talk with Luisa and John at the wedding. Perhaps they know something," Giovanni added. "Felicia did not know much, but I did not expect a lot of information from her."

"Use whatever means necessary, Giovanni. Compel them if you must," Hale insisted. Giovanni reluctantly nodded his agreement which surprised us all.

*****

The next day, Arianna and I attended the Weymouth University Thanksgiving Day football game. We both wore blue Weymouth sweatshirts, jeans, and sneakers. When we arrived, we walked up the steps to the faculty and alumni section.

"Arianna and James, so glad you could make it," Dean Branson's booming and perpetually jolly voice greeted us. He wore a blue Weymouth University sweater, jeans, and a Weymouth ski hat with a large blue and white pom pom on top. Dean Branson was a large, jolly man with flawless taste, a good heart, and a rosy outlook on life. "I know this year we are going to win," he cheered.

It was a cloudy day, and the temperature was in the forties. It was a perfect day for football. We filed in the row and took our seats. A few minutes later, Arianna handed me a blue and white ribbon flag to cheer on the team. She kept the blue and white pom-pom on a stick for herself.

I leaned forward and watched the game. The group cheered at completed passes and groaned when the quarterback was sacked.

Arianna nudged me and handed me a silver flask. I looked at her questioningly. "It's from the dean. To keep us warm." She raised her eyebrows and smiled.

"Really?" I took a drink and passed it on.

During the first half, the game was remarkably close. Weymouth scored twice and was ahead by three points at halftime.

Arianna stood up. "I'm going to the concession stand with Dean Branson to get food. Be right back." She followed him down the steps.

I leaned back and watched as the opposing team's band took to the field.

A short while later, Arianna returned with two hotdogs, fries, a large drink, and a bright pink cotton candy. "Oh, good, I didn't miss the Weymouth band." She handed me the cotton candy, set her drink down between us, and took her seat. She started eating one of the hotdogs. "These are good." She continued to eat.

I sneered at the cotton candy I held out at arm's length in front of me.

"That cotton candy isn't going to bite, you know," she said between bites of hotdog.

"I know."

"Try some, you might like it."

"No, thank you." Then I leaned close to her. "You know, the color reminds me of those bridesmaid dresses."

Arianna gave me a pained look. "I thought the same thing."

The second half of the game was less exciting. Weymouth lost, but it was a close game. At least closer than the score had been in previous years.

"I thought for certain we would win this year," Dean Branson moaned as he slowly and carefully walked down the steps. "Oh well, maybe next year. Party starts in an hour," he cheerfully reminded us, all thought of the loss forgotten.

"Can't wait." Arianna hooked her arm in mine as we walked through the parking lot and headed toward downtown. When we were out of the crowd, she leaned close to me. "Last year, I was still unconscious when the dean had his party."

I nodded yes. I didn't know what to say. I worried that being back at Weymouth on the anniversary of the first attack by Darius that resulted in her transformation might cause flash backs and anxiety for Arianna, and to be honest for me too. I squeezed her hand. When she lay dying in my arms, I never felt so scared in my life. I shuddered and pulled her closer.

We walked around downtown and looked in the closed store windows then made our way to the alumni center. The dean's party was informal and relaxed, but the food and decorations were extravagant and sophisticated as was typical of all his parties. Blue and white streamers crisscrossed the ceiling, and there were bunches of blue and white balloons scattered all around the room. On the tables and intermittently along the buffet line, there were blue and white flower arrangements accented with small footballs and streamers.

Arianna and I joined the buffet line. We each took a plate and picked up silverware wrapped in a napkin. Each white napkin was tied with a football charm and a blue and white band that said Weymouth. Naturally, there was an abundance of food including a turkey carving station and all the traditional Thanksgiving side dishes. The beverages flowed freely, and when we sat down at a table, a waiter came by with glasses of red wine.

Arianna's friend Joan and her daughter joined us at the table, and then to my surprise, so did Montgomery Hale. He carried a glass of red wine but did not have a plate of food. I was immediately alarmed because he rarely attended any university functions. "Is something wrong," I whispered.

He shook his head no, leaned back, and took a drink.

Joan and her daughter had to leave early, so Arianna said good-bye to them and then went back to the buffet line giving Hale and I a chance to talk.

"James, I wanted to ask you how things are really going with the wolves. Last night, I had a feeling you were not saying something because of Giovanni."

Now I took a long drink and let out a sigh. "One of the wolves, Jason, has made it his personal mission to protect Arianna."

Hale looked at me over the rim of his glass. "And that makes you uncomfortable?"

"He intentionally touches her arm, her shoulder, or her hand every time he sees her which believe me is often." I took another drink. "Marie doesn't like the way he follows Arianna either."

"What does Arianna think?"

"She finds him annoying, but she doesn't want to be rude. Giovanni made her promise to be nice. He told her hunters and wolves are traditional allies." I shrugged. "Salem is a small town, and to be fair, the others are not bad. It's just Jason."

"You may need the packs' help at some point, James. This is not over. That old vampire wants to finish what Darius started, and I am convinced it is because of something Arianna's great grandfather did."

"I know Hale."

"Keep me informed." He stood up when Arianna returned. "Enjoy the party."

"Thanks," Arianna replied cheerfully as he walked toward the door. "Is everything ok?" She sat down next to me.

"Yes, everything is fine." I leaned over and kissed her delicately.

Later, we milled around and mingled.

"Hello, James," Doris Campbell from the library waved. "It is good to see you." She was tall and willowy, and she reached me in a couple of strides. She too wore a Weymouth sweater. Her slightly greying shoulder length hair was perfectly curled under at her shoulders as always.

"Doris, I am happy to see you. I wasn't sure if you were coming since you did not attend the game. I wanted to thank you for reading my manuscript. You had very constructive comments that I am working into the new draft."

"James, I am very honored to help. Your story was intriguing. It was so rich in detail. I pictured myself in Salem in the 1800s."

"Thank you."

"Really, James, the story is captivating. I could not put it down. I think it will sell."

"Thank you, Doris."

She shook my hand. "I wish you much success. Please keep in touch."

"I will. And thank you again."

I made my way around the room and stopped to chat with several people. I saw Arianna laughing and talking to three women from the English department. To my dismay, Kevin Caro walked over to her and said hello. I saw him give her a hug. They talked briefly, and she put her hand on his arm. A few minutes later, she came up to me. "Do you think Kevin is safe?"

"Why do you ask?"

"He's having weird dreams about being attacked, and he doesn't look good. Do you see how pale he is?"

I looked closer at him. I had to admit he did not look well. Kevin was unfortunately used by Darius last March in Darius' second attempt to kill Arianna. She compelled him to believe he was attacked by an animal. "I'll ask Marcus to keep an eye on him and make sure no one is harming him," I told Arianna.

She nodded, but she continued to look at Kevin. "I'll talk to him."

I laughed silently to myself. I knew what that meant. I watched her walk over to Kevin, and then she led him down the hallway where they were alone.

She returned a few minutes later. "So, what did you discover?" I asked.

"Well, I think Kevin was just having weird dreams, sort of flash backs of the attack in March," Arianna explained. "Unfortunately, he describes the rogues almost perfectly. Apparently, he has disturbing dreams every night, and he wakes up more tired than when he went to bed. But I think he will be ok now. I compelled him to not dream about the attack, and I gave him a more bear like description of what attacked him. Do you think that will work?"

"It might. Compelling someone is tricky, and it isn't always long lasting."

"Should we ask Hale to keep an eye on him? After all, he has more opportunities to be around Kevin than Marcus since their offices are across the hall from one another at the university."

"Hale? That may not be a good idea. There is ongoing dislike between Hale and Caro."

She wrinkled her nose and nodded. "I'll talk to Giovanni. See what he thinks."

Marcus and Trina were already at Marena's house when we arrived. Giovanni, who now lived with Marena, was in the kitchen cooking.

Arianna took a deep breath. "Yum. It smells good in here." She sat down at the table next to Trina and pulled out her phone. "Oh Trina, let me show you the latest pink nightmare bridesmaid dress possibility."

Trina gasped, "Oh no. You will look like a ball of cotton candy."

Marcus leaned in to look. His eyes went wide, and he looked at me.

"And she told me she would pick a nice dress." Arianna rolled her eyes and shook her head.

"I feel so sorry for you." Trina could not take her eyes off that dress.

"Ready?" Marcus asked Trina.

"Yeah."

I kissed Arianna. "We will be back soon."

"Have fun."

"Will you and Giovanni be ok together?"

She kissed me. "Yes, we will be fine."

Giovanni walked in the kitchen carrying a platter of grilled steaks. I went outside and joined Marcus and Trina.

"Giovanni is really happy to be invited to the wedding," Trina said as we walked toward the entrance to the forest. "Those dresses though. Wow. I feel sorry for Arianna."

"Yes, she is not happy about the dresses, and she is very busy with rehearsal dinner details," I said as we left the trail and looked for game.

We hunted for a couple of hours then sat on the large rocks by the stream.

"Oh, Marcus, Arianna says Kevin Caro is having weird dreams. Apparently, he is remembering the rogues, and it's affecting his health. Can you keep an eye on him, and make sure no one is using him again?"

"No problem."

"It's probably nothing. Arianna compelled him to get information, and she's pretty certain it's not a vampire."

"Is she telling Giovanni?" Marcus asked.

"Yes, she said she planned to talk to him and see what he suggests."

Marcus sighed, "Oh boy. And we left them alone. I hope Marena is back."

His comment made me nervous. I looked at them. "Maybe we should head back?" I asked very seriously. Marcus and Trina laughed and nodded yes.

The first thing I noticed when Arianna and I walked into Marcus' cabin was the more feminine feel. There was a flower arrangement and placemats on the kitchen table and pots and pans on the stove. There were curtains over the mini blinds, and when I glanced in the bedroom as we walked by, I saw a brand-new floral bed comforter and bed skirt on the bed.

"Are you hungry, Arianna?" Trina asked.

"Always." They went in the small kitchen together.

Trina still ate quite a lot of human food even though she derived little nourishment from it. She was turned less than two years earlier, and she liked to cook. She and Arianna sat down to eat enchiladas.

"It's nice to have someone over who eats real food." Trina passed a bowl of Spanish rice to Arianna.

I followed Marcus into the living room, and we sat down in the recliners in front of the large flat screen TV that took up most of the room.

"Trina, you are such a good cook," I heard Arianna say.

They continued eating and talking at full speed while Marcus and I had a drink and watched the football game.

"I'm glad they get along so well." Marcus refilled our glasses with whiskey.

"They are both newly turned. They still relate to their human lives." I glanced back at them to make sure they were still talking. "Marcus," I whispered very very softly, "I'm concerned about this old vampire and Arianna's great grandfather. Giovanni was not kidding when he said Giuseppe made a lot of enemies and never followed the rules. Giovanni left his village for a while so Giuseppe could be in charge. I think Hale is right, the old vampire wants revenge on Giuseppe for something he did."

"Makes sense, and you are convinced Giuseppe is still alive?"

"Yes, I would bet on it. I think he had enemies here and decided the best way to keep his family safe was to make everyone believe that he actually died in the accident. He probably hoped with his death, his enemies would forget about him and his family."

"It all fits," Marcus muttered.

"Giovanni told me Giuseppe taunted a vampire who turned him when he was a child." I shook my head. "Marcus, there are so many unanswered questions. We hope to get some leads at the wedding, and it really worries me that Giovanni is willing to compel Luisa and John to get answers."

"I hope you do get some information. But if Giuseppe is sly enough to fake his death so vampires believe he is dead, I doubt the family will be much help."

"It's obvious that he compelled them to make them think he was aging," I paused. "There are so many questions surrounding him. I don't like it, Marcus." I leaned back in the recliner as the girls came in the room. Marcus and I would have to finish the conversation later.

Chapter X
New Opportunities

Arianna

I took Albert's advice and sent resumes out to colleges and universities in the area with openings for adjunct teaching positions. On Monday morning, I was pleasantly surprised when I opened my email. "James, I have an interview at Salem College on Thursday."

He looked up from his computer and smiled. "That is fantastic."

I sat down next to him. "I decided I'm not going to tell my parents about the interview."

"Ok."

I let out a breath. "I have been thinking. I always tell them everything, but maybe Albert is right. They don't need to know everything."

James looked at me for a moment. "I agree with Albert. It certainly is ok to keep some things from them. You are an adult, and you do not need to clear everything with them." Then he laughed. "I hope you haven't told them about everything we do."

"Well, no." I wrinkled my nose and smirked.

"So, don't worry about not telling them about the interview."

"Thanks. I feel less guilty already."

James went back to working on his manuscript, so after a hearty breakfast, I climbed up to the attic and brought down the holiday boxes. I turned on soft Christmas music to get in the mood then I started by decorating a small white tree in the kitchen with an assortment of mini glass ornaments, glittery snowflakes, and small pipe cleaner candy canes. Around the base of the tree, I set up a miniature nativity scene that I had when I was a child.

There was a narrow table on the landing going up to the second floor. I had a variety of small houses, so I laid out a blanket of fake snow on the table and set up a village. I used quite a few of my bottle brush trees to create a backdrop for the houses.

In my office, I set up a larger white tree that I recently purchased. I always wanted a large, white, beach themed Christmas tree, so I decorated it with a variety of coastal ornaments and seashells and topped it with a sugar starfish. By lunchtime, most of the house looked festive.

I surveyed the formal living room. I needed greens for the mantle. Because the house was historic, I wanted to decorate with a candle in every window and lots of greens both inside and outside the house. I needed to go into the forest to gather the ground pine, holly, spruce, and other evergreens I needed to make wreaths, swags, and garlands. Satisfied with my progress, I went in the kitchen, turned up the Christmas music, and prepared my lunch.

James came in the kitchen while I was eating. "The house is looking festive." He leaned over and kissed me.

"Thank you."

"Did you want to get the tree today?"

I nodded yes. "I also plan to go with you when you hunt."

"You do?"

"Yes, I need greens, pinecones, and other materials for the mantle and the outside decorations."

"Why don't you just purchase the greens and pinecones when we get the tree?"

I lowered my sandwich and looked over at him. "James, harvesting greens and making decorations is part of the fun."

James shook his head and shrugged. "Ok," he mumbled.

*****

On Thursday morning, I brushed my hair one more time and touched up my makeup. I was unusually nervous about this interview. I decided to wear a black skirt and jacket with a maroon blouse and a print infinity scarf. I put on earrings and headed downstairs.

"James, how do I look?"

"Very nice. Professional, but not stuffy."

"Good." It was raining, so I grabbed my trench coat and an umbrella out of the coat closet. "Well, I'm off."

James kissed me and handed me my bag. "Good luck."

"Thanks."

I drove to campus and fortunately found a close space. The campus was smaller than Weymouth University, but just as old. I stepped out of the car, opened my umbrella, and walked quickly up the grand stone front steps of the building where the dean's Office was located.

"Hello, I am Arianna Sabini. I am here to see Dean Reynolds."

The administrative assistant looked annoyed at the newest puddle of water on the entry floor. "Yes. She will be with you shortly. You can hang your coat on the rack."

"Thank you." I hung up my coat, looped the wrist band of the umbrella over the hanger, and sat down to wait.

Within a couple minutes, Dean Reynolds came down the hall. She was a short woman with slightly graying hair. She wore a plain grey suit with a white blouse. "Arianna?" I rose and shook her hand. "It's nice to meet you."

"Thank you. It is nice to meet you."

We walked back to her office. She closed the door and motioned for me to sit down. On the desk was a cluster of photographs of her children. The windows had classic mini blinds with no curtains. A large bookshelf was packed with books and there was another pile of books on the floor. Dean Reynolds sat down behind the very neat desk and flipped through my resume.

"Your transcripts are impressive, and you have some teaching experience. Our students certainly would benefit from your expertise." She looked up at me. "So, tell me more about your teaching experience and the classes you have taught."

I relaxed a little because I had a good feeling about this woman. She was professional and to the point. Her students were her number one concern. I described my experience and the ways that I could enhance student learning. She asked what brought me to Salem. I told her about James and his family's home. I wanted to be honest with her, so I told her I was taking time to evaluate my options and see what I genuinely wanted to do for my career.

"Well, I started at the college ten years ago, became department head seven years ago, and became the dean last year," she told me. "We have a very dedicated group of professors, and we are expanding our online offerings next Fall."

My instincts about her were right. Thirty minutes later, I left Dean Reynolds' office with a commitment to teach two online mythology classes during the Fall semester. Since they had space, I was assigned a shared office beginning in January and invited to attend department and curriculum meetings. I took a deep breath as I drove home.

James came out when he heard my car in the driveway. He saw my smile and knew. "Congratulations!" he called as he came out to the car.

"I'll be teaching two Mythology classes online in the Fall."

"Your father will be happy."

I gave him a smirk, "Maybe? It is online teaching."

"It's teaching."

We went inside. He took my coat and umbrella and hung them up in the hall to dry. I kicked off my wet shoes.

"I think you will like Salem College. It is very much like Weymouth."

"I liked what I saw of it." I made a turkey sandwich, and then took a bag of potato chips off the top of the refrigerator, poured myself a tall glass of iced tea, and sat down.

James pulled a chair alongside me, and he leaned over and kissed me. "Your mother called while you were out. I told her you were running an errand."

I took a bite of my sandwich and nodded. "I'll call her after I call my father and tell him the good news. I'm sure she wants to discuss the rehearsal dinner."

"I thought she settled on a place for the dinner and a menu?"

"She did. Now, we need to discuss table linens and favors." James raised his eyebrows. I continued, "apparently since the wedding color is pink, Mom believes pink should be incorporated into our color scheme and favors."

"You don't agree?"

"No." I said flatly. "The rehearsal dinner is the groom's party, and the colors should reflect his taste." I went round and round about this with my mother. I was not really in the mood to discuss the wedding, and sensing I was annoyed, James wisely did not respond.

The next morning was still rainy. I did not have many plans, but James had a meeting with an agent, so he was up and showering before seven. He came out of the bathroom whistling.

"Good morning." He leaned down and kissed me.

"Morning," I grumbled. Although I did not require much sleep, I still was not a morning person.

"I hope I didn't wake you."

"No, but I don't feel like getting out of bed."

"Then don't." He walked over to his closet and pulled out a suit. I watched him as he dressed. James' taste in clothes was impeccable. His shirts fit well, not too tight but tight enough to show his muscular body. I particularly liked the black suit he chose to wear today. He picked out a patterned tie with the thinnest line of purple running through it which gave it an artsy character.

"Are you working at the Historical Society today?" He tied his tie and then straightened it.

"Yes, for a couple hours, but not until after lunch."

"More wedding planning this morning?"

I rolled my eyes and let out a deep sigh. "Yes. I hope we can iron out the last of the details today. I need to shop for the supplies for the favors."

"Well, I am certain whatever you two decide, they will be beautiful."

I rolled my eyes again.

"How do I look?"

"Handsome. Did you say this potential agent is a woman?"

He sauntered over to the bed and sat down. "Yes, why?"

"No reason, just wondering."

He laughed and kissed me passionately. "You are my soul mate, Arianna. There will never be anyone else for me. Don't forget it."

I kissed him back. "Well, you better be off. You don't want to miss your train."

"I will text you." He kissed me again. "Have a good day."

"Good luck."

He went downstairs, and a few minutes later, I heard the front door open and close. I debated whether I should get up or stay in bed, and bed won out. I nodded off for a few minutes. It was very nice not having any firm plans. I was discovering my non-student/non-teacher self. I lay listening to the rain drumming on the roof. It was so peaceful.

Eventually, I got out of bed just long enough to wash my face and brush my teeth. On my way back to bed, I grabbed my laptop. I checked email and was grateful not to have received one from my mother. The phone rang. I looked at the clock, 8:30; it must be Caroline. "Good morning, Caroline."

"Good morning. How are you today?"

"Good and you?" It was unusually quiet on her end.

"I just put the kids in front of a sing-a-long video." She took a deep breath. "Does that make me a bad parent?"

"Absolutely not. Videos can be entertaining and educational. And besides, sometimes you just need a break."

"Thanks." She sounded exhausted.

"Are you ok, Caroline?"

"Oh, yes. Just tired. All the preparations for Christmas and the in-laws coming up on the 23rd and staying with us for a week. I have been cleaning and baking for days."

I almost said the in-laws are visiting to see everyone not to see how clean the house is, but I knew better. People were judgmental, and unfortunately, Caroline's mother in-law was going to judge everything she did or did not do. "I know, hang in there," I replied sympathetically.

"How is the rehearsal planning coming along?"

"Oh, that's not a good subject. Who knew planning a wedding was this complicated? Was it this complicated when you got married?"

"Yes."

"Really?"

"Yes. Coordinating flowers, menus, favors, and decorations is a lot of work."

"I planned the bachelorette party."

"And it was a good one," Caroline laughed.

"Thanks." It was good to hear her laugh. We talked more often now that I was not always running off to class, a meeting, or grading papers.

"Have you told your dad about the new job?"

I sighed. "He's not happy that it's online teaching, but he seems satisfied that I will at least be teaching. He expects me to be at a major university doing research and teaching. But, you know, I really enjoy teaching at a smaller school. He just doesn't understand."

"I know. Your father always had big expectations for you. But it's your life. If you want to teach at a small school, then do it."

"Ah! That's easier said than done."

"Don't I know it. Well, the video is ending, so I need to get back to the kids. Call me."

"Ok, I will talk to you again soon." I looked at the clock. My mother would be calling shortly. I got up and slipped on a pair of leggings and a sweatshirt, and then I went downstairs to have breakfast and a very large cup of tea before her call.

I put up my umbrella and ran from my car to the building jumping over several large puddles on the way. The rain was so heavy it was difficult to see even a few feet ahead. I shook out my umbrella and set it just inside of the door to dry.

"Hi, Arianna." Pamela, the Historical Society intern looked up from her computer.

"Hi." I hung up my wet coat. "I imagine we aren't very busy today."

"No one has been in all day." She stood up and stretched. "Terrible weather. No one wants to be out in it."

"I wish it would stop raining."

"Shh." She put her index finger to her lips. "When it stops raining, it will start snowing."

I made a face. I was not in the mood for snow. "I'll be in the next room."

"Have fun."

I worked on a box containing *Salem Mercury* newspapers from the 1870s. The collection did not contain every paper from 1874, the year I knew James was turned, but I hoped to come across something about him. I went to the kitchen and made a cup of tea, and then I sat down and pulled the stack of papers out of the box. For each issue, I checked the page numbers, read the headlines, and made notes of missing pages. Occasionally, a section of a page was cut out. I flagged these areas. Eventually, the papers would be digitized.

I sipped my tea and read. It was close to the end of my shift when I found James' name in a notice. 'Mr. James Merden of Salem returned from Edinburgh, Scotland having completed his medical education and training. Mr. Merden will be practicing medicine at New York Presbyterian Hospital.'

There was a picture of James. He looked exactly as he does now. He was not smiling but looked proud and confident. I took out my camera and took a picture of the announcement. I looked at the date: June 3, 1874. I did not know that he became a doctor and was turned in the same year. James said little about his life at that time, and eager for more information, I flipped to the three November issues in the box because James said he was turned around the holidays. I read quickly but found no mention of James.

I started on the December issues and still nothing, so I looked for January 1875 issues. Finally, I found his name on January 12, 1875. 'Mr. James Merden having mysteriously recovered from what should have been a fatal stabbing on 28 December has gone to a warmer climate to continue his recovery.' I looked up from the paper "That's it?" I said out loud. I took a picture of the notice and carefully returned the papers to their box indicating where I left off.

It finally stopped raining, and as I slowly walked to my car, I sensed someone. "Hi Marie."

She walked up beside me. "Has James returned yet?"

"No. He's still in Boston."

"Good," she replied firmly. I looked at her. "Why don't we have a cup of tea and talk?"

"Would you like to come home with me?"

"Why don't you come to my home?"

"Ok." I was a little apprehensive, but I unlocked the car doors, and she got in on the passenger's side. "Which way?"

"Turn right and head toward the mall. I will direct you."

I followed her directions and pulled off the road onto a narrow dirt path. Once out of sight of the road, she told me to stop. We got out of the car and walked along a foot path to a small cream colored house with black shutters in a clearing. It looked…ordinary.

Marie opened the door, and I followed her inside. The lingering sent of incense tickled my nose. She walked over to a small table in the entry hall and lit a hurricane lamp. "Come to the kitchen, and we can talk while I make tea."

The kitchen was large with an island that divided the space into two uneven sections. In the larger area, there was a small table and two chairs. Several cutting boards were placed on a dark counter in the smaller section, and there was a set of knives at either end. On the counter by the sink was a large glass container full of a dark murky liquid. She motioned for me to sit at the table.

"You dry a lot of herbs." I marveled at the array of bunches of dried herbs and flowers that hung from the ceiling almost covering it completely.

She went to the sink and filled a tea kettle with water. "What kind of tea would you like? I have chamomile, Ceylon, Peach.

"Peach sounds good."

She pulled a metal canister from the cabinet and filled two tea balls with the dried ingredients. "I thought it would be nice for us to talk."

I smiled at her. "You have a charming home."

"Thank you." She took two mugs off the rack. "James said you were applying for teaching positions. How is the job hunt going?"

"Very well. I have an online teaching position for the Fall semester at Salem College."

She stopped and looked at me. "Congratulations. It did not take you long to find a position." She placed two saucers, napkins, and spoons on the table.

"I was surprised to be hired so quickly."

"From what James has told me, you are an exceptionally good professor. They are lucky to have you."

"Thank you."

"I understand your brother is getting married soon."

I nodded yes. "I am going to be a bridesmaid."

"You don't seem happy about it."

"Oh, I am happy to be in the wedding to support my brother." I paused and took a breath. "It's just there are so many things to do, and the dresses are pink and poufy. Definitely not my style." I took out my phone and showed her pictures of the potential gowns.

Marie looked from the pictures to me and back to the pictures. "I see what you mean."

As soon as the water started to boil, she turned off the gas, poured water into the two large mugs, and dropped a tea ball into each mug. The aroma of fresh peaches filled the room. Marie set the mugs on the table and sat down.

"How is your work going at the Historical Society?"

"It is going well. There are so many interesting items in the old newspapers."

She cleared her throat. "Did you see the notices about James in the old newspapers?"

So, that is what this is about. I had a feeling she wanted to talk to me about James. "Yes, I did." I dunked my tea ball.

"And what do you think?"

"Well, the notices were not detailed, but I was disturbed by the words, mysteriously recovered from what should have been a fatal stabbing."

"Yes, the townspeople were scared. They called me a witch and a monster." She took a sip of tea and chuckled, "Of course, it's true." She took another sip. "Did James tell you what happened?"

I shook my head. "Not really. He said he was seriously injured in an incident at a bar when he was home for the holidays and that you turned him to save his life."

"Well, essentially that is what happened. However, I was not, and still am not, in the habit of saving people from death by turning them."

"But you chose to turn James."

She smiled, "yes." She closed her eyes and began her story.

"Back then, I lived on the edge of town, but I stayed to myself as I do now. However, I am always aware of what is going on in the town. I remember James when he was a very young boy. He played ball in the street with the other boys, but he also spent a great deal of time reading. I often saw him stretched out in a nearby field reading a book while the other boys played pranks, bullied younger children, and were unruly. The first time I talked to him. He was ten or eleven years old. He sat on a wall near the square close to his home reading. I walked by and asked him why he was not running around with the other boys.

'I want to be a doctor someday, and I have to read everything I can,' he replied.

"What struck me was not his answer, but the fact that he did answer. Most children ran away when I approached. I'm sure it was because their parents warned them to stay away from me."

Marie took a long drink of tea and continued. "When I saw James a couple of days later, I offered him a book on herbs. I told him if he wanted to be a doctor, he needed to know how to use herbs. He took the book and thanked me. To my surprise, when I walked home from the market the next day, he was waiting for me. 'Thank you for the book. I stayed up late reading and taking notes. Do you have any others?' he asked.

'I can bring you one tomorrow,' I suggested.

"He thought for a moment, 'Can I get one today? I'll carry your bags home for you.' Then he took my shopping bags and walked beside me. I was surprised that he was not afraid to come home with me.

"Well, James was astonished at my collection of herbs. He recognized many of them, and he was eager to learn more. He looked through my book collection and selected two books. 'I'll bring them back tomorrow,' he said. I told him he could keep them for a few days. His eyes sparkled. He said thank you and went home."

Marie took another sip of tea. "When I was in town a couple of days later, James' mother approached me. 'Miss St. Claire?' she called. I turned to look at her. I was emotionless. I thought she was going to tell me to stay away from her son, but instead, she thanked me for lending James my books. She then assured me that he would be very careful with them.

'James reads everything, but if he becomes a bother, you just send him home,' she told me. Well, everyone in town avoided me, and I could not believe that she was giving her son permission to visit my home."

"From what James has said about her, his mother sounds like she was a very nice woman," I commented.

"Yes, she was, Arianna." Marie dabbed her eyes dry with a corner of a napkin. "I told her James was no bother at all. Then she thanked me again, and she even took my hand in hers. Well, James was a frequent visitor. His mother often sent me muffins or some other item she baked. At first, he came by to ask about herbs or to borrow a book. Later, he accompanied me into the forest to gather herbs. I taught him how to dry them and use them for medicine. Then I took him on house calls."

I looked at her. "House calls?"

"Oh yes. Everyone in town believed I was a witch and avoided me, but when illness struck, they called on me for help."

I stared at her. I opened my mouth but did not know what to say.

Marie continued. "When James was seventeen, he went to New York to study, but when he came home on school break, he always came to visit me. He still wanted to be a doctor, but he knew his father needed help with the shipping business. When he finished school, James came back to Salem and worked with his father. He continued to learn about herbs and accompany me to tend to the sick. His mother was always genuinely nice to me. She even invited me to tea at her home which upset the neighbors," Marie chuckled.

"Well, James was a good businessman, but his heart was in medicine. His father knew this and eventually decided to sell the business and send James to Edinburgh, Scotland to study. James was so excited when he came to tell me the news. I gave him my herb book to take with him."

"Oh," I gasped. "I have seen that book. He has it in a prominent place on his bookshelf to this day."

Marie smiled. "James was gone for three years studying medicine, and when he returned, he went to New York to work in the hospital there. He was an exceptionally good doctor, and he enjoyed helping people. He came home for the Christmas holidays and went out with a few of his childhood friends. His closest friends were decent men who had grown up to become businessmen, and one was even a minister. However, there were also bullies in town. These men cornered a young woman outside the pub. She was a poor woman from a poor family, but she was also a new witch in the coven. The men taunted her, and being young and inexperienced, she tried to run away, but they surrounded her. James and his friends came out of the pub and saw what was happening. His friends did not want to get involved, but James approached the men and told them to leave the woman alone. He walked up to her and took her by the arm to escort her home when one of the cowards stabbed him in the back. James' friends rushed to him, and the others fled. They got a cart and moved him to his parent's home, and one ran for the doctor. The doctor sewed the wound closed but said James would not survive because the internal damage was too severe. When I heard what happened, I rushed to the house. I looked at his wounds. The doctor was correct, James would not survive his injuries.

"His parents were heartbroken. His mother cried hysterically and begged me to help her son. James' father was in shock and looked like he might pass away at any moment.

'Do you want me to save your son?' I asked them both. 'I have to warn you. He is gravely injured, and this may not work. But, if I can save him, he won't be exactly the same.'

"His mother sobbed, 'I can't bear to lose my only child. Save him.' I looked at James' father. He nodded yes."

Marie stopped and dabbed her eyes again. I was absolutely riveted to her story. She remembered everything in such detail. I looked down at my barely touched cup of tea then took a long drink.

Marie took a deep breath. "I told James' father to get everyone out of the house while I prepared myself. I turned only a few people, and I knew I needed to stay in control, or I would kill James faster than the knife. Once the house was empty, I told James' parents to go downstairs and not come upstairs no matter what they heard, and under no circumstances were they to let anyone in the house. They nodded and left the room. I locked the door behind them and then went to the bed to talk to James. I would not turn him unless he consented. 'James, can you hear me?' He squeezed my hand. 'I can save you, James, but you won't be the same.'

"He opened his eyes. 'I know what you are Marie. I've known for a while. I want to live. I want desperately to live. Help me.' He collapsed and his hand went limp. I frantically felt for a pulse. It was faint but there. I took a deep breath, closed my eyes, and bit him."

She smiled, let out a big sigh, and looked at me. "His parents agonized downstairs when they heard him scream, but it worked, and two days later he was changed. He looked different, paler, but more handsome, and stronger. His parents wept and hugged him. They were immensely grateful.

"I snuck James out of the house in the middle of the night and taught him to hunt. I knew the townspeople were scared. The doctor came by and wanted to speak to James. People talked about James' recovery, and they suspected I did something unnatural to him. We decided that James and I would visit my sister in the South and let things calm down here."

"He knew you were a vampire? Did he say how he knew?" I asked.

"No, he didn't, but James is very perceptive."

"Thank you for sharing the story with me, Marie. It explains a lot."

"He is a very special man, and he loves you very much, Arianna."

"I love him too."

She smiled and placed her hand over mine. "I know and that makes me very happy."

We sat quietly for a few moments. "When did you meet Giovanni?" I asked suddenly.

"When he first came to America many years ago. He always looked so sad. But I will tell you about him another day."

"Marie, when my mother visited, she brought some jewelry and other items from my childhood. Would you come by and see if anything is enchanted like my locket?"

"Of course."

My phone chimed. "Excuse me."

"It's James," she said.

"Yes, he is on the train and will be here in thirty minutes."

"Well, you better be going then."

I stood up. "Thank you, Marie. I enjoyed our chat this afternoon." I started to walk toward the door but stopped. "Should I tell James you told me the story?" I did not know how I would keep it a secret, but I thought I better ask.

She smiled. "Yes, you should tell him. I know he wanted to tell you, but he was not sure how to do it."

I was relieved. I did not want to keep anything from James.

"He worries about scaring you, Arianna, but I believe you are stronger than he realizes."

"I know he loves me. I did not take my transformation well. I didn't know I was a hunter. I did not know he was a vampire. Then I was attacked, and I awoke and discovered a world I thought only existed in stories." I took a breath and wiped my eyes. "I regret what I said and did to James. I pushed him away. I hurt him, and I never want to hurt him again."

"Arianna, it is all in the past. Think about the future." At the door, she took my hands just as I have seen her take James' hands. "I am glad you are in his life. Be well."

It was raining again when I left Marie's house. I stopped at the grocery store for a rotisserie chicken and potato salad and arrived home just before James. I opened the door before he came to a full stop. "Well?"

He smiled broadly and reached me in several long strides. "She will represent me."

"That's wonderful!" I flung my arms around his neck and kissed him soundly. I ushered him inside and took his wet coat.

James took off his wet shoes. "Will it ever stop raining."

I held my finger to my lips. "Shh. It could be worse; it could be snow."

He gave me a sideways look. "True."

"So, tell me the details."

"She likes what she read so far. I left the draft with her, and she thinks it will sell. She wants to get the manuscript to a publisher early in the new year, preferably by late February or early March."

"Wow. Will you have it edited by then?"

"I think so. The date is a target, so it can be adjusted if necessary."

"I'm so proud of you, James." I gave him a big hug. "Let's celebrate." I took a bottle of champagne out of the chiller, and James popped the cork. I took two gold rimmed glasses out of the hutch, and he poured us each a glass.

"To a successful publication," I toasted.

"Thank you."

James refilled our glasses, while I set my dinner on a plate. We sat down at the table.

He drank down some wine. "How was your day?"

"Good. I stayed in bed for a while, talked to Caroline, talked to my mother, worked at the Historical Society, and had tea at Marie's house."

James put his glass down. "Marie brought you to her home?"

"Yes, we had tea and talked." I put my fork down. "She knew I was going through the old newspapers, and she wanted to tell me why she turned you. She said you wanted to tell me, but you didn't know how to because you were afraid it might scare me and bring up bad memories." James nodded his head yes, but he still did not speak. "You told her you wanted to live, just as I told you I wanted to live. You also knew Marie could help you, and I think subconsciously, I knew you could help me too."

"Arianna, I was afraid to tell you because I feared it would upset you. There are similarities between our stories, and I did not want you to have flash backs."

I took his hands in mine. "Thank you for worrying about me, but I am stronger than you think, and I am ok with my transformation now. In fact, I think I can say that I am happy it happened to me."

He raised his eyebrows and looked steadily at me.

"Ok, granted, I wish some crazed vampires were not trying to kill me, but I love my life, and I love you, and I would not change a thing."

James pulled me off my chair onto his lap. He kissed me long and hard. One of those kisses that melted my bones and reminded me that nothing mattered but the two of us.

Chapter XI
House Party

James

It was just after two am when I closed the front door and walked toward my car. I knew she was close by, so I got in and waited. A few seconds later, the passenger door opened, and Marie slid inside.

"Hello Marie." I turned and smiled at her.

"I'll hunt with you tonight, James."

"Good." At first, we drove in silence. We did not have to drive, but we never wanted to draw attention to ourselves. This close to the holiday there was traffic on the roads even at this hour.

"I saw Arianna in town last week buying glass ornaments."

I laughed. "Yes, she needed more for the banister garland because she said it was too plain."

"I noticed she put a ground pine garland and wreath on the front door. It is traditional and looks very nice."

"You know, she made them herself."

Marie turned her head and looked at me. "Really? Where did she learn that skill?"

"Apparently, she and her mother made garlands and wreaths every Christmas."

"Interesting," Marie muttered.

I drove to the state park, pulled in the entrance, and parked in front of the barricade. It began to snow as we got out of the car and headed into the forest. We circled around and then headed toward the stream. The air was crisp and cold, and a few frozen leaves crunched under our feet as we ran. The moonlight glistened off the ice crystals at the edge of the stream. It snowed lightly during the early evening hours as well, and the little snow that had accumulated on the ground blew around as we passed. There was a herd of deer close by, and the two of us stayed upwind of the animals. In a few minutes we each had a deer.

"Are you finished?" I asked Marie as she walked toward me.

"No, I think one more."

I led the way up a hill deeper into the forest. We were not in a rush, so we walked slowly in search of more game. It was a pleasant night, and we stopped while Marie picked bark. She put pieces in the bag she carried. An owl flew overhead, and I wondered if it was looking for Arianna.

Eventually, Marie and I turned to head back toward the car and came upon a pack of large coyotes. "Their numbers are multiplying." I did a quick count of the animals.

"Yes, there are too many of them. They will struggle if we have a bad winter."

I signaled to Marie to circle around the other way. Coyotes were not as dangerous as wolves, but they were smart and tricky animals, so we had to be cautious when hunting them. She nodded, and we both maneuvered silently into position. I nodded, and we sprung out into the clearing, and each took an older animal.

When we finished feeding, we went to the stream and washed up. I sat down and waited while Marie gathered pinecones. An owl flew silently over our heads. We stayed out until the sun was beginning to crest the horizon. Just before we reached the car, we heard footfalls and leaves crunching.

"Deer hunters," Marie whispered.

I motioned for her to follow me and swung around to give them a wide berth.

We exited the forest and walked down the road to the barrier. Two pickup trucks were parked next to my car.

"Marie, you are coming to the party tonight. Right?"

"Oh yes. It was gracious of you both to invite me." She actually sounded excited. "Is Giovanni going to be at the party?"

"No. He and Marena are in Vermont settling a dispute."

"Will he be coming to Salem for the holidays?"

I shook my head. "No. He wants to spend a quiet Christmas with Marena since we leave the day after Christmas and will be away for the start of the new year." I started the car and turned it around.

Marie made a throaty sound. I swiveled my head to look at her. "What's wrong, Marie?"

"Nothing, I am just worried about your trip to Montana. The three of you will be in unfamiliar territory. Two hunters and a vampire may draw a great deal of attention." She paused. "It is also a wild area."

I laughed. "You know, Arianna said the same thing."

Marie nodded. "She is a wise young woman."

I smiled. "Yes, she is."

"Will there be many vampires at the party tonight." Marie changed the subject.

"Marcus and his girlfriend will be there."

"Who is this girlfriend?"

"Her name is Trina. She's an architect. She works for a firm in New York City."

"How did he meet her?'

"He was a consultant on a project she worked on."

Marie sat quietly. I wanted things to go smoothly this evening. Arianna put extraordinary effort into this party, and sometimes, vampires and humans do not mix well. Several people from her undergraduate days were coming, but I worried most about the three local women and their husbands that were invited.

"Arianna appears excited about the wedding."

"She said you two had tea again last week."

"We did, and we had another pleasant chat. She is especially kind, and she loves you so very much." Marie normally did not open up to others, and I was pleasantly surprised that she and Arianna actually cared for each other considering their rocky first encounter.

"I never did thank you for telling her the story of why you turned me."

"She took it well. Your fears were unfounded. Arianna appears to have come to terms with her new life." Marie turned slightly in her seat and looked at me. "I have been receiving regular reports from the wolves," she said changing the subject again. "They are taking their role quite seriously, patrolling the town and checking on vampires that pass through."

"I guess that is good."

"John prefers to report to Arianna. Giovanni and I told him that she is not ready to fully embrace her position, but he, and Jason, think otherwise."

"Arianna runs into Jason regularly."

"Well, it is a small town, James. They are bound to run into one another." I grunted, but Marie continued. "If Arianna embraced her status, it would make the situation with the wolves easier." She sat back. "It would also make Giovanni happy."

I glanced over at her. "Maybe in time, but I don't think Arianna is ready for that yet, Marie."

"Maybe you should talk to her after the wedding and the new year."

I did not reply. "How is your sister?" I asked changing the subject.

"Oh, she is doing well. You know she purchased a computer."

"You should get a computer too," I suggested. Typically, Marie did not embrace change or modern conveniences. She still used candles around her house even though she has electricity, and it took quite a while to convince her to use a cell phone.

"I have thought about it." I raised my eyebrows at her. "Yes," she paused, "I think it may be time to get one. My sister and I could video chat."

"Really? Well, I will be happy to help you purchase one when I return from the wedding."

"Thank you."

We drove for a few minutes in silence. "Can I take you home?"

"No, to your home will be fine."

I turned down Chestnut Street, pulled into the driveway, and parked the car. "Would you like to come in?"

"Thank you, no. I will see you at seven." She looked at the house. "Arianna appears very busy."

I listened, and I heard Arianna working in the kitchen preparing food. I kissed Marie lightly on the cheek. "Thank you."

"For what?"

"For accepting Arianna."

Marie smiled and took my hands. "How can I not like her? She makes you incredibly happy." She gave my hands a squeeze. "I will see you later."

I watched her walk away. Arianna opened the door. "Hi. Was that Marie?"

"Yes. She accompanied me today."

"Is she coming tonight?"

"Yes, she is." I stepped into the kitchen, stopped, and looked at the bowls and platters drying on the counter. "You've been busy. Did you sleep?"

"I did for an hour or so, and then I decided to start preparing the food. I made two seafood lasagnas. The shrimp is chilling. I have everything washed and chopped for Cesare salad and fruit salad. I also have the garlic bread sticks prepared and ready to bake.

"What smells so good?"

"I have three cakes baking in the oven for dessert: red velvet, chocolate, and French vanilla."

I followed her into the front room. Everything sparkled and glistened. The banister up to the second floor was draped with a long needle pine garland accented with natural pinecones, white ribbon, glittery ornaments, and tiny white lights. The foyer table held a large floral arrangement, and I saw another on the dining room table. The front room's mantle and the doorways were also decorated with garlands. The tree twinkled with white lights reflecting off the ornaments and tinsel. "This is … amazing."

"Thanks." She picked up a white basket of party favors and placed it on the entry table in the foyer between two large, velvet red poinsettia plants. The table was trimmed with a thick garland of white tulle and white lights. Arianna straightened the big white bows on either end of the table. "Can you put the wine in the chiller please, James?"

I wrapped my arms around her waist and kissed her. "I love you." I kissed her again. "Thank you for making this house our home."

She rose up on her toes and kissed me. "I love you too."

The timer beeped. She kissed me again and walked back in the kitchen to take the cakes out of the oven. She set them on cooling racks beside bowls of frosting. "That is all I can do until later. After you put the wine in the chiller, why don't you join me upstairs?" Arianna trailed her fingers up my arm then brushed her lips lightly over mine.

When I tried to deepen the kiss, she pulled away teasingly. I took a step forward and pulled her back to me. I kissed her eagerly as I slid my hands up inside her shirt.

She leaned back and smiled. "I guess that is a yes."

I watched as she slid out of my arms and slowly walked away from me. At the doorway, she turned, blew me a kiss, and pulled her shirt off before she headed up to the second floor.

*****

"James you should mix the punch," Arianna called from the bathroom.

"Ok. What else should I do?"

"I think that is all. I will start to put out the hor d'overs. Everything else is heating or chilling."

I adjusted my tie and brushed my hair. "Do you think a tie is too much?"

"No! It's a Christmas tie. It's festive."

I heard the blow dryer turn on. I sat on the bed and put on my shoes.

"Oh, James?"

"Yes?"

"I need you to light the candles in the front room too."

"Ok." I stood up and picked up my jacket from the bed. The bathroom door opened, and Arianna stepped out. I was speechless.

"Wow! That is a beautiful dress," I finally managed to get out. "Wow!"

"Thanks." She smoothed the front of the dress and went over to the full-length mirror. She adjusted the dress again and looked at the back. It was a short, silky, red dress with spaghetti straps and a black belt. "I really like the plunging neckline of this dress. I can wear a longer necklace with it. Can you help me?" She pulled her hair to one side, and I put the necklace on her. She put on long gold earrings that matched. "What do you think?"

"Beautiful." I kissed the back of her neck. "Absolutely beautiful." I trailed a string of kisses up her neck.

"Thank you."

We went downstairs and finished the preparations. "The house not only looks spectacular, love, but it smells like Christmas."

"I'm glad you like it. I worried that it might be too much for you." Arianna picked up the sound system remote and pushed play. Soft holiday music filled the room.

"No, it's not too much. It's festive."

A short time later, the first car pulled up to the house. It was Marcus and Trina. I went to the door and opened it. "Welcome."

"Nice to see you." Trina walked in with a garment bag over her arm.

"Hi, Trina. Hi, Marcus. Thank you for coming." Arianna and Trina hugged.

"Marcus, it's good to see you," I shook his hand.

"Thank you for inviting us." Marcus looked around. "The house looks great, Arianna."

"Thank you."

Trina peeked in the other rooms. "It's amazing. How can you plan a party and get ready for a wedding?"

Arianna sighed. "Believe me, the party was much easier than the wedding, and we are only in charge of the rehearsal dinner. Honestly, who knew weddings were so much work."

"I think it's better to elope." Trina said seriously.

"I'm beginning to agree," Arianna nodded. "Do you need to put on your dress, Trina?"

"Yes, but my dress isn't as cute as yours."

"Come on, I'll show you to your room. Would you like a tour of the house too?"

"Yes! Marcus, are you coming?"

"No, I'm going to have a drink with James. I've seen the house." Marcus followed me into the front room, and I poured two glasses of brandy. We sat down in the wing backed chairs in front of the fireplace. "Have you seen Tony or any of the others around Salem?"

"No sign of Tony. A few vampires have passed through, but the town has been noticeably quiet since Halloween." I took a drink.

"How are things with the wolves?"

I shook my head. "Marie told me that the wolves prefer to report to Arianna."

"And that Jason guy?"

"Every time Arianna sees him, and believe me that is often, he finds a way to touch her arm or her shoulder. I think he does it on purpose to let me know that he talked to her."

"I'm sure he does." Marcus sat back and took a drink. "Traditionally, hunters and vampires have not lived together."

"Giovanni said years ago, hunters often married female werewolves. It ensured the children would either be hunters or wolves."

"Makes sense. They both age slowly and live a long time. But Arianna is not a regular hunter. It makes more sense for her to be with a vampire because physiologically she is more like us."

"Tell that to Jason," I replied sarcastically.

"Speaking of aging. James, I didn't want to say anything in front of Arianna, but Giovanni is aging."

"I've noticed it too."

"Has Arianna?"

"I don't think so. Not yet."

"Well, spending time with him in Montana she may notice."

The doorbell rang, and more quests arrived. Marcus and I stood up and went to answer the door. Arianna and Trina came downstairs, and the house started to fill with people. Several of Arianna's college friends arrived. They hugged and immediately all started talking at once. I knew Arianna was disappointed that Caroline could not come to the party because big Jack and little Jack were both sick.

Marie was the last guest to arrive. I took her cloak, and Arianna introduced her to the other guests. Several of the neighbors looked scared, but Arianna distracted them with food.

Arianna bustled over to me. "Things are going well." She beamed with happiness.

"Yes, considering we have vampires and humans together drinking copious amounts of alcohol what can possibly go wrong?" She laughed, and I kissed her gently. Then I think I turned white. Mrs. Ballard was talking with Marie.

Arianna followed my gaze. "Ah, maybe I should go over there." She headed toward the two women.

Marcus sauntered over to me. "There certainly is a mix of people at this party," he laughed.

I felt relief when Arianna successfully turned Mrs. Ballard away from Marie.

Trina came bouncing over holding a glass of champagne. "Great party. And Arianna's college friends are super nice. Are you ok, Marcus?"

"Yes."

"Good. Just checking." Arianna waved at Trina. "Oh, Arianna needs me to help set up the buffet."

"I will…" I started to say, but Trina held up her hand to stop me.

"Nope, you check the drinks. Arianna and I will set up the buffet. By the way, the food smells delicious." She practically skipped away to help Arianna.

Marcus and I opened several more bottles of champagne and wine, and then we restocked the buckets holding cold bottles of water, beer, and soda. Arianna announced the buffet was ready, and everyone moved to the dining room. Food and drinks were plentiful, and the neighbors looked like they were finally relaxing and enjoying themselves.

I noticed Marie in the buffet line. She took a small scoop of sea food lasagna, refilled her wine glass, and came over to sit with Marcus and me near the fire.

"This is very good," she said between bites, "I think I may have a bit more."

"I occasionally have a few bites of Arianna's seafood dishes too. They are exceptionally good."

"Do you think we should eat something?" Marcus looked around nervously.

"I've always found that at a buffet party, most people don't notice who eats what," I replied. "I keep a full glass of wine in my hand, and no one asks questions."

"Trina's eating enough for both of us, anyway." Marcus laughed.

Marie studied Trina. "I noticed she still acts very human, Marcus."

"She hasn't been turned long," Marcus explained. "She was in denial when she was first turned and kept going about her life as if nothing changed for quite some time."

Marie raised her eyebrows and looked at Marcus and then at me. "Another one who denied her transformation?" she shook her head. Marcus and I shrugged.

"Who turned her?" Marie asked.

"She doesn't know. No one knew the guy, and her friend said she did not invite him."

Marie stopped eating and lowered her fork. "What?"

"She was at a party in New York City, and a guy asked her if she wanted to live forever. She thought it was metaphorical, so she said sure. He took her hand and led her outside. She thought they were going out on the balcony for conversation since it was very loud in the apartment. Once there, she asked his name. He told her his name was Savior, and the next thing she knew, he bit her. She said she could not do anything to stop him, and she felt a searing hot pain. He released her, and she screamed. Several people heard and rushed outside, but he climbed down the balcony and was gone. She was scared, and they thought about calling the police, but they decided it was a drunken prank. Of course, she was sick for several days, and she ran a high fever. She thought she caught the flu. She returned to work, and one of the other architects where she works, who is also a vampire, recognized the transformation. He asked her quite a few questions, but she told him she was fine. Apparently, it took several tries until he convinced Trina what happened to her."

"She never saw the vampire who turned her again?" Marie asked. Marcus shook his head no. "That is strange and disturbing."

"There are many strange things happening lately," I absentmindedly commented. "I don't like mysteries."

"And there are too many mysteries surrounding Arianna and Trina," Marie added. "Marcus, does Trina have a lot of family?"

"Just her parents. She's an only child. They live in Wisconsin." He fidgeted around. "We are flying out there for a few days and coming home late on Christmas day. Fortunately, Trina can't be gone long. She's working on a big project." The relief was clearly evident in his voice.

"Think of me in Montana for a week and at a wedding. Then add that I have to try and keep Arianna and Giovanni civil."

"Wait. Arianna wanted Giovanni to attend the wedding. You think they will still be snippy with one another?" Marcus asked.

I smirked at him. "This is Arianna and Giovanni."

"There is a bright side. At least you won't have Jason around."

That made me smile. "True, Marcus. The trip is looking better already."

Chapter XII
Quiet Christmas

Arianna

It was one am when the last guest left. I sat down on the couch next to Trina and kicked off my heels. "That was fun."

"I agree, Arianna. I haven't been to such a good party in a long time. More champagne?"

"Thanks." Trina refilled my glass, and I took a long drink. "Where are James and Marcus?"

"In the back room."

"The man cave," I informed her.

"Your friends are super nice."

"Thanks. It was so great to see them and catch up. You know, I was worried with so many different people in one house, but the party was a success." Trina and I drank more champagne. "Do you still hang around with your friends from before you were turned, Trina?"

"I don't have many friends in the area. I moved to New York only a month before I was turned. I was at a work party."

"Well, you are making friends now." I touched my glass to hers.

A short while later, Marcus and James went out to the car and brought in the luggage. We turned off the lights to make it look like we went to bed.

"Are you hunting with the guys?" I asked Trina.

She shook her head. "I'm good. Besides, they need guy time."

I laughed.

James came in the room, walked over to me, leaned down, and kissed me. "We will be back around dawn."

"Have fun."

James and Marcus left, and Trina and I stayed up talking and drinking for another hour before going upstairs to rest.

The next morning, I was cooking bacon when Trina joined me. "Would you like bacon and eggs, Trina?"

"Yes, thanks." I got a plate out of the cabinet for her, and she sat down at the table. "I know it's weird, but I still love food."

"I'm always starving. My metabolism is fast. Trina, how many eggs and how do you like them cooked?"

"Two or three. How do you normally cook them?"

"I usually scramble them and put them in a tortilla with bacon and chipotle cheese."

"Yum. That sounds good."

"Would you like tea?"

"Definitely."

I scrambled up half a dozen eggs and heated tortillas in a tortilla basket. I poured two large cups of tea and set everything on the table.

"It smells delicious," Trina said with a sigh.

"Thanks" We started to make our breakfast burritos. I really enjoyed having Trina eat breakfast with me. James often sat with me while I ate, but there was something nice about sharing a meal with someone. Maybe that was one reason why James wanted me to hunt and feed with him. We would be sharing a meal. It was something I needed to think more about.

"Good morning, ladies." James and Marcus joined us. "So, what should we do today?" James asked.

"Would you like to visit Historical sites, the museum, or maybe go to the Christmas bazaar?" I asked.

"The bazaar sounds fun. I need to buy a few more gifts," Trina replied.

"Oh Trina, we have to go to the candy shop. The fudge is so good even James will eat a piece."

"Candy makes a great gift too."

"Absolutely. I'm bringing fudge to my family when we go to Montana."

"Don't forget the pumpkin muffins," James added.

"Pumpkin muffins?" Trina asked.

"Oh, yes. The pumpkin muffins are amazing. We'll get a dozen while we are out. More tea?" Trina nodded yes, so I heated up the tea kettle. James and Marcus looked fidgety. "Is there a football game on today that you guys want to watch?"

"Yes," Marcus answered.

"You guys can stay here, and Arianna and I can go out alone," Trina suggested.

"Why don't you two watch the games, and Trina and I can go to the bazaar and the shops. And, if you want Trina, we can go to the mall." The two guys looked relieved.

Trina enthusiastically nodded her agreement. "I need a New Year's Eve dress, and I'm not really good at shopping."

"I need a dress too." I poured water in the cups and added tea bags. "Patty said we can change out of our bridesmaid dresses before midnight."

"The bridesmaid dress will probably be hideous. You will need to change into something nice," Trina commented.

"I know. I'm seriously afraid I am going to look like a pink pigmy puff."

"The bride wouldn't pick something hideous," Marcus chimed in.

"You don't know much about weddings, do you?" Trina snickered. "It's common for the bride to pick big, puffy, unflattering dresses for the bridesmaids. It makes her look better."

On the way to the bazaar, Trina and I stopped at a variety of shops. "My mother loves anything Egyptian," she told me.

"Then we need to stop in the Trolley Shop." I pointed to the building up ahead. "They have Egyptian statues."

We each had a couple of shopping bags by the time we reached the bazaar. The venders had many beautiful, handcrafted items including wooden puzzles. "Jack loves trains," I told Trina.

"Your godchild?"

I nodded yes. I purchased a train puzzle with a variety of animals in the cars behind the locomotive.

We strolled through the booths. Trina bought several items. I stopped to look at handmade fountain pens.

"For James?" Trina asked.

"Yes. He keeps a journal and often writes out scenes by hand."

We left the bazaar and walked over to the wharf. Trina took several pictures of the Friendship. The ship was closed today.

Our next stop was the café for pumpkin muffins. I ordered a Pumpkin Chai tea and Trina ordered a soda. While I was there, I placed my orders for the coming week. I planned to bring muffins to Caroline when I visited her, and I wanted to bring three dozen to Montana.

We sat outside the café and watched as people walked by doing their holiday shopping. The city was full of holiday spirit. Christmas Carols played in cars and in the shops, the sky threatened snow, and there was a briskness to the air. Most people were smiling and talking. Some people were singing. Many people wore stocking hats, and they all carried shopping bags.

"Do you think we will meet any of the wolves today?" Trina asked excitedly. "I really want to meet one."

"I am sure we will meet up with one eventually. Probably Jason. He has a habit of showing up. James thinks it's intentional, and I'm beginning to agree."

"I hope we run into him."

We continued up the street to the candy shop. It was crowded as usual. We stood in line and watched through the window as several workers made saltwater taffy. While we waited, Trina ate a sample piece of fudge. "Oh wow, this fudge is amazing!" She took another sample.

"It is the best." I took a sample as well.

"Hi, Arianna."

I turned around. "Hi, Jason," I replied. Trina looked at me with wide eyes, and I nodded my head ever so slightly.

He walked over to us. "It's nice to see you, Arianna."

"Jason this is my friend, Trina. Trina, Jason."

Jason shook Trina's hand. "How long are you in town, Trina?"

"Just a couple days. Why?" Trina narrowed her eyes, and there was tension in her voice.

Jason gave a casual off handed laugh. "Oh, no reason. I'm just making conversation. Is this your first trip to Salem?"

"It is." She relaxed slightly.

"It looks like you two have been doing a lot of shopping. Do you need help getting back home, Arianna? I am happy to carry your bags for you." He reached over and tried to take them.

"No thanks, Jason." I held onto the bags. "I think Trina and I can manage."

He removed his hand. "Ok. Everything is quiet in town today. Mostly people out shopping."

I nodded.

"Well, you have my number. Call me if you need me, Arianna. I am always available to help."

"Thanks. We should be fine. James and Marcus are at home if we need anything."

"Ah, James' friend Marcus." Jason looked at Trina. "Is he your mate?"

Trina glared at him.

"Marcus is my friend as well, Jason."

"And yes, he is my boyfriend," Trina added.

Jason nodded his head. "I guess they are watching the games. Well, have a good day."

"You too," I replied without enthusiasm.

"It was nice to meet you, Trina." He waved and left the store without buying anything.

"You have his number?" Trina asked.

"Yes. Giovanni said even if they weren't going to report to me, we needed to exchange phone numbers, so we can contact one another in an emergency."

"How many emergencies have there been for Jason to call you?" Trina laughed.

"None yet. But as I said, he shows up everywhere."

"He's passive aggressive," Trina stated flatly.

"That he is."

Trina bought several items, and I bought my usual jelly pumpkins for us to munch on while we made our way back to the house. "Jason looks like a normal guy. A big guy, but a normal one. Wolves do have a pungent smell though," Trina commented.

"He does?"

"Can't you smell him, Arianna? His scent is quite strong, and not at all like a human."

"To me he has a slightly musky scent, but it is pleasant." I shook my head. "I have to ask Giovanni how to tell if someone is something other than human. You know, I had no idea there were werewolves when I first met Jason and his family."

"I never knew about werewolves either."

"Of course, when I met them, the little brother was a dog."

Trina's gasped. "Really?"

I nodded yes.

When we arrived back at the house, James and Marcus were in the man cave watching a game. We poked our heads in to say hello. The guys sniffed the air and suddenly stood up.

"Did you see Jason while you were out?" James asked.

"Yes, in the candy store." No matter how quick the encounter with Jason, James always knew.

"I can smell him." Marcus wrinkled his nose. He sniffed Trina.

"I told you he had a strong smell, Arianna."

"He doesn't smell bad to me." I shrugged.

Trina and I went in the kitchen. I heated up a plate of leftover seafood lasagna, and by the time I finished eating, the guys were engrossed in another football game. We kissed our guy good-bye and headed to the mall.

Trina was quiet as I drove.

"Are you ok, Trina?"

"Arianna, can I ask you a super personal question?"

"Sure."

"And if it is too personal, you don't have to answer. I can't believe I'm asking you this, so really if it's too personal, don't answer."

"Trina what is the question?"

"Have you ever," she paused and took a deep breath. She let it out slowly. "Has James ever bitten you when you two were …you know…" She waved her hand.

It was a very personal question. I glanced over at her. Her hands were twisting in her lap, and her eyes were teary. I took a breath. "Yes, James and I have bonded."

"You both have bonded? Wait. Can you bite him? Do you even have fangs?"

"Yes, I have fangs," I assured her. "Fangs were one of the changes with my second transformation. If I had them after the first transformation, I would have known I wasn't entirely human."

"Don't be too sure of that."

"Oh, Trina, I am so sorry. I forgot."

She waved her hand dismissively. "Don't worry about it. I was in deep denial. It took being nearly crazed by a lack of blood for me to accept that I was turned."

"You aren't the only one," I replied sadly.

"You too?"

"I knew I transformed, but I didn't want to accept it. I left James, told Giovanni to go away, and tried to continue with my life as if nothing happened." I shrugged. "That is until I became so crazed, I found James in the woods, dropped down, and drank from the doe he killed."

"Wow."

"Marcus didn't tell you? He was there."

"Nope, he just told me that you also had trouble adjusting to the change."

"That's an understatement," I laughed.

"Arianna, can I see your fangs?"

I extended them.

Trina jumped and covered her mouth. "Omg, you do have fangs, but they are so tiny. Oh no, Arianna, I'm so sorry. I shouldn't have said that."

"It's ok, Trina. Mine are small, but they do allow me to feed like you, and of course they are used in a fight." I paused. "Although, I have never actually killed an animal on my own. I only have hunted with James, and he did all the work." I glanced over at her. "Back to your original question. What happened, Trina?"

She looked down at her hands. "Marcus bit me last week while …" she twirled her finger. "I completely flipped out. He looked so hurt. I felt terrible, but it brought back memories of being bitten and turned."

"Trina," I said softly, "that is understandable. I'm certain Marcus understands."

"He apologized and said he was sorry. He said he should have asked first."

"Marcus is very kind, and such a good man." I paused. I was not sure if I should ask the question on my mind. "Can I ask? Have you two had sex since?"

"We have."

"See, I know Marcus understands. Your turning was traumatic, but maybe in time, you will be more comfortable and want to do it."

Trina sighed. "I want to, Arianna. I know he wanted to show his commitment to our relationship, and I do too. I love him." She looked down. "I don't think he will ever do it again though."

"Trina, he doesn't have to be the one to initiate it, you know."

She looked up and smiled. "You're right. Why didn't I think of that? Thanks. I feel better."

"You're welcome. I'm glad I had an answer for you. I have been doing research, but I know so little about being a hunter. I know even less about being a vampire, or for that matter, a wolf."

"It's not like there's a manual we can read."

I looked at Trina. "You know. That's a clever idea."

"What writing a book?"

"Why not? A story about a woman becoming a vampire, or even better a vampire hunter, and learning about the supernatural world. Of course, it must be sold as a fictional story, but it would be factual for people like us."

"That is a great idea. You can write it. Aren't you doing some writing?"

"I am."

"I really think you should, Arianna. Heck, I'd buy it," Trina laughed.

We were in great spirits when we arrived at the mall. There was a line of traffic getting in the parking lot, but that was expected this close to Christmas. I found a space, and we stopped at one of the large anchor stores first.

I looked at a rack full of dresses. "I want something short and sleek for New Year's Eve."

"Something that makes you look hot because you know that bridesmaid dress won't make you look hot."

There were several possibilities in the first store but nothing that really hit the mark.

"Trina, is it me, or are there a lot of pink dresses?" I flipped through the dresses in the next store.

"I was thinking the same thing." She pushed several pink dresses aside.

"I don't wear a lot of pink."

Trina gave me a sympathetic smile.

"There's a very trendy new store in this mall." I led the way out of the store. "Let's try it."

The window display had several short sequined dresses. Trina and I liked what we saw, so we went in. We selected dresses and stood in line for a dressing room. Finally, one opened up, and we decided to share the room.

I had several dresses, but one in particular caught my eye. It was a short, one shouldered, white and silver sequined sheath dress. I put it on. "What do you think?" I turned from side to side and looked at myself in the mirror.

"Wow! Arianna that dress is hot."

I smoothed the dress down in front. It hugged my curves perfectly. "I think this is my dress."

Trina pulled a similar green sequined dress out of our dress pile and put it on. It looked good with her spiky, short, blonde hair and green eyes.

"Wow. I look amazing in this dress. I can tip my hair green to match." She turned from side to side. "Marcus will be shocked." She raised her eyebrows and had a devilish look on her face. "But he will love it."

"I think we each have a dress, Trina."

We posed side by side in front of the mirror, and I snapped a picture of us.

"Are you sending that to James?"

"No. I'm not even going to show him the dress until New Year's Eve."

"Oh, that is a great idea. I think I will do the same."

I took off the dress. "I wish we were spending New Year's Eve with you and Marcus."

"Me too. We would look super hot together."

"We should have James and Marcus take us to a night club in the city when we get back from the wedding." I put my sweater and jeans back on.

Trina looked down at her chunky, low heeled boots. "I need shoes to go with that dress, Arianna."

I looked down and nodded. "Next stop, the shoe store."

One look at Trina's face as we entered the shoe store told me this was going to be difficult. I took her straight to the strappy high heel aisle. "What do you think, Trina?"

She shook her head. "I'm not sure I can walk in those."

"Sure, you can. It just takes practice. What size shoe do you take?"

"Nine."

"Oh, me too. Let's try on shoes."

The games were over when Trina and I returned from shopping. James and Marcus were sitting in front of the fireplace having a drink.

"How was your shopping trip?" James called when he heard the door open.

"Great," Trina and I replied together. We entered the living room.

"Can we see what you bought?" James tried to look in my bags. I knew he hoped I bought skimpy lingerie which of course I did.

"You can see a few of the things," I said mischievously. I pulled out a white sweater that had cutouts of lace at the shoulders and a low V neck.

"Nice," the guys said.

Trina pulled out a pair of high heeled, strappy, silver sandals that she bought to go with her New Year's Eve dress.

"Wow, I've never seen you wear shoes like that," Marcus commented.

"It is a different look for me." Trina smiled at Marcus. "In fact, Arianna helped me pick out several new things."

I nodded and pulled a gold pair of high heeled, strappy sandals out of my bag. James raised his eyebrows and nodded appreciatively.

"What else did you get?" Marcus asked excitedly as he tried to look in the shopping bag.

"No peaking." She closed it up.

"We picked up a few surprises," I told them.

Trina giggled, and she and I left to put our purchases away. As we started up the stairs, I heard James say, "that usually means something that I will really like, so I'm sure you will like what Trina bought too."

"Really?" Marcus replied. "I have to encourage Trina to shop with Arianna more often."

Trina and Marcus headed back to New York late Sunday night. After they left, James and I sat on the sofa in front of the fireplace. We sipped wine and worked on our laptops. I really liked the idea of writing a story, and I wanted to write down ideas and questions I needed to research. James looked over at me as I intently typed, but he did not interrupt me.

As we headed up to bed a few hours later, James asked what I was working on tonight, and I told him about my idea.

"That is an exceptional story line," he said as we got into bed.

"I am really excited. I had some ideas and wanted to get them written down. I thought I might have my character compare and contrast known mythology to what is true in the supernatural world."

"Sort of a here's the myths about vampires, but here's the reality, but it is a fictional story."

"Exactly."

He nodded his head. "I like it."

"Thanks" I made a few updates to my planner. "I'm going to wrap everything up at the Historical Society tomorrow."

"Ok." James poured us more wine and then picked up his book.

I took a sip, but it was late, and the wine made me sleepy. I yawned, put the glass on the night table, and closed my eyes. I crossed my leg and arm over James, and he turned out the light and pulled me close.

Monday morning, I brought a basket of cookies to the Historical Society. I finished the box I was working on and labeled it completed. I stacked the remaining boxes neatly, and then I chatted with my coworkers while we snacked on tea and cookies. They asked about the wedding and my travel plans. Finally, I wished everyone a Merry Christmas and left.

I made my way to the café and picked up a pumpkin muffin order to bring to Caroline in Connecticut. I also picked up a chocolate Santa each for Jack and Bobby at the candy shop. I knew Caroline would not be thrilled, but children need to be spoiled at Christmas time.

While James hunted Monday night, I finished packing and then sat in bed with my laptop and worked on my story. Now that I was out of school, my creativity returned. I really missed having time to write, and I wanted to make certain I kept a balance in my life going forward.

My mother called about ten o'clock. She was nervous about the rehearsal dinner and the wedding. I really did not pay attention to everything she said.

"Oh, Mom," I interjected, "remember I'm going to Connecticut tomorrow."

"How are the two Jacks doing?"

"All better."

"Are you sure? You don't want to be sick for the wedding."

"I'm sure they are fine."

She made a huff noise. I couldn't tell her that it didn't matter what illness they had because I was not going to get sick anyway. I really was discovering that there were many advantages to this transformation.

"When are you visiting Aunt Rose?"

"Wednesday. We are taking her to an early dinner."

"Well, have a safe trip."

"Thanks, good night."

"Good night, honey. I will call you if anything comes up."

*****

Tuesday was a beautiful day to drive to Connecticut. It was warm for December, and the sun was shining. So far, we only had a few light snowfalls, and the temperature was above normal. I was not complaining because I had a lot to do and did not need snow to complicate matters. James helped me load the car. I had several large gifts for the boys, overnight bags, and food gifts, but we crammed everything into James' little sports car.

"We need to buy a family car in the new year." James placed a large bag containing a toy piano on the back seat.

"We can take my car. It's bigger."

"We need to get you a new car."

"I will when I'm working a steady job."

James said nothing. We had this discussion before. He wanted to buy me a new car, and I wanted to wait until I could afford one on my own. I got into the passenger's seat and felt claustrophobic. A stuffed animal sat in the tiny space between the driver's and passenger's seats. "It won't be this crowded on the way home," I said quietly.

James sighed and started the car. "We are buying a family car," he said firmly, and I knew better than to argue right now.

It was after rush hour, but the traffic was still heavy. I leaned across the stuffed animal and kissed him. James smiled and kissed me back. "What would you like to do for Christmas Eve this year?" he asked.

"Stay in, open presents, maybe watch a movie."

"The Hawthorne Hotel has a special Christmas Eve dinner, or if you prefer, they have a Christmas Day brunch."

"I like the idea of Christmas Day brunch."

"Good, I'll call for reservations."

When we pulled into Caroline's driveway, I saw Jack at the kitchen window. As soon as the car stopped, the door opened, and Jack ran out. I got out of the car and scooped him up into my arms and gave him a kiss. "You are getting so big."

"I missed you, Auntie." Jack kissed me several times.

"Jack baby, I missed you too."

James came over to us. "Hello, Jack."

Jack mumbled hello grumpily. He kept his arms around my neck, and I carried him inside.

Caroline squealed when we walked through the door. She held little Bobby who was fussing. "I am so happy you two are here."

"It is good to see you." I shifted Jack and tried to lean over to give Caroline a hug.

"Caroline, it's nice to see you" James carried in our overnight bags.

"You remember where the guest room is, James." She gestured upstairs.

James nodded and left the room.

"Tea?" Caroline asked me.

"Definitely." We walked into the kitchen. The walls were painted mint green, and there were oak cabinets and black granite style countertops. I remembered the Summer Caroline and Jack purchased the house. She was pregnant, and because I was at the university nearby, I spent most weekends helping her and Jack paint and decorate.

I set Jack on a chair in front of his toy cars on the table. James came back in the kitchen. "We can wait to empty the car," I said to him.

"No, no. You ladies sit and chat. I will empty the car. After the ride, I can use the stretch."

"Thanks, honey." I blew him a kiss, and he headed out.

Caroline put Bobbie in the highchair and then turned on the burner to heat the tea water. "It's so nice to see you." We hugged properly now.

Caroline took two mugs out of the cabinet and then put a handful of dry cereal on the highchair's tray for Bobbie.

I sat down, and Jack climbed onto my lap. "When Bobbie naps do you want to go to the mall for ice cream?" I whispered to him. He smiled and nodded eagerly.

"Jack, do you want a bowl of cereal?" Caroline asked.

"No," he snapped.

She looked at him sternly.

"No thank you, Mom."

The water boiled, so Caroline stood up and poured tea. "Would James like tea?"

"Probably not."

Caroline set two mugs on the table, sat down, and dunked her tea bag. She looked tired. "Jack, why don't you sit in the other chair so Auntie can have her tea?"

"No," he whined.

"He's ok." I reached around him for my mug.

We chatted about the wedding and Christmas, but I sensed she had something she wanted to tell me. A few minutes later, James came in. He looked at Jack sitting in my lap but did not say anything.

"James, would you like a beer?"

"Yes, thank you." Caroline started to get up, but James stopped her. "You sit. I can get it."

She smiled at him and drank her tea. She reached over and pushed more cereal toward Bobbie.

"What time does Jack get home from work?" I asked.

"He's going to get out about three o'clock, and it takes forty-five minutes to get home."

I looked at my watch. It was almost eleven o'clock. Jack was getting antsy, and Bobbie was getting fussy.

"I should make lunch," Caroline said.

"Actually, we want to take Jack to the mall, and give you a little time for yourself. It looks like Bobbie is going to nap soon."

Caroline let out a sigh of relief. "Thanks." She turned to Jack. "Go get ready."

"Yay!" He jumped down and ran to his room.

"You are going to get him real food, right?" There was a touch of sarcasm in her voice.

"Oh course." I rolled my eyes.

Jack ran back into the kitchen with his sneakers. "I need help." He climbed up into a chair, and I put on his sneakers.

"Go get your coat," I told him. He jumped down and ran to the hallway. "Caroline, you relax, and don't worry, James and I will take good care of Jack."

"Take my car. I'm not sure the car seat will fit in James' little car." Caroline handed me her car keys then she adjusted Jack's jacket. "Now, you be a good boy for Auntie Arianna and James."

"I will." He kissed Caroline, and she kissed him back.

Caroline picked up the baby and walked us to the door. "Have fun."

"We will, and don't worry." I sat Jack in his car seat and then slid behind the wheel and drove to the mall which was packed with holiday shoppers. I didn't bother looking for a close space but took the first one I came to in the back of the lot. I took Jack out of his car seat. "We should take the stroller," I said to James.

"I can walk." Jack took my hand.

"Ok, but we'll take the stroller just in case." James took the stroller from me.

"James, will you take Jack's other hand, please, so we can all walk together."

"Oh course." James took Jack's hand. There was a lot of traffic, and it was a long walk to the door, so I wanted Jack safely between us. Our first stop was the food court. We found a table, and James stayed with Jack while I bought pizza and drinks. Kids can be very curious, but Jack did not ask why James wasn't eating pizza. While he ate, Jack told us about his school. He liked to play on the jungle gym. He also liked to draw and color. He ate most of the pizza slice and drank all the milk. He stood up on the chair, and I wiped his mouth clean.

He looked at James and then looked at me. "Are you going to marry James, Auntie?"

"Ah, well, maybe someday, but people can love one another and not be married."

"Good," he replied curtly.

"Good?"

"When I grow up, I will marry you." Jack put his arms around my neck and kissed me.

"When you grow up, you won't want to marry me. I'll be old."

"I want to marry you."

"Well, I love you, but I'm your auntie."

"Auntie Jen says you aren't an auntie like she is."

I sighed, but I smiled at Jack. "That is true, Auntie Jen is your Daddy's sister. I am your Mommy and Daddy's friend." I had no idea why Jen disliked me; she was usually very cold to me.

Jack kissed me. "Can I go in the play area?"

"Yes, you can." James and I walked over to the entrance to the play area with Jack. I took off his shoes, and he ran in.

James put his arm around my waist. "So, I have a rival for your affections."

"Yes, you do. And he is a younger man," I laughed.

"Auntie, watch me slide," Jack called.

"I'm watching." He climbed the ladder and slid down the slide with his arms over his head. "Yay!" I clapped. He jumped up and ran to get back in line to do it again.

After the play area, we started shopping. We took Jack to the toy store and bought him several toy cars. Then we went to the big department store, and I bought Jack a pair of character sneakers. I also bought a pair of lined suede boots. As we walked through the store, I saw a pretty red dress. I looked at the guys. "Can you two sit down and relax while I try the dress on?"

"Sure, we can. Right, Jack?" James asked.

"Ok," he grumbled.

"Good." I took the dress, and Jack sat with James on the chairs outside the dressing room while I tried it on. It was an A line dress with red lace cap sleeves and a lace bodice. I looked at myself in the mirror. I liked it, so I went out to show my guys. "What do you think?"

"Very nice," James said.

"Very nice," Jack imitated him.

"I think I will get it for Christmas Day brunch." I turned and looked in the three-way mirror. "I'll be right out." I changed, paid for the dress, and went back to get them. "Ok, who is ready for ice cream?"

"Meeeee!!!" Jack screamed.

James stood up, took my bag, and put it in the stroller. I took Jack's hand, and we headed to the ice cream stand.

Jack wanted a chocolate cone with sprinkles.

"Can I have an empty cup too?" I asked the clerk.

I decided on two scoops of chocolate ice cream in a cup, and we sat down at a small café table. I tucked a couple of napkins into the neck of Jack's shirt in an effort to keep him clean. Jack ate fast, but the ice cream melted faster. He took a bite out of the pointy end of the cone, so I put it in the cup and gave him a spoon. To my surprise, he nearly finished it. I took a hand wipe out of my purse and wiped his hands and face. "Do you want to ride in the stroller?" I asked him.

"Noooo." he was getting whinny he was so tired.

I put Jack's jacket on and took his hand. He shuffled along, so I picked him up and carried him. James pushed the stroller full of our purchases.

We walked back to the food court. "I can carry him," James said. He tried to take Jack from me, but Jack held on tighter and said no.

"I can get him." Jack relaxed, put his head on my shoulder, and closed his eyes. Carrying him was no problem for me which was yet another advantage to having these new abilities. He was sound asleep before we got to the car.

James was quiet on the way back to Caroline's house. He had led a quiet life until he met me. Now, he had people visiting his home, and we were taking trips to visit people. I reached over and took his hand. "I love you."

He squeezed my hand. "And I love you."

We arrived at Caroline's right at three o'clock. She opened the door, and I carried Jack in and placed him on the couch. "He's exhausted. He had fun."

Caroline looked much better. She napped and showered while Bobbie slept. "I'm going to start dinner."

"Caroline, I told you don't fuss."

"I made lasagna over the weekend, so we are going to have it, garlic bread, and green beans."

"Ok let me help." We went into the kitchen. James went upstairs to check his email giving Caroline and I time to talk before Jack arrived home. "So how are you doing?" I asked.

"Pregnant."

"What?"

"I'm pregnant."

"Oh, that's ...," I started to say wonderful but the look on her face stopped me. "What's wrong?"

"I don't know." Caroline sat down and started to cry. "I'm tired, and the pregnancy was a surprise."

"Oh." I was not sure what to say. I put my arm around her shoulder. "What did Jack say?"

"He was surprised too. We took precautions, but it happened."

I was at a loss for words. I gave her a hug. "I'm sure everything will work out."

She smiled, "I know. I will be ok. I just found out Sunday, and it was a bit of a shock."

"When is the baby due?"

"August. We aren't telling anyone yet. It's too soon."

"Ok."

She got up and dried her eyes on a kitchen towel. "I actually feel better after telling you."

"It's going to be ok." I hugged her again.

"I know."

"Maybe it will be a girl this time."

"Actually, I hope it is. I want a little girl." She smiled and looked more like herself.

By the time Jack came home, her eyes were dry, and she was smiling.

Jack and James got along very well. They sat in the kitchen and talked while we prepared dinner. "Cape Codder, anyone?" Jack asked.

"I'd like one," I called.

"Let me help you." James followed Jack into the dining room to make drinks.

"Let's eat in the kitchen, Caroline."

"No, we should eat in the dining room."

"Sit," I said. "I will take the lasagna out of the oven, and we can eat right here." I set the table and pulled out the lasagna to cool. Caroline sat next to Bobby in his highchair and fed him. James walked in carrying a pitcher of drinks. Jack poured cranberry juice into a highball glass for Caroline.

While we were eating, Jack woke up from his nap and came in the kitchen. His father picked him up. "Did you have fun at the mall today?"

Jack yawned and nodded yes. "I played on the slide and had ice cream."

I put lasagna on a small plate for Jack. He held out his arms to me, and I picked him up and set him on my lap.

"You aren't going to feed him?" Caroline said with a sigh. "You spoil him so much," she laughed.

I shrugged. I looked over at James. He stared at me. I could not read the expression on his face. Jack ate all the lasagna on his plate, and he had a garlic stick.

Caroline took a covered cake dish from the pantry.

"Pistachio cake?" I asked hopefully. Chocolate cake and pistachio cake were my two favorites. Chocolate was easy to find, but not pistachio. I really needed to get the recipe from Caroline.

"Yes." She sliced the cake and started passing it around.

"No thank you, Caroline." James leaned back in his seat. "I'm full, but Arianna can have my piece."

"Absolutely," I mumbled between bites. I offered Jack a bite of cake.

"Oh, he doesn't like pistachio," Caroline commented.

"Yes, I do," Jack snapped back.

Caroline stood with her hands on her hips and gave her son a stern look.

"Sorry, Mom," he said meekly.

After dinner, Caroline decided to give Bobby a bath while James, Jack, little Jack, and I cleaned up. When the perishables were put away, I told Jack and James to go in the living room. "Jack and I can finish up here, right?"

"Right." Jack stood on a chair in front of the sink playing with the soap bubbles. I stood right behind him, and together we finished rinsing off the dishes and putting them in the dish washer. Jack was very wet by the time Caroline came back with Bobby who was all cleaned up and in a fresh onesie for bed. She brought him in to Jack and then came back in the kitchen. "He's almost had a bath already."

I wiped the water off the kitchen floor. "And your floor is clean," I said with a laugh.

"Bath time," Jack yelled. "Auntie will give me my bath." He took my hand and pulled me down the hall. I waved bye to Caroline who laughed and went in to join Jack and James.

I filled the tub with bubbles and got out the bath toys. Jack put the foam shapes on the tub wall. I spelled out Jack with the foam letters.

"Spell your name," he said to me.

I spelled out Arianna next to his. Then I spelled out Bobby, Mommy, Daddy, and finally James. Jack took down James' name.

"You don't want James' name on the wall?"

"Nope." Jack started putting more foam shapes on the tub wall.

"Why are you mean to James? He is always nice to you."

"He smells funny?"

"Oh, you don't like his cologne?"

"Nope. The other smell."

"What other smell?"

"He smells like candy."

"Like candy? But you like candy."

"He smells too sweet. I get a headache."

James did have a sweet smell. I guess all vampire's do. I shook my head. Jack was jealous of James. I opened the shampoo bottle and started washing his hair.

After he was dressed in PJs, he said good night to everyone, and then he jumped in bed and waited for me to read him a story. I took *Put Me in The Zoo*, a Dr. Seuss series book off the shelf, laid down next to him, and started to read. "This was one of my favorites when I was little," I told him.

"It's one of my favorite's too." He snuggled close to me. "Sing to me, please."

"I started to softly sing *Twinkle Twinkle Little Star* because I knew it was one of his favorites, and soon, he fell asleep.

I went downstairs and sat next to James on the sofa.

"I am so glad you came to visit," Caroline said. "I wasn't sure you had time since you are leaving for the wedding in a few days." She shivered. "It's going to be cold up there."

I nodded. I could not tell her that the temperature was not a concern for me. "I hope there isn't a lot of snow. I had to purchase sturdy boots for the trip."

"Your whole family is making the trip, Arianna?" Jack asked. "Another drink?" He motioned to James.

"Yes, please," James got up, and Jack refilled their glasses.

"Even Grandma is making the trip," I replied. "I haven't seen her in a while, but I'm worried about her traveling to Montana, especially in the winter."

We talked for some time. It was nice to catch up with them. It was well past eleven o'clock when Caroline started to get sleepy, so we said good night and went to the guest room. I put on a night shirt and got in bed next to James.

We read for a while. "I'm tired." I yawned.

James ran his fingers through my hair. "Rest."

I snuggled close to him.

The next morning, I rolled over, hugged James, and kissed him. "Good morning." I looked around. "Oh, Jack didn't come in last night. That's weird."

James closed his book and set it down on the nightstand next to him. "He tried to. You were asleep, and I heard him get up and start to walk down the hall. I got out of bed and returned him to his own bed."

"James."

"Call me old fashioned, but I think children should sleep in their own bed." James picked up his book, opened it, and started reading again.

I stifled a laugh. James was as jealous of Jack as Jack was of him.

Unfortunately, we could only stay over the one night. After we showered and dressed, I took the sheets off the bed and put them in the washing machine, and then remade the bed with clean sheets. Caroline's in-laws were arriving later. I cleaned and wiped down the bathroom and put out fresh towels. Jack stayed home from work in the morning, so we could all have breakfast and exchange gifts.

Little Jack handed me a present that he obviously wrapped. "Thank you." I kissed his head.

"He picked that out himself," Caroline told me.

I peeled off the wrapping paper and inside was an emerald green necklace. "Wow," I said. "You picked this out Jack? It is beautiful."

He smiled and nodded. "It's your birthstone."

"It is." I took the necklace out of the box and put it on. "Thank you," I said to Caroline. "I love it."

When Jack left for work a short while later, James brought our things out to the car while Caroline and I had a cup of tea. I was happy Caroline looked rested today.

"It's too bad you can't stay longer," she said, "but you have to get ready for your trip and the wedding."

"And your in-laws are coming," I added. I let out a sigh. "It has been so nice. Mom hasn't called, but I am sure she will call later with the newest problems and concerns." We both laughed.

"I was so surprised when you said Albert was getting married. I never thought he was the type."

"I agree."

"And she is so much younger than he is."

"She is younger than us," I reminded her.

"He hasn't known her very long, has he?"

I shook my head. "He moved to Montana during the Summer and met Patty."

Caroline raised her eyebrows and shook her head then drank down some of her tea.

Jack came in the kitchen, crawled into my lap, and handed me a drawing of flowers that he made for me. "This is going on my refrigerator," I told him. He hugged me.

James came back in and sat down. He looked at Jack in my lap but did not say anything.

"James, can I get you something to eat or drink before you go?"

"No thank you, Caroline. Thank you for having us."

"Anytime, you are always welcome."

"Well, Jack, I'm sorry, but Auntie has to go home now."

"No." He tightened his grip.

"I'm going to visit Montana."

He looked up at me. "Wow."

"I'm going to bring you back something cool."

"You are? What?"

"It's a surprise. Promise me you will be good and help Mommy."

He nodded his head vigorously. "Will you call me from Montana?"

"Yes, I will."

He hugged me tightly and kissed me. I set him down and stood up. I kissed Bobby then hugged Caroline. "Be well."

"Please, be careful, Arianna."

I nodded. "I will."

"Call and text me."

James got my coat, and I gave Jack and Caroline another hug and kiss. "Merry Christmas."

"Merry Christmas," they said.

James led the way out the door, and we got in the car. I rolled down my window. "Bye, I love you guys." I waved to them.

"Love you, Auntie," Jack called.

"Love you. Call me." Caroline emphasized the later.

James started the car, backed out of the driveway, and turned onto the street.

I sighed and looked at him. "Thank you." I took his hand.

"You're welcome, love." He brought my hand to his lips and kissed it.

I wanted a quiet Christmas Eve and Christmas Day with James before the jam-packed wedding festivities. We planned to have dinner, sit in front of a fire, take a walk around midnight, and come back home and open our presents.

The morning of Christmas Eve, I had a few last-minute errands to run, and I picked up an order of pumpkin muffins.

"How are the arrangements going?" Julie, the shop owner, asked as I checked out.

"I think we are set. I've never attended such a complicated wedding."

"It's the bride's day," she said with a big sigh.

"So, I have been told many times."

"Have fun. Merry Christmas."

"Thanks. Merry Christmas and Happy New Year." I gathered up the box and a cup of Pumpkin Chai tea then headed toward the door.

"Take lots of pictures," Julie called.

I nodded and waved.

Next, I stopped at the candy shop. I bought fudge for Dad and a bag of pumpkin jelly candies. I was really addicted to those things. Then I stopped at the market for shrimp and broccoli for my Christmas Eve dinner. I grabbed a couple boxes of cereal bars for the trip, and then I headed to the check out. I saw my neighbor standing in line. "Hi, Mrs. Butler."

"Oh, hello, Arianna." She fumbled with the items in her hands.

"Can I help you?" I reached toward her, but she pulled back quickly and nearly dropped her asparagus.

"No, thank you. I have it." She adjusted the items in her arms.

I checked out and turned back to Mrs. Butler. "Merry Christmas."

"Merry Christmas."

It started to snow while I was in the market, so I put my hood up as I walked out of the store. Just before I reached my car, Jason suddenly appeared. "Hi, Arianna."

"Hi, Jason."

"I want to let you know we'll watch your house while you are away."

"Thank you. James and I appreciate it."

Jason nodded. "Please be careful, Arianna."

I looked at him. "I will have James and Giovanni with me."

"There are definitely werewolves there," Jason paused, "and not all of them are like us."

"I thought hunters and wolves were traditional allies?"

He bobbed his head from side to side. "Yes and no. Wolves have allegiances, and they fiercely protect those they are loyal to. Be careful."

This conversation made me even more anxious about the trip. "I'll be careful."

"Call me if you have any questions."

"Well, I better get going." My voice reflected the concern I felt. I put my bag of groceries in the car.

"Merry Christmas, Arianna."

"Merry Christmas, Jason." I got in, started my car, and headed home.

I went inside the house. James was back from hunting, and I heard him in the shower. I quickly put the perishables away and went upstairs. "Hi. I'm back," I called to him all thoughts of wolves and Montana gone now that I was with James.

"Want to join me?" he asked.

I was already undressed, and I opened the shower door and got in.

After dinner, James and I took a bottle of red wine and glasses and lounged on the sofa in front of the fireplace. The fire cast a soft glow, and the Christmas tree lights twinkled. It was still snowing outside, and everything was so peaceful and quiet. Just before midnight, we put on our coats and boots and went for a walk. I hooked my arm in James' arm as we strolled down the street. The snow dampened the sounds of our footsteps. We heard church bells in the distance.

"It must be midnight. Merry Christmas." James leaned over and kissed me.

I wrapped my arms around his neck and kissed him. "Merry Christmas."

We leisurely walked through the empty square where the reenactors were in October. The stores and the museum were closed but most had Christmas lights on in the windows. A few cars were out on the roads, and as we passed a bar, we heard revelers singing carols. We turned the corner and walked down the main street. We stopped and listened to the choir singing in the church and then walked down to the wharf.

"Hi, Marie," James called. Up ahead, Marie came out of a doorway.

"James, Arianna," she replied cheerfully as she walked toward us. "Merry Christmas."

"Merry Christmas," we said.

"I was visiting with friends. You two look like you are enjoying a bit of quiet time."

I closed my eyes and took a deep breath. "It is the calm before the storm."

"Let's stop and have a drink," Marie suggested.

"Yes," James and I replied together.

Marie and I hooked arms with James, and the three of us strolled off to the local pub to toast Christmas.

Chapter XIII
Onward to Montana

James

I put the last of the bags in the trunk and closed it. I saw Arianna moving around inside the house, checking things, looking at her list, and gathering up items. She was nervous. She was like this every time she was going to see her family. It was not that the family didn't get along; they did. It was the expectations each of them had that seemed to make them so… intense.

I walked in the house. "The car is packed, and I am ready when you are."

"Ok, good."

I checked the door to the basement to ensure it was locked. Not that anyone would come near the house, even the neighbors stayed away. And of course, the wolves would be watching the house. Not for me, but for Arianna. I sensed Marie and went back outside to greet her. "Hello, Marie."

She walked up to me and took my hands in hers. "Safe journey."

"Thank you. Happy New Year."

Marie looked past me to Arianna. "Is she ok?"

"She gets like that when she is going to visit with her family."

Marie watched Arianna intently as she took a very deep breath and turned toward the open door. "Hello, Marie."

"Hello, dear. Do you have everything?"

Arianna waved her list as she locked the front door. "I think so. I'm bringing most of the items for the rehearsal dinner favors. Weddings are so much work."

Marie nodded as Arianna approached. "I'm sure the wedding will be beautiful." She gave my hands another squeeze. "You two be safe."

"We will," we replied together.

"Giovanni will be with us," Arianna added as she put her purse and carry-on on the backseat of the car.

"Yes, the two of you may attract attention. Be careful."

"Bye, Marie. We'll see you soon." I walked toward the car. I noticed Mr. Butler was looking out the window. "And thanks for watching the house for us. Feel free to make yourself at home," I called loudly to Marie, and I saw him gasp and move back from the window.

Marie held in a laugh and waved as she headed down the street. Arianna suppressed a laugh in the front seat of the car. I settled into the driver's seat and started it up. "Montana, here we come." I stepped hard on the gas, and Arianna burst out laughing.

I parked in the long-term lot, and we made our way to the terminal. Arianna was more relaxed now. "Marena, Marcus, and Giovanni are waiting for us inside," she said as she juggled the phone in her hand. We walked in and saw the three of them standing awkwardly near the check-in counter.

Marcus walked toward us. "Hi. How are you?" He took one of the bags from Arianna.

"Hi, Marcus, thanks." Arianna walked over to Giovanni.

"Marcus, thanks for coming to the airport." I shook his hand. "How was Wisconsin?"

"It actually went well. Trina's parents were nice."

"Great. Let's hope my trip is as good."

Arianna looked at the departure board. "The plane is on time. We should check in."

Giovanni, Arianna, and I went to the counter with the bags we needed to check. When we finished, we returned to Marcus and Marena, and we all walked to the security check point.

"I like this new bag tracker APP." Arianna tapped her phone and smiled. "The bags have been scanned in and are on the way to the plane."

"Have a wonderful time," Marena said to Giovanni as she gave him a light kiss. "Be careful." Giovanni kissed her back, and the three of us smiled at them. That is until Giovanni glared at us.

"We'll be home soon. Happy New Year." I kissed Marena on the cheek and shook Marcus' hand.

"Happy New Year." Arianna waved goodbye. "Tell Trina I will text her pictures."

"Have a good time," Marcus called back as we took our place in the security line.

We went through the long line without any problems, but Giovanni looked unhappy. It was a long walk through the terminal, and finally, we reached our gate. The three of us sat down. I took out my reader. Giovanni sat next to me. He was unnaturally still. Arianna, on the other hand, was antsy.

"I'm going to go get something to eat and see what the shops have." She stuffed her phone in her back pocket and took her wallet out of her bag. "Giovanni, can I get you anything?" He shook his head no. I smiled at her, and she leaned down and kissed me. "I'll be back soon."

Giovanni and I sat quietly. I occasionally glanced at him out of the corner of my eye. He sat like a statue. "Are you ok?" I finally asked.

"Umm," he grunted.

I took that to mean that he was fine, but he looked extremely nervous.

About thirty minutes later, Arianna returned with two large bags, a bag of food, and a tall drink. She sat down and looked over at Giovanni. "Is he ok?" she whispered.

"He says he is."

"I found a nice bag to use as a second carryon bag on the way home." She opened the bag and showed me. "I bought one for mom too."

"They are very nice."

Arianna leaned back and pulled out a chicken sandwich from the small bag. "I love a chicken biscuit sandwich. Giovanni, I bought two. Would you like one?'

"No, thank you," he said softly.

"Are you ok?"

"Umm." He nodded.

Arianna finished both sandwiches and an order of fries. She put her earbuds in and leaned back in the chair. Giovanni continued to sit very still and stared straight ahead.

Sometime later, the attendant announced that boarding would begin shortly. Giovanni shifted in his seat then he abruptly stood up, picked up his bag, and headed to the boarding line that had begun to form.

Arianna and I looked at one another. "I'm not sure he is ok, James."

"He'll be fine." I picked up my bag and started toward him. Arianna shrugged and joined us in line.

We were seated three across with Arianna in the middle in the center section of the plane. She fidgeted in her seat and adjusted her pillow. Giovanni fastened his seatbelt then studied the emergency manual. He listened intently as the flight attendant went through the emergency procedures, and then he sat very rigid in his seat and stared straight ahead. The plane took off and Giovanni did not even blink. In fact, Giovanni did not seem to move, and he did not utter a single word until the flight attendant came by with drinks.

"Can I get you a beverage sir?" she asked me.

"Red wine, please."

"Beverage Miss?"

"Red wine, please."

"Sir, something for you?" she asked Giovanni.

Giovanni looked at her "Red too, please."

She passed out plastic glasses and handed each of us a small bottle of red wine. Giovanni grunted again. He fumbled with the wine.

"Here, let me." Arianna took the bottle and opened it. "Giovanni are you sure you're ok?" His hands were unsteady as he began pouring wine into the little plastic glass. "Are you afraid of flying?" she asked.

"Umm," he grunted in reply.

"Would you like to watch a movie?"

He shook his head no. He drank the wine in his glass, refilled it with the remainder of the wine, and drank it straight down. He took a deep breath, leaned his head back, and closed his eyes.

We had two flights to get to Missoula, Montana. On the first flight, Giovanni never seemed to relax despite a few bottles of wine and a meal. He ate, leaned only his head back, and closed his eyes, but he was still very stiff, and his breathing was shallow. After dinner was served, Arianna started a movie on her laptop. She plugged in a splitter so we could both listen, she moved closer to me, and she put her head on my shoulder. The movie began, *Christmas in Connecticut* the 1945 version, her favorite holiday movie. I put my arm around her and kissed her head.

We had a long layover in Minneapolis. Again, Arianna walked around the terminal while Giovanni and I waited at the gate. The second flight was shorter but there was quite a bit of turbulence. Giovanni clenched the arm rest and stared straight ahead the entire flight. Arianna fell asleep. I read so as not to disturb either of them. Giovanni seemed to breathe again when we landed.

Arianna's mother called and waved enthusiastically when she saw us exit the terminal.

"Hi!" Arianna called back as she rushed forward to greet her family. She and her mother hugged.

"I hope you three brought warm clothes," Felicia commented as she looked wearily at Arianna's jean leggings and thin white sweater. Felicia wore a pair of navy slacks, a thick cream colored sweater, and a bright red vest that looked bulky on her petite frame.

"We did." Arianna turned and hugged her grandmother. "Hi, Grandma."

"Oh, my dear, I missed you." Luisa had tears in her eyes. For a ninety-eight-year-old woman, Luisa looked remarkably fit. Her hair was not completely grey, she stood straight, and she looked sturdy. She wore jeans and a heavy cable knit turtleneck sweater under a thick, black, wool coat.

"Hi, honey." Arianna's dad kissed her and took her rolling bag. John looked out of place. He wore a tweed cap on his balding head and was dressed in a suit, but his pant legs were tucked into floppy black snow boots. "How was your flight?"

"Good." Arianna turned to Albert. "Hi. Congratulations again."

"Hey, Baby Sis." Albert hugged her and took her two shopping bags. "Bought a couple things at the airport I see."

Arianna reached for my hand and pulled me to her. "Grandma, Albert, this is James."

Luisa took my hands and pulled me down to her. She kissed one cheek and then the other. "So nice to meet you, James." Arianna had her grandmother's dark brown, almost black eyes, and they both had long, strong, and sharp fingernails.

"It is nice to finally meet you too." I said with a smile.

"Good to meet you." Albert shook my hand.

Albert was the most relaxed. He smiled and talked much slower than the rest of his family. He was tall, just over six feet, and he had a full head of chestnut brown, curly hair that came down almost to his shoulders. He wore jeans, boots, and a red plaid flannel shirt with a black quilted vest.

"And this is Giovanni, James' uncle," Arianna said, and Luisa and Albert welcomed him and shook his hand. To my surprise, Giovanni kissed Luisa on the cheek. Arianna smiled at him. She did not call Giovanni, grandpa, but I knew she cared for him. He was gruff and often grumpy, but I saw tiny tears in his eyes when he met the family he never knew he had.

We talked, or I should say they talked all at the same time as we walked to the car rental booth. "Why aren't you staying at the hotel in town?" I heard Arianna's father grumble.

"Because James and Giovanni like to hike and there are trails near the cabins," Arianna replied. "Besides it's not far from your hotel, and we thought the cabins had more ambiance."

"Thank you." I took the keys from the woman at the desk and went over to the group. I leaned over and whispered to Arianna, "wait here. I'll get the car."

"Ok. Thanks." She smiled at me. Luisa watched her granddaughter then looked at me and smiled. I picked up several bags and started heading outside.

"Hang on, James." I turned around, and Albert was hurrying toward me with bags in his hands. "I'm going to get Dad's car too." We walked across the street to the parking lot. "My sister looks very happy."

"She is happy."

"She looks relatively relaxed."

"In part, it is thanks to you. She took your advice, and it has helped get John off her back."

"Dad means well, but he is intense, especially with Arianna." We reached the rental car section and we stopped. "Thanks for coming to the wedding."

"And thank you for inviting my uncle. He was staying with us for the holidays, and I didn't want to leave him alone."

"No problem. The more the merrier."

"Where is John's car parked?" I asked.

"A couple aisles over." He pointed toward the short-term parking area. "Let's get them loaded in the cars, and then we'll head to the Pancake Palace for lunch."

I nodded, unlocked the car, and popped the truck. We stowed the bags then Albert went to get the other car. I sat down in the driver's seat and sighed. This was going to be a long week, and I knew I better hunt often.

Arianna rode with her parents and grandmother, and Albert rode with me and Giovanni. "This will be quieter," Albert said as he settled into the back seat. Once we exited the airport, we saw the vastness of Montana, and why it is called big sky country. Mountains, sky, trees. The vastness seemed to extend out in every direction.

"Giovanni have you ever seen anything like this?" Albert asked.

"No, this is impressive."

The mountain peaks were covered with snow, but alongside the road, the drifts were small. "I expected to see more snow on the ground. Not that I am complaining," I added quickly.

"We have not had a big snow since early November," Albert commented.

Faulkes, the town were Albert lived, was close to the airport and the university where he worked. It took less than twenty minutes to get to the Pancake Palace. It was an older building with a large pancake sign that read, '24-hour Pancakes'. I pulled in next to John's car, parked, and got out.

"I'm starving," Arianna said as she walked around the car to help her grandmother.

"If she would eat properly, she wouldn't always be hungry," Giovanni muttered.

I gave him a stern look, something I rarely did. I respected Giovanni not only because he was a hunter but because he was Arianna's grandfather. Truthfully, I afforded him more respect than she did at times. Arianna had difficulties accepting all the changes of the past year, and this was not the time to bring up anything hunter related. Giovanni looked at me with a blank expression. "I don't want anything to upset Arianna," I explained.

"Humm," Giovanni grunted in reply.

We were seated right away, and the waitress brought over two pitchers of water. She went around the table taking orders. Arianna pointed to chocolate chip pancakes, so I ordered them knowing she would eat majority of it. She ordered a two egg omelet with cheese, a stack of buttermilk pancakes, and to my surprise bacon on the side.

"So Giovanni does not complain," she whispered.

The family kept up a rousing conversation, often all talking at the same time, while we waited for the food and throughout the meal. They each carried on several conversations and continuously interjected into other conversations. Even Luisa kept up.

"James, what is your book about?" Luisa asked. It took me a moment to realize the question was for me.

I stuttered, "Oh, excuse me, Luisa. My book. Well, it is an Historical novel set in Salem, Massachusetts."

"And Arianna tells me you have an agent and a contract, congratulations."

"Thank you. I am incredibly pleased with the contract."

"Yes, congratulations," John said picking up the conversation. "It is a difficult publishing market."

"It is." Arianna gave my arm a squeeze. "I am very proud."

As quickly as the conversation turned to me, it turned away again.

John sat on the other side of Arianna, and I heard him ask about her new job. "Online, though. Is that real course work?"

"Absolutely, Dad. Online learning has become exceedingly popular because it appeals to the traditional as well as the nontraditional student."

"Yeah, most universities are offering more and more online classes," Albert added through a mouthful of pancakes.

"I don't know though. It's online, and the school is small." John was a traditionalist. He believed in traditional classes where the professor lectured, and the students listened. He taught Physics at a large university, and he wanted his daughter at a comparably sized school. "Have you considered coming to California? I am sure the Classics department would be interested in having you teach, and since you are teaching online you can continue for the small school as well."

I saw Arianna close her eyes, and she took a deep breath. "Dad, I told you, I am not moving to California. I am incredibly happy living in Salem with James. We have been over this," she said very quietly. He started to speak when I noticed Luisa giving John a stern look from across the table. I heard him grunt, and he resumed eating. Arianna looked at me with a pained expression. I squeezed her hand under the table.

"I think it's great that you found something for Fall, Baby Sis."

I felt Arianna shudder. "Thanks."

After lunch, we divided up and went to our respective accommodations. Albert went with John, Felicia, and Luisa back to their hotel, and I drove to the cabins we rented.

Arianna sat up front. She was noticeably quiet. She looked around at the panoramic view as I drove. "It's beautiful, but different than I imagined." I smiled at her to try and ease her nervousness, and she reached over and took my hand.

I was not worried about the vastness of Montana. If I was worried about anything, it was about the vampires and wolves that lived here. "There were several wolves in the restaurant," I commented.

"There were?" Arianna turned to Giovanni. "You need to give me some hints to help me recognize wolves."

"I will teach you," Giovanni replied. "Yes, I smelled the wolves." He let out a sigh. "I am sure word is already spreading about us. We don't know who we will encounter here," Giovanni paused again. "We need to be careful."

"Let's hope no one really cares about us," I added.

"We won't get much down time at this wedding. There are a lot of activities planned, and we have to prepare for the rehearsal dinner." Arianna took out her phone. "I'm making a list of items I need to finish the favors. We also need to get a wedding gift."

"I am giving cash," Giovanni replied. "I have the card all set."

I had not been to a wedding in many years. I wanted to marry Arianna, and I hoped that she might be more open to marriage after being in the wedding party. Yes, there were difficulties with the rehearsal dinner planning, but I was certain Arianna was also excited about the wedding. I wanted her to be my wife. I laughed to myself. I guess I am old fashioned, but I wanted to see Arianna walk down the aisle to me. I wanted to stand side by side with her and take our vows to love one another forever.

Chapter XIV
Meeting

Arianna

We stopped for groceries and then went to the cabins. The owners lived in the main building near the entrance. Fortunately, because of the time of year, we were the only guests. After we checked in, James drove down an exceptionally long driveway. There were five log cabins in a row, and we had the last two which were spaced furthest apart. James parked the car, and we began unloading the luggage. Without a word, Giovanni just picked up his bags, went in his cabin, and closed the door.

I shook my head. "Something isn't right with him, James."

"He has been acting strangely. I have a feeling that was his first time in an airplane."

We brought some of the luggage into our cabin. "He seemed happy to meet Grandma. In fact, she was really the only one he talked to during lunch." We went back outside for the remaining bags and the groceries.

"You talked to her quite a bit too. You had a lot of catching up to do with her."

"I miss her. I haven't visited her in a couple of years. She doesn't travel often anymore. She was sick when I graduated and could not make the trip. This is an exceedingly difficult trip for her to make, but she had to see Albert get married."

"We should visit her."

James and I put down the last of the bags and closed the door. "Yes, we should."

I looked around. The cabin was essentially one expansive room and a bathroom. There was a bed, two nightstands, and two dressers in one area near the closet. Another area was set up as a living room with a TV, a fireplace, a love seat, and a chair. The kitchenette had a two-burner stove, refrigerator, sink, and microwave, and between the kitchenette and living room area was a small table and two chairs. There was a door near the stove that led into the rather small bathroom. The wooden furnishings were rustic which added to the ambiance. Two overhead lights and several floor lamps provided lighting. On the walls was an assortment of wilderness landscape paintings.

I hung up my dresses and James hung his suits in the closet. We both took comfortable clothes out of our suitcases. I took off my sweater and was distracted when James took his shirt off. I peeled off my leggings and walked over to him. I ran my hands up his arms and hugged him. I kissed him on the neck, and he moaned and returned the kiss. It felt good to be in his arms.

"You better go hunt." I leaned back and sighed a few minutes later.

James nodded. "I guess I should." He pulled me close and kissed me. Reluctantly, we stepped back and finished dressing. James sat down to put on his boots. "I won't be long, and I will not go far."

"Take your time. I heard a hawk call when we arrived. I think I'll go out and look around."

"Be careful, Arianna." James kissed me again and headed out the door.

I stacked up the dry goods on the counter in the kitchenette and put the perishables in the refrigerator while I had a granola bar. I heard the call again, so I opened my suitcase, took out my arm guards, and went outside.

"Arianna," Giovanni's rough voice called. I turned to look at him. "Be cautious. I have an uneasy feeling about this place."

"I'll be careful." I put on the guards as I walked toward the trees. Before entering the forest, I looked back and saw Giovanni take a chair from inside the cabin and set it outside. He sat down and waved. I waved to him and moved into the forest. I walked for a while and came to a small clearing. I heard a hawk land up ahead, so I slowed down. As I approached, I saw myself. I stopped and used my mind to reach out to the bird. The hawk took flight and soared down toward me. I held up my arm, and he landed heavily on the guard. He looked like a young bird. I slowly brought up my other hand and gently stroked the hawk's head. He responded by pushing his head into my hand. Suddenly, he took flight, and I started to receive images of men. I suspected they were vampires. I concentrated and hoped I was sending the images to James and Giovanni.

The hawk soared above then let out a shrill shriek as the four men approached. I quickly passed on the vision. I removed my arm guards and tucked them in my waist band at my back then pulled my shirt out to cover them just as the four strangers arrived.

They stopped a good distance from me and sized me up.

"Hello," one of them said. He was a tall rather thin man, and I was pretty certain he was a vampire hunter. Two others were vampires. I could tell because of their sweet scent. The other I suspected was a wolf; although, he had a different scent than the wolves I knew. The hunter approached me, then stopped, and stared at me. He bowed his head slightly, "I'm sorry. I did not realize what you are."

Suddenly, Giovanni arrived behind me. The hunter cautiously looked up at me and stepped back. We heard commotion in the forest. Giovanni and I exchanged nervous looks. Was James in trouble? We heard a howl and then a thud, and then James arrived. His shirt was wrinkled, and his hair was tousled, but he looked unharmed. He took in the scene around him and came and stood next to me.

Two men burst out of the cover of the trees snarling, but they stopped dead in their tracks. They looked around. The hunter said nothing but jerked his head back. The two took up their places behind the others. Everyone was very tense.

The hunter straightened up and took a step forward. "May I inquire why you are in the area?"

"We are here to attend a wedding." I replied.

"You must be Albert's baby sister," one of the vampires blurted out. It caught me off guard, and I chuckled, but the hunter's eyes widened.

"I'm sorry, Miss. We meant no disrespect." He glared at the vampire.

His submissive demeanor surprised me. Obviously, he was concerned that I was offended, but I did not understand why. "Yes, I am Albert's younger sister, Arianna, and who are you?"

"Oh, apologies," the hunter stammered. "I am Ray; this is Sebastian, Bruno, Trevor, Joe, and Clayton. And these are your clansmen?"

I nodded. "Yes, this is James, and this is Giovanni."

"A vampire and a hunter."

"Yes."

"We were unaware that Albert had a hunter in his family. We were on patrol when we caught unfamiliar scents and needed to investigate. We will leave you now, and we will inform Redman, our clan leader, of your arrival. I am sure he will see you tonight as he is also invited to the wedding." They each bowed slightly. They seemed to be waiting for something, so I bowed slightly in return. They straightened up and took off into the forest.

Once they were gone, I called to the hawk, and he came down and landed close-by. I put my arm guards on. He landed on my arm, and I gave a message of guarding and watching for others. He nudged me, and I gently stroked his head. He shifted around and then hopped up and landed on my shoulder. He rubbed his head against mine, and I once again thought watch for others.

"Have you hunted enough James?" Giovanni's voice sounded uneasy.

"Yes. I was heading back when I received the images from Arianna. I knew there were two wolves following me."

I looked at James. "So, they were wolves?" He nodded yes.

"Let's get back to the cabins," Giovanni said. There was urgency in his voice which made me nervous.

They did not move and waited for me. I pictured the cabins for the bird. As he took off, I heard my jacket rip and felt his talons cut my shoulder. "Great."

The three of us quietly headed back. I thought it best to come out of the forest one at a time, but James and Giovanni thought otherwise. Giovanni came into our cabin, and we closed the door. The hawk did a sweep of the area. No one was in sight, and he settled in a nearby tree.

"It's safe to talk." I took off my jacket and went in the bathroom to clean my shoulder and change my shirt which was also ripped.

When I finished, I grabbed a bottle of juice out of the refrigerator. "Giovanni, would you like a juice?"

"Yes, thank you." I handed him a bottle and sat on the back of the sofa. Giovanni sat in a chair by the table, and James paced. Neither spoke.

"So, what was that?' I drank down half the bottle of juice. "Why were they bowing to me?"

"You don't get it." Giovanni let out an exasperated sigh. "You are a super hunter. You are someone to be respected and feared."

"Vampires never bowed to me before. In fact, some of them just wanted to kill me."

"Was it respect or fear?" James interjected.

"I'd say more fear, but also respect," Giovanni said flatly.

"So, who do you think this Redman is?" I asked.

"Probably like you." James stopped and leaned against the counter. "The way they bowed to you suggests someone is enforcing a hierarchy."

"Redman is another super hunter?" I shook my head. "So what?"

"He may see you as a threat." Giovanni definitely looked worried.

"Or an ally," James suggested. "They were curious and confused."

"Because she's a woman." Giovanni took a deep breath and let it out slowly. "I'm sure they have never seen a female hunter." His eyebrows were creased together, and he rubbed his forehead. He breathed shallowly, and his eyes were sullen. He looked tired. "They know Albert that is clear. I expect we will be meeting this Redman tonight." He stood up and gave James and I a stern look. "No one goes into the forest alone," he said gruffly.

"Agreed," James and I replied at the same time.

"I'm going to rest until it's time to go to the restaurant." He slowly walked to the door, opened it, and left.

James started to pace again.

"What's wrong James?"

He stopped and looked at me. "This Redman will be very interested in you." He closed his eyes. "Not just because you are very beautiful, but together, you would be quite powerful."

"I don't care if he's interested in me. I love you." Was James actually worried I might fall in love with this Redman? Giovanni was acting strangely and now so was James. I walked up to James and pressed my body to his. He put his arms around me, and I kissed him. "I love you," I repeated.

When we arrived at the restaurant and I saw a stuffed moose out front, I immediately knew I was overdressed. My black and white sheath dress was fitted, short, and more city than country. "Maybe I should have asked what to wear?"

James got out of the car and came around to open my door. "You look beautiful." He was dressed more appropriately in a tweed sport jacket, dark blue jeans, and a white shirt.

"Patty said dinner, drinks, and dancing. My shoes are too cityish." I looked down at my black strappy heels.

Giovanni got out of the car and headed into the restaurant without saying a word.

"Your shoes are fine, and you look great in the dress. Don't worry." James took my hand and led me to the front door. Loud country music hit us as he opened it.

We walked up to the podium, and before we gave our names, the hostess said, "Oh, you Must be the groom's family."

We followed the hostess to the room in the back. I felt everyone's eyes on us, so I looked straight ahead and did not make eye contact. James put a protective hand at the small of my back as we walked. The hostess led us to a set of double doors and opened them.

Immediately a very perky young woman with long blonde hair ran up to us. "Hi. Arianna!" I recognized Patty from our video chats. "Wow, nice dress."

"Thanks. This is my boyfriend, James, and his uncle, Giovanni."

"Nice to meet you." She gave each of them an enthusiastic hug.

I took James' hand and walked over to the table where my family was seated. I gave my purse to my mother, and I took off my long leather coat and draped it over the chair with her long wool coat. Mom wore a plum satin dress with matching heels, and Dad wore a grey suit and tie. No wonder the hostess knew we were with the groom.

Patty grabbed my arm. "Sorry to take her away so soon. Come on Arianna, let me introduce you to the girls in the wedding party."

The tables had white tablecloths with a light pink fabric overlay and dark pink napkins. There were clusters of pink balloons at the ends of the head table. She pulled me toward a small group of women. I gave a pleading look at James, but he just smiled back as I was pulled away.

I was relieved to see Brittany, a thin, petite brunette, wearing a floral party dress. It helped me look less out of place because Carrie, Jesse, Patty, and almost everyone else was dressed in jeans.

"Brittany helped pick out the dresses, Arianna. I think you will really like your dress." Patty was so excited and happy she was breathless.

I caught a scent and turned maybe a little too quickly. A vampire approached dressed in jeans and a white Western shirt that had black embroidery along the yoke.

"Oh, Janus, you're finally here. What took you so long?" Patty ran up to him and hugged him.

"Sorry I'm late."

"Meet Arianna."

"Hello." Janus tentatively held out his hand. He obviously knew about me.

I took his hand and shook it firmly. "It's nice to meet you." I took a rather deep breath and memorized his scent.

"Janus is the best man, but he knows fashion and style, so he's also my wedding planner," Patty explained.

Brittany walked over. She pursed her lips. "Janus."

"Brittany," he replied. It was obvious there was tension between those two.

The waitress approached. "Patty, everyone is here so we are going to start setting out the buffet."

"Oh, let me go make sure everything is puurrrfect." Janus purred and rushed off.

Albert walked over, put his arm around Patty, and kissed her. "Arianna, let me introduce you to the guys." He pulled me toward him. "This is Tom, Jake, and Joe." They each reached over and shook my hand. The three men and Albert were all wearing blue jeans and Western shirts, and all were human.

"Ok, let's sit down." Patty ushered me to the girl's side of the table. Once we were all seated, the staff passed out champagne. Patty's father stood in front of the table. He was a tall man with greying hair. He also wore jeans and a Western shirt.

"Excuse me. Can I have your attention, please." Immediately the room quieted down. "I want to thank you all for coming this evening." Everyone clapped. "So, let us all raise our glasses to Patty and Albert. Here's to a long, happy life together."

"Patty and Albert!" everyone exclaimed. I looked over at my family. My mother and father sat side by side, and she had her arm through his. They leaned close together and were smiling broadly. I noticed James and Giovanni sat opposite one another at the table, no doubt to watch all directions.

After dinner, the lights were turned down, and the big double doors between the main room with the stage and the dining room were opened so we could hear the band. "Shall we dance?" James whispered as he took my hand. We glided onto the dance floor. James pulled me close. "By the doors do you see them?"

At a table near the doors, sat a huge, burly man whose presence commanded attention. He had wavy, light brown hair and a short beard. He was dressed in jeans, a white shirt, and an expensive looking tweed jacket with leather shoulder and elbow patches. He had a drink in his hand, and he leaned back and looked, no stared, directly at me.

"What do we do?"

"We wait to be approached."

When the song ended, Janus appeared quite suddenly. He bowed his head and addressed only me. "Arianna, Redman requests the pleasure of your company."

I looked at James who nodded. I saw Giovanni walk toward the table where Redman sat. There were two men sitting with Redman, one was the hunter we met in the forest. I let Janus lead the way. As I approached, the three men stood up. Redman extended his hand. "Arianna, it is a great pleasure to meet you." I took his hand to shake it, but he pulled my hand toward him and kissed it. "I've never met someone like you. Please sit." We sat down, and the other two nodded and moved away from the table. James joined Giovanni.

"Would you like a drink?" Redman continued to hold my hand.

"No, thank you."

He smiled and signaled to one of the vampires for another drink. "I was surprised when my clansmen said they met you and your clansmen in the forest. I hope they were respectful to you."

"Yes, they were very polite." I sat up a little straighter in my chair affording the opportunity to slide my hand out from under his. I placed my hands in my lap. James was right, Redman was interested in me. "As I told them, we are just here for the wedding."

"Oh," Redman said with a sad tone of voice. "There is no rush to leave. It is nice to have a visitor, especially one as beautiful as you."

"Thank you." I nodded. "However, we will be leaving the day after the wedding."

"Arianna, tell me about yourself. How long have you been this way?"

I looked at Giovanni. He nodded and moved a little closer. "Why do you ask?"

Redman leaned forward and laughed. "The old one is a hunter. He stays close to you. Training you no doubt. And am I right to guess that the vampire is the one who turned you?"

I knew I should not disclose too much to him, so I was careful. "No," I began slowly, "James did not turn me. I was turned in battle. And what about you?" This was an egotistical man, and I knew if I asked about him, he would gladly carry the conversation.

The vampire brought him another whiskey, and Redman leaned back in his chair. "I've been one for many years. I was twenty-two when I came to Montana. I fell in love with the wide open spaces. One Winter day, I was out checking my traps when I came across a vampire. He was hungry and bit me. Nearly killed me. Probably would have if I didn't have the gene. He realized he went too far. I didn't know that it was against the law to kill a human. Not that anyone would have found my body until Spring, but the vampire carried me back to my one room cabin, and I lived. We've been friends ever since." He nodded to Janus.

"When were you transformed again?" I knew it was important to find out as much as possible about this man.

"It was a few years later. My leg caught in one of my traps, and I fell down a steep hillside. I was severely injured. Janus turned me again." He took a long drink of whiskey. "I repaid him by purchasing a track of land for him." He took another long drink. "So, tell me when you were turned."

"My second transformation occurred last Fall when I was living in New York State."

"And you live in Salem, Massachusetts now?"

There was no denying it. He obviously did research on me, and I wondered if that included compelling Albert or another family member. "Yes. I live with James."

"You were turned in New York?"

I nodded yes.

"Things are falling into place. We had several vampires from New York pass through here a couple of months ago."

Giovanni and James moved a step closer. "Do you know who they were?" I asked.

Redman signaled to one of the vampires who came immediately to the table. "Get those pictures of the New York vampires, quickly." The vampire left. "You said you were turned in battle, with whom?"

Giovanni nodded for me to tell him. "His name was Darius. He was a leader in New York, but he also was killing hunters and those with the hunter gene. He used rogues and wished to kill me because I was a hunter." I purposely did not tell Redman that I did not know that I was a hunter when Darius attacked me. "However, instead of killing me, Darius turned me."

"And he killed Darius?" Redman inclined his head toward Giovanni.

"No, after Darius attacked me, he got away. Eventually, a vampire killed Darius, but that was in another battle months later."

"Your vampire?"

"James was there, but he did not kill Darius." It occurred to me that back in March, it was part of the plan to have Marcus kill Darius instead of having James do it.

The vampire returned with the pictures. Redman laid the pictures on the table. "Janus caught one of them talking to Albert."

"You mean compelling him."

"He denied it, and at the time there was no reason to think otherwise. However, since you are a hunter, Albert's sister, and turned in New York, it seems likely there is a connection. Do you know these vampires?"

"Oh, yes I do." I signaled for James and Giovanni to look at the pictures. "This one is Tony." I pointed to the youngest vampire. This one I have encountered twice, but I don't know his name." I did not think it was wise to tell Redman that the old vampire said he knew me as a child.

"This one is Cody; he was one of Darius' men," James added.

"We caught Tony with Albert." Redman pointed to the old vampire. "This one's name is Jacob. He is crazy, erratic. I don't trust him. He seems to have a grudge against all hunters. I first met him sixty or seventy years ago. He too spoke of a Darius, but I never met this, Darius. Jacob came here several times, but not in oh probably fifteen years. He never stayed long in the area."

I was not sure if it was safe to probe Redman for information, but I needed to know more. "Did he tell you what he was doing here?"

"Years ago, he brought vampires in from other countries. The remoteness makes it an easy entry point for vampires. This time, he said he was just passing through. He told me he turned Tony and was training him and showing him the country. He did say things were unsettled in New York, and there was a power struggle going on. I have no interest in New York, so I did not press him for details."

"Jacob wants to kill me, so any information you can give me is appreciated."

Redman looked concerned. "I don't know much about him, but I will investigate. Now, it is obvious he was not just passing through, and I don't think it was a coincidence that Tony was alone talking to Albert."

"I don't think it was coincidence either. They were here probing Albert for information."

"Agreed." Redman looked off to the side. "Your mother is wondering who I am, and why you are sitting here talking to me. Perhaps we should continue our conversation later." He stood up. He took a card out of his pocket and handed it to me. "If you need anything, anytime, or place, call me. You and I are alike Arianna. No one will be able to understand you like me, and if someone threatens you, it is a threat to me too." I stood up, and he once again kissed my hand. "It was a pleasure to meet you, Arianna."

I looked around and saw the expression on my mother's face. "Who should I say you are?"

"The people in town know me as an entrepreneur. I own the lumber yards in the area. I am friends with Albert and Patty, so if anyone asks, say we were discussing possible wedding gifts. I will be in touch." He and the others left just as my mother walked up.

"Who was that?" she asked.

"Oh, some big wig in town." I tried to sound as casual as possible.

"What did he want with you?"

I leaned in toward my mother and looked deep into her eyes. "Wedding gifts, bachelor party, you know."

"Ah," she smiled and walked away. I looked over at Giovanni. He had a pout on his face, his eyes were narrowed, and his hands were on his hips. I knew I would hear about it later.

James came up behind me, and he wrapped his arms around my waist. "I'm glad you can't compel me. Let's dance."

Chapter XV
Pre-Wedding Parties

James

I ran my fingers through her hair and Arianna stirred. "Good morning." I kissed her softly.

"Good morning."

"Your dress fitting is at nine o'clock."

She sighed. "What time is it?"

"6:40." She turned toward me. I kissed her head and ran my hands over her back. "How are you this morning?"

"Ok."

"Just ok?" I snuggled close to her.

"Patty told me Brittany picked out the bridesmaid's dresses. She has good taste, but I'm worried. Did you see how much pink there was last night?"

"Yes." Last night, the other girls' mostly pink wardrobe contrasted with Arianna's black and white dress and black heels.

"I think I will need a splash of alcohol in my tea this morning to fortify me for shopping today," Arianna said seriously.

I laughed and rolled out of bed. "I'll start the shower." I turned on the water and got in. I was finishing rinsing when I heard Arianna come in and close the door.

"Well, last night was interesting," she said.

"It certainly was interesting, and we did get some useful information. Jacob seems to have a grudge against everyone." Redman came to the cabins just after midnight. He spoke mostly to Arianna and Giovanni, but at least he acknowledged me.

The shower curtain moved, and Arianna joined me. The shower was tiny, but we managed to squeeze together. "I don't think we can trust Redman," she whispered.

I looked out the small window in the shower.

"Don't worry," she said, "no one is around. The hawk showed me it is clear. He is roosting in the tree right outside the door."

"I think Redman would kill me if given the chance."

"Giovanni says he will not harm you."

"Only because he fears alienating you."

"That will have to do then. And I agree with Giovanni, he won't do anything with the wedding in a few days."

I helped Arianna soap up. I really enjoyed our showers together. It gave us time to take care of one another. I took the shower head and sprayed away the soap while she lathered up her hair. After rinsing, I worked a dollop of conditioner through her hair.

"You spoil me, James."

"That's my job." I kissed her nose.

When we finished, we dried off and dressed, and while Arianna combed out and dried her hair, I put on water for tea and set a box of cereal and a carton of milk on the table.

Giovanni knocked on the door. "Come on in," I called.

He walked in carrying a big mug of coffee then sat at the table. "What are your plans for today?" he asked in his typical gruff manner.

"I have to drop Arianna off downtown for her dress fitting, and then I'm free until we all meet for a late lunch.

"You should hunt today."

"I hunted yesterday."

"Yes, but now we have threats all around us. You need to keep up your strength."

"I thought you said they wouldn't do anything because of the wedding?"

"Best to be vigilant," he barked.

Arianna came out of the bathroom. "How do I look? More appropriate for Montana?" She wore a black pair of jeans, a cream colored silky blouse, and a pair of low boots.

I laughed. "Yes, come eat."

Giovanni stared at Arianna while she ate. "I think you should hunt with James later," he grumbled.

"Why?" she asked.

"Because it will make you stronger. I'm certain Redman and the other hunters feed on blood often."

Arianna ignored what he said and poured herself a second bowl of cereal. "I wanted to ask you about the hunters," she said between bites. "Most vampires haven't seen a hunter in years, yet there are several in this small town. Why?"

Giovanni grunted, "I don't know. The population of hunters has diminished everywhere but apparently not here. I haven't seen this many in one area in many years."

"That worries you," I stated.

"It does. You must feel it." He looked at the two of us. "Something is not right in this town." Arianna and I both agreed with him. "We all need to be vigilant," he said loudly. "Although," he paused, "Arianna, you are safest. In fact, you are probably safer here than anywhere. No one would dare touch you because Redman would kill anyone who touches you without a second thought."

"At least we now know about Jacob," Arianna said between bites of cereal.

"Yes, and I am certain that if Jacob or Tony come back here, Redman will do whatever he needs to do to find out what they know about you."

"He might eliminate the problem for us if they are uncooperative," I added hopefully.

"True," Giovanni replied, but there was worry in his voice.

*****

We arrived at the dress shop at almost the same time as Arianna's parents and grandmother pulled up in their car. Giovanni stood on the sidewalk and opened the door for Luisa. "Oh, thank you, Giovanni, but I'm not getting out here."

"You aren't going to see the dresses, Grandma?" Arianna sounded disappointed.

"Not today. I will be surprised with everyone the day of the wedding. Your daddy is taking me to the mall to get a wedding gift."

"Do you guys want to come?" John asked Giovanni and me.

"Actually, we plan to hike this morning, but thank you for inviting us," I replied.

"Hiking?" John shook his head.

"Fresh air and exercise are good for you," Giovanni added.

"I'm sure," John mumbled. He gave Felicia and Arianna a kiss on the cheek. "Lunch is at two o'clock, correct?"

"Yes, at The Forum where we were last night," Felicia replied. John got back behind the wheel and drove off.

Patty, her mother, and the bridesmaids arrived with Janus. "We are going to have a fabulous time today, ladies." Janus opened the door and swept his hand to motion them in.

"Aren't you getting your tux with the guys?" Arianna's voice dripped with sarcasm.

"I already have my tux. So, I am here to help the bride today."

Arianna rolled her eyes at him.

"Oh no, no men allowed." Janus blocked the door for me and Giovanni. "We don't want to spoil the surprise."

I was not thrilled about Janus being with Arianna in some ways, but he was Redman's right hand man. If there was trouble, Janus would contact Redman immediately, so Arianna would be safe.

I took Arianna's hand. "I'll pick you up later. Have fun." I gave her a quick peck on the lips.

She looked at me with slanted eyes then pulled me to her and gave me a longer kiss. "You are so old fashioned," she whispered.

"I guess I am." I gave her a longer kiss in return.

"That's better." She walked past Janus and into the shop.

"Text me," I called to Arianna. She waved, and Janus closed the door. I turned toward Giovanni. "Do you think she will be ok?"

"Yes. No one would dare harm her."

"What I meant was, will she be ok dress shopping with all those women?"

Giovanni laughed. "Now, that is debatable."

We got back in the car, and I pulled out onto the street. "Where should we go? Back to the cabins?"

"Let's go somewhere else. Just in case Redman has men patrolling near the cabins. There are also a number of wolves in this town, and they are likely out patrolling whether Redman asks them to or not."

"Yes, last night when we walked through the bar, I smelled quite a few wolves."

"Wolves are generally not friendly to vampires, so watch out for them. Treat any wolf you see as if it is a shifter until you are certain what it is. Better to be cautious."

I looked at him and chuckled. "If you or Arianna are with me, I should be fine. These wolves are loyal to Redman, and he has accepted you and Arianna, so they will too."

"True." Giovanni almost sounded cheerful.

We drove for a while to get an idea where we could stop. The scenery was magnificent. The sky was clear and blue. What I noticed most was the quiet, and at night, all the stars in the open sky.

I turned around and headed back the way we came.

"There's a turn-off up ahead; you can park there," Giovanni instructed.

I pulled in and parked. Giovanni and I walked into the trees. I did not intend to hunt long. I planned to take the first animal I came across. The less time we spent in the forest the better. An hour later, there was still no game. We started to circle back around when we came to a small stream.

"Let's follow the stream," Giovanni suggested.

I knew the stream was the best chance for game, but I reluctantly headed down stream and away from the car. Sure enough, fifteen minutes later there was a herd of elk. Giovanni sat down on a rock at the edge of the stream to wait. I chose an older female, and in a few seconds, I was feeding.

"Is one enough?" Giovanni asked as I approached him.

"Yes, it is. I feel good."

Giovanni got up slowly. He seemed to be moving slower lately. I caught a glimpse of his arm as he reached down to rinse his hands in the icy water and saw a cut I noticed at the airport. He saw me looking at his arm and stood up.

"Are you ok, Giovanni?"

"Yes, of course."

"That cut still has not healed.

He took a deep breath. "I don't seem to be regenerating as quickly as I once did." He started to walk back toward the car. "It's nothing to worry about. Don't tell her. Promise me."

I hesitated. I did not like keeping things from Arianna. However, I knew it was best not to tell her just yet. "I won't, for now, but she may notice the cut too."

Giovanni grumbled, and we walked back in silence. We got in the car, and I started driving back to the cabins. As soon as I had cell service, I received several texts. "Arianna sent me a picture."

Giovanni grunted as he often did.

"Oh wow!" I said and showed the picture she sent to Giovanni.

His eyes went wide. "I've never seen her wear that color pink before." He stared at the picture for a few moments. "Is the dress supposed to be so big and round?"

I looked at the picture again. "I think so. It looks like a princess gown."

Another message came through. It was a picture of pink shoes with *OMG!* as a message. I showed Giovanni.

"Those shoes are the color of cotton candy." He shook his head.

You look good in everything. Kiss. I replied to Arianna.

When we arrived at our cabins, Giovanni got out of the car slowly. "I'm going to shower," he said, and he walked away without looking back.

"We should head back downtown about 1:30," I called to him. Giovanni grunted, so I assumed he agreed.

I took a quick shower and then sat at the table and wrote. I had a few ideas for additional scenes that I wanted to get down. I planned to get the next installment to my agent when we returned from the wedding.

Another text came in. *Dad picked Mom up, and Janus took Patty and her mom home to change for lunch. Brittany, Carrie, Jesse, and I are shopping for the bride's gifts. They will give me a ride to the restaurant, so meet me there.*

Ok. We will meet you there. I texted back.

Giovanni knocked on the door right at 1:30. "Come on in," I called.

He wore a pair of khaki pants and a blue and brown plaid shirt with a dark blue blazer.

"We are going to meet Arianna at the restaurant. She and the girls are bridal gift shopping."

Without saying a word, Giovanni sat down at the table to wait. I saved my work and closed the laptop. I tucked my light blue button-down shirt into my jeans and grabbed my leather sport coat and keys. "Ready?"

"Yes."

When we were driving, Giovanni cleared his throat. "I don't want Arianna to know about my regeneration because I don't want her to worry."

"But if it comes up."

"I don't expect you to lie to her, James, but it's something she doesn't need to worry about for some time."

"I understand."

We arrived at the restaurant, and I parked the car. Arianna had not yet arrived, so Giovanni went in, and I lingered outside. I received a text. *On our way.*

I'm waiting outside. I texted back.

Good. I need to put my shopping bags in the car.

Brittany's small red car turned off the road and came down the driveway within five minutes of Arianna's text. Music blared and the girls were talking excitedly. They spilled out of the car, and I walked toward them. I took several bags from Arianna's hands. "You did some shopping."

Carrie blushed and giggled.

"Yes, I did." Arianna hooked her arm in mine as we walked to our car. "And you are going to like some of what I bought," she whispered mischievously, and I had a feeling it may have something to do with the girl's giggling and blushing.

Lunch was casual and relaxed. Felicia wrinkled her nose and looked down at the moose burger then looked at Arianna who wore the same expression. Giovanni took a bite of his burger and nodded his approval.

"Is it good?" John asked him.

"It is." He took another big bite.

Arianna took a nibble.

"How is it?" Felicia whispered to her.

"It's not too bad."

Felicia took a tiny bite.

Luisa called the waitress over. "Dear, do you have any chicken?"

The waitress looked surprised, but she recovered quickly and smiled. "We do, would you like a chicken sandwich?"

"Yes, please. Thank you."

The waitress reached for the burger. "Would anyone like an extra burger?"

"I'll take it," Giovanni replied.

Arianna and Felicia looked at one another. They had already started their burgers. Arianna cut hers in half and offered it to Giovanni who gladly accepted it. John ate most of Felicia's burger.

Fortunately, lunch finished quickly, and we left the restaurant an hour later. "Get some rest," Patty yelled to Arianna from the open window of Brittany's car. "We're going to P A R T Y tonight!!"

Arianna gave a weak wave and got in the car. "Stop at the store please, James. I need something to eat."

I drove to the trading post which was a combination of several shops and food places all in one big log cabin style building. Arianna went to the pizza counter and ordered a large pepperoni and sausage pizza. While we waited for the pizza to cook, we walked around and looked at the shops.

"This is real fur." Arianna slipped her hand inside the fox fur lined slipper. "It is so soft. I will get them."

I noticed Giovanni in a shop that sold jewelry. He walked over to a case with necklaces. No doubt he was getting a present for Marena, but I knew better than to ask him about it.

When we returned to the cabins, Giovanni went to his cabin without saying a word. I unlocked the door to our cabin, and I brought in Arianna's shopping bags. She carried the pizza to the table then went back outside. The young hawk came down, and I watched her interact with the bird. She pet his head, and then he hopped up on her shoulder. When she finished, she came inside and started to eat, so I sat down on the love seat and opened my laptop to work on my novel revision.

After eating the entire pizza, Arianna pulled items out of the shopping bags and set them on the table. Everything was pink. "I'm wrapping our gifts to the bride because Patty will be with the girls this afternoon. I wanted to get traditional white bridal lingerie, but they insisted on pink. We settled on a baby pink camisole with darker pink panties, a pink and white robe, and pink slippers." She placed everything neatly in a pink tissue lined white basket, placed the basket in a clear plastic bag, and then tied it up with pink and white ribbons.

"You seemed to have fun shopping today," I commented.

"I did. The girls are nice, especially Carrie." Arianna walked over to the refrigerator and grabbed a bottle of juice then took a cereal bar out of the box on top of the fridge.

"Are you still hungry?"

"No, I just need something sweet." Arianna went back to the table and took a small rectangular box out of a bag. "How do you like these?" She opened the box and showed me a strand of pale pink pearls.

"They are beautiful."

"It's my personal gift to the bride. I saw them in the jewelry shop window."

"Patty will love them."

Arianna closed the box and wrapped it in silver paper, and then added pink ribbon curls and a bow. I saw something else in the bag, and I craned my neck to see what it was, but she closed it. "That is a surprise for later tonight," Arianna replied with a very seductive smile.

Lucky me. I went back to writing, but my mind kept thinking about Arianna's surprise.

I finished the chapter I was revising, saved, and backed up the file when my phone rang.

"Hello, Marie. How are you? Is everything ok?"

"Yes, everything is fine here. How are you?" she asked.

Where to start, I thought to myself. I gave her a quick overview of what was happening.

"Hum," she grunted. "Be careful of the wolves, and I don't like the sound of this Redman."

"I don't like him either, but we did get a little useful information from him." I paused unsure how much to tell Marie on the phone. "I am concerned that Tony was caught with Albert. They must have been trying to get information from him."

Marie was quiet for a few moments. "I agree. I will tell John, and I am certain he will increase patrols. Be careful, James. I don't like all that is going on."

"I will Marie. Good-bye."

I hung up and listened. Arianna was still in the shower, so I quickly took off my clothes and joined her. She was conditioning her hair, so I helped her rinse which took longer than if she did it herself, but doing it alone was not as much fun.

"Thank you," she stretched up and kissed me. Her naked body pressed against mine, and it was an effort not to pick her up and make love with her. I gave her a long passionate kiss. A promise of what was to come later.

With a deep sigh, she stepped out of the shower and dried off.

"James, did you see a black belt on the bed?" Arianna asked as I came out of the bathroom rubbing my hair with a towel.

"I put it on the dresser."

Arianna wore tight black leggings, a black camisole with a dark, multicolored sheer blouse over it, and her favorite black strappy heels. She clipped on the belt over the blouse at her waist. "How do I look?" She turned to look in the mirror on the dresser.

I stared for a few moments. "Very good. Where are you girls going?"

"The Tune. It's a night club on the outskirts of Missoula. You guys are going to a lodge?"

"That's what I'm told," I said unenthusiastically. I selected a pair of black slacks and a cream dress shirt with a tiny design. I was not thrilled about being so far away from Arianna, or about going to a bachelor party at a lodge. I let out a sigh and tied my tie.

Arianna walked over to me, leaned close, and straightened my tie. "I'd rather stay with you," she pouted.

I kissed her. "Me too."

Arianna's phone rang. "Hello." I heard Patty's voice on the other end. "Ok, I'm ready." She hung up and looked at me. "The limo will be here in a few minutes."

"I'm taking my car and driving your father and Giovanni. If you want to leave, just call me, and I will pick you up."

"Are you worried?" She looked back at me over her shoulder.

"A little. You look hot."

"I can take care of myself." She turned back and kissed me.

"Oh, I know you can, but still, be careful."

"You too," she said seriously. We heard the limo pull up and one of the girls knocked on the door. "Come on in," Arianna called. It was Brittany. She had on a black dress, tights, and boots. "I like that outfit, Brittany," Arianna said as she put the cabin key in her wristlet.

"Hi James." Brittany looked down and blushed. She saw Arianna's shoes. "Wow, I couldn't walk in those."

"It just takes practice."

"Is that the gift? You did a nice job."

"Thanks." Arianna picked it up and handed it to Brittany.

"I'll get in the limo." Brittany blushed again and gave me a little wave.

Arianna slipped into her long, black leather coat then picked up the little bag that held her gift for Patty. She grabbed my arms and pulled me close then kissed me long and hard. "I miss you already. I love you," she whispered.

I wrapped my arms around her and held tight. "I love you too." I passionately returned the kiss. Reluctantly, I released her. I watched from the door as she stepped into the limo, and I waved as it drove down the long driveway and out onto the road.

I went back inside and finished getting ready. Giovanni went to Arianna's parent's hotel early, so I put on my sport coat, locked up, got in the car, and drove to pick up Giovanni and John and take them to the bachelor party.

*****

I knew the three of us looked uncomfortable. We stood together drinking scotch, John and Giovanni's drink of choice. Some of the younger guys were drinking beer and playing beer pong. Redman and several other men were at the other end of the room sitting at a table, drinking, and talking amongst themselves.

A short while later, Janus and a few of Albert's friends made their way over to us and chatted for a while. I saw Giovanni was nervous, and to be honest, so was I. We stood or sat always facing in opposite directions, so we could watch everyone and the doors.

Around ten o'clock, the lights dimmed, the disco ball flashed, and three topless dancers came in the room. They danced around Albert while his friends teased him that he better enjoy himself because he was getting hitched. The three of us stayed back, and I noticed Redman did the same.

About eleven o'clock, John asked if we were ready to leave. "Yes," Giovanni and I eagerly replied at the same time. We walked over to Albert to say good night.

"You guys are leaving already?" He was quite drunk.

"How are you getting home?" John asked sternly.

"That's my job," Janus informed him. "Don't you worry; he is safe with me."

John grunted much like Giovanni, and we left. I dropped John off at his hotel, and it was just before 11:30 pm when I pulled up to the cabins. Suddenly, Giovanni sat up straight. Arianna stood in the doorway.

I stopped the car and opened the door. "Is everything ok?"

"Yes. Everything is great." She sounded cheerful.

"You are back early."

"Carrie didn't feel well, so she and I left early. The limo driver took us back, and now he's going to the club for the rest of the girls. It was boring anyway."

Giovanni looked relieved. "Well, good night."

"Good night," we called to him. I walked up to her, and Arianna pulled me inside and closed the door. She opened her silky, black robe to reveal a lacy, black bra and tiny, black panties. "So how was the Bachelor Party?" she asked as she moved her hips and turned her head from side to side.

"Not as enjoyable as looking at you."

"Weren't there strippers?"

"Topless dancers do nothing for me." I leaned closer to her and whispered in her ear, "unless it's you."

She smiled and placed delicate kisses up my throat. "I think that can be arranged." She kissed me very passionately, and I wrapped my arms around her and eagerly kissed her back. She wove her fingers through my hair, and after some time, she leaned back. "Take off your jacket and get comfortable."

I kicked off my shoes and took off my jacket. As I loosened my tie and started to unbutton my shirt, Arianna walked over to the bed. She let her robe drop to the floor then she turned around and slowly and deliberately crawled on the bed on her hands and knees. I gulped. The panties were a thong. "Oh, I want you."

"Then take me." She smiled mischievously looking back at me over her shoulder.

I could not take my eyes off her. I came up behind her and ran my hands up her thighs to her soft round bottom. I climbed on the bed behind her and unhooked her bra.

She turned toward me. "Slide back on the bed."

I moved quickly and sat up against the headboard. She straddled me and started dancing in front of me, her breasts only inches from my face. I reached over and started kissing them. She moaned softly spiking the desire already consuming me. I needed her now. I hooked my fingers in the thong string, and in my haste to get it off, I pulled it down too hard, and ripped it.

Arianna gave a soft laugh. I rolled her over, and her hair flowed over the bed. "You are so beautiful."

She smiled and reached up to undo my pants. I got up to remove them, and she sat up, turned around, and knelt on the bed. She looked back at me with a devilish smile. My mind went blank, and my body was driven by my lust and hunger for her. I got up on the bed behind her then slid into her in one smooth motion. She gasped and moaned with pleasure as she arched her back. I closed my eyes and let the sensations engulf me. We moved mindlessly together. Frantic in our need for one another, we moved with force and speed as we changed positions multiple times.

My mouth streaked down her body, and I brought her to climax several times, each one more intense than the last one. "James, I need you, now." Her eyes were clouded in passion as I moved over her until our hips were touching. "Now," she demanded. She arched her back and wrapped her long legs around my back as we joined together again.

My mind exploded, and I had an overwhelming urge to bite her. Instead, I devoured her mouth. She returned my passion and nipped at my lower lip. "Do it." She leaned back exposing the full length of her neck to me. She wove her fingers in my hair. "Do it, now." Her voice was rough was passion.

I ran a finger down her throat and felt her pounding pulse. Blood pumped through her veins, and I dropped my head and bit her. She gasped and her nails dug into my back as she exploded with an orgasm that shook her entire body. I hung on as long as I could as wave after wave ripped through her and when I could not hold off any longer, I lost myself in her.

Chapter XVI
Strange Revelations

Arianna

"Good morning." James nibbled at my shoulder. "Did you sleep well?"

"I did." I rolled on top of him.

"What's on the agenda for today?"

"As far as I know, we are free until tonight. There is a get together at the lodge. My mother said she ordered pies and a cake." I leaned over and laid tiny kisses along his shoulder and up to his ear.

"Umm. What should we do today then?"

"We should get a wedding gift."

James let out a contented sigh. "Ok…the mall?"

"Uh-huh, at some point." I kissed him then leaned back and ran my hands up and down his chest. His muscles tensed and a groan escaped him. "Staying in bed all morning sounds good too."

James grabbed my hips and pulled me down to him. With a growl, he started kissing his way down my neck. We were laughing and kissing, and things were heating up when Giovanni knocked on the door.

"Are you two up?"

"What is it?" I asked impatiently.

"I want to talk with you both."

"Now? It's 6:00 am." I was not amused.

"I think it is best to talk now, yes."

I sighed and rolled off James. "This better be important," I grumbled.

James shrugged his shoulders and called to Giovanni. "Give us a few minutes."

We put on clothes. James pulled the covers over the bed. I gave him a questioning look.

"Let's not make it obvious what we were doing."

"We weren't doing anything," I mumbled grumpily. Then it occurred to me that James was uncomfortable. Giovanni was technically my grandfather, but I did not see him in that context. I smiled and shook my head. "You are so old fashioned." He shrugged his shoulders. I rolled my eyes at him and went to put on a kettle of water for tea.

"Ok, come on in," James called as he opened the door.

Giovanni came in and sat down at the table. He got right to the point. "I think you should hunt with James today, Arianna."

"Ok, it's not safe for any of us to be in the forest alone."

"No, I mean you should feed as well. And you two need to get out of town to hunt."

I stopped eating my cereal bar and looked at him. "Why?"

"I don't like this town, and I think we should all be prepared just in case there is trouble. I doubt they will do anything, but there is something strange about these hunters and vampires. There is something they aren't telling us."

"I'm certain of that," James added.

"Ok, fine. I'll hunt with James." Giovanni and James both stared at me. "What! I said yes."

"With no argument?" James was obviously shocked.

"I agree there is something odd about this group, and it's not just this bizarre hierarchy they have. Patty knows a lot about vampires, and she believes they exist."

They both raised their eyebrows in surprise, and they waited for me to continue.

"After the gown fitting, my mom and Patty's mom went to have coffee while Janus, the girls, and I walked around downtown. We stopped to look at the books in a store window. Patty pointed to that new vampire best seller and said, 'that book is a load of crock. Vampires don't act like that.' Well, Janus started to laugh, and I noticed that Carrie, Jesse, and Brittany didn't seem surprised by her comments." I took the tea pot off the stove and poured Giovanni and I each a cup of tea. "I told them there are many legends about vampires. The author may be combining elements of various vampire legends she researched to put a different spin on her story. Patty laughed and said, 'well she knows nothing about real vampires.' So, I think she knows Janus is a vampire."

James and Giovanni shook their heads in disbelief. "I will be glad to leave this town," Giovanni said.

"You and me both," James agreed.

"We need more information." I pulled out my laptop and turned it on. "We need to find out more about Redman."

James took out his laptop too. It did not take long for us to find information on Redman Burke.

"According to land records, Redman purchased his first piece of land in 1914," James informed us.

"Redman said he came here when he was twenty-two," I added.

"And it looks like he continued to purchase land." James skimmed the records. "Oh, and here is a purchase with Janus Jones in October 1917."

"So, he became a super hunter sometime in 1917." They looked at me. "Redman told me he purchased land for Janus in payment for transforming him after he was badly injured." I continued reading the archives of the town's newspaper. "The townspeople know about vampires!" I blurted out.

"What?" they both shouted.

"Well, they don't say vampires specifically but listen to this. 'Redman, Janus, and Connor were injured in the attack of the undead but will make a full recovery. It is with sadness that we report the death of Brock, one of our newest residents who was killed in the attack.' There is a picture of Redman and Janus, and they look exactly as they do today."

"The undead?" Giovanni asked. "Vampires?"

"Maybe rogues," James suggested thinking out loud. "Rogues are crazed. They look like zombies."

"Yeah, fast moving screeching zombies." I shuddered thinking of the two attacks on me by rogues.

"Well, clearly the townspeople knew the attackers were not human," Giovanni added. "The question is, did they know Redman, Janus, and Connor were not human?"

"Yes, I think so." I looked at the picture on my screen. "Redman and Janus were in the town records from many years earlier. They should have been old men, but they don't look old. People must have known and accepted that they were not human."

"Couldn't they just compel the necessary people?" James asked.

"I don't think so," Giovanni sighed. "I think Arianna is right. At least some of these people know about vampires and hunters and probably about the wolves too."

"And they are ok with the knowledge that there are vampires in the world. That is quite scary to me," I added.

James and I continued scanning the archived newspapers.

My phone rang. "Hello, Mom."

She talked fast.

"A what?" I asked. "Hold on."

I muted the phone and took a very deep breath. "Apparently, tonight's dinner is a luau!" I closed my eyes. "They forgot to tell me." Neither James nor Giovanni said anything. I took another deep calming breath and returned to the phone.

"I'm sorry, dear. I thought someone told you. Do you have anything you can wear? The girls are wearing bathing suits and grass skirts." At least Mom sounded sympathetic and annoyed for me.

"James and I need to get a wedding present, so I will see what is available at the mall."

"Ok. Would Giovanni like to spend the day with us?"

"I'll ask him." I muted the phone. "Giovanni, would you like to spend the day with Grandma and my parents while James and I go to the mall?"

"Yes, thank you," he replied very cordially.

"Mom, Giovanni said yes. We'll stop by your hotel about nine and drop him off. I think it's best to get out early."

"I agree, dear. See you soon."

"Bye, Mom."

I hung up and looked at the two men. They were silent. "Who has a luau, in December, in Montana?!"

James and Giovanni said nothing.

"This town is insane! I need a shower." I put my phone down hard on the table and marched to the bathroom.

Giovanni was gone when I stepped out of the bathroom thirty minutes later. James kissed me on his way in. "Feeling better?"

"Yes."

"Good."

Before getting dressed, I looked through my suitcase for something to wear to the luau. I didn't bring a swimsuit, but I had a black camisole tank top. I looked through James' clothes and pulled out his khaki pants. It was a start.

I decided to wear jeans and a sweater to the mall. I combed out my hair and applied mascara. James came out of the bathroom naked and still dripping a little water from his hair. He looked good, really good, and I wanted to stay in bed with him this morning rather than going to the mall to look for luau outfits.

"You can wear the khaki pants tonight, and maybe we can find a tropical shirt at the mall," I said without taking my eyes off him.

He looked at the clothes I had on the bed. "I have a white shirt that I can wear."

"That will work if we don't find anything tropical. I hope we can get some leis at the party store." I went to my computer and checked the mall's website. "There's a fabric store there too, so if nothing else, I can get material and wrap it around my waist to make a skirt to wear with the black top. Do you think any stores have flip flops at this time of year?"

"I think we should be able to get flip flops. People use them year round at gyms."

We finished getting ready. We put sweatshirts and hiking boots in a tote bag for later when we hunted, and then locked up and knocked on Giovanni's door.

"Do you have khaki pants for tonight?" I asked.

"Yes," he replied.

"If I get you a lei, will you wear it?"

"If I have to." He was not amused.

We got in the car and drove the short distance to my parent's hotel. "Hi, Mom." I gave her a kiss on the cheek as I walked in their room.

"Hi, honey."

"Where's Dad."

"We're in here," he called from the adjacent room.

"Hi, Dad. Hi, Grandma." I kissed them both and sat down next to Grandma.

"Would you like a cup of tea?" Mom asked.

"No thanks. James and I have to get to the mall."

"Hello, Luisa," James and Giovanni said as they came in the room.

"Nice to see you both."

"We shouldn't be too long, but it does take time to get anywhere up here." I folded my arms. "A luau! Really?!" I said to Grandma.

"It's what the bride wants," she reminded me.

"I know it is all about the bride, but does a wedding need to be so… involved?"

"When it's your day, you can decide what to do." Grandma patted my leg.

"Ok, fair enough. I won't be having anything so involved I can tell you that." I took a cookie from the package on the table.

"Are you planning a wedding?" There was excitement in her voice.

"No, I'm not," I replied firmly.

"Uh huh."

I did not want to think what that implied. I grabbed a few more cookies to sustain me. "Well, we better be off, so we can get back and get ready for the luau." I gave Grandma a kiss on her cheek.

Giovanni sat down when I stood up. "Be careful you two," he said.

"We will." I replied. "Have a fun day." James and I went back into the other room. "We're heading out."

"Drive carefully." Dad directed his comment at James.

"Do not worry. I am a careful driver," James replied.

"I'll text you and let you know how it's going, Mom."

"I'm sure you will find something, Arianna."

It was a quiet drive to the mall. "What are you thinking about?" I finally asked James breaking the silence. He did not answer right away. I didn't push.

Finally, he spoke. "I was thinking about what your grandmother said."

"About?"

"When it is your day, you can do what you want."

James mentioned marriage before, but I was not very receptive. I knew James loved me, and I loved him. That was all I needed. "She was just saying that it is Patty's day."

He reached over and took my hand. "When will you be ready for it to be your day?"

I squeezed his hand. I did not have an answer. I loved James, and I knew there would never be anyone else for me, but I did not have an answer.

Chapter XVII
The Bear

James

The mall was in sight. I was not going to say anything more to Arianna about marriage. I did not want to scare her or spoil the trip. I needed to lighten the mood. I pulled into the mall parking lot. "Are you ready to luau shop?" I did a little dance in my seat.

"Grrr," she growled. "It's the bride's day. It's the bride's day." She gave me an exaggerated smile. I was glad she was in a better mood.

We started in the men's department of the large department store. I really did not want a tropical shirt. Fortunately, I spotted a cream shirt with very pale fern leaves that I could live with. "Will this do?" I asked hopefully.

Arianna smiled. "Yes, that is nice. Hopefully, we can find leis and flip flops." We checked out then looked around the ladies' department. "I really don't see anything that will work." She shook her head. "I am beginning to think making a wrap is going to be my best option."

"Where to next?" I asked.

Arianna looked over the mall directory. "Eventually, we will go to the party store and then the fabric store. There is also a drug store, but first, I want to look for a wedding gift. There's a gift store and a mall cart that does engraving."

I took her hand, and we strolled through the mall which was packed with people. Christmas music still played, and since the decorations were still up, there was a festive feel in the air. I was not sure what we were going to find because most of the stores had heavy clothing, not something appropriate for a luau. I agreed with Arianna; who has a luau in December?

We looked at a number of potential gifts and then stopped at a food cart. Arianna bought a pretzel. "I like the wedding frames," she said as she ate. "What do you think?"

"I like the frames. I think we should get one." We went back to the cart and ordered the frame then continued shopping while it was being engraved.

"Let's stop in the drug store, James." Arianna led me inside the store. Thankfully, we did not find flip flops. We made our way to the opposite end of the mall. Arianna looked over her list. "I need a few more items for the favors," she commented more to herself than to me.

Our next stop was the party store. "Luck is with us. Tropical items," I said surveying the items on display.

Arianna looked relieved. She headed to the rack of leis and picked a package of white ones and an assorted color package.

"Your mom said the girls are wearing grass skirts. They have some here." I pointed to them on the shelf below the leis. Arianna wrinkled her nose. I figured she did not like the idea of a grass skirt. It was just not her style. In the back of the store was a rack of leftover Halloween costumes, so I started looking through them. There were nurse costumes, bar maid costumes, princess costumes. Then I saw it. "Arianna, dear," I called sweetly. She looked over at me. I held up a Hawaiian dancer costume consisting of a sarong style skirt, white lei, flip flops, a hair tie, and a coconut bra.

Her face lit up. "That's perfect, except for the coconut bra." She came over and took the costume from me. She looked it over carefully. "I'll wear a tank top, add a few accessories and it will be complete." She stretched up and kissed me on the cheek then went back to the area with the leis and picked out several floral ones. She held them up to the costume. "Perfect. Let's pay for these, get the rest of the items on my list, and go pick up the wedding frame."

After the fabric store, we crossed the aisle to the card shop. While we were walking around the store, Arianna stopped and looked at a display of small statues that commemorate milestones in life. She picked up a statue of a man and woman looking at each other in a tender embrace. I saw those statues at other shops back home, and they were extremely popular. She put a boxed statue in her shopping basket.

We decided on a card and gift wrap, and then we stood in line to check out. "I'm not sure I will wear those flip flops." Arianna looked at me and shrugged. "They really aren't me. Not for a party. It's not like the luau is on the beach. I have gold heels, and I think they will look better." I nodded my agreement.

We picked up the wedding gift, and Arianna looked over her list one more time. "I think we have everything. Now, I want to get something for friends."

Arianna pulled me over to a store with a variety of locally made items. In the toy section, she purchased a stuffed moose for Jack, and a stuffed rabbit for Bobby.

There was a display of real racoon fur hats nearby. "What do you think about a hat for Jack?" Arianna asked me.

"I think that is a good gift for him."

"I'm not sure Caroline will be ok with it," she pondered, but she bought it for Jack.

"There are food items over here." I led Arianna over to a display of local foods. She bought several jars of jelly for Jack senior. Then she went to the jewelry counter and picked out a necklace each for Caroline and Trina.

I bought a sun catcher of a mountain scene for Marie, and then saw a gift set consisting of a small wooden crate with whiskey and two moose shot glasses. "This is perfect for Marcus. What do you think?" I asked Arianna.

She looked over and smiled. "That is a great idea."

We went back to the car, and we were both in good moods as we drove back. Arianna leaned her seat back and smiled up at me. "This turned out to be a good day." She reached over and ran her hand up my arm. "I love you."

"I love you, and it has been a good day." I reached over and took her hand. "There is a pull off up ahead. It's probably used by game hunters and hikers, but it doesn't look like it's been used in some time. Hopefully, there is game nearby."

Arianna nodded. "Did you think it would be constant parties for days?" she asked in a profoundly serious tone of voice.

I sighed. "Honestly, no. I don't think it's worth all the money being spent."

She sat quietly for a few minutes. "I agree. I think a wedding should be simple. A ceremony and a reception with close family and friends."

I hoped this meant that she was considering marriage. I desperately wanted to tell her I wanted us to get married, but I thought it was best to lighten the mood. "What, no bachelor party?" I held back a laugh.

She looked at me and rolled her eyes, but she gave me a big smile. Arianna called me old fashioned, and maybe I was in some respects. I knew in modern society marriage was not required as it once was. But, for me, marriage was the ultimate sign of commitment, and I wanted that commitment with Arianna.

As if she knew what I was thinking, she gave my hand a squeeze. "I love you."

I looked at her and smiled. "I love you too."

I pulled off the road. We took off our regular shoes and put on hiking boots. We also took off our coats and put on sweatshirts.

Arianna looked at her phone. "No service. I'll leave the phone in the car." She put her hair up in a ponytail and tucked her arm guards into the waist of her jeans. We stood outside the car quietly listening and surveying the area. We were alone. "Should we run awhile James?"

I nodded yes, and we headed down a very rough path. There was a light covering of snow, but I had expected it to be much deeper at this time of year. We ran for about a half hour then circled back. I watched Arianna as we ran. Her hair flowed behind her, and the taut muscles in her legs moved as she jumped over a fallen log. Every now and then, she closed her eyes for a couple of strides searching for a hawk with her mind. It truly was a rare and unusual gift that Arianna had. Giovanni's wife, Arianna's great great grandmother, who was a first level hunter, had a similar gift and communicated with animals.

Suddenly, Arianna stopped. She pulled her arm guards out from the waistband of her jeans and put them on.

I stopped and stood beside her. "A hawk?"

She shook her head no and looked up. I looked up too and gasped. Dropping fast was a magnificent bald eagle. I backed up to give it room and watched in amazement as Arianna held up her arm for the bird. When the eagle landed, her arm dipped down, but she straightened it quickly. Delicately, she stroked the bird's head and stared into its eyes communicating with it. We heard a call and looked up. Another eagle, possibly this one's mate, soared down and landed nearby. Arianna walked over to it and stroked its head. The two birds nudged each other, and then the second bird hopped on Arianna's other arm. She couldn't pet the birds with one on each arm, but they rubbed their heads against her head.

"They are beautiful. Aren't they, James?"

"Yes, they are beautiful. And they are big." I turned my head sharply and sniffed the air.

"What is it?" Arianna stiffened, and she looked around nervously which made the eagles jumpy.

"Bear."

"A bear?!" Arianna's eyes widened. She stared into the birds' eyes, and they took off into the air and circled overhead. A few seconds later, I saw through the eagles' eyes as Arianna transmitted what she saw to me. The bear was close by in a small clearing just on the other side of a narrow band of trees.

"Why are there bears out at this time of year?" she whispered as we made our way through the trees. She tightened her ponytail as we crept along and tucked her hair down inside her sweatshirt. "Don't bears hibernate?"

"Grizzlies go into hibernation sometime between October and December. Males go into hibernation later than females, and I guess because the weather has been unusually warm, and there isn't much snow yet, he has stayed out longer."

Arianna kept close to me.

The eagles circled overhead.

"We need to stay upwind of him," I told her.

We peeked out from behind a tree. "That's a big bear." Arianna sounded both excited and nervous.

"Grizzly bears are much larger than the black bears we have in the East. Maybe we should let it go." It was an exceptionally large bear, and Arianna was inexperienced.

"No way. We can do this." She sounded confident and determined.

"Ok. We will attack him from behind. Be careful; he will have a long reach."

She nodded that she understood. We separated, and we each moved silently toward the bear. The closer we could get to him before he sensed us, the better our chances. We were both in position and poised to attack. Arianna looked at me and waited. I nodded go, and we ran toward him. I grabbed the bear's head and Arianna caught him around the middle. The eagles screeched and dove at the bear. He was caught off guard and pawed at the eagles, but they were too fast. The bear reared and roared. The sound echoed all around us. I hoped there was no one in the area because that roar would attract attention.

We hung on tight while the eagles took turns diving and pecking at him. The bear dropped down then suddenly reared up with such force that Arianna and I were thrown off. Arianna was first on her feet, and she advanced on him. I watched in horror as the bear took a swipe at her. He missed her body, but his claws caught her sweatshirt and tore it. The two eagles dove on the bear at once protecting her.

"Great one of my favorite sweatshirts," she groaned, and before I could stop her, she leapt on top of the bear and had it around the neck. It flailed its front paws and roared. The eagles kept diving at it, so the bear did not know what to swipe at first. I leapt up and wrapped my arms around the bear's middle to restrict its movements. Under both of our grips, and with the eagles attacking from above, eventually the bear started to tire and give up. We struggled, but we both hung on. Finally, when the bear dropped his head down, I bit him. The bear roared and reared one more time, but we had it, and the three of us tumbled to the ground. I bit him again to be sure he was dead.

"Wow, that was so exciting and invigorating!" Arianna glowed with the exertion.

"Yes, it was. Ladies first." I motioned for her to begin feeding.

Arianna knelt down and drank. She drank quite a bit more than she did the last time she hunted with me. She stood up and moved aside for me to take over. It took some time, but I drained the bear. When I finished, I took out my knife and cut fur and skin exposing the meat. As soon as I stepped aside, the eagles came down and began to feast.

I looked over at Arianna. She sat in the snow watching the eagles. Her hair was a tussled mess, her shirt was torn and hung limply exposing her firm body, and her knees were bent. She leaned back seductively as she watched the eagles pulling at the bear's flesh. There were traces of blood at the corners of her mouth. As I watched, she pulled her hair out of the ponytail holder then shook her head. Her hair fell in a long sheet down her back. She looked unbelievably delectable. As she tossed her head back, her creamy neck was exposed to me, and her intoxicating scent became impossibly strong. My head swam. I could not resist, and in an instant, I was on top of her sucking at the soft skin of her neck.

A seductive moan escaped her lips. "James," she breathed.

With surprising strength and speed, Arianna reversed our positions. She lay on top of me and kissed me passionately, our tongues dancing and colliding with one another.

I nibbled on her lower lip, and I rolled us over. We continued to kiss, and she rolled us back the other way. We rolled and continued to grope at one another's body. We sat up, and I pulled off what remained of her sweatshirt and unclasped her bra freeing her breasts. I kissed each one. Then I stood us up, and I removed her jeans and panties.

"James. Now James," she whispered as she unbuttoned my shirt and slid her arms up my back. I caressed and kissed her body. She leaned back, reached down, and unzipped my jeans.

I backed her up against a tree, grabbed her wrists in one hand, and stretched them over her head. She did not resist me. She leaned back and closed her eyes. She quivered in anticipation and moaned softly. I drank in her beauty. She was exquisite. I sucked at her neck while I explored her body with my other hand. I looked up and her mouth was slightly open, so I covered it with mine as I pushed my body against hers. When I let go of her arms, she wrapped them around my neck. I grabbed her legs with my hands and lifted her up and onto me. Her body shuddered, and she threw her head back and moaned loudly as our bodies joined. Instinctively, I bit her which intensified the emotions for both of us, and immediately, we began to move together at a frenzied pace.

"Yes, James." Her breathing was ragged, her eyes were half closed. Her nails dug into my back as her body tensed.

We dropped to the ground, and I pulled her on top of me. I grabbed her hips, and she rode up and down on me as her moisture soaked us both. I increased the speed of my thrusts and held onto her hips. I was so close, but I held on until she had another orgasm. I felt it building inside her. A few more thrusts, and she exploded in release. Arianna fell forward onto me and bit me. I felt a surge of desire, and I bit her again. We were primal and lost in one another. Nothing mattered but her, and as long as I had her, the world was right. I held her firmly as I rolled her over, and I too found release.

Slowly, I opened my eyes. I rolled onto my back and pulled Arianna on top of me.

She kissed me softly. "That was phenomenal."

"It certainly was." I devoured her mouth with mine once again.

Eventually, we stood up and gathered up our discarded clothes. "What time is it, James?"

"2:30, we don't have much time."

"Do you need to feed again?"

"I probably should after making love like we did, but I'm sure everything is scared off."

"Not the eagles," she laughed. The eagles were preening in a nearby tree.

We dressed and one of the eagles hopped up on Arianna's arm. The other took off into the sky. Arianna closed her eyes, and her head moved from side to side as if she were soaring through the air. Her hair fanned out behind her. "There are elk nearby, James." The other eagle took off into the sky. "This way."

We ran after the bird, and in no time, I smelled them. Up ahead was a small herd of elk. "Stay here." I said to Arianna. She crouched down and waited while I took down a large buck then quickly turned and took down a smaller animal. "One each," I called to her. I quickly drained the large animal. Arianna drank what she could, and I finished the smaller animal.

The eagles sat in a nearby tree. They made eye contact with Arianna, and I waited while she communicated with them.

"Ok, we can go," she said. It was getting very late, so we moved swiftly in the direction of the car.

As we approached the bear carcass again, I yanked Arianna behind a tree.

"What's?" she started to say, but I covered her mouth with my hand.

A pack of wolves had found the bear. "We need to make sure those are real wolves."

Arianna nodded, and we crept forward staying upwind of the animals.

When several animals lifted their heads, I saw their black eyes. I breathed a sigh of relief. "They are actual wolves."

"How can you tell?" Arianna stared at the animals. "Giovanni never explained it to me."

"The eyes. A wolf has jet black eyes, but a werewolf has golden eyes."

She thought for a moment. "Yes. I remember thinking the puppy's eyes were a pretty golden color. I never saw an animal with that color eyes." She looked at me. "Can't a shifter mix in with real wolves?"

"Fortunately, they do not seem to get along well. The alpha wolf usually attacks the shifter."

I took her hand, and we skirted cautiously around the pack. As soon as we were clear, we raced back to the car, and I sped away.

Arianna called to see where her parents were as soon as she had service. "Hi, Mom. What are you guys doing? Oh ok. Well, James and I will shower and get dressed. It took longer to shop than we planned, but we got everything on the list." She listened. "Ok. We'll meet you at your hotel. Does Giovanni need anything from his cabin?" She listened and nodded her head. "Ok, we'll see you soon." She let out a sigh of relief. "Giovanni went back to the cabin earlier and showered. My parents picked him up about a half hour ago. He is with them. They are waiting for us at their hotel."

I parked the car, we got out, and the hawk immediately flew down onto Arianna's arm. She communicated with it. "The area is clear," she informed me.

The hawk did not leave her arm, so I opened the cabin door, and Arianna walked inside with him. The hawk did a short hop and flew to the back of a kitchen chair and settled himself.

Arianna pulled off the remains of her sweatshirt and tossed it in the garbage pail. "Start the shower please, James."

I stared at the hawk for a few moments.

Arianna took the clothes we purchased out of the bags and started to remove the tags.

I shrugged and went into the bathroom. I turned on the water, leaned against the sink, and looked in the mirror. The mark from Arianna's bite was beginning to disappear. I ran my finger over it and smiled. Arianna was amazing, and she was mine.

Chapter XVIII
Luau

Arianna

I carried my hawk outside, and he flew up into the tree. I tossed my bag of extra supplies in the back seat and got in. The tires squealed as James pulled the car out onto the road. He flicked the two white leis I had him wear and smirked.

"You look festive," I assured him.

"I guess."

It was 4:25 pm, and we did not want to be late. He sped to the hotel, and we arrived at 4:32, close enough.

"Oh, good, you are here." My father greeted us at the door.

We went inside. Giovanni wore a blue shirt, so I took a blue lei and a white lei out of my bag, twisted them together, and showed it to him. To my surprise, he took it and put it on without complaint.

"Nice shirt, Dad." I gave him two white leis because his shirt had a tropical print.

"Thanks. I had it in my closet."

I turned to Grandma. "Hi, Grandma." I bent down and gave her a kiss. She had on a turquoise dress and big white flower earrings. I took a floral lei out of my bag with lots of pink and twisted it with a white lei then put them on her.

"This is very pretty. Thank you, dear."

Mom came out of the bathroom in a floral strapless sundress and sandals. She wore pearl earrings and a matching bracelet. I twisted a white lei and a fuchsia one together for her.

"Oh, you look very pretty, Arianna." She looked at my outfit. "A tropical sarong. Where did you find it?"

"James found it at the party shop." I turned from side to side and looked in the mirror. I wore three floral leis twisted together over the black camisole tank top. I straighten my hair, so it laid flat whether I wore it down or put it in a ponytail. I added long gold earrings to match my shoes.

Mom looked at my gold, strappy high heels. "I guess you couldn't find flip flops."

I made a face. "Actually, flip flops came with the outfit, but I just can't wear them."

Mom smiled. "You look very pretty."

"We do have one more accessory." I reached into my bag and pulled out two pairs of sunglasses. I handed a pair to James, and we put them on. "What do you think?" We posed together.

"It's dark outside," Dad commented. "You don't need sunglasses."

"But they make us look cool."

"You two should visit me in Florida. You look like natives." Grandma could not suppress her laugh.

"We will come visit you, Luisa," James said. "Arianna loves the ocean."

"And the seashells," I added.

"Ah yes," James laughed, "we definitely don't have enough bowls of seashells."

I rolled my eyes at him.

"We should head out if everyone is ready." Dad looked down at his watch. He did not like to arrive anywhere late.

James handed me my coat. "It's snowing," he whispered.

I looked at him over the top of my sunglasses. "Terrific. A dark and snowy luau."

"Arianna," my mother narrowed her eyes in warning. I just smiled at her.

Giovanni went with my parents and grandmother, and we followed them in our car. I flipped down the visor and used the mirror to apply reddish lip gloss then I freshened my mascara. I pulled my hair back and fastened it with a hair band and then twisted a floral lei around the ponytail holder. James kept looking over at me. "Is something wrong?" I asked.

"No," he replied with a smile. "I like your hair in a ponytail." He paused. "I like the way it bounces when you move." He raised his eyebrows and gave me a seductive grin.

"I'll have to remember that."

James let me out at the door, so I did not have to walk far in my shoes. I took off my coat, and as I waited for him to park, Redman and several of his clan arrived.

"Good evening, Arianna." He looked me up and down and let out a deep sigh. "You look absolutely beautiful tonight."

His gaze made me nervous, but I stood up straight. I would not let him intimidate me. "Thank you," I replied without any enthusiasm.

He moved uncomfortably close, but I refused to give ground to him. I peered out the door looking for James.

"Are you going in?" he asked holding open the inner door.

"Not yet. I'm waiting for James." I did not turn to look at him. I hoped if I showed no interest in him, he might lose interest in me. I saw James approach, and I opened the outer door for him. He came inside and slid his left arm around my waist.

"Hello Redman." James held out his right hand.

Redman took his hand and shook it. "Good evening."

The three of us stood in the doorway for what seemed like a long time, but it had to be only seconds. Finally, Redman motioned for us to go in first. We made our way to the function room at the back of the steak house. We walked through the door and stopped. It was all decked out in pink: dark pink tablecloths, pink and white flowers, pink and white balloons, pink streamers.

"Wow," I said quietly as I looked at the pink overload. James and Redman's eyes were wide, and their mouths were slightly open. Neither said a word. "It certainly is pink in there," I commented.

"Yeah," they both muttered.

"Ah, Arianna. There you are." Patty came rushing over to me. "Oh wow. You look so pretty. Sorry, I forgot to tell you about the luau. I really thought I did. I'm glad you found something to wear." She pulled me in the direction of the other bridesmaids leaving James and Redman standing there still staring at all the pink in the room.

Patty had on a bright fuchsia swimsuit, multiple pink leis, and a grass skirt. The other girls were all wearing assorted shades of pink swimsuits with grass skirts, and they were barefooted.

"I'm sorry we forgot to get you a skirt, Arianna." Brittany scrutinized my outfit. "You look good. Where did you get the sarong?"

I didn't want to say the party store because they might ask why I didn't get a grass skirt, so I told a version of the truth. "Actually, James found it." It was the truth. I just did not say where James found it.

"Oh," Brittany looked over at James with puppy dog eyes. It was obvious she thought he was handsome. I caught her staring at him several times the past couple of days. "He seems very thoughtful," she said more to herself than to me or the others.

"Oh, he is extremely thoughtful." I gave him a little wave. He sat with Giovanni and Grandma, and they all gave a wave back.

"Hey, Baby Sis." Albert kissed me. "You look nice."

"Thanks."

He turned to Patty and took her hand. "The buffet is almost ready. We should take our seats."

The bridal party sat together at the head table. I found my place card and sat down. Carrie sat next to me. She was the quietest of the girls. She took everything in, but unlike the others, she was soft spoken and said little. She smiled and sat down. "Hi, Arianna."

"Hi, Carrie. You look really pretty." Her shoulder length blonde hair was in a ponytail. "Oh here." I handed her a floral lei from my bag. "You can wrap this around your ponytail holder."

"Thank you." She wrapped the lei and then flattened the front of her skirt. "The skirt is itchy." I noticed she had on panty hose. "I like what you have on a lot better."

"Thanks."

Janus bounced around and fussed over everyone and everything. He was best man and the wedding planner, and he took his jobs very seriously. He was dressed in tropical pants, a sleeveless white tee shirt, and he too was barefooted. He poured champagne for everyone at the head table while the waitresses filled the guest's glasses. "And how are you two tonight?" he asked Carrie and me as he filled our glasses.

"Fine thank you." I replied. I noticed Carrie did not look directly at Janus. She kept her eyes down and away from his face.

"Good." He moved on to fill more glasses. Carrie looked up at me.

"You don't like Janus?"

She shook her head slightly. "No, I don't. I don't trust him."

"Did he do something to lose your trust?"

"No. I don't trust him because of what he is."

I watched Janus bustling around. He was loud, bold, and seemed to always draw attention to himself. "Oh. Yes, he is flamboyant."

"That's not the problem." Carrie leaned close to me and whispered, "he's a vampire."

My mouth dropped open. I stared at her and blinked my eyes. I started to speak then stopped and closed my mouth. I was shocked and did not know how to respond.

Carrie smiled. "I know you don't believe it. You think there is no such thing as vampires. Well, vampires are real, and Janus is one. Believe me. Stay away from him, Arianna, and never ever be alone with him or look directly in his eyes."

I swallowed hard and finally recovered enough to ask, "Carrie, why do you think he's a vampire?"

"Because I've seen him drinking Patty's blood."

The look on my face must have said shock and astonishment because Carrie quickly added, "oh, he doesn't hurt her, but he does drink her blood occasionally."

I closed my eyes for a few moments to regain my composure. "Does he know that you know he's a vampire?"

"Oh. Yes. Most people in this town know that vampires exist and that we have a number of them living here." She whispered very softly now.

"You know, Redman has lived here for more than a hundred years, but he doesn't look old, does he? And that's not all. He helped rid the town of evil vampires years ago. It's in the archives. Most everyone knows." She paused. "Well, many people know. Maybe not everyone, but many people think he and his gang are some kind of protectors."

"What does Albert say about all this?"

"I don't think Albert knows about Janus. He's one of the few who don't believe in vampires. He thinks it's just folklore."

"And you say Redman is a vampire too?" Of course, I knew he wasn't one, but I was curious what Carrie thought.

"No, I don't think he is one, but he's something. As I said, he's over one hundred years old." She looked guilty. "Maybe I shouldn't have told you."

"No, Carrie. I'm glad you told me."

"Well, I think you need to know. I see the way they look at you, especially Redman."

I followed her gaze over to Redman's table. He leaned back casually, smiled, and watched my every move.

"Arianna, you should stay away from them for your own safety." Carrie put her hand over mine. "Never ever be alone with any of them."

"I will be careful, Carrie. Thank you for telling me."

Janus tinged the side of his glass with a fork, and we both turned to look at him. "Attention everyone, attention. I would like to propose a toast."

I looked over at James and Giovanni. They were looking at Albert and Patty, but they were also scanning the room. I knew it was impossible to tell them what Carrie said here. It was too dangerous. As it was, I worried someone might have overheard what Carrie said to me. The residents of this town worried me. How can they know about vampires and not be afraid?

And how can Patty allow Janus to drink her blood. I looked over at Albert. He was smiling at Patty. Was he in danger? How would he react if he knew about Patty? How would he react if he knew about me? About James? There were so many questions. I had to talk to James and Giovanni, but unfortunately that had to wait.

After dinner, James and I danced and even did the limbo, but when Janus brought out hula hoops, I went over to sit with and talk to Grandma. I plopped down in the chair next to her with a heavy sigh.

She looked over at me. "Having fun?"

"Tons."

"Don't be sarcastic. Come on, smile." She patted my knee.

I gave her a big, wide, fake smile. She looked at me over the top rim of her glasses. I sat up in the chair. "This is too much."

"It is." Grandma agreed to my surprise. "Your parents are having fun though."

I looked at them. Mom and Dad were having a wonderful time on the dance floor. They were laughing and smiling as they glided around. They loved to dance and took full advantage of any opportunity to get out on the dance floor. "Just think," I looked at Grandma and put on another fake smile, "we have to do this again tomorrow night."

"It'll be ok," she laughed and patted my knee.

A few minutes later Giovanni and James came back to the table and sat down. James handed me a drink. I looked at my watch. "When can we leave?" I drank down quite a bit of the drink.

Giovanni sat down across from me and sighed. I knew he also did not like all the parties. He looked at me and then at James. "You better tell her."

"Tell me what?" I sat up straighter.

"Well," James cleared his throat and sat down next to me. "Apparently, the wedding party is going out to look at the Northern Lights after the luau."

"Are you kidding me?" I said a little too loudly. I was not happy. James and I planned a quiet night gazing at the stars and the lights by ourselves. James just gave a sad smile and shrugged his shoulders.

"Terrific," I grumbled. "Have you seen the lights, Grandma?"

"Yes, I saw them last night. They are beautiful. I think I will sit outside for a few minutes again tonight and look at them."

When we finished our drinks, James stood up and held out his hand. "Would you like to dance?"

"Yes." I took his hand, and he led me onto the dance floor. The lights were turned down, and the strobe light cast multiple colors around the room. James wrapped his arms around my waist, and I entwined my arms around his neck. I took a deep breath and laid my head on his shoulder. I glanced over at Redman. He continued to stare at me, and I wondered what was going on in his mind.

About 8:30 pm, the party started to break up. I helped the other bridesmaids take down the decorations and clean up. I noticed Redman, one of the wolves, and several of his vampires hanging around. I also noticed Carrie stayed away from them. She cleaned up on the other side of the room, and she glanced over at the group often.

I went over to her, "Are you ok?"

"I don't like them hanging around so long," she replied nervously.

"I wonder why they are still here?"

"I don't know, but I wish they would leave." She picked up a trash bag and continued to clean off a table.

"That was fun." Mom picked up the other trash bag. "We are going to take Grandma back to the hotel." She kissed me. "Be careful outdoors tonight."

"I will."

"Call me when you get up in the morning. Grandma and I will come over, and we'll get everything ready for the rehearsal dinner. Good night, dear."

"Good night, Mom. I love you."

"I love you too." She kissed me again then carried the trash bag over to the pile and left.

"Good night, Arianna, and be very careful tonight," Dad called from the doorway.

"I will. Good night, Dad."

As I finished putting the last of the tablecloths in a trash bag, Redman came up to me. I saw James and Giovanni move slowly in my direction. "Arianna, I want to let you know one of my men found a grizzly carcass not too far off the road about seventeen miles south of here. It might be vampires just passing through, or it might be the ones from New York again. I have several patrols of wolves out making certain the area is clear."

I looked at him. "Oh, no. I'm so sorry. It was James and I who killed the bear this afternoon."

"You and James?" He stuttered in surprise and a bit of awe. He looked over at James and then back to me.

"Yes, we hunted on our way back from the mall this afternoon. I didn't think we needed to tell you, but in hindsight, maybe we should have mentioned it."

"The two of you killed the grizzly?" He shook his head.

"Yes, why?" I looked over, and James was smiling now. Giovanni had no expression.

"The old one wasn't with you?"

"No, he wasn't. As I said, James and I hunted after shopping at the mall." I looked at the shocked expression on his face and inwardly smiled. Outwardly, I said, "surely you hunt sometimes." I knew full well that he did.

He cleared his throat. "Yes, I actually hunt often. It keeps up my strength." He puffed out his chest. He nodded his head and stared at me, and I wasn't sure what he was thinking. "Well, I must say, I am impressed. It normally takes three sometimes four to kill a grizzly." Redman cleared his throat again.

"Really?" I said coyly.

"Well, I guess we don't have a mystery then." He smiled, took my hand, and kissed it. "Good night."

"Good night."

"Ready?" James asked after Redman and his men left the building. He clearly felt immensely proud.

"Definitely." I piled the trash bag with the others. "Patty," I called, "James and I need to bring Giovanni back to the cabin, and we need to change our clothes, so we'll meet you guys shortly."

"Ok, Arianna. Hurry. Oh, dress warm and bring blankets. It gets cold watching the lights," Patty called to me.

I waved in acknowledgement and left the building.

Chapter XIX
Northern Lights

James

The three of us left the restaurant and walked to the car. Giovanni and Arianna got in, and I dusted the light snow off the windows. The sky cleared while we were inside, so it should be a good night for Northern Light gazing. I sat down behind the wheel and started the car.

"What is this about a grizzly," Giovanni asked once we were on the road and our conversation could not be overheard.

"You told us to hunt, so we hunted and took down a grizzly," Arianna replied rather smugly.

"By yourselves?! Are you two crazy? James, I thought you had more sense than to take on a grizzly bear. That is a dangerous animal, and Arianna is inexperienced."

Giovanni then directed his comments directly to Arianna. "And you were very smug when you told Redman. I'm not sure what he is thinking."

"Well, I couldn't lie to him. He thought there were strangers in the area. He sent out extra patrols. Besides, he was impressed." She smirked, but she also looked angry.

"Still, you two might have been injured or killed. A bear is dangerous," he repeated.

"We did have some help." I added quickly hoping to defuse the situation.

"Help? What kind of help?"

"Well," I smiled at him, "two bald eagles helped us. They swooped down and attacked the bear and distracted it. Their attacks gave Arianna and I time to get a better grip and allowed us to take it down."

Giovanni almost smiled. "Arianna, you can communicate with eagles?" His tone definitely softened.

"Apparently," she said with confidence.

"Interesting." Now, Giovanni sounded impressed. "That can be useful. Eagles are immensely powerful birds."

We arrived at the cabins, and Arianna contacted an owl that was in a nearby tree. It took flight and circled the area looking for others. "Clear," she said.

We got out of the car. The owl flew down and Arianna petted it. When it took flight, she walked over to a nearby tree and stared up. I saw her hawk ruffle its feathers and knew she was communicating with it. "No one approached our cabins," she informed us. She turned and walked toward the cabin. Giovanni followed her inside.

"Well, you certainly did impressed Redman." Giovanni's voice was somewhat cheerful now.

"Is that good or bad?" I asked.

"It can go either way. He now knows you two are formidable, but that can be a threat to him and his authority. I'll be glad when we are heading home." Giovanni stopped and looked in the trash can. He bent down and picked up Arianna's torn shirt. "I guess it wasn't all that easy, was it?" he asked sarcastically.

"My shirt was a casualty." Arianna gave a little laugh.

Giovanni turned angry again. "The bear took a swipe at you?! You might have been severely injured or killed!" he yelled.

"Yes, but that is not what happened," I said firmly before the two of them started arguing again.

"All he got was my shirt. It wasn't even that close. The sweatshirt was baggy, and his claws caught it and tore it." She looked sadly at the shirt Giovanni held up. "I liked that sweatshirt."

"You two were incredibly lucky. I'm glad you didn't tell Redman about the shirt. Let him think you two had no problems with the grizzly."

Arianna went in the bathroom to change into jeans and a sweatshirt.

"It wasn't easy, but it was exciting, Giovanni." He watched me as I took a blanket off the bed and put it in one of Arianna's large tote bags. "We ran into some wolves on our way back to the car. I told Arianna how to tell if it's a real wolf or a shifter."

"That's good," he grunted.

"Watching the eagles with Arianna was amazing. I have never seen anything like it." I took a bottle of wine from the refrigerator and added it to the bag. I decided to wrap two glasses in a towel to keep them from breaking and added them to the bag.

"Northern Lights watching." Giovanni shook his head.

"They are beautiful."

"Yes," he grunted. "But why do you all have to do it together?"

I shrugged my shoulders. As long as Arianna and I were together, I was willing to do whatever was needed.

Giovanni waited for Arianna to come out of the bathroom. "You two be cautious tonight. No bears. Do you hear me?"

"Yes," we said together. It was highly unlikely we would run into another bear.

Giovanni let out a huff. "And watch out for vampires. And wolves. I have a feeling Redman is going to have us watched more closely now. And Arianna, I don't want him to know you can communicate with birds."

"We will be careful," Arianna said to him.

"Don't worry Giovanni," I added.

"Ok. Good night." Giovanni headed to the door. He still had the torn shirt in his hands.

"Why are you are taking my shirt?" Arianna asked.

He turned and gave us a small smile. "I feel like a fire tonight, and I'll get rid of this evidence." He looked at Arianna. "Please be careful," he said softly. "I worry about you."

"I know you do, and we will be careful. Good night." She smiled at him, and he left the cabin.

I changed into jeans and a sweatshirt, and Arianna and I both put on boots. By the time we arrived at the meeting place, the others had already set up a little camp. "We have chairs for you guys," Albert called.

Arianna went over and sat down. I sat down next to her and pulled the bottle of wine and two wine glasses from the bag. Albert gave me a funny look. "You said it was BYOB, Albert."

"Yeah. It is. We usually just drink beer out of a can. No need for glasses."

I took a corkscrew out of my jacket pocket and opened the wine. I handed the glasses to Arianna, and then I poured wine into them. I re-corked the bottle and stuck it in the snow. "Ah, but Arianna prefers red wine," I said to Albert as I took one of the glasses from her.

"I do." She clicked my glass with hers and took a long drink. She smiled at me, "Thank you." I leaned over and kissed her then took the blanket out of the bag and pulled it over us. Arianna leaned her head back and looked up into the night sky. There were so many stars, and long streams of green light stretched across the sky.

"The lights are so beautiful. Look at that James." She pointed up at the lights. They shimmered, and the colors swirled in the night sky.

"They certainly are beautiful." I took her hand, and she squeezed it. For the most part, everyone was quiet. The Northern Lights awed us all. We sat staring up at the sky for well over an hour. The light show was spectacular.

I refreshed our glasses of wine.

"Popcorn?" Albert handed me a tin full of several flavors of popcorn and a stack of napkins. I immediately passed it to Arianna.

"Oh, I love caramel popcorn." She opened a napkin, took a big handful, and put the popcorn on it.

"Yeah, you always did love it," Albert laughed. "I remember we were lucky to get any because you ate it so quickly."

"I haven't had it in a long time."

"These popcorn tins are in all the stores. I'll get you one."

"Thanks." Arianna munched on popcorn.

The tin came around several times, and we continued to sip our wine. The Northern Lights were putting on a spectacular show tonight. Occasionally, someone gasped or said ahh at a particularly brilliant display of color.

"Did you know, it is supposed to be good luck to make love under the Northern Lights?" Patty said quietly. She cuddled closer to Albert and kissed him.

"Really?" Jesse replied in a very squeaky tone of voice. I noticed Tom scooted his chair closer to her. According to Arianna, they recently started dating.

"I thought it was Japanese folklore that a child conceived under the lights was more likely to be a boy or to be gifted?" Carrie corrected.

Patty sighed and shrugged her shoulders. "That's making love, isn't it?" she giggled.

"Well, I like Patty's version better. It's romantic," Jesse retorted.

"It definitely is," Patty replied with a giggle.

There was a pulse in the green aurora and several people let out audible gasps.

"Wow, the colors are brilliant tonight. Aren't you glad you are here, Sis?"

"Yes. This is absolutely amazing." Arianna sounded genuinely happy, and it was nice to see her and her brother reconnecting. She told me they were not close growing up. The age difference certainly played a role, but she said they never were able to talk, and he left for college when she was still quite young. I reached for the bottle of wine and emptied it into our glasses.

Even with blankets and propane heaters, it was getting very cold for the others, and they wrapped the blankets tighter around them. I tucked the blanket around Arianna even though I knew she was not cold. She snuggled close to me, hooked her arm in mine, and laid her head on my shoulder. Her other hand skimmed up my chest, and I slid my hand over her hip.

A short while later, Tom and Jesse were the first to say good night. We heard Jesse giggling as they walked back to the car. The tires squealed as Tom pulled out quickly, and we heard the car drive away. Arianna looked at me and smiled. "I don't think they are going home," she whispered in my ear.

Not long after they left, Carrie, Brittany, and Jake decided to leave.

"Good night, Arianna," Carrie said. "We're freezing and going to the diner for coffee."

"Have fun. See you tomorrow."

We heard them drive off. Patty and Albert were whispering to one another and kissing. They had a blanket pulled over their heads, and Patty was giggling.

Arianna squeezed my hand. "Ready to go?" she whispered.

I nodded yes, and when Joe and his date left, Arianna and I took the opportunity to leave as well. It looked like Patty and Albert were staying for a while. They were wrapped up beneath a big quilt. I moved the heater a little closer to them.

"Good night you two," Arianna said as I gathered up our blanket and the wine glasses.

"Good night," they said together.

Albert poked his head out from under the blanket. "Oh, Sis, what time should I come over tomorrow morning?"

"I'll call you when Mom and Grandma come over. Most likely it will be midmorning."

"Ok, night."

"Good night." Arianna took my hand, and we heard Patty whispering softly under the quilt as we walked away.

I put the two chairs we used in the back of Albert's truck. Before we reached our car, I pulled Arianna into an embrace and kissed her. "Do you want to make love under the Northern Lights?"

Arianna gave an uncharacteristic giggle. "I do." She grabbed my arm and pulled me with her. We veered off the path, found a well-hidden spot, and spread out the blanket. "We have to be very quiet," she whispered in my ear. She pushed me back and slid on top of me. She ground her hips into mine as she gave me a scorching kiss.

When we returned to our cabin, I was certain Giovanni was still awake, but he did not come out. Arianna had a snack, and I checked email. Marcus asked if there was anything more to report on Redman. I sent him a short email before starting to work on my manuscript.

Arianna took out her laptop and worked on her manuscript. She asked more questions about how to tell wolves from shifters. She worked the information into short stories, and each was a chapter that relayed essential information to vampires and hunters. Of course, it was being written under the guise of fiction.

Around three o'clock, Arianna kissed me and went to bed. I continued to work at the table with the display only dimly lit. When I finished a chapter revision, I looked up and gazed at Arianna as she slept. Her hair spilled over her shoulder and off the edge of the bed. Her breathing was shallow and even, and her face was calm and serene. I liked the idea of the two of us being writers. It was romantic, and I imagined us sitting side by side working on our respective projects. Life really was wonderful. I opened a file and dug in for the next chapter revision.

Arianna woke up just after six o'clock. She stretched and sighed.

"Good morning." I closed my laptop, walked over to the bed, and slid down under the blanket with her.

"Good morning." She slid half on top of me, her bare breasts rubbed against my chest. She reached down. "What's this?" She pulled at my boxers. "You are overdressed, my love."

"Sorry." I slid them off quickly.

"Much better. I don't like being naked alone." She rolled fully on top of me and kissed me. Kissing was enough to arouse me, and I grabbed her hips and lifted her up. "See you couldn't do that dressed," she giggled. She was in a very playful mood this morning. I hoped the phone did not ring, and Giovanni did not knock on the door.

I came out of the bathroom and kissed Arianna. "I love you."

She smiled at me, "I love you too."

"You should dry your hair and get dressed soon. I'm certain Giovanni will be knocking on the door at any moment."

"He's not back from his walk yet," Arianna casually replied as she continued to eat her breakfast.

"His walk?"

"Yes, he went out for an early morning walk."

"He went out alone? What happened to no one goes into the forest alone?" I mimicked Giovanni's stern tone.

"He's close-by."

"The hawk showed you?"

"Yes." She got up and put her cereal bowl in the sink. She turned and opened her robe as she walked toward me. "Do you still want me to get dressed?"

I shook my head no, moved toward her, and slid my hands inside her robe. I caressed her back and then skimmed my hands over her hips and up to her breasts.

She let out a happy sigh.

Suddenly she gasped, and her body stiffened.

"What is it?" I asked. I knew she was getting a vision.

"Bear." She moved her head. "Do you see what I see James?"

"Yes! Giovanni is moving closer to that bear."

"Why isn't he responding?" Arianna closed her robe. The hawk swooped down on Giovanni several times, but he just waved it away.

I knew where Giovanni was and ran out the door heading in his direction. Arianna was right behind me. We did not know why Giovanni could not see what Arianna saw, or if he did, why he was not responding. "You go to Giovanni, and I'll scare away the bear," I called to her.

Arianna nodded. Fortunately, it did not take much to scare the bear off, and I quickly went to Arianna and Giovanni's location.

"What's wrong with you?" I heard Arianna ask as I approached. Her voice was tense.

"Nothing." Giovanni snapped angrily.

"Nothing? Didn't you smell or see that bear. I know I transmitted the image to you. It could have killed you."

"And I don't like your bird spying on me," he shouted at her.

"If it wasn't for that bird, you might have been the bear's breakfast. What were you doing anyway?"

"I was gathering bark from the larch trees."

"Why?" Her hands were on her hips, and she glared at the bundle he had in his hands.

"To make a tea if you must know." He was very gruff with her.

"A tea? For what?" Arianna demanded.

"For those of us who are ordinary hunters, it helps keep us healthy."

Arianna squinted at him. I was not sure she believed him. "You never mentioned this before."

"Well, you don't need it, but I think I should give you a lesson in herb uses when we get back." Giovanni looked from Arianna to me. We were both barefooted. Arianna wore only a robe, and I had on nothing but a pair of lounge pants. "If anyone sees you two, they will know something is different about you," Giovanni said angrily.

"Frankly, in this town, I don't think it matters," Arianna snapped back as she tied her robe tighter. We both gave her a questioning look. "I'll tell you what Carrie told me last night at dinner on the way back to the cabin."

Arianna went inside, got her guards on, and went back outside. When we went to the fabric store, she purchased a piece of faux leather for her shoulder, so the young hawk could perch there. He stayed on Arianna's shoulder, and she came inside with him. He hopped up onto the back of one of the chairs.

Giovanni sat at the small table while Arianna went in the bathroom to dry her hair and get dressed.

"I don't like this at all," Giovanni muttered. "The townspeople know about vampires and hunters? That violates all treaties and agreements." He shook his head. "I can't believe that Carrie actually saw Janus drinking Patty's blood." He paused and shook his head again. "And Patty allows it!" He looked at me. "That is not normal. She is a human. Her instincts should resist him."

"They seem to have their own rules up here." I put on a shirt. "And Redman seems to be the one making the rules."

"Yes. I don't like it," he grumbled. "I wonder if Redman knows Janus feeds on Patty?"

"Arianna is concerned about Albert. Carrie told her Albert doesn't believe in vampires, yet Patty and Albert are close to Janus."

"There are so many questions." Giovanni shook his head.

I was going to ask about the bark and the tea. I thought it might be to help with his reduced regenerative powers, but I decided not to ask at this time. Arianna seemed satisfied with Giovanni's explanation, so it was probably best not to bring it up. I quickly straightened up the cabin, made the bed, and put on a kettle of water for tea. Arianna came out of the bathroom dressed in jeans and a long-sleeved shirt. "James, you should start a fire. I think it's chilly in here for Mom and Grandma."

"Ok." I went over to the fireplace and added wood. It did not take long for the fire to start burning and warming up the cabin.

Arianna ate a bowl of cereal. She tossed several pieces of cereal to the hawk.

Giovanni asked her more questions about her and Carrie's conversation. He shook his head. "I don't like this at all. Is your father coming over too, Arianna?"

"No, just Mom and Grandma. We need to make the favors for the rehearsal dinner tonight. Have you found out anything from Grandma about Giuseppe?"

"I have talked to her quite extensively, and John too, but I have found nothing out of the ordinary."

Arianna shook her head. "Did you compel her like Hale suggested?"

Giovanni gave Arianna a stern look. "Not yet." His annoyed tone returned. "I am attempting to talk first. Something you should try before compelling someone."

Arianna did not reply. She stood up and the hawk hopped up onto her shoulder. She pet his head, and then brought him outside. A few minutes later, she came back in and started unpacking the bag of supplies she brought with her.

Giovanni stood up. "James be careful today."

"I will."

Giovanni gathered up his pile of bark. "I'm going to go to my cabin for a while." He started to walk towards the door and then turned around. "Thanks for saving me from that bear."

Arianna and I nodded.

He sighed and left.

I changed into jeans and a sweater then packed my notes and laptop in my computer bag. I planned to write at the library, and I also planned to do more research and a little reconnaissance work on Redman and the other vampires in town. I planned to talk to people under the pretense of doing research for a book. I found people opened up to writers, but unlike Giovanni, I planned to compel people if necessary to get more information from them.

Chapter XX
Rehearsal

Arianna

We heard the car pull up. James opened the door and went outside. "Hello, Luisa. Let me help you." Her jacket had a little snow on it, so James helped her out of it and dusted off the snow.

"It's snowing again." I stated flatly.

"Yes, it is," Mom replied with a deep sigh as she came in and closed the door. "It's nice and warm in here." She shook the snow off her coat and put it on the bed with my grandmother's coat. She walked over and looked at the supplies on the table. I chose royal blue, gold, and white as the color scheme for the favors and decorations. Mom let out another big sigh.

"What's wrong?" I asked.

"I was thinking about the table linens and decorations." She pouted her lips. "I really do think we need to make some changes and include the bridal party color."

I shook my head. "Personally, I have had enough pink. This is the rehearsal dinner put on by the groom and his family. I feel we need to do something more to his taste."

"I'm in pink overload too, but the wedding color should be represented," Mom insisted.

James sat Grandma close to the fire, and then he sat down next to her. They were quiet and did not get involved in the discussion. There was no way I was having an overload of pink tonight. Mom and I had this argument before, and I was standing firm. Yes, it's the bride's day, but it's also the groom's day, and tonight is his night. However, for the sake of peace, and because I knew the wedding color should not totally be ignored, I proposed a compromise.

"Ok, I have an idea. The floral arrangements we ordered are white with royal blue and gold curly ribbons for accent. Why don't we call the florist and have them add a few, just a few, pale pink sweetheart roses to each arrangement."

Mom smiled. "That's a great idea. Yes, I like that idea."

I reached into another bag. "I also have pink curling ribbon leftover. We can add it to the bow on the bridal party gifts."

"Where are the gifts?" Mom asked.

"Albert is bringing them over in about an hour."

When the tea kettle whistled, James walked to the kitchen area, and poured three cups of tea. "Well ladies, if you have everything under control, I think I will excuse myself for a while." He gathered up his laptop bag and put on his coat.

"Where are you going?" Mom asked.

"I plan to go to the library to work on my manuscript."

"Is Giovanni going with you?"

"No, Giovanni is staying here. He said he was tired," I told my mother. I was concerned that Giovanni was tired. However, I felt overwhelmed, and I was certain he was too. Maybe being tired was his excuse to spend time alone. He felt certain James would be fine in town alone, and there was the added bonus that without Giovanni, James was free to "talk" with the librarian.

I walked with James to the door and gave him a hug. "Be careful. I love you," I whispered in his ear.

"I will. I love you too." He leaned over and gave me a peck on the lips.

I took a deep breath and closed the door before I turned back to Mom. "I'll call the florist and then we'll put the favors together." She nodded, and Grandma let out an audible sigh of relief.

We set up an assembly line for the favors: plastic bag, almond candies, kisses, truffles, mints with the bride and groom's names on the wrapper, tulle, ribbons, and ring and flower decorations. Back in Salem, I experimented around with the number of candies to put in each bag. I demonstrated the process. "Ok, six almond candies, four kisses, two truffles, and two wrapped mints per bag. We will have extra candy that we can put in a bowl for people to nibble on after dinner. Twist tie the bag then put it in the center of the tulle circle. Pull up the tulle. Use one printed ribbon with the bride and groom's names, a royal blue ribbon, and a gold ribbon, slip on the decoration and tie it all up." I showed them the finished product.

"It looks beautiful, Arianna," Grandma said.

"I have the ribbons precut."

"Why don't I fill the bags with candy and twist tie them closed, and you and Grandma put them in the tulle," Mom suggested.

"Ok, tying them up will take the most time."

We got to work. Mom filled bags quickly. Grandma and I placed them in the tulle and then tied on a decoration with the ribbons. When we finished a bundle, we placed it in a large, white, wicker basket.

"Where did you get this basket?" Grandma asked as we worked. "It's pretty, but I'm not sure one basket will be enough."

"I found them at the fabric store in the mall when James and I went shopping for the luau supplies." I pulled a second basket from the large bag under the table. "I bought two."

"Should we add pink ribbons to the baskets?" Mom asked.

"Oh, I guess so," I replied with a sigh.

"It's the bride's day. When it's your turn to be a bride, you can do what you want," Grandma reminded me, yet again.

Mom finished more candy bags then put water on for tea. Even with two of us putting them in the tulle, it took us much longer to tie them up.

I heard a car drive up, and in a few moments, Albert knocked and came in. "Hey, those look great. Can I have a candy?"

"Of course, you can." Mom handed him a truffle. They were his favorite candy which was why I chose to include them. Afterall, it's the groom's night.

"I like the favors," Albert mumbled with a mouth full of candy.

"Thanks," I replied.

Grandma tied a ribbon around a bundle and set it in the basket. Mom came back over to make more candy bags while she waited for the tea water to boil.

The tea kettle whistled. "I'll pour the tea, so you won't break your rhythm." Albert rinsed our mugs then poured in water. "What kind of tea do you want, Earl Grey, English Breakfast, or Peach tea?" He looked at me. "Arianna, you brought three kinds of tea with you for less than a week's stay?"

"No, I bought three kinds of tea when I got here."

"Earl Grey," Mom replied ignoring our bickering.

"Peach for me," Grandma said. "I like that the peach tea is made with black tea. I need the caffeine boost," she chuckled.

"Peach for me too. Thanks."

Albert put in the tea bags and set the mugs near each of us.

"Last one," Mom said a few minutes later. She dunked her tea bag. "That wasn't so bad."

"We still have more to tie up." Grandma stopped and took a sip of her tea.

"Arianna, I really like this cabin. The kitchenette is very handy." Mom squeezed lemon in her tea, stirred it, and took a sip.

"I know. I love it. I really like the ambiance too. I'm so glad James found these cabins."

Grandma smiled at me. "James is very considerate. I can see why you love him, Arianna." She reached over and squeezed my hand.

"I love him very much."

Mom took the bags of leftover candy and set them aside in two of the clear plastic bowls I purchased at the party store. "Albert let me see the bridal party gifts." He brought her the bag of gifts. She took them out and placed them on the table in place of the candy. "Bottle openers?" She gave him a stern look.

"Personalized bottle openers for the guys," he replied sheepishly.

She wrinkled her nose. "I guess." She took out the personalized jewelry boxes for the girls.

"Patty said to put the jewelry boxes in these bags." He pulled small pink bags out of the larger bag. "She has each bag labeled. She has something else for the girls too, but she wants to give it to them personally."

"Well, the wedding color will be represented on the table," I whispered to Grandma, and she laughed.

Mom gave me a stern look, and I gave her a wry smile back. "I'll start wrapping these up then," she said ignoring me.

Albert took another truffle and popped it into his mouth.

Mom finished wrapping the gifts and put them all into a larger pink gift bag that Patty provided. Grandma and I only had three more bundles to tie.

"Done," Grandma said as she tied off her last favor. She leaned back and took a long sip of tea.

"Are you tired, Grandma?" I asked.

"A little."

"Would you like to lie down?"

"No, I am fine."

"Are you sure, Mom?" my mother asked. "It will be a long evening again."

"I'll rest after lunch."

Albert took another truffle. "Want one, Baby Sis."

I nodded, and he tossed one to me. "Thanks."

"Don't fill up on junk you two." Mom picked up the bowl of candy. I snagged another truffle when she walked by, and she gave me another stern look.

"I'm going to have a bowl of cereal to tie me over until lunch." I took a box off the top of the fridge. "Would anyone like a bowl?"

Grandma and Mom said no. "I'll have one. I'm starved," Albert said, so I poured us each a bowl of cereal and set out the milk. As Albert and I started our second bowl each, his phone rang. "Hey, Patty." He listened and chewed. "Ok." He kept eating. "Ok, so, do you want me to come there?" He listened more. "I'll bring Arianna."

I gave him a questioning look.

"Ok, we'll be there soon. Bye." He hung up and kept eating.

"Bring me where?"

"We have to stop at my apartment and get the glasses and serving pieces, and then Patty needs us at the hall. The balloon lady came to set up the arch, and she said a single arch is too small for the room. She wants to do a triple arch, but Patty wants my opinion."

276

"So why does she need me?"

"You are going to stand in for me, so she and I can see how it looks."

"Should I change?" I looked down at my clothes.

"Why?"

"Are you sure this outfit is ok for lunch?"

"It's fine. We're just going to the diner." Albert stood up and washed his bowl.

"You look gorgeous," Grandma agreed.

I smiled at Grandma. "You are biased."

"Yes, I am, but you are still gorgeous."

"Ok, let me freshen up and change my shoes." I kicked off my new slippers.

"Where are your socks?" Grandma asked.

"If I wore socks, I wouldn't feel the soft fur between my toes," I explained.

She shook her head and laughed.

"I will wear socks with my boots," I assured her. I put on fancier earrings and a bracelet then I brushed my hair, put on a silky scarf, and put on my boots. "Let me text James." I picked up my phone. "I'll tell him to pick up Giovanni and meet us at the diner at 1:15."

"Since Giovanni is in his cabin, we can take him over. No need for James to come back."

"Ok." I texted James then called Giovanni and explained the situation. "Giovanni will be right over."

Giovanni knocked a few minutes later.

"How are you today, Giovanni?" Grandma asked.

"I am well, thank you. How are you?"

"Cold, but otherwise I am well."

"Tea, Giovanni?" Mom asked.

"No, thank you."

"Ok, if you are all set, Arianna and I will head out then meet you at the diner. Arianna, I'll warm up the car." Albert put on his coat, went outside, and started his car.

I put on my leather jacket and gave Mom and Grandma a kiss.

"Where are your mittens?" Mom asked.

I grabbed the mittens off the table. "I have them."

Mom shook her head. "When you were little, I always had to remind you to wear your hat and mittens."

"I was never cold." I shrugged. "Just lock the door when you leave. Bye."

"Have fun," Grandma called as I left.

This was my first opportunity to be alone with Albert. I wanted to try and find out what Tony wanted from him. I sat down in the car.

"All set?" Albert asked. I nodded. He drove to his apartment, and we went inside. The apartment was small, just three rooms, and looked lived in. Albert was not a good housekeeper. "It's not much, but it works for me."

"It's a guy's place," I chuckled. "Albert?"

He looked at me, and I locked eyes with him. Giovanni believed compelling was a last resort, but this was my only opportunity to be alone with Albert, and I needed to see if I could get some answers. Hopefully, Tony did not have time to erase Albert's memory.

"Albert, do you believe in vampires?" I asked.

He looked anxious and squinted his eyes. "There are no such things as vampires."

"Does Patty believe in vampires?"

"Yes."

"What did Tony from New York want when he talked to you in the Fall?"

Albert moved his head from side to side. "Great Grandpa."

"What about him?"

"Asked if I have seen him. Told him no. He's long dead."

"Did he ask about me?"

"Asked if you have seen Great Grandpa."

"What did you tell him?"

"Said no. Great Grandpa is long dead."

"What else did he ask you, Albert?"

Albert shook his head. "Asked about the wedding. Said I should call you. He said he was in the area and just wanted to say hi. He said he knew you."

Tony knew me. It was nearly a disaster when we met in New York City last year. James and I could have been killed. Fortunately, Tony was a newly turned vampire, and Jacob did not seem anxious to kill me. We were lucky to get away without a fight that day.

"Did Tony ask anything else?"

Albert closed his eyes as if trying to remember. "I, I don't know."

I tried a few other questions, but that was all Albert remembered. I sighed. "Let's get going."

"Oh, ok." Albert blinked and stared at me.

"What did you need to get here?" I asked when I had his full attention.

"Oh," Albert went to the bedroom and came out with a box. We left the house, got into the car, and Albert drove to the hall.

It was past 1:30 when Albert, Patty, Carrie, Brittany, and I arrived at the diner. Patty could not decide on the balloon arches. Albert walked in, looked at both, said three arches, and sat down. Patty had the lady set up one, then three, then one again. Brittany, and I posed as the bride and groom. Carrie stood in for the cake. Finally, Patty decided on three arches, but she was not confident in her decision.

Dad looked a little annoyed when we finally arrived. He liked punctuality.

"Sorry, my fault we're late." Patty sounded a little breathless.

James stood up and held my chair for me. Grandma looked at James and smiled.

"Thank you." I gave James a peck on the cheek and then sat down between him and Grandma. I picked up the menu. "I'm starving."

Patty looked at us, and even though she whispered to Albert, I heard her say, "Why don't you hold my chair." Albert just shrugged his shoulders.

James took my hand under the table and gave it a squeeze. I looked over the menu. "I know what I want."

"We do too," Albert said.

"Let's order." Dad signaled the waitress.

Patty seemed tense. Her phone rang several times, and she went outside to take one call. "Patty doesn't look good," I whispered to Grandma.

She looked over at Patty. "Wedding jitters. Everyone gets them."

As soon as we finished eating, Patty said she had some things to attend to before the rehearsal. "No dessert for me thanks. Lunch was nice. Thank you," she put on her coat and nudged Albert.

"We'll see everyone tonight. Thanks." He put on his coat, and they quickly left.

"Who wants dessert?" Dad asked.

"I do," I said a little too eagerly which drew a look from my mother.

"There's always room for dessert," Grandma chuckled.

*****

When we were back at the cabins, James, Giovanni, and I sat down at the table.

"What did you find out, James," Giovanni asked.

"Many people in the town know about vampires. They think it's normal." He shook his head. "The librarian showed me several more newspaper articles from the archives regarding Redman, Janus, and others protecting the town, helping build the school, and even sponsoring community activities. I did not even compel her. I simply asked about vampires." He paused and took a deep breath. "It was very disturbing."

"I hope we never have to come back to this town," Giovanni said.

I nodded my agreement, but I knew I might have to come back as long as Albert lived here. "Well, I have some information too. I talked to Albert when we went to his apartment to get a few wedding items."

Giovanni sighed loudly but did not say anything, so I continued. "He does not believe in vampires; although, he said Patty does. Then I asked him what Tony from New York wanted, and Albert said Tony asked if he had seen our great grandfather."

Giovanni sat up. "They asked Albert about Giuseppe?"

I nodded yes. "Albert said he told Tony that Great Grandpa was dead. They also asked if I had seen Great Grandpa, and Albert said no. And," I paused, "Tony did suggest that Albert call me about the wedding." I shrugged. "I'm certain there was more, but I think Albert's memory had been altered."

"Why?" James asked.

"It seemed like Albert struggled to answer my questions."

James looked at Giovanni and then back to me. "Sometimes that is what happens when someone's memory has been erased."

Giovanni grunted. "Well, it is clear that they also believe Giuseppe may still be alive." He started to say something else, then shook his head, and looked at us. "I'm going back to my cabin." He stood up and left.

James reached over and covered my hand with his. "It may take time, but we will figure it all out."

I squeezed his hand and nodded.

That evening, the priest talked to Patty, and she felt less stressed. We ran through the ceremony several times. Everyone was comfortable with how to walk and where to stand. Carrie and I stood together while we waited for our turn. She did not mention the vampires again, but I noticed she stepped back whenever Janus was near her. When we were finished at the church, I rode in the car with Carrie and Jake to the rehearsal dinner venue.

Carrie sat sideways to talk to me as we drove. "It's so nice that your grandmother came to the wedding, Arianna."

"This was a hard trip for her, but she had to see Albert get married."

"I dreamt about my grandmother last night. I guess I thought about her because your grandmother is here. I need to call her."

"Where does she live, Carrie?"

"In Canada. She is in her eighties, and she lives alone in the woods."

"Really?"

"She's tough. She used to live further East in Canada, but she moved West after my grandfather died. My father was just a baby."

"Does she visit you often?"

Carrie shook her head no. "She came here once, but she didn't like it here. She said there were too many people in the town."

I raised an eyebrow. "Really?"

"Some people like to live alone." Jake pulled in the parking lot, and we got out of the car and walked over to where everyone was gathered. Jake went to talk with the guys.

"This has been a whirl wind week," Carrie said with a deep sigh. She adjusted her dress which was a floral basic A line style.

"It certainly has been crazy," I agreed.

"And you had a cross country flight too."

"And another to return."

Carrie adjusted her dress again.

"You look nice, Carrie," I said to boost her confidence.

She smoothed the front of her dress again. "I'm not comfortable wearing a dress, not like you."

"I wear dresses often that's why I'm comfortable."

"I like your dress."

"Thanks." My dress was royal blue. The neckline had a deep V which showed off my great grandfather's locket. I wore long gold earrings, and my purse and shoes were also gold.

"I usually just wear jeans and sweaters. I start my last undergraduate semester in a couple of weeks," she mused.

I smiled at her, "Enjoy it."

"Oh, I plan to."

"Have you applied to grad school?"

"Yes. I am hoping for Seattle or California, but I also applied to two schools on the East coast, so maybe if I go there, we can visit."

"Absolutely. You should consider Weymouth University. It is a great school."

"Actually, when you said you taught there, I went to the website. I think I will apply there as well."

"Good luck."

Joe and Tom came and stood by us as we waited for the DJ to announce the bridal party. They were both graduate students who worked with Albert, and they were not very talkative except with Albert.

Finally, our names were called. Joe offered me his arm, and we strode into the hall. We parted, and I took my place next to Jesse on the bride's side. Carrie joined me a minute later.

"And the bride and groom to be, Patty and Albert," the DJ shouted above the wedding march.

Patty smiled broadly and looked radiant. Albert whispered something to her, and she blushed slightly. They filed in behind the table and we followed suit.

My father and mother moved in front of the table with their champagne glasses in hand.

"Good evening. It is Felicia's and my pleasure to welcome you here tonight as we celebrate the upcoming wedding of our son Albert Sabini to Patricia DeGeorge. Albert and Patty may your marriage be long and full of happiness and love. Congratulations!"

"Congratulations!" we shouted and drank.

Everyone sat down, and the wait staff began serving dinner. The meal began with salad, and then guests had a choice of chicken or prime rib. I chose the chicken. It was grilled perfectly and was moist and delicious.

While we ate, Carrie and I chatted. I really liked her. Apparently, she and Patty lived next door to one another growing up. Carrie went away to college in Colorado, so they were not as close as they once were.

After dinner, the DJ got the wedding party up dancing. Joe was a good dancer, and we moved across the floor to the music. I heard Carrie laugh, and I looked over at her. I noticed she and Jake were dancing fairly close together. More of the guests came out on the dance floor, and James cut in. Joe nodded and let go of my hand, and then he went over and asked one of Patty's cousins to dance.

"Having fun?" James asked. He took my right hand in his and pulled me close with his left.

"Yes, I am. Are you?"

"I am now." He moved us across the dance floor and twirled me around when the tempo picked up. We had a couple dances then I danced with Dad. Mom danced with Albert, and James danced with Patty.

After a few more dances, Dad and James went to get drinks, and Albert, Mom, and I sat down at the table with Grandma and Giovanni.

"I see you are wearing your locket," Mom remarked.

"Of course, she is," Albert commented.

"What does that mean?" I was slightly offended by his tone.

"Great Grandpa spent a lot of time with you, Arianna. You were his favorite."

"Well, you had him for years before I was born, Albert."

"No, I didn't. I hardly ever saw him."

I looked at Mom, and she nodded yes. "He's right, we hardly ever saw him until you were born."

"That's because she was his favorite," Albert sighed.

I opened my mouth to rebut Albert, but Grandma laughed. "Now that was certainly true. Arianna was absolutely my father's favorite." She took a sip of her tea. "It's because she looks like his mother."

The look on Giovanni's face told me her comment took him completely by surprise. He cleared his throat. "She looks like his mother?" Giovanni's voice sounded tense.

"Arianna has the same alabaster skin and long silky hair as my Grandmother."

"Did you know your grandmother, Luisa?" Giovanni asked.

"No, sadly, she and my mother died in an accident when I was an infant." I put my arms around her. I knew it was difficult for her to talk about her mother. Grandma cleared her throat and took a long drink of tea. "Any way that's why he gave you that locket, Arianna. He carried a picture of his mother in there. He did not like to talk about her, but he really loved her, and her death was traumatic for him."

I looked at Giovanni, and he looked perplexed. There was a moment of awkward silence, but Albert broke it. "Yep, she inherited a necklace and got a trip to Italy." We all looked at him. "Well, she did. I wanted to go, but he said no I had to go to school."

"He never took Arianna to Italy," Mom said with an exasperated sigh. "Honestly, I don't know why you made up that story."

"I remember it clearly."

"I think you dreamed it," Dad interjected. He and James had returned with drinks. "You were very upset when Grandpa took Arianna to New Jersey for two weeks, but you were in school, and you could not go."

"How old was I?" I asked. "I don't remember a trip?"

"You were four," Albert informed me.

"Yes, it was right after you had your tonsils out. Do you remember being in the hospital?"

"Sort of. I remember Albert was in the room, and there was another kid in a plastic tent next to me."

"That's right," Mom said. "The girl in the bed next to you had pneumonia and was in an oxygen tent. Albert was in the hospital for observation after his bicycle accident."

"And I went to New Jersey? I don't remember the trip, but I remember being with Great Grandpa and going places with him. I just don't remember it being Italy or New Jersey. And I think I was sick on the trip."

"No, you were not sick, Arianna. In fact, you haven't been sick since you had your tonsils out."

"Are you sure?"

"Of course, I'm sure. I am your mother. It was a very quick trip to New Jersey. Joseph wanted to visit some friends from Italy. I think because his friends were from Italy, Albert thought he took you to Italy."

"No, that's not it," Albert contradicted. He was getting agitated and shook his head. "You guys insist they were only gone two weeks to New Jersey, but I know they were in Italy for six weeks." He let out a huge sigh.

I looked over at Giovanni. His face reflected the confusion I felt. "Luisa, you say Arianna resembles Joseph's mother. What was her name?"

"Maria," Grandma replied.

Giovanni gasped. "Luisa, your grandmother's name was Maria?" I looked at Giovanni's expression, and I knew something was wrong.

"Yes. Why?"

Giovanni cleared his throat again. "Oh, you never mentioned her name that is all." He knew something, but he obviously could not say anything right now.

"Well, let's dance." My father held out a hand to my mother, she stood up, and the two of them twirled out into the crowd.

"That is a good idea." James took my hand, I stood up, and we joined my parents on the dance floor.

Chapter XXI
Wedding Bells

James

The rehearsal dinner ended late. Arianna picked up one of the table arrangements, put it in a bag, and set it by her purse. Giovanni came back inside after helping Luisa to the car. "Are we almost ready to leave?" He looked at his watch.

"Almost," Arianna replied.

"Felicia, I have the car out front, are you ready?" John called from the door.

"I'll be right out."

"Good night, Arianna." Carrie put her coat on.

Arianna handed her a table arrangement. "Good night and thanks." Carrie and Jake left the hall together.

I helped Arianna and her mother put on their coats. Felicia got in the car and waved as John pulled out of the parking lot. Giovanni, Arianna, and I got in our car. Because a moving car was the safest place to talk, I pulled onto the main road and started driving. The snow had stopped, and now the stars were out.

Giovanni started talking immediately. "First, Arianna does not look like Giuseppe's mother. My daughter in law, Rosalie, had auburn hair and hazel eyes."

"So then why is Giuseppe calling a different woman his mother?" Arianna wondered.

"I don't think Giuseppe is Luisa's father," Giovanni replied, and Arianna gave a gasp. "Do you have any pictures of this Maria?" He was very gruff.

Arianna shook her head no. "Maybe Mom or Grandma has a picture. I can ask. I'm not even sure I ever saw a picture of her. I don't remember a picture inside the locket.

"A picture would definitely help, but it really does not matter. If the woman Giuseppe claimed was his mother looked like Arianna, then he was lying. Why? I do not know." Giovanni let out a deep sigh.

I shook my head. "So, we don't completely know Arianna's family tree, and Giuseppe is the key. He obviously survived when you thought he died, Giovanni, and he had at least one child before being turned a second time. At some point, Luisa was born, and he took her here as her father, but we don't know why."

"That sums it up," Giovanni commented.

I looked over at Arianna. She was visibly upset. Her head was down, and I saw small tears at the corners of her eyes. "You have a complicated past, Arianna. But we will find the answers together." I took her hand.

She let out a breath. "Well, Albert is confused. I have never been to Italy."

"I venture to say you have," Giovanni replied calmly. "I believe Albert's memory is the correct one."

Arianna turned around and looked at him. "Why?"

"I am certain he didn't dream it. Often when a person has been compelled, the person thinks it was a dream," Giovanni explained. "However, in this case, your parents think Albert's memory is a dream brought on by jealousy and confusion because you were supposed to be visiting people from Italy. That suggests they were the ones who were compelled, not Albert." Giovanni paused. "Albert's memory is most likely the correct one."

Arianna leaned her head back against the seat. "This is so confusing."

"It is also strange that you remember being sick when you were with your great grandfather, but your mother says no," I added.

"I definitely remember being sick. Perhaps Great Grandpa didn't tell my mother I was sick."

"That's possible," Giovanni replied. "There's one more thing I didn't mention. You said you were never cold, and that's why you always forgot your hat and mittens."

"Yeah, so?"

"Hunters don't get cold."

Arianna's mouth opened, but she did not respond.

"I'm going to turn around and head back to the cabins," I told them. We drove in silence for a while. "Arianna, should I stop for something to eat? The diner is open until two am."

"No, thank you," she replied. "I have a few items left if I get hungry." She sounded very tired and maybe even a little depressed.

When we returned to the cabins, the hawk was once again roosting in the tree right outside the cabin. The great horned owl was also in a nearby tree. Arianna got out of the car, and he beat his wings, rose into the air, and circled the area.

"No one is around." She went inside and changed into comfortable clothes. As she came back outside, she put on her arm guards. Giovanni and I sat on the chairs outside the cabin doors and watched as the owl landed on her arm. She stroked the bird and then it took flight. He circled around, and then once again landed on her arm.

Giovanni stood up. "Well, I am off to bed, Good night," he said as he opened his cabin door.

"Good night," we replied.

"The Northern Lights are beautiful again tonight," Arianna commented as she reached up and pet the owl's head. He nudged against her hand then took flight.

"They are." I leaned back against the wall of the cabin and watched the swirls of color in the sky. Arianna walked over and sat down.

For quite some time, we watched the aurora swirl in the sky.

I wished there were something I might do to help her. I never met Giuseppe, and I already did not like him. After tonight's revelations, it was clear that Giuseppe was hiding something when he fled to America with Luisa. Something he did was likely the reason Jacob and Darius wanted to kill Arianna, and he most certainly was the reason they knew her as a child. There were so many puzzle pieces. I was thankful for my own relatively uneventful childhood. My father was a respectable businessman, and my mother was a woman devoted to her family and her community.

I stood up. "Let's walk." I held out my hand to her.

"Do you need to hunt?" Arianna stood up and took my hand.

"If we see something. Do you think he can look around?"

She shrugged her shoulders. "Maybe? I think this is a very young owl." The bird came down and landed on her arm. Arianna looked into the bird's eyes, and then he took off into the air. We continued walking. Arianna's head moved as she looked around through the owl's eyes. I was not in a hurry. It was a beautiful evening, and the streaks of color of the Northern Lights illuminated the sky. There were so many stars. We were far away from light pollution, and the night sky was breathtaking.

"Yes," she said at last. "About a mile south of us is a herd of elk." We turned and picked up the pace.

When we reached the herd, I had Arianna stop a good distance away. "You stay here. I'll be right back." As I stood up, the owl flew straight toward me, and I had to duck. The movement made the elk lift their heads. Arianna and I stood very still hoping the herd would not spook. After a few minutes, they lowered their heads again. It took only seconds for me to take down a large older doe. I went back to where Arianna stood watching, took her hand, and led her to the animal. The owl hopped down onto a nearby fallen tree and watched. I inclined my head, and Arianna dropped down and drank her fill then I finished the animal.

She yawned. "I'm getting tired."

"It's three o'clock," I told her. I cut a piece of meat for the owl and handed it to Arianna. I cut a second piece for the hawk.

She walked over to the owl, pet his head, and fed him then we walked back to the cabin. Arianna went up to the tree where the hawk roosted. He hopped down to a lower branch, and she reached up and fed him the meat. I looked over and saw Giovanni in the window of his cabin. He pointed to Arianna. I nodded yes. He smiled and stepped away from the window.

Once inside the cabin, we did not turn on any lights. We washed up, and she kicked off her shoes, undressed, and put on a robe. Arianna stood by the window and let out a deep sigh. I undressed then came up behind her and wrapped my arms around her waist. She leaned back into me, and I kissed her forehead.

She let out another big sigh. "I want to go home."

I turned her around and pulled her close then picked her up, carried her to the bed, and laid her down. "Rest." I kissed her. "Tomorrow is a big day."

She closed her eyes, and I saw small droplets glistening at the corners. I got in bed beside her, and she wrapped her arm around me and crossed one of her legs over mine. I smoothed back her hair, and in a few minutes, her breathing became shallow and even as she fell asleep.

*****

The next morning, Arianna went outside. The hawk finished doing a wide circle then landed on her shoulder. "No one is around," she said as she pet the hawk and brought him inside the cabin. He hopped to his favored spot on a chair back and waited while Arianna went to take a shower. I heard her humming.

When the water turned off, I poured her a cup of tea. She came out of the bathroom drying her hair with a towel and wearing, nothing. She dunked the tea bag a few times, grabbed a cereal bar, kissed me as she passed me, and went back into the bathroom.

I cleared my throat. "When is the limo coming to pick you up?"

"About ten."

I looked at my watch. "Why do you have to be there so early? The ceremony isn't until five o'clock."

"We are getting our hair and nails done and having lunch." Arianna came back into the room, smiled, and kissed me again. "It's a tradition."

I watched as she slipped on white bikini panties and a white strapless bra. I brought her over the mug of tea, and she sat down on the edge of the bed. "It's going to be a nice wedding." She sipped her tea. "But it has been a long week." She finished the tea and handed me the cup. "Thank you for everything this week."

"I would do anything for you." I kissed her. "You better get dressed."

She dressed then took the hawk back outside. It circled again and then flew up into a nearby tree.

When the limo arrived, Giovanni came out of his cabin. Several of the girls were already inside talking excitedly. Arianna handed her bag to the driver, kissed me, then got in the limo. "See you two at the church," she called as she closed the door. Giovanni and I waved as the limo slowly drove down the driveway to the road.

"I will be glad when this wedding is over, and we are on a plane back home," Giovanni said as we went inside. I put on my boots. He stood watching me. "She looks better this morning. It was a smart idea to get her to feed with you. It strengthened her."

"She was so drained last night. I knew it would help. She came in and went right to sleep."

"Are you going to hunt?" he asked.

"I think I better. It will be a long evening."

"I'll come with you."

We headed into the forest. The hawk passed over us looking for Arianna. He swooped down several times, and Giovanni shooed him away. Even though Giovanni was not a talkative man, I was glad to have his company. We came upon game fairly quickly. After I fed, I tossed a piece of meat to the hawk, and then we slowly walked back.

"I need to have something to eat." Giovanni walked toward his cabin.

"I want to do a little work, and then I will shower," I told him.

I checked my email and sent a note to my agent. I was ready to send her the chapters I revised when we returned to Salem. I felt exceptionally good about the revision. I spent time working on a chapter and then showered. I just started to get dressed when Giovanni knocked on the door. "Come on in," I called.

"I want to get there early."

It was only three o'clock. "Ok. It won't take me long to finish getting dressed." I went back in the bathroom and dried my hair. I put on my dress shirt, tucked it in my black suit pants, and tied my tie. "I was thinking about Tony being with Albert. I think they knew months ago about Arianna's Italy trip," I said to Giovanni when I went back in the kitchen area. "We know Tony told Albert to call Arianna. Is it possible they wanted to ensure we came to Montana?"

"It is possible." He was quiet for a few moments. "We are just catching up to what they know."

"I think they are planning something."

"I am sure of it." Giovanni shook his head. "Marena is sending out extra patrols."

"I told Marie to tell John to be extra vigilant."

"I have been in touch with Marie and John as well. Why would Tony suggest Albert call Arianna if they were not planning something? And Redman? I don't know what to expect from him. It's been an uneventful week; I don't like it."

"Giovanni, you said you didn't think Redman would do anything before the wedding. Are you expecting trouble after?"

"I don't know." He shook his head.

I knew how he felt. I had an uneasy feeling every time I was around Redman. The way he looked at Arianna. He made no secret of his desire for her. He confidently sat back and watched her every move. He believed it was only a matter of time before she would be with him. I straightened my tie and put on my suit jacket. "It will be nice to get on that plane tomorrow." I picked up Arianna's bag of after wedding clothes, and we got into the car.

"Let's drive around."

"Ok where do you want to go?" I started the car and slowly drove toward the road.

"Arianna is at Patty's house?"

"Yes. They had lunch, and now the stylist is doing their hair, makeup, and nails before they get dressed."

"Has she texted you?"

"A couple of times. She hasn't sent any pictures. I guess she wants her hair and dress to be a surprise."

Giovanni leaned back in his seat. "Let's go there and see if anyone else is helping them."

I sped up and headed to Patty's house. We drove by but did not stop because we did not want to be seen. I pulled down a side street, and we saw Janus going from his car to the house with several boxes. Only Janus was there which was expected. Satisfied that all was well, we left and drove around town.

"I'm glad I made the trip," Giovanni said after a while. "It's a good thing I was here because of Redman, but I also enjoyed meeting Luisa and the rest of the family." I looked over at him. He stared straight ahead. "They are my family after all."

"Yes," I replied quietly. It must be unsettling for Giovanni. For many years, he believed he was the last surviving member of his family, and now suddenly, he had a family he never knew existed.

"What do you think of John," he asked.

I thought for a moment before replying. "He is difficult to get to know. He's very private about his life." I paused. "I know he loves his daughter."

"More like he's obsessed with her career," Giovanni said loudly.

I nodded. "It is odd. I'm not surprised that Albert lives in Montana and Arianna on the East coast."

Giovanni grunted. "Work is important, but John thinks of nothing else. There is so much more to life."

"I agree." I thought about life. Humans had one limited life span. We had multiple human life spans to accomplish our goals. I looked over at Giovanni. "But do we look at life differently because of what we are? Would we be different if we were in John's shoes? He thinks Arianna and Albert only have a brief time to make their mark and accomplish goals."

Giovanni grunted but did not reply. I continued to drive. We had time before we needed to be at the church. Giovanni watched the scenery go by and was quiet for a few minutes while he contemplated my words.

"What you say is true. But, James, his obsession over his children's careers is not normal. Every father wants his children to succeed, but he takes it to the extreme. He wants to know everything they do, and he expects them, well Arianna mostly, to be perfect."

"He's a micromanager and a workaholic. He expects his children to be the same. Still, I know he loves them and wants the best for them."

"He loves them, yes," Giovanni agreed.

I turned around and began to drive back to town. We were both quiet, but it was an easy silence.

It started snowing very lightly when we arrived at the church. I dropped Giovanni at the door, and he waited with Felicia and Luisa while I parked the car next to Arianna's parent's rental car. John waited for me, and we walked across the parking lot together.

"I guess we have the easy part this time," he commented as we walked.

"Easy part?" I asked.

"When Arianna gets married, as parents of the bride, it will be our responsibility to host the wedding and the reception."

"Ah, yes." I did not know if that was just a remark or a hint. I wanted to marry Arianna. I've never wanted anyone else, but I did not want to rush her. Instead of opening her up to the idea of marriage, I was afraid this week scared her even further away from marriage. I knew one thing, if, no not if, when Arianna and I married, I knew she would not want so many pre-wedding parties.

Once inside the church, one of Patty's friends came bustling over to us. She was a short, pretty girl with curly blonde hair and bright blue eyes. She wore a very pink dress and pink shoes. "Please come to the table in front of the doors after you've hung up your coats. There are flowers for the parents and grandparents."

We hung our coats up on the rack in the vestibule then John, Felicia, and Luisa walked over to the table. The girl who greeted us pinned white rose corsages with white bows on Felicia and Luisa, and she put a single white rose boutonniere on John's lapel. The doors into the main part of the church were open, and an usher led us to our seats in the front row on the groom's side. I went in the row first followed by Giovanni, Luisa, John, and then Felicia.

Felicia took out a white handkerchief and dabbed her eyes. "The church looks so beautiful." She dabbed her eyes again.

Each row was decorated with a bunch of white chrysanthemums and a large, light pink bow. On the Altar were several arrangements of assorted pink and white flowers in large white vases tied with big pink bows. Soft music played in the background. Slowly, the church began to fill with guests. Redman came in with several other people and sat toward the back on the groom's side.

An usher led Patty's mother down the aisle to her seat. She filed into the row opposite us. She smiled, but her eyes were wet. A few minutes later, an usher unrolled a white aisle runner. Albert and Janus came out of the door next to the altar and took their places on the right side. Albert looked relaxed in his black tuxedo. He wore a white shirt and a pink cummerbund and bow tie. He surveyed the guests and acknowledged people with a smile. Janus seemed a little tense and uncomfortable. He looked around nervously, and I could tell he was not breathing.

It was just after five o'clock when the usher closed the doors at the back of the church. People waited patiently, and a few minutes later, the priest took his place in front of the altar. He arranged a few items on the altar then nodded to the organist who began playing the processional music.

The doors at the back of the church opened, and everyone turned and looked back. Jessie and Jake appeared in the doorway. They paused and smiled for the photographer then they slowly walked down the aisle and took their places on either side of the altar. Next to enter were Carrie and Tom. I did not watch them all the way down the aisle because I saw Arianna and Joe in the shadows. When Carrie and Tom were at the altar, Arianna and Joe stepped into the doorway and paused while the photographer took several pictures. They smiled and slowly walked down the aisle to the front of the church.

Felicia gave a small gasp. I am biased, but Arianna was a vision. Her gown had a strapless sweetheart top in a pale shade of pink. Tiny rhinestones rimmed the top edge of the dress, and another line of rhinestones rimmed the drop waist where the dark pink, full, tulle skirt began and flowed to the floor. Her matching pink shoes peeked out from under the gown as she walked. She wore a long rhinestone necklace with matching earrings. Her hair was straightened. The front sections of hair were pulled behind her head in an elaborate knotted design that was dotted with baby's breath. She carried a bouquet of pink roses and white baby's breath.

Arianna smiled as she approached us, and I took pictures of her. Then I watched her intently as she gracefully let go of Joe's arm and turned to walk in front of the altar.

Luisa dabbed her eyes with her handkerchief. Giovanni took her hand. Arianna took her place next to Carrie, and then she looked over at us and smiled. She was so radiant that I did not want to look at anyone else. Finally, I looked back, and Brittany, the Maid of Honor, was more than half-way down the aisle. She took her place on the left side of the altar.

She was followed by the flower girl. Courtney wore a puffy white tulle dress with a big pink satin bow tied at her waist. She walked very slowly down the aisle and sprinkled pale pink and white rose petals. She even paused and posed for pictures. She emptied her basket and stood next to the bridesmaids.

The music changed to the Wedding March, and everyone rose and turned to look at the back of the church. Patty and her father appeared in the doorway. They smiled at each other, and Patty's father kissed her and lowered the veil. Patty took his arm, and they started their slow walk down the aisle. Patty's white satin ball gown was trimmed with rhinestones, and it had an exceptionally long train. She carried a bouquet of large white roses and pink sweetheart roses. "She's so beautiful," I heard Felicia whisper to John, and she wiped her eyes.

When they reached the altar, Patty's father lifted the sheer veil that covered her face and kissed her again. He shook hands with Albert, took Patty's hand and placed it in Albert's hand, and then he took his place by his wife's side. She handed him a tissue to dry his eyes.

Brittany fluffed the train of Patty's gown, took the bride's bouquet, and then took her place at Patty's side. The priest smiled at everyone then said a blessing. When he finished, he motioned for us to sit, and he began the wedding ceremony.

I could not keep my eyes off Arianna. She listened intently to the ceremony, and she just beamed with happiness. I loved her more than I could ever express, and when she glanced over at me and our eyes met, I knew she felt the same deep and unwavering love. She closed her eyes for a moment and smiled.

I clearly imagined her in a white bridal gown walking down the aisle toward me. In my mind, I saw her standing by my side as we took our vows and became husband and wife. I put my hand in my pocket and turned the tiny box I had in there. I knew I had to proceed cautiously. However, seeing Arianna in a gown intensified my desire to marry her, and I did not want to wait much longer.

Chapter XXII
Reception

Arianna

"More champagne, Arianna?" Brittany held up the nearly empty bottle.

"Absolutely." I held out my glass for her to refill.

"Can you turn up the heat please?" Carrie called to the limo driver. We just had a long photo session outside, and the girls were freezing. The bridesmaids were in one limo, the groomsmen in another, and Patty and Albert in the third.

"Now, it is time to p a r t y!" Brittany exclaimed, and we all gave a cheer. The limo pulled up to the reception hall. Brittany took a compact mirror out of her purse and checked her hair and makeup.

I flipped by hair back. "Can I borrow that?" She handed me the mirror. My hair was sprayed, so it really did not move even in the light breeze outside.

"You look gorgeous." Brittany took the mirror from me. "Too perfect actually."

"I'm not perfect."

"Yes, you are, and I know why." Her voice was low and intended for only me. I did not reply.

The driver opened the door, and Brittany stepped out of the limo. Carrie held my arm to stop me from moving ahead with the others. "See I told you. They believe in vampires, and they think you are too beautiful."

"Carrie, I am not a vampire."

"Oh, I know."

"How do you know?"

"You don't smell like them."

"I don't?"

"No. Haven't you noticed that Janus has a really sickeningly sweet smell?

I hesitated for a moment. Vampires did have an overly sweet smell, and Janus' scent was quite pungent. "Well, yes. I did notice that he smells overly sweet." I stared at Carrie not knowing what else to say.

"Carrie, Arianna, come on," Brittany called in a very snippy and annoyed tone of voice. "We need to be ready."

Carrie and I stepped out of the limo and hurried over to take our places in line.

Brittany and Janus checked everyone over to make sure we looked picture-perfect while we waited for Albert and Patty to emerge from their limo. It was quite cold outside, and everyone moved around to keep warm, so I did as well.

The DJ's assistant looked at his watch. "We are running about fifteen minutes behind schedule." He glanced at the limo. "Ok. Send them out. It's almost time," he said into his walkie-talkie.

A few moments later, Mom and Dad and Patty's parents came outside. Finally, the limo door opened. We clapped, and Patty blushed. Patty and Albert came forward and took their places at the end of the line right behind Brittany and Janus.

The assistant looked relieved. "We are ready," he called into his walkie-talkie. He turned to address us. "Ok, when you hear your names called, walk in together arm in arm. Stop so the photographer can take pictures. Make sure you smile, and then take your places in front of the head table." He looked at us. "Does everyone understand?" We all nodded and mumbled yes.

The bride's parents were called first followed by my parents. Jesse and Jake were called next. Carrie flattened the front of her dress and took a deep breath. Their names were announced, so Carrie took Tom's arm, and they walked in.

"Ready?" Joe asked.

"I am." I straightened up and smiled. We heard our names, and Joe and I walked into the reception hall. The photographer moved around us taking pictures. All the guests stood and cheered. I saw my family clapping enthusiastically. James stared directly at me. He smiled and gave a small wave. Grandma wiped her eyes, and Giovanni actually smiled and looked happy. Mom and Dad had resumed their places at the family table and were smiling broadly and clapping. Joe and I walked slowly up to the head table, took our places, and began clapping along.

Brittany and Janus danced in. People hooted as he twirled her to the head table, and they too began clapping.

When the DJ played a drum roll, there was a long pause, and the room went quiet. "Ladies and Gentlemen," he announced, "I have the pleasure to introduce, for the first time in public, Mr. and Mrs. Albert Sabini!!!" The wedding march played, and everyone clapped and cheered. Albert and Patty entered the room then stopped as the photographer and guests took pictures. They waved to people and then stopped for more pictures. Very slowly, they walked up to the head table.

Immediately, the guests tapped their glasses with a piece of silverware. "Kiss, Kiss," they chanted. Albert dipped Patty low and gave her a long kiss, and the crowd cheered.

The DJ waited for the applause to die down. "If everyone would please pick up your glass, the best man will make the first toast."

Janus raised his glass. "Ladies and Gentlemen. I would like to propose a toast to the happy couple. Patty, I have known you for many years. Albert, I have not known you long, but I remember the day you and Patty met. It was love at first sight. But Albert, you needed a little push." Everyone laughed. "Patty persisted, and soon, Albert overcame his shyness. Today, you begin your journey as husband and wife. So, everyone, please raise your glass, and join me in wishing the newlyweds a long, happy life together, filled with more joy than sadness, and always filled with excitement, respect, and love. To Albert and Patty."

"To Albert and Patty." Everyone drank and clapped. Only moments after everyone sat down, the tapping on the glasses started again. It got louder until Albert and Patty kissed. Then everyone cheered.

"This group isn't going to let up," Carrie laughed.

I nodded my agreement, and sure enough as the salad was served, the tapping started yet again.

The dinner was delicious. I was going to get chicken, but Giovanni insisted I order the prime rib, and to my surprise, it was tender and juicy. Unlike the other girls, well except for Carrie, I ate everything on the plate including the asparagus which I normally do not eat. "How was the chicken, Carrie?"

"Delicious. And the prime rib?"

"Surprisingly good. I enjoyed it."

"I'm glad to be sitting next to you, Arianna," Carrie said with a sigh. She leaned closer to me. "Don't say anything, but I really don't like Jesse or Brittany very much."

"Your secret is safe with me."

When Albert and Patty moved from table to table talking to people, I went over to sit with my family. James stood up. "You look incredibly gorgeous." He gave me a longer than normal kiss then went to get an extra chair.

I sat in his chair. "It was a beautiful ceremony."

"It was," Mom and Grandma agreed.

"You look so pretty, Arianna," Dad said.

"Thanks. I know it's odd, but I really like this dress."

"You are radiant, Arianna." Mom added.

"You look great too, Mom." She had on a powder blue, long sleeved lace dress. She wore a triple long strand of pearls, drop pearl earrings, and a pearl comb accented her hair. "I like that color on you."

I looked at Grandma's dusty rose dress. It had long sleeves and she had on a thick white cardigan sweater. "You look nice too, Grandma. Are you cold?" She touched my arm with her hand. "Wow, you are cold." I noticed she had a hot cup of tea next to her champagne flute.

James came back with a chair, and he sat down next to me. "That dress looks fantastic on you." He looked closely at the dress. "It looks different than the one you sent me a picture of a couple days ago."

"It's the same one, but they took out the crinoline under the skirt because with it, the dress was too short for me. That is why the dress is less poufy now."

"It's much nicer." James took my hand.

"It is." I looked over, and Brittany was signaling me back. "I've got to go. Duty calls. See you soon." I returned to my seat at the head table.

Janus made his way back to the front of the room, but instead of taking his seat, he took the DJ's microphone. "Well, now that everyone is all nice and fed," he smiled and paused. I sat up straighter, and I noticed Giovanni did as well.

I reminded myself that this was not a horror movie. Vampires do not feed people then feed on them. I shook my head and let out a breath.

Janus continued, "It is time for some dancing. Let's welcome Albert and Patty to the floor for their first dance as husband and wife." The DJ started the music, and Albert led Patty to the center of the dance floor. They whispered to one another and moved slowly around the floor while people snapped pictures. I took a couple pictures of them dancing, and I took a few pictures of my family. It was so nice for us all to be here together.

A new song started, and this time the DJ took the microphone. "Would the bridal party join the happy couple, please. Joe came over and offered his arm then we walked to the dance floor. Again, the photographer moved in between us taking pictures. Joe seemed more relaxed than at the church. My fine sense of smell detected vodka as well as champagne.

"And would the parents of the bride and groom please join in." Dad danced Mom out onto the floor. They moved and twirled their way over to us. Joe's back suddenly stiffened, and he gripped my hand a little tighter.

"Hi, Mom and Dad," I said as they glided by.

"They dance really well," Joe said as we watched them spin their way around the dance floor.

"Yes, they do. They love to dance," I laughed. The song ended, and I stepped back from Joe.

"Thank you that was beautiful." The DJ started another song. "Can I have the bride and the father of the bride on the dance floor, please." Carrie and I joined my family's table while we watched Patty and her father. He talked to her as they danced, and occasionally, he dabbed his eyes with a handkerchief. I took a couple of pictures.

"Would the mother of the groom and the groom please join them on the dance floor." Albert came over and took mom's hand, and they started to dance. I took more pictures. I stood close to James. He had one hand at my waist, and his other hand rubbed the small of my back. I leaned into him and rested my head on his shoulder.

"That was beautiful," the DJ said as he too clapped. "Well, it's cake time!" he announced enthusiastically.

Carrie and I joined the rest of the wedding party near the cake which stood under the middle balloon arch near the head table. The cake was five double tier layers with white frosting. Real pink roses cascaded down one side and spilled out onto the table. A bride and groom figurine stood on the top tier. People took pictures and gathered around. Albert and Patty positioned themselves to one side of the cake. Patty picked up the cake knife, and Albert placed his hand over hers as they carefully sliced into the bottom tier. They made a couple more cuts. Patty placed two small pieces on a plate. There was a drum roll. They each picked up a piece of cake with their fingers and delicately fed the other. There were a few moans from the crowd who wanted to see a messy cake feeding.

Albert suddenly dipped his finger into the frosting and placed a dollop on Patty's nose. She and the crowd roared with laughter. Then he bent down and sucked off the frosting. A huge applause and more laughter erupted from the crowd. The music started again, and Albert and Patty returned to the dance floor.

I sat down next to James at the family's table. Carrie and Jake brought up chairs and squeezed around the table too. The head table was empty because the attendants were sitting elsewhere. The hostess cut the cake and servers appeared and began passing cake out to the guests. James thoughtfully took a piece of the chocolate cake knowing I would finish it.

"Don't you eat sweets, James?" Mom asked.

"No, I eat few sweets. Arianna loves them though." James took a couple small bites. I swapped plates with him and started on his piece. When I finished, James held out his hand. "Would you like to dance?"

"I'd love to."

Like my dad, James liked to show off on the dance floor. He twirled me to an open spot then pulled me close. "You look ravishing, and you smell so good," he whispered in my ear. "Are the necklace and earrings from Patty?"

"Yes. Do you like them?"

"They are pretty."

We stayed on the dance floor for several songs. Carrie and Jake danced very close to one another. Mom and Dad danced over to us, and we switched partners. Then Dad twirled me back to James, and he retook Mom's hand and off they went again.

Grandma and Giovanni sat next to each other at the table. They talked, drank tea, and watched the dancing.

"Let's switch," Albert said as he and Patty approached. I took Albert's hand, and James took Patty's hand.

"Thanks for coming, Sis."

"I wouldn't miss your wedding."

"You seemed overwhelmed sometimes."

"There was a lot going on."

"It's ok," he laughed. "It overwhelmed me too sometimes."

I was surprised. "Then why did you have so many functions?"

"It's the bride's day. It's what Patty wanted."

I smiled at him. "You'll be a great husband."

"I hope so."

The song ended, and people clapped and returned to their seats. The DJ put on soft instrumental music while he took a short break. I sat down next to my grandmother.

"Would you like a Cape Codder?" James asked, and I nodded yes. "Would you like anything Luisa? Giovanni?"

"No, thank you, dear," Luisa said, and Giovanni shook his head no.

"Are you having fun, Grandma?" I asked her.

"Oh yes." She patted my hand. "How are you holding up?"

"So far ok."

"I like James, Arianna."

"I'm glad."

"You two act like you have known one another all your lives."

"We are extremely comfortable together. It was like that from the beginning."

She smiled and patted my hand again. "He's old fashioned in some ways, and I like that."

I thought for a moment. "Me too," I said very seriously. I had to admit that James' old-fashioned manners were something I enjoyed.

When James returned with drinks, I pulled him down to me and gave him a peck on the lips. "Thank you."

"You are welcome." James sat down and took my hand under the table. I drank down half of the drink in one go, and Grandma gave me a disapproving look. I shrugged my shoulders.

"Can I have the bridal party on the dance floor please," the DJ announced.

I gave a sigh, "Now what?"

"Gentlemen, now is your chance to dance with the beautiful bride and her lovely attendants. And ladies, you will have the opportunity to dance with the groom and his attendants."

I looked at James. He was taking money out of his wallet.

"It is one dollar a dance, and every time the song changes, it's time for a new partner."

I looked at Grandma. "I guess they forgot to tell me about this event too." I drank down the remainder of my Cape Codder, took a deep breath, put on a smile, and stepped onto the dance floor.

"Ok ladies and gentlemen, let's raise some money for the honeymoon!"

The music started to play, and James was right there with a wad of dollars in his hand. He danced with me through two song changes then Dad showed up when the song changed again. At the next change, I was surprised when Giovanni danced with me.

"Thank you for getting me invited to the wedding," he said quietly as we danced.

I smiled at him. "I thought it was important for you to be here to see Albert get married."

James danced with me after Giovanni, and I thought I might make it through the dancing, but then Redman showed up at the next song change.

He took my right hand and placed his left hand very lightly at my waist. "You are very beautiful, Arianna."

"Thank you."

"I hope you will come back to visit again soon. I would like the opportunity to get to know you better."

"Perhaps one day," I said casually. I did not want him to think I was in any way interested in him. He just smiled and danced. He was a gentleman.

He did not try to get too close to me. James danced with Carrie, and I noticed they both watched Redman and stayed close by.

"Thank you for the dance," Redman said when the song changed. He bowed slightly and left to dance with Patty.

James grabbed my hand and was once again my partner.

"How long is this going to go on?" I demanded.

"I knew he would dance with you."

"I did too. I've really had enough of these wedding obligations," I said sternly. "This is not my idea of a wedding. I know it's the bride's day, but I have had quite enough."

The song changed, and Redman was back. I smiled and took his dollar. He was more talkative this time. "I want you to know that if you ever need me, you have but to call."

"Thank you, I appreciate your willingness to help me."

"I will watch for those vampires and contact you if they return, or if I discover any additional information."

"Thank you." It was wise to have each other's contact information I told myself. However, I still did not trust him. I thought the song should have changed by this time, and I looked over at the DJ table where Janus was obviously keeping the song from changing until Redman was finished talking to me.

"I am very happy we met." He paused and looked at me. "I know in my heart that one day we will be together, Arianna. We are alike."

"You know that I am with James."

"Yes, I do. You are with him for now, but forever is a long time." He nodded to Janus, and the song changed. Redman kissed my hand, bowed, and left.

James was instantly at my side. "Are you ok?"

"I am now." I pulled him tight against me. Thankfully, that was the last dance. I gave the money I collected to Patty. I looked at my watch; it was after ten o'clock.

"Thank you everyone," the DJ boomed.

"Can I have all the single ladies on the dance floor, please." It was time for the bouquet toss. I joined Carrie who stood near the back of the group. "And the bride please stand here. Yes, your back to the girls. Ok ladies, are you ready for the bouquet toss?"

Most of the girls cheered and moved forward. Carrie looked as uneasy as I felt. "Aren't you going to the front Arianna?"

I shook my head no. "Carrie, I don't need to catch a bouquet."

"Do you think you and James will marry one day?"

I looked over at him. "James is the only one for me whether we formally marry or not."

"I understand." Carrie looked at the anxious women and inclined her head back. I nodded yes, and we edged to the back wall behind all the women.

The DJ played a drum roll. "Patty, when the music stops, toss the bouquet." The drum roll continued then stopped. Patty tossed it. The little clump of flowers hit the ceiling and several flowers fell from the main group. Girls scrambled to get a flower, but Brittany snagged what was left of the bouquet before it hit the floor. She screamed and jumped up and down with delight.

Next, Janus placed a chair at the center of the dance floor, and Albert led Patty to it. The DJ played strip tease music, and everyone hooted as Albert reached up Patty's gown and very slowly removed her garter. Patty blushed and laughed. "Ok single gentlemen take your places for the garter toss."

"James, aren't you going up?" Mom asked.

"I prefer not to thank you."

But Albert thought otherwise. "Come on James, you too." James looked to me for help, but I gave a little smile and waved, so he took his place in the back. The drum roll started and stopped. Albert tossed the garter, and Connor caught it. James looked relieved as he came back to the table.

"Now, Brittany, sit right here." The DJ pointed to the chair on the dance floor. "Connor, you can put the garter on Brittany. Let's see how far he gets folks." The strip tease music played again. Connor slowly moved the garter over Brittany's foot and up her leg. They both looked uncomfortable. Finally, about mid-thigh, Brittany stopped him, and he slid the garter off her leg. "Give them a big round of applause everyone." Connor took Brittany's hand, she stood up, and they bowed to the cheering audience.

"Albert took the microphone. "Thank you everyone for coming to our wedding. We appreciate having you all here as we begin our life as husband and wife."

"Thank you, everyone." Patty said into the microphone. "It's an hour until midnight. So, let's party and ring in the New Year together," she hooted.

"Well, we made it. The wedding is officially over." I let out a thankful sigh.

"Arianna, are you going to change?" Carrie called as she walked toward the ladies' room.

"I'll be right there." I walked over to James who held up my bag. "Thanks." I took the bag and hurried off to join Carrie.

Chapter XXIII
The Question

James

The mood in the room was light, and the DJ played lively dance music. Arianna came out of the ladies' room and walked to the table. My mouth fell open. Her dress was made of tight fitting, shimmery white and silver sequined material that picked up the colors of the strobe light. The colors danced in patterns and glistened off the sequins. It was incredibly short, and she had on platform black stilettos. I rose and went to meet her.

"What do you think?" she asked.

I could only nod my approval. I was very thankful that Redman left.

"I'm glad you like it. Shall we dance?" She led me to the dance floor. In those stilettos, we looked nearly eye to eye.

I pulled her close even though it was a fairly fast song. "You are gorgeous," I gushed. She leaned toward me and kissed me.

A short while later, Patty and Albert rejoined the party. I kept a tight hold of Arianna's hand as we walked over to talk to them.

"Wow! Baby Sis, you look good in that dress."

"Thanks Albert."

"Would you ladies like drinks?" I asked.

"Yes, thank you," they replied.

"I'll help you, James," Albert called as he caught up to me. "Wow, Arianna sure has changed." He shook his head.

"Changed?"

"Well, she was a kid when I went to college. I haven't seen her much since then."

"Ah, yes. She said you two rarely see each other."

"Can you blame me?" He picked up two glasses of champagne. "Dad is intense. You see how he is with Arianna."

"Still, they are your family."

"True, but family looks better from a couple thousand miles away." He grinned and headed back to the ladies.

I ordered two Cape Codders at the bar then walked back to Arianna. I handed one of the drinks to her.

"Thank you." She smiled and took my hand.

"I'm so glad you were a bridesmaid, Arianna," Patty said. "Thank you."

"Thank you for asking me."

We chatted while we watched people dancing and sipped at our drinks.

"So, Sis, how are things going with Dad?" Albert gave a little chuckle. "Has he given you any more advice? I'll bet he isn't happy."

Arianna shrugged her shoulders and drank down the remainder of her drink. "Oh, a slow song. Ready to dance again, James?"

I finished my drink, took her glass, and set both on a nearby table. "Let's go."

I circled my arms around her waist, and Arianna slid her hands inside my jacket. I felt her fingernails through my shirt as she moved her hands around on my back. "I will be glad when we leave this crazy town," she whispered.

The next song had a faster beat, but Arianna pulled me to her and kept dancing slowly. She closed her eyes and placed her head on my shoulder as we danced. I kissed her head and resented that I could not close my eyes and relish this moment, but we were in hostile territory, and I had to remain aware of my surroundings. I looked over at Giovanni. He sat up straight and tense in his chair. His eyes continuously moved around the room.

"It's five minutes until Midnight. Everyone, grab a party hat and horn." The DJ tooted his party horn into the microphone.

Arianna took my hand and led me to the table. "Here Grandma." She handed her grandmother a hat and horn. "Giovanni?" He took the items she offered him and put on the hat.

"This is fun. I haven't been out for New Year's Eve in years." Luisa tooted her horn a couple times.

"Last year was the first time I celebrated New Year's Eve in many years," Giovanni added.

The waiter came by, and Arianna and I took glasses of champagne for everyone.

John and Felicia joined us. "It's almost time!" Felicia giggled a bit too loudly.

"I think she's had too much to drink," Arianna whispered.

"Are we ready to count down?" The DJ asked.

"Yes," came the response from the crowd.

"Oh, come on. You can do better than that. I said, are you ready to count down!"

"Yes!!" This time the response was much more enthusiastic.

"Ok everyone. Here we go! 10, 9, 8, 7, 6, 5, 4, 3, 2, 1 – Happy New Year!" The music played, and I didn't care that we were in public or that her parents were there. I pulled Arianna into a tight embrace and gave her a long, deep, passionate kiss.

When I started to step back, she pulled me toward her. "Happy New Year, James." She wrapped her arms around my neck and kissed me back just as passionately.

When Arianna stepped back and wished her parents Happy New Year, I noticed Luisa smiling at me, and her eyes glistened with happy tears. I leaned down and kissed her cheek. "Happy New Year, Luisa."

"The same to you, dear."

It was nearly 2:00 am when the party broke up. When we arrived at the cabins, Giovanni slowly got out of the car. He looked tired. "Good night, Giovanni," Arianna and I said together.

"Good night." He gave a little wave as he opened his cabin door and went inside.

Arianna wrapped her arms around my neck. "It was a beautiful wedding, wasn't it?"

"It was. Are you happy?"

"Very." She kissed me, and I moved her toward our cabin.

I opened the door, and we went inside. She took her coat off, and what little moonlight came in through the window shimmered off her sequined dress. "Arianna, I want to ask you something."

She turned toward me. "Yes?"

I reached my right hand into my pocket and pulled out a tiny box. Her eyes widened, and she stared at it in my hand. I opened it to reveal a marquise cut, two karat diamond ring in a gold setting.

"Ah," she gasped.

I went the traditional route and got down on one knee. "Arianna, will you marry me?"

"Yes!" She did not hesitate at all. Happy tears ran down her cheeks as I put the ring on her finger and kissed her.

"This is such a surprise." She wrapped her arms around my neck. Between kisses she looked at the ring on her finger. "The ring is gorgeous."

"I'm glad you like it." I ran a hand down her hair and kissed her again and again.

She held up her hand and looked at the ring again. "It really is so beautiful."

I never felt happier. Arianna said yes. It was definitely the best night of my life.

Eventually, I took off my jacket and tie and unzippered Arianna's dress and helped her out of it. She unbuttoned my shirt and took it off. "James. Are you going to make passionate love to me all night?" she whispered seductively in my ear. She ran her fingers through my hair then brought her mouth up to mine.

"Oh yes." I kissed my way down her neck. "I love you."

"I love you."

*****

Just as the sky began to lighten, Arianna slipped out of bed. She put on sweatpants and a sweatshirt, slipped her feet into her boots, and went outside. I went to the door and watched. She put on the arm guards and put the faux leather patch on her shoulder. The red-tailed hawk flew down to her and landed on her shoulder. Arianna walked into the forest. Giovanni opened his door and sat down on the chair. Since he was outside, I quickly dressed and joined him.

"She isn't far," he said as I walked over to where he sat.

I heard her walking on the snow, so I made my way toward her. I looked up at the soft sound of wings and saw the great horned owl fly off her arm and up onto a tree branch to roost. Remarkably the hawk remained on her shoulder.

Arianna slipped her arm around my waist. "What a beautiful day." She looked up at the brightening sky. "I noticed that the sun feels more intense here."

"The air is cleaner."

We strolled back to the cabins.

"Hi Giovanni," she called as we approached him. "James and I have news. We are engaged." She held her hand out and showed him the ring.

Giovanni actually smiled. He stood up and shook my hand. "Congratulations." He turned to Arianna and hugged her. "I am very happy for you both."

"Thank you," we replied.

"Well, I guess we better pack," Arianna took off the arm guards. "After breakfast, of course. I'm starving," she added. Giovanni and I shook our heads.

"Actually, I am already packed, and I've also had breakfast." Giovanni waved as he went back inside his cabin and closed the door.

Arianna shrugged. "Well, I'm starving." We went inside. The hawk hopped onto the back of the chair and watched as she put a kettle of water on for tea and grabbed a cereal bar. She tossed him a piece which he gobbled down. We had plenty of time to get ready to leave. Brunch was scheduled for one o'clock and our flight was very late in the evening. Arianna hummed happily while she made breakfast.

I got in the shower and let the water flow over me. We just needed to get through the day, and we would be on our way home. As the water ran over me, I relaxed my shoulders. I carried the engagement ring for weeks. I did not plan to propose to Arianna last night, but everything seemed perfect, and I did not want to wait any longer. I shampooed my hair, rinsed, and got out of the shower.

The smell of bacon and eggs wafted in as I opened the door. "It smells good."

Arianna sat at the small table. The hawk still sat on the chair next to her. She typed with her right hand and ate with her left. "It's delicious." She took another bite of egg and followed it with a bite of toast. "We had 4 eggs left, so I figured I would eat them." She held out a piece of bacon for the hawk, and he gobbled it down.

I dressed then put my suitcase on the bed and packed my clothes. I looked at the pile of bags by the side of the bed. Arianna had a lot of packing to do. "I'll get your dress and shoes from the car, so you can pack them." She nodded and continued eating and typing. I brought everything in from the car and then sat down with my laptop. Arianna was still typing one handed. "Anything interesting in email?" I asked.

"Caroline and the kids are good. I am working on my book. I want to get some ideas down."

"I know the feeling."

She clicked save and closed her laptop. She stood up, kissed me, and pet the hawk then washed the plate and frying pan and set them on the rack to dry. "I'm going to shower and then pack."

"Ok." I had a scene in my mind, and I was so engrossed in writing that I barely noticed when Arianna came out of the bathroom. She kissed my cheek as she walked by me and quietly started to pack.

Sometime later, I stopped typing and looked up. Amazingly, Arianna fit everything in the suitcases. The bridesmaid gown was in a garment bag with her sequined dress. I looked at my watch, it was almost noon.

"I will miss my hawk, but I'm glad we are heading home today," Arianna said with a sigh. "I can't wait to put a lot of distance between us and this weird town."

"Me too." I closed my laptop.

She put her laptop and cord in her carry-on bag. "I need a vacation after this week." Her phone rang. She rolled her eyes. "My mother."

Fortunately, there was no crisis. After talking to her mother, Arianna bent down, and the hawk hopped onto her shoulder. She went outside with him. She stroked his body. I could tell she was communicating with the bird. She lifted her arm, and he hopped on it. I joined her, and Arianna continued to pet his head as we walked into the forest.

I chuckled. "He's a pet."

"He really is. I wish I could take him home."

When the bird took flight, Arianna watched him as he flew off. She let out a sad sigh. I took her hand, and we walked back to the cabin.

"I'll load the car."

Giovanni sat outside his cabin, and when I opened the trunk, he brought over his suitcase and carry-on bag. Once everything was loaded in the car, we did a last check of the cabins to be certain we packed everything. We stopped at the main house and returned the keys then drove to the brunch.

"Last party for this trip." Arianna checked her hair in the mirror. "I hope I don't have to sit too close to Janus. He has such a sickeningly sweet scent."

"Humm, I noticed," Giovanni grunted from the back.

"He does?" I asked.

"All vampires smell sweet." Arianna flipped up the visor.

"Do I smell sweet to you?"

"Yes, but in a unique way. I love your scent."

"I love yours too." I put my hand on her leg. "But Janus smells different?"

"Oh, yes. It is quite strong. That's why Carrie and I try to sit far away from him."

Giovanni sat upright. "Carrie finds Janus' scent sweet?"

"Yes. Why? Don't vampires smell sweet to humans?" Arianna asked me.

I shrugged, "I always thought our scent was appealing to humans. It's supposed to be part of what attracts them to us."

"It is," Giovanni said roughly. "Humans find a vampire's scent appealing."

"How do we smell to humans, Giovanni?"

"We have a different scent, but hunters smell basically like other humans. Sort of neutral."

"Then why does Carrie find Janus' scent sweet?" He did not respond. "Well?" Arianna asked impatiently. I saw Giovanni glance at me.

"Giovanni, do you need to talk to Arianna alone?"

"No. No, it's not necessary." He waved his hand dismissively. "Carrie might have the hunter gene."

"Really!" Arianna and I exclaimed almost at once.

Giovanni continued, "Yes, that was one way we identified people with the gene. Vampires smell overly sweet to them." Giovanni looked directly at me. "No one must know this. It is a secret we have kept to protect people with the gene. I trust you, James." He emphasized each word.

"Giovanni, I will never tell anyone. You can trust me. Remember, Hale and I worked for years trying to figure out who was killing potential hunters."

"I know," he mumbled.

"So, Carrie can become a hunter?" Arianna shook her head, "Wow!"

"It isn't completely full proof, but yes, she likely has the gene. How old is she?"

"I'm not sure. She's at least twenty-one. She came to the club and had an ID." Arianna paused, "Giovanni, why hasn't Redman turned her?"

"Perhaps he doesn't know about the scent. He wasn't properly trained, and he is somewhat isolated up here."

"Why didn't you tell me about it?" She sounded annoyed.

"Because you didn't want formal training, and, I didn't think to tell you," he snapped back.

"Is there a training manual for hunters? Really, no one tells me the things I need to know."

"No," Giovanni grunted. "Ours is an oral tradition."

"The problem with an oral tradition is things get forgotten and changed." Arianna smirked. "That's why I'm writing a book." She looked back at Giovanni. "So, what do we do?"

"I'm not sure. She should be turned if she carries the gene. We have so few hunters."

"Only if she consents." Arianna's voice was very firm.

"We need more hunters."

"No!" Arianna practically shouted. "She must be given the choice."

For once, Giovanni realized he would get nowhere with her. He grunted and sat back. "Well, we need a plan because today is not the day to turn her. However, she must not tell anyone about the vampire's sweet scent. Redman may know, or he may figure it out. Then she won't be given a choice. We also need to know her exact age."

"I'll find out her birth date, and I will make sure she doesn't tell anyone about the scent," Arianna said confidently. While she was still human, Carrie could be compelled. I knew Arianna planned to compel her. Giovanni knew it too, but he said nothing.

Suddenly, Arianna gasped and sat up straight. "Oh my god!"

"What?!" Giovanni and I exclaimed in unison.

"Jack has the gene."

"Jack? Caroline's son?" I asked.

"Yes. When we visited, I asked him why he was so mean to you. He said because you smell funny. I said to him, 'Don't you like James' cologne?' Jack said it was the other smell. Jack told me, 'He smells too sweet. I get a headache.' Jack must have the gene."

"Great, eternity with Jack," I said out loud without meaning to do so.

"James, he's a child!" Arianna gave me a stern look.

"I'm sorry. Yes, of course, he's just a child." Arianna gave a little huff, but she smiled at me. We arrived at the restaurant, and I parked the car. Arianna saw her parents and waved. She got out of the car and ran toward them.

Giovanni stayed back. "The kid is that bad?"

I shrugged. "As you heard, he doesn't like me. You will have to judge for yourself when you meet him."

Chapter XXIV
Leaving Montana

Arianna

"Hi, Mom," I called. I gave her a hug, and together we walked into the restaurant. James and Giovanni were right behind us. Once inside, I took James' hand and led him over to the table.

"You look very perky today, Arianna," Mom said.

I looked around. "No head table?"

"Not today," Mom waved to a couple of chairs. "It's just family, the wedding party, and a few close friends, so you can sit with us."

"Thank god." I pulled out a chair next to Grandma and sat down. James sat next to me, and Giovanni sat across from him.

I put my hands on the table and moved my fingers.

"That is a pretty…" Mom stopped. "Is that an engagement ring?!"

I smiled. "Yes. James asked me to marry him last night, and I said yes."

Dad and Mom got up and came over to us to offer congratulations. Grandma whispered congratulations and kissed me. She and Mom examined the ring on my finger. People around us realized what was happening. Carrie and the other girls rushed over to see the ring too.

Grandma called James to her. "You have made me so happy." She kissed his cheek. "So happy. I know you will love her and protect her." She was crying, and I squeezed her hand.

Albert came over and hit James on the back. "Wow, why didn't you tell us?"

"I didn't really plan it. I carried the ring for weeks. I wanted it to be a surprise."

"Well, it's a surprise," he laughed. "Congratulations, she's a great girl."

Dad did not look as excited as everyone else. When the crowd around me finally dispersed, he pulled up a chair and sat next to me. "I haven't had much time to talk to you, Arianna. I hope you are making the right decision. Taking another semester off may not be advisable."

"Well, I will be getting ready for my Fall classes. Teaching online is not that different from teaching in a traditional classroom. I am using the same book and power points I used in previous classes, but I will make some revisions." I paused and looked at him. I knew he was just concerned about me, but I was happy, and I wanted him to be happy for me. "Plus, I will be on campus going to meetings and working with other faculty members on new department wide course outcomes."

Dad made a face. "But online classes. I don't know."

"Dad, online classes are the wave of the future. This is a terrific opportunity that will help my career."

"Are you applying elsewhere? Salem College is a small school. I think you should look for a position at a larger school in Boston. The commute would not be bad. You can take the train in." He leaned back in his chair, but he did not look comfortable or relaxed.

"Teaching at a small school is extremely rewarding. You can really get to know the students. But I have several job agents set up online, and I will be applying when open positions are posted," I added quickly.

Dad still did not look happy.

Fortunately, some of the other bridesmaids were already walking around chatting with people, and I needed to get away. "I guess I should mingle a bit and help out." I squeezed James' hand and headed off toward

Carrie. I also needed to get her alone to compel her. Giovanni did not object, but of course it was to protect Carrie. She needed to be given the option of being turned at some point. If she decided no, I would compel her again, so she would have no memory of the choice.

"Wow, what a week." Carry sighed heavily.

I nodded my agreement. "It sure has been a busy week."

"It's too bad you didn't have a lot of time to sight see or ski."

"I did see the Northern Lights, and they were breath taking."

"You'll just have to come back and visit."

Secretly, I hated the thought of coming back to this town, but I smiled and nodded yes. Brittany and Janus came out of the kitchen. Janus carried a box of cupcakes. Tom and Jake followed, each carrying a box. Carrie and I placed a cupcake tree on the round table. Janus opened his box, and Carrie, Brittany, and I began setting cupcakes on the multileveled display.

"Should we make one level chocolate, one lemon, or mix them up?" Brittany asked.

"I think separate them, so people won't have to move cupcakes to get what they want," Carrie suggested as she placed a few cupcakes on a level.

"I agree." Brittany moved cupcakes around, and we continued loading the display. There were lemon cupcakes with bright pink frosting and edible glitter, and chocolate fudge cupcakes with chocolate frosting and sprinkled with mini chocolate chips. We loaded the top tier with half lemon cupcakes and half chocolate cupcakes.

"They look delicious," Carrie remarked as we put the final touches on the display.

"Oh look!" Tom licked his lips, "we have extra cupcakes." His eyes sparkled as he reached for one, but Brittany slapped his hand.

"You can have one in a few minutes, Tom. Put the extras on the table around the display," she said with a huff. Janus smoothed the tablecloth, and Brittany stashed the boxes out of sight under the table.

"Do you want to sit with us," I asked Carrie.

"Definitely."

We walked back to the table. I sat down next to James, and Carrie sat across from me. Jake sat on one side of her, and Giovanni sat on her other side. The restaurant staff came into the room carrying trays of food. They set them out on the buffet table and lit the sterno cans under the hot food.

Patty's parents stood up, and Patty and Albert joined them. "Thank you again everyone for sharing this special time with our family. Safe travels to all who are heading home, and please visit us again soon."

"Thank you," Patty and Albert said together, and everyone clapped.

They started the buffet line, and the rest of us stood and got into line. I was starved. I filled my plate and made suggestions to James.

"Would you like a drink, Arianna?" James asked when we returned to the table.

"Yes, honey. Thank you."

"Carrie, can I get you a drink?"

"No thank you, James. I'll just have water." Carrie poured herself a glass of water from the pitcher on the table, and she started cutting up a piece of chicken. "The food is delicious," she mumbled between bites. I nodded yes because my mouth was full. "I'm always starving." Carrie took another bite. "I don't gain weight, so I must have a fast metabolism," she chuckled. Giovanni gave me a long look.

James returned with drinks and sat down. He slid his plate closer to me.

"I don't know about anyone else, but I am exhausted." Mom picked at her food as she always did. She looked at me because I was eating so much.

She believed women should eat lightly when out. I guess it was something her generation thought appropriate. I continued eating.

"I'll be glad to get home," Grandma rubbed her hands together. "I don't think I ever warmed up." She took another drink of hot coffee.

"When are you leaving, Dad?" I asked between bites.

"Early, 4:00 am. The flight leaves at 8:40."

"Wow, that's early." I looked at my mother who made a face.

James leaned over and whispered, "Giovanni thinks it's best if we all stay together. Let's see if we can get them to come to the airport with us."

I nodded slightly. "Why don't you come to the airport with us? We're going tonight, and this way you won't have to get up so early in the morning." I knew Dad would not like paying for two hotel rooms, but he also did not like getting up that early and driving in the dark.

"I don't know." He looked at Mom and Grandma. "Can we pack up and leave later this afternoon?"

"I'm already packed," Grandma was clearly ready to get back to the warmth of Florida.

"I'm mostly packed," Mom added. "I would rather go to the airport this afternoon than in the morning, John."

Dad nodded his head. "That is a good idea. We'll follow you to the airport," Dad said, and I heard James's groan. He liked to drive fast. "When does your flight leave?"

"At 1:00 am. We're flying during the night and straight to JFK," I told him.

"I can call and get you a room at the airport hotel, John," James offered.

"Thank you, James. The three of you can stay in our room until you have to check in," Dad added.

James went outside to make the call. Giovanni stood up and went outside to join him. He was incredibly nervous which made James and I nervous.

Carrie moved into James' seat. "I really liked getting to know you, Arianna."

"I enjoyed getting to know you too, Carrie." It was true. I liked Carrie even before I knew she might be a hunter.

"It looks like you are heading home just in time. Heavy snow is forecast later this week. You wouldn't want to be snowed in."

"No, that would not be good. It's been a nice holiday, but I am anxious to return home."

"You have my email and my phone number, let's keep in touch, Arianna."

"Absolutely, Carrie." We hugged. I looked around. Most people were still eating. Now might be an opportunity to get Carrie alone. "I need to use the ladies' room," I whispered.

Carrie nodded. "Me too."

We went in and there was a lady washing her hands. I washed mine as well, and when she left, I locked the door. I ducked into a stall and exited when I heard Carrie washing her hands. As I talked to her, I looked intently into her eyes and compelled her. First, I asked her several questions, and then I told her not to reveal anything about vampires smelling sweet. I added that if strange vampires came to town, she should contact me immediately. I hoped it was enough to keep her safe until we could talk to her about the possibilities. I unlocked the door.

"I want at least one each of those cupcakes," I said as I led her out of the bathroom.

"Oh, oh, yeah, me too. They look delicious."

We loaded cupcakes on two small plates and went back to the table. Giovanni sat next to Grandma, and they were deep in conversation. James stood up and held my chair as I approached. He also had a fresh drink waiting for me, and I needed one.

"They are all set with a hotel at the airport." James took a long drink. I leaned back into him and ate one of the cupcakes.

"When do you think you two will get married?" Mom asked.

I looked at James. "I'm not sure. When were you thinking, James?"

"I'll marry you today. I love you."

"I love you too." We kissed.

Albert pulled up a chair and sat down. "I hope you guys had a fun time."

"We did," I said.

"Yes, we did." James shook his hand.

"Are you all packed for the honeymoon?" I leaned back into James a little more, and he brought his arm around my waist.

"All packed and ready to sit on a warm and sunny beach." We all laughed. He looked at James and me for a long, quiet moment. "When do you plan on getting married?"

I stiffened a little. It was what I feared. My family was going to start pressuring me. James rubbed my back lightly. I took a deep breath and smiled. "We haven't thought about a date yet. I'm just enjoying being engaged."

"Ok." Albert raised his eyebrows. "Let us know."

"We will."

Patty came over and sat on Albert's lap. "I'm so excited for you, Arianna. Let me know if you need any advice or any help with the wedding planning."

"Thanks, Patty."

"Oh, people are getting their coats. We need to say goodbye to them, Albert." She pulled him up. "We'll be back."

I put my head on James' shoulder. "Wedding planning. I don't think so. I'm thinking the two of us on a Caribbean Island."

"Don't you dare," Grandma said sharply. I sat up and looked at her. "James, don't you allow it. She cannot deprive me of a wedding."

James laughed. "Luisa, I think she's kidding." He looked at me and smiled, but it faded when he saw my face. "You are kidding, right?" I rolled my eyes. "We better give her a little time, Luisa. It's been a tough week."

The remainder of the brunch went well. We said our goodbyes, and then we went to Mom and Dad's hotel to help them pack. Grandma was not kidding; she was entirely packed and ready to go home. James and I went outside to load the bags in the car. "Arianna, do you want to drive with your parents to the airport? It will give you time alone with them."

"I think I will."

"Here's the last bag," Dad called from the doorway.

I went to get it from him. "Dad, I'm going to ride to the airport in your car."

"Good. You can sit up front with me."

We warmed up the cars and settled in for the ride. "Arianna, when will you start to attend meetings at the college?" Dad asked as soon as we were underway.

"I volunteered to help at the welcome desk, and there is a department meeting the first week of classes," I informed my father. He grunted.

"And what is James doing this semester?" Mom politely inquired.

"He is revising and publishing his novel."

"He doesn't work at all?" Mom questioned.

"He has money saved. He will be getting an advance too. Our living expenses are minimal, just utilities and food."

"What about taxes?" Dad glanced over at me.

"There is a trust fund set up for the taxes and maintenance of the house." I felt uncomfortable telling them so much, but James emphasized that it was ok to tell them about his finances to ease their minds.

Dad grunted again.

"She's an intelligent woman, and James is a mature and intelligent man. I am quite certain they can manage their finances." Grandma was stern, and her tone ended that conversation. Dad grunted again but did not ask more questions.

There were a few minutes of silence, and then Mom asked the question I dreaded. "Arianna, should we send out engagement announcements? Do you have a date in mind?"

I took a deep breath and gathered my thoughts. "The engagement was a complete surprise to me and only happened last night, so we do not have a date in mind."

"What about announcements?"

"I think we can wait on sending out announcements. James and I may wait a year or two before getting married." Now, Mom grunted.

"There is no rush, Felicia. There is plenty of time, and there's nothing wrong with a long engagement," Dad told her. I was not entirely surprised that Dad thought there was no rush.

"Well, don't wait too long," Grandma piped in. "I'm not going to be around forever."

"You'll be with us for a while, Grandma."

"I hope so," she laughed.

We were all quiet for a few moments. I began to rethink driving with them, but I knew it was best. We had very little time alone on the trip with the wedding preparations and pre-wedding functions.

Finally, Mom spoke. "Since you are getting married, would you like us to send your things that are in your room at our house to Salem?"

"Oh," I replied. I did not have many items at my parent's house in California, but there were a few pieces of furniture I had since I was a child. I had clothes there, but nothing I had to have, and there were some small decorative items. "I guess, yeah. I would like the wardrobe and toy box."

"Good. I will pack up those two, and we can ship them to you."

"Thanks."

"You know, the wardrobe will fit nicely in the spare room Giovanni stayed in."

"I have some family linens I would like to send to Arianna for her new home, Felicia. You can take them and pack them with the items you send to her."

"Of course," my mother replied.

"Thank you, both." I turned in my seat and smiled at my mother and grandmother. The reality of marriage and not returning to my parent's house was sobering. Truthfully, I never moved into the California house. I was already on my own in college when they moved there, but I knew there was a room in the house for me. Now the furniture and the linens would be part of James and my home in Salem.

With those conversations out of the way, the rest of the trip was very pleasant. We were all laughing by the time we pulled into the car rental return. James, Giovanni, and I helped them get settled into their hotel room, and then we all went to the airport restaurant for a nice relaxing dinner. Dad did not ask any more questions about my teaching, and thankfully, there was no mention of a wedding.

*****

Later that evening, we said our cheerful, but tearful, goodbyes.

"We'll call you when we get to Florida," Dad said.

"Ok, Dad. Are you all set for the morning flight?"

"I have a wakeup call at 5:30. We'll have a quick breakfast right at 6:00 and the porter will bring us to the check in counter at 6:30."

I kissed him. "I love you."

"I love you too. I'll call you."

"Love you, Mom."

"Arianna." She hugged me close. "Be careful and call me if you need anything."

"I will."

I walked over to Grandma and waited for her to release James from a tight hug. "Oh, I am so happy for you both." She took my hand, and I leaned down and hugged her.

"I love you, Grandma."

"Oh, baby, I love you too. Come visit me."

"We will."

"You two take care of one another," she said, and I nodded and wiped my eyes.

Giovanni picked up his bags, and James took our big bags. I grabbed our carry-ons. "Well, this is a first," I laughed. "My luggage is lighter going home than going out. Bye, love you."

The three of us walked rather quickly to the check in counter. Giovanni went first. He put his bag on the conveyor belt then stepped aside. James put our checked bags on the conveyor belt and turned to answer the attendant's questions. With our boarding passes in hand, we walked to the security check point. We put our bags through the x-ray and went through the scanners. Once we gathered our belongings again, we walked to the gate.

Giovanni sat down and looked relieved. "I enjoyed talking with Luisa. She has given me insight into Giuseppe."

"This was a good trip, overall." I sat down to wait. I did not feel comfortable walking around the terminal. I shook my head. "But we still don't have the answers?"

"No, Arianna, we have more questions."

James sat down next to me and took out his tablet to read. I took out my tablet. "Now we have Carrie to deal with too." I planned to email Carrie often to make certain she was ok.

Giovanni nodded. "Yes, but that can wait. All I know is, I will be happy when we touch down in New York."

"Me too," I sighed.

James looked up from his tablet. "Me three."

Chapter XXV
Discussions

James

On the flight back, Giovanni actually closed his eyes and slept. I was concerned about him. He looked older. I stroked Arianna's hair back from her face. Her head rested on my shoulder, and she was fast asleep. The two of them still had difficulties communicating, but she needed his guidance. Neither would admit it, but they were alike in many ways. I felt the trip brought them closer. They woke up when the flight attendants came by with beverages.

"I need a big cup of tea not this little thing," Arianna complained. She finished the tea, put her headphones on, and leaned back.

"James, are you two staying in New York or going straight back to Salem?" Giovanni asked.

"We were planning to go back tonight, but we can stay. There is much to discuss with Marcus and Marena."

"Good. I think we should tell Hale too." I nodded my agreement, and Giovanni leaned back and closed his eyes again.

We landed about an hour later and made the long walk to the baggage claim area. Giovanni looked tired, and I offered to carry his small carry-on bag, but he shook his head no and gave me a stern stare.

Marcus, Trina, and Marena were waiting in the baggage claim area. "Welcome back," Marcus said as we approached them.

I grasped his hand. "You don't know how good it is to be back."

Marena hugged Giovanni. "It's good to be back," he said quietly to her. She smiled. "Welcome home."

"Hi everyone," Arianna said cheerfully.

"Arianna let me see the ring!" Arianna held out her left hand. Trina gasped. "Oh, it is gorgeous!"

"Thank you!"

"Congratulations." Marcus shook my hand again.

Marena hugged us both. "I am so happy for you two. Should I ask? Is there a date?"

"Not yet," I quickly answered for us since Arianna looked uncomfortable again. "Marcus and I will get the bags." He and I walked over to the baggage claim area and waited.

Marcus glanced back at Giovanni, and I knew he thought that Giovanni did not look well. "We can all fit in my car, and I'll drive you over to the long-term lot," Marcus said as he took one of our bags off the belt. I grabbed the other two.

"Thanks, Marcus. Arianna and I will check in at the hotel, and we'll meet you at Marena's house."

"Sounds good. We should hunt tonight, James."

"We have a lot to discuss," I said as we walked back to the others.

We gathered around Marena's kitchen table late in the day. Arianna, Giovanni, and I recounted our trip to Montana. Marcus, Hale, Trina, and Marena listened and occasionally someone raised an eyebrow or sighed. Marcus was impressed with our grizzly bear encounter, and they all marveled at Arianna's ability to communicate with eagles.

Marena shook her head when Arianna told them the townspeople knew about vampires. "That is unimaginable. It violates the treaty that ended the last war."

"Exactly," Giovanni added. "That is a strange group up there. They seem to have their own rules; Redman's rules."

"Well, there are a number of disturbing issues," Hale said in a long drawl. "I am concerned that Jacob and Tony were up in Montana, and Tony was obviously getting information from Albert." Hale paced the room as was his habit when he was thinking. "Are you certain Redman will inform you if they return?"

"Definitely," Arianna replied without hesitation.

"Although, Redman is likely to kill them if they go back to the area since they are a threat to Arianna," I added.

"That would save us the trouble," Hale stated quite seriously.

"But it would not answer the questions." There was anxiety in Arianna's voice. "Maybe I should email Redman and remind him we want Jacob alive."

"I don't think it will matter, Arianna," Marcus added. "It sounds like this Redman has a mind of his own and does what he pleases."

We talked for several hours. Arianna looked at her watch. "I'm getting hungry. Giovanni, should I order dinner for us?"

"I have steaks," Marena replied.

"Thanks, Marena, but I really would like a pepperoni and sausage pizza and a chicken parmesan grinder. The pizza was lacking there." Arianna rolled her eyes.

Marena laughed, "No problem."

"Pizza sounds good but make my sub meatball." We were all a bit surprised that Giovanni agreed so easily. Going to the wedding and meeting his family seemed to have a positive effect on him.

"I'll be in touch, James. Let me know if there are any developments." Hale left mumbling to himself.

Trina got up and stretched. "I'll go with you to get the food, Arianna. You can tell me about the wedding."

"You aren't hunting with Marcus and James?" she asked.

"No, I hunted last night." Trina leaned closer to Arianna, "I want to hear everything about that wedding, and I'm sure the guys want to talk alone." They both laughed.

I gave Arianna the car keys. "I'll meet you here later." I kissed her, and Marcus and I headed out. We walked in silence to the edge of the forest. It was dark, so once we broke the tree line, we quickly ran deep into the forest. We came upon a herd of deer very quickly, so Marcus and I made quick work of feeding, and then we headed to our favorite spot in the forest. We leapt up onto the top of the large boulder, leaned back, and looked up at the stars.

"The Aurora Borealis was spectacular, Marcus. I never saw anything like it."

"I saw it a couple of times in Canada."

"The night sky was amazing. So many stars. It was one of the best parts of the trip." I smiled. "Of course, Arianna saying yes was the highlight of the trip for me."

We sat quietly looking up at the stars until finally I was ready to tell my friend about Redman. "He loves her, Marcus," I said flatly. "At least he thinks he does. He's biding his time."

Marcus shook his head. "I'm sure he wouldn't hesitate to have you killed."

"Not if the opportunity came up to kill me and keep his hands clean, but he won't risk alienating Arianna." I gave Marcus details on everything that happened. I knew he would keep the information to himself, and I needed to tell someone about my observations and fears. I began to feel better with every word.

"I don't know how you managed to keep so calm, James."

"Believe me, Marcus, it took every ounce of will that I have in me." I turned to look at him. "Another thing, Marcus, I haven't said this to anyone, but I need to tell someone. I have a feeling Giuseppe had something to do with Arianna becoming a hunter and being unmarked."

"But Arianna was so young when he left. If she had been bitten again."

"He took her to Italy when she was four. She doesn't really remember much about the trip. She does remember she was sick, but her mother denies it. Her parents said Giuseppe took her to New Jersey for two weeks, but her brother said they were gone six weeks to Italy. Giovanni is certain Albert's memory is the correct one, and the others were compelled."

"And you think he had a vampire bite her in Italy and make her a hunter?"

"It sounds crazy, but it is a plausible explanation. Remember, Giuseppe became a hunter at a very young age because he taunted a vampire and was bitten."

Marcus shook his head. "I see why you haven't told anyone, but I agree, it is a possibility." He was quiet and thoughtful for a few minutes. "I have to ask, how bad is Giovanni?"

I wasn't sure how much I should tell Marcus since Giovanni practically swore me to secrecy. "Well, he is quite old. His regeneration is slowing down."

"Marena was worried."

I looked at Marcus. "Really?"

"Yes. She was ready to fly out when he told her about Redman and his clan. She was terrified of a battle and Giovanni getting hurt. He assured her that Redman would not do anything to harm either of you because he would not risk angering Arianna." Marcus bobbed his head back and forth. "Honestly, I'm not sure if that made Marena more tense, or if it calmed her fears."

"Why didn't either of you tell me?"

Marcus shrugged his shoulders. "Marena said you had enough going on. She made me promise not to say anything until you returned."

"It will be impossible to keep Giovanni out of any battles."

Marcus nodded his head in agreement.

"I guess we will just have to look out for him."

"Does Arianna know?" Marcus asked.

I thought about it for a minute. Did she know? "No, Marcus. I don't think she realizes what is happening yet. Although, she did question him when he gathered bark for a tea." I sighed. "She was so busy with that wedding."

"I never knew weddings were so involved."

"Neither did we." I let out a nervous laugh. "I think it made Arianna more afraid to get married."

"But she said yes," Marcus laughed. "Besides, you two can elope."

"Oh no. No way. Her grandmother made me promise I would not agree to it. She wants to see Arianna walk down the aisle, and she said we better not wait too long."

Marcus made a face and shuddered. "I have a feeling Trina's family will be the same way."

"Are you getting engaged?"

"I have thought about it. Trina was very excited about you and Arianna getting engaged." He paused, tilted his head, and looked at me. "I've looked at rings," he admitted.

"So, weddings run in threes." I laughed.

"Yeah, I guess so," Marcus chuckled.

I looked up at the stars. I loved living in Salem, but it was nice to be back with my friend. It was late, so we headed back to town. Marena opened the door and let us in. Giovanni was in bed sleeping.

I looked around. "Where's Arianna and Trina?"

"After they ate, Giovanni was exhausted, so Trina went to the hotel with Arianna."

I glanced over at Giovanni. "How is he doing?"

Marena sighed and closed her eyes. "He won't admit it, but the trip was hard on him. He said he told you about his regeneration slowing down." I nodded. "I told him he needs to tell Arianna soon."

"I agree. We will stop by in the morning before we leave for Salem."

"Good. I'm glad you are all back safe, James." She took my hand and squeezed it.

"I am happy to be back. Good night."

Chapter XXVI
Home at Last

Arianna

We arrived back in Salem in the early afternoon.

"Let's stop at the grocery store before going home, James."

He turned into the parking lot and parked. I needed quite a few items since we had been away. An hour later, we pulled up to the house and brought everything inside. I put the perishables away, and we went upstairs to start unpacking.

"Come on in, Marie," James called down when we heard a knock on the door.

"James, I will be down in a few minutes." I wanted to give him time to talk to Marie alone.

"Ok, love. I will open a bottle of wine." He gave me a little kiss and went downstairs.

I hung up the garment bag in my closet, took off my shoes, and stepped into my fur lined slippers. I hung up most of my clothes and put my dirty laundry in the hamper. Then I brushed my hair and quickly checked my email before going downstairs. Marie and James were sitting at the kitchen table. "Hi, Marie."

"Hello, Arianna. It sounds like you two had an eventful trip." She stood up and hugged me. "Congratulations on your engagement. I am so happy for you both."

"Thank you. I was completely surprised." We sat down at the table, and James poured me a glass of wine. "What do you think about the situation in Montana, Marie?"

She thought for a few moments. She took a drink of wine. Finally, she answered. "I have never heard of anything like it. Humans knowing about vampires and accepting them as normal." She shook her head.

"James told you what Albert said about my great grandfather taking me to Italy for six weeks?"

"Yes. I wonder why he took you there. He had obviously been in this country for many years. He must have had a reason."

"And why leave Albert's memory intact? That is what I do not understand." I took a sip of wine. There were so many more questions.

"Hale believes Giuseppe had enemies, and he wanted them to believe that his planned fake death actually went wrong and killed him," James added.

"That makes a lot of sense." Marie was thoughtful again. "More investigation is needed."

"Yes, we plan to go to Italy soon," James informed Marie. "We need to get Giovanni a passport to make flying internationally easier."

"Meanwhile, we need to watch for Jacob, Tony, or anyone suspicious," I added.

James refilled our wine glasses.

"Here is a picture of Jacob, Marie." I handed her the picture that Redman gave me. It was much better than the one James took in the stairwell last year.

"I will pass this on to John, so he can alert the pack." She looked at me. "Unless you would like to tell them, Arianna."

I shook my head no.

Marie visited for a couple of hours. When she left, I made dinner for myself and then James and I took a bottle of wine and reclined on the sofa in front of the fireplace. "It is so good to be home." I leaned against him and stared into the fire.

He wrapped his arm around me. "It certainly is."

*****

I attended the start of the semester meetings at the college, and I brought in a few personal items to decorate my on-campus office. I planned to work on campus two days a week, most weeks.

"What are your plans today?" James asked as he dressed for his appointment with his agent.

I sat at the edge of the bed and brushed my hair. "I will go to the Historical society for a couple of hours and then go to campus. I am manning the welcome back table from noon until three o'clock."

James leaned over and kissed me. "Be careful."

"You too." Things were quiet. The wolves patrolled and saw no signs of strange vampires. I drove James to the train station and saw him off. I went back home and called Caroline while I packed a snack and drink for later. I told her James and I planned to visit in the next few weeks. I wanted to secretly ask little Jack some questions about James' scent, and I needed to make certain he told no one about it. I gathered up my bags and then went to the Historical Society. I still worked on Mr. Tanner's collection and had recently found the notice in the paper about James purchasing the building lot on Chestnut.

About eleven o'clock, I marked where I left off and put the boxes away. "I am heading out," I called to Pamela who waved as I passed by her.

I was hungry, so when I arrived on campus, I stopped at the cafeteria for a sandwich. I sat at a booth and looked around as I ate. It was strange not to be worried about classes and grades. In the fall, I was so thankful to have time off that I did not think about the new school year. But sitting here now, looking around, I wasn't sure how I felt. On one hand, it was nice to be moving into my career, but it was also sad because a new school year always brought so much promise. I was so happy to be finished with classes and the dissertation, but I missed it too.

Some students sat alone pouring over a textbook or a planner, and some were hanging out in groups and talking. I truly enjoyed the energy of a new semester. And as I sat and took in the scene around me, I thought that although I was not going to be taking classes, I was going to be on campus interacting with students and peers. I really was excited to be back on a campus.

When I walked to the welcome desk at noon, I was feeling better about life. There were six of us working. We handed out welcome bags to students and answered questions. I was talking to a student when I smelled a wolf. I turned and saw one of the young pack members. I smiled, "Susan, right?"

She hesitated and then approached me. "Yes, hello."

"Is this your first semester at Salem College?"

"Yes."

"Welcome." I handed her a bag.

"Thanks." She tentatively reached out and took the bag. "I didn't know you worked here."

"This is my first semester at the college. I will be teaching online classes in the Fall. What is your major, Susan?"

"General studies right now. I really would like to go into the medical field."

I nodded. "Good. Well, I hope to see you around campus."

"Thank you. I hope to see you too." She walked away, and I greeted another student.

After working, I did not feel like cooking, so I stopped at the grocery store on my way home. I had not even put one item in my basket when I saw Jason. "Hi, Arianna." He walked toward me.

"Hi, Jason."

"Susan said she saw you at the college today."

I looked at him. Susan probably called her father right after she talked to me. I should have expected it. "Yes, I did see her."

"She said you were very nice to her."

"Of course, I was nice to her. I am nice to all of you when I see you." I was offended that he would think I would be anything but nice. I had nothing against them. I started to tell him off, but someone called his name.

"Jason, there's a stranger in the area." I turned around and saw Trey coming toward us. "Oh, Arianna. Hello."

"What's going on," Jason asked.

"We picked up a strange scent. Come on. We need you."

Jason looked at me then at Trey. "We can't leave her here."

"I can take care of myself, Jason," I replied.

"Don't leave the store alone. Call James to meet you here."

"He's in Boston."

"Then call Marie."

"I'm coming with you." I put down the empty shopping basket.

Jason looked at me. "Does this mean you are assuming your role?"

"No. It means that I need to know who is here. I am not going to go home to wait for someone to come after me." I walked toward the exit, and Jason and Trey followed. "Where was this stranger?"

"Follow me." Trey walked very quickly to his pickup truck. "Get in."

The three of us got in, and Trey drove to an area close to Marie's house. We got out of the truck, and Trey howled. We heard a howl in reply. "Let's go," he said.

I watched in amazement as they stripped off their clothes and transformed into wolves right before my eyes. They quickly ran off. I was so startled by their transformation that I did not follow immediately. I heard another howl. I looked toward the sound and ran to catch up to them. We met up with another wolf, but I didn't know who it was. I couldn't communicate easily with them when they were in wolf form. They pawed at the ground and sniffed. I took a deep breath. It was a vampire scent, but I did not recognize it. We split up. Jason and I went in one direction, and Trey and the other wolf went in the opposite direction. We walked around for quite a while, and finally Jason found the scent again. He howled and took off. I followed him closely.

I searched for a hawk with my mind. I was not sure if I should tell them about my ability, but we needed help. We continued to follow the scent. The other two wolves joined us. Suddenly, the scent overwhelmed us. We stopped. The scent was everywhere. We spread out in a circle and nervously looked around. I heard a noise and looked up.

I screamed and tried to run as a vampire jumped out of a tree and landed right on top of me. We fell to the ground, and he bit me hard on the neck. I screamed in agony. Blood gushed out of the wound and onto the plants and ground. I was in so much pain my eyes were blurry, but I managed to grab him behind his head and throw him against a tree. The wolves were on top of him quickly, but he bit one of them and gouged the other. Jason leapt up and bit him. The vampire screamed and took off with Jason in pursuit.

Trey and what turned out to be Maxwell transformed back into human form. The three of us were bleeding badly. Trey was in the worst shape, and Maxwell put pressure on the wound. I rushed over to them. Suddenly, we smelled another vampire. We turned quickly ready to attack but then saw it was Marie.

"What happened?" She ran toward me.

"I'm fine. Help Trey."

Marie went to him and looked at the wound. She reached into her bag and drew out a clump of herbs. She applied them to his wound, and she chanted something. At first, Trey looked scared, but then he visibly relaxed.

"You will heal," Marie said to him. She took his hand and placed it over the herbs. "Hold this tight here until we can get it bandaged."

She applied herbs to the gouge marks on Maxwell's side, and again she chanted. They were healing already. "Are you ok, Arianna?"

"Yes. He bit me, but I can feel it healing." She looked at my neck and applied herbs. When she started to chant, I drew back. "What are you saying?"

"A healing spell," she replied. "It will help you heal quicker."

I nodded, and I was surprised when I immediately felt it working to help me heal.

Jason returned in human form. "He got away."

"Who was it?" Marie asked.

"The scent wasn't familiar," Jason replied. "Did you recognize him, Arianna?" I shook my head no.

"Let's get out of here," Marie said. Trey was very weak from the loss of blood, and Maxwell helped him up. "We will take him to my home."

"You go ahead," Jason said. "I want to take one more look around."

"I'll come with you, Jason."

"No! Arianna, go with Marie. I'm just going to make certain he is gone. I will be right behind you."

"Yes, Arianna, you need to come with me," Marie urged.

Reluctantly, I got on Trey's other side, and we helped him back to Marie's house.

Jason arrived a few minutes later with their clothes, and when Trey felt stronger, the three of them left to report to John.

I stayed with Marie until James returned. We had a cup of tea, and I felt much better.

James burst through the door. "Arianna, are you alright?" He pulled me close and looked at my neck. The bite was almost entirely healed.

"Yes, I am ok."

"I should not have left you."

"You cannot stay by my side day and night, James."

"Next time, you come to Boston with me."

"I don't think it was a coincidence that the vampire was here when James was out of town," Marie stated.

James looked at Marie. "You think they are watching us?"

"They must be, or they have someone in town reporting on your activities."

"They must be compelling someone we know, Arianna." James paused, "I should have known."

"There have been no strangers in the area until today. Who knew you were away?" Marie asked.

"Perhaps someone saw me get on the train," he suggested.

I shook my head. "I would bet it is one of the neighbors. They must have seen us leave this morning, and then they saw me return home alone."

"Yes, it must be one of them," James agreed.

I shuddered. "It's Kevin Caro all over again. This has to stop."

The doorbell rang. "That's Jason," I said. "We figured you would come straight here from the train station, so he is going to drive us home. John doesn't want us to walk."

James shook his head. "I should have picked up the car, but I was in a rush to see you, Arianna." He ran his hands up and down my arms. "I was so scared."

When Jason came in, James shook his hand. "Thank you for being with Arianna today."

"That's our job," Jason replied. "I'm sorry she was bitten. That vampire got the jump on us today, but it won't happen again."

"Let's go home, Arianna." James took my arm.

"My car is at the market."

"We'll get it later."

"Thank you for your help today, Marie."

She took my hand and James' hand. "John has increased patrols, but you two be careful."

"We will," we replied together.

On the drive home, we told Jason our suspicions about one of the neighbor's being compelled. "How do we figure out which one?" he asked. "It could be anyone."

"There are signs. We will have to watch and see if we can figure it out," James told him.

"Jason, would you like to come in and have a drink?" I asked.

"No thanks, not tonight. Dad and Sam are checking your house, and then we are going on patrol. He stopped the car in the driveway. Give me your car keys, Arianna. We will get your car and drop it off here." He held out his hand. I hesitated but gave him the key. I was grateful for the help, but I felt uneasy accepting the help.

John and Sam came around from the back of the house. "The house is clear," John announced. "There are vampire scents in the area, but that doesn't mean anything. Chestnut is a busy street and many people, and vampires, walk by."

James and I got out of the car. "Thank you." James shook each man's hand.

"Yes, thank you," I also shook their hands.

"Do not hesitate to call us if you see anyone," John replied, and he and Sam got in the car with Jason.

"Thanks again, Jason," I called. He nodded and backed the car down the driveway.

We went inside. James closed the door, flipped the lock, and pulled me into his arms. He held me tight. Suddenly, the weight of the day's events caught up to me, and I sunk into him. I could not stop the tears that ran down my cheeks. My arms were limp, and my legs felt heavy. James picked me up and carried me upstairs.

Chapter XXVII
Regrets

James

I intended to stay close to Arianna. We knew we were being watched, and until we found out who was reporting to Jacob, we had to be cautious. Marie and I planned to hunt together as a precaution, and Arianna accompanied us. I thought we might even get her to feed and strengthen her. The three of us stepped out of the car and started to make our way toward the stream. Arianna put on her arm guards. We heard a screech and looked up. A hawk circled overhead. The bird suddenly dove toward us. It slowed and grabbed onto Arianna's arm.

Marie took a couple steps back. "That was amazing," she whispered to me.

"It always is. You should have seen the eagles."

Arianna stroked the bird's head and looked into its eyes. The bird took flight and looked for game. We followed it, but suddenly Arianna stopped.

"What's wrong, Arianna?" I took a few deep breaths and searched for a scent. Marie assumed a defensive stance and looked around.

Arianna shook her head and squeezed her eyes shut. "Someone else is in my head." She shook her head from side to side, and suddenly, her eyes opened wide. "Someone else can see my vision."

"What? Who?" I asked.

"Jason!" She closed her eyes. The vision stopped. "He can see what I see."

"How is that possible."

"I don't know. Oh my god. I don't know." She started to panic, and I grabbed hold of her.

Marie and I both took a deep breath.

"What's wrong?" Arianna asked.

"Wolf," we said together.

I knew it had to be Jason, and anger welled up inside me. I let go of Arianna, and in a couple quick steps, I intercepted him. I grabbed him by the throat. "Explain!" I commanded. He shifted back into human form in my hand.

Jason struggled, but I had a firm hold of him. "I don't know what happened," he choked out. "Let me go."

I turned my head sharply. Another wolf arrived. He transformed into John. "What's going on? Let Jason go!" he demanded. Marie stepped in front of him and stopped him from advancing on me.

"That is what we are trying to discover." Marie glared at John. "James, let him go," she said forcefully. I reluctantly released Jason, and he fell hard to the ground.

"What happened?" John asked. "Jason, why did you take off?"

Jason stood up and looked at Arianna. "I don't know. I suddenly saw Arianna in the woods. The image filled my mind, and I followed it and found her." He shook his head. "What the hell was that?"

Arianna looked at me and then at Marie. "I guess you should tell him," I said.

She took a shaky breath. "I can see through some bird's eyes."

"How the hell is that possible?" Jason asked.

"It is a gift I have. But no one except James or Giovanni has ever been able to see my visions." Her voice was abnormally high. I walked to her and put my arm around her to try and calm her down.

"Giovanni believes he sees Arianna's visions because he is a blood relative," I informed them. I was not certain Giovanni wanted them to know he and Arianna were related, but the connection needed to be explained.

"You and Giovanni are related?" John asked Arianna. She nodded yes. "And you?" John glared at me.

"James and I are bonded," Arianna answered.

"You bonded with a vampire?!" John shouted.

His anger brought out Arianna's anger. She stepped forward. "Yes, I have," she said firmly. "And who I choose to bond with is none of your concern."

I looked at Arianna. "Did you bond with Jason?"

She turned and glared at me. "Absolutely not!" She was quite angry. "How could you think I would do that with anyone but you?!"

"Then how can he see?"

"I don't know, but I know I did not bond with him!" Arianna visibly shook she was so angry.

I was angry with myself. How could I think she would bond with someone else? I turned to Jason. "What did you do?!" I picked him up and threw him hard. He hit the ground with a thud. John advanced on me again, but Marie held him back. Arianna glared down at Jason waiting for an explanation.

"I wanted to bond with Arianna," he finally grudgingly admitted. Arianna stepped back and clutched her neck. "I drank your blood, Arianna."

"How?" she stammered.

"When you were injured."

"You did not!" Arianna scowled at him. "I would never allow you to do that!"

Now John moved toward his son. He picked him up off the ground and growled. "Explain. How did you drink her blood if she did not allow it?"

"I wanted to bond with her. When the vampire bit her, her blood spurted out everywhere. When she and the guys went to Marie's, I transformed back into a wolf, and licked the blood off the foliage." He looked down at the ground.

Arianna gasped. "That is so gross." She made a face, but then turned angry again. "And you had no right!"

Now John was so furious his hands were tightly fisted. "No, Jason, you had no right to do that without consent." His face was bright red and only inches from his son's face.

"How was I supposed to know she communicated with birds," he pleaded and looked at Arianna. "You would never have known, Arianna. I just wanted to be able to sense you more easily, so I could protect you. It's my job." He looked down at the ground.

"I don't need you to protect me!" she yelled at him.

"Very few people know about Arianna's ability," I said to John. "If the wrong people discover her ability, it can put her in grave danger. Command him not to reveal it to anyone."

John stared at me. "I don't like being told what to do by a vampire," he snarled.

"Then I will tell you," Arianna said loudly and firmly. "You must order Jason not to reveal my secret."

John looked at her for a few moments. Then he nodded. "As you wish." He looked at his son. "You heard her. You do not reveal her ability to anyone." As alpha, his order was binding.

"Arianna, I would never do anything to harm you. Your secret is safe with me," Jason pleaded, but she continued to glare at him.

"Let's go, Jason." John grabbed his son's arm and the two of them left.

I reached for Arianna, but she pushed my hand away. "I can't believe you asked if I shared blood with him."

"I'm sorry," I replied. "I feel terrible. I should never have thought for a moment that you would willingly give Jason, or anyone else, your blood." I tentatively took her hand. She did not pull it away. "I am truly sorry, Arianna. I was just so angry. I wasn't thinking." I squeezed her hand. "Please. Forgive me."

Her hand shook. "Now is not the time to discuss it." She pulled her hand away.

By this time, it was nearly dark. We had planned to be out of the forest by night fall, and we still had not fed.

Marie walked over to us. "Let's find game," she said softly, and we walked toward the stream.

Arianna said very little while we hunted. I apologized several times as we drove back to the house, but my words were met with an icy quiet stare. We walked inside. Arianna refused to feed with me, so she went to the kitchen to make dinner without saying a word to me.

I thought it best to leave her alone, so I went upstairs to shower. I let the water run over me for a long time. I knew I had to make it up to her. She was justifiably angry with me, and I was angry with myself. I regretted my words as soon as they left my mouth. Why would I ever think she would willingly bond with Jason? I shook my head. It felt like someone, first Redman and now Jason, was trying to undermine our relationship. I hated to admit it, but I was jealous and overprotective.

I hoped Arianna would join me in the shower, but she did not. I turned off the water. I dried off and opened the door into the bedroom hoping she was in our room, but she was not.

I dressed and went downstairs. All the lights were off. Arianna was not in the kitchen or the den. I looked down the hall and saw a light under the door to her office. The closed door. I thought about knocking, but I decided to give her some space, and I slowly went back upstairs. I went to my study and checked email then started to revise my manuscript. I gave the revisions I made thus far to my agent today, and I told her I would have the rest in a few weeks.

Marie called me about midnight. "How are you and Arianna doing?" she asked. I sighed and did not answer right away. "I guess she is still upset."

"Yes." I let out a long sad sigh.

"Have you tried to talk to her?'

"I apologized again on the way home, but she won't speak to me, and she is now in her office with the door closed."

Marie was quiet for a few moments. "She loves you, James. She will come around. Give her time."

"Thanks, Marie. Good night."

Just before two am, I quietly went downstairs. The light was off in Arianna's office, but the door was still closed. I carefully put my ear to the door, and I heard Arianna's rhythmic breathing. "Good night. I love you," I whispered, and I went back upstairs.

*****

The next morning, I came out of my study when I heard Arianna come upstairs. "Good morning."

She looked at me. "Good morning." She went in the bedroom. I followed her but stayed just inside the door. She went to her closet and took out clothes. "I am going to shower and go to the college this morning. I have a lot to do today."

"Ok. Should I drive you?"

"No. I am certain no one is going to attack me between here and the school."

I approached her. "Arianna, I want to say again that I am sorry." I reached for her hand. She allowed me to take it, but she did not move closer to me. "Truly, I am sorry."

"I know you are sorry." She pulled her hand away. "I need to shower."

I stepped aside, and she went into the bathroom and closed the door. I went back to my study. Obviously, she needed more time. I sat at my desk and pretended to work, but I listened to her movements. She dressed and then went downstairs and ate breakfast. When I heard her rinsing her breakfast dishes and putting them in the dishwasher, I went downstairs.

"Are you going to the college now?" I asked.

"Yes, I am almost ready." She put a sandwich and several drinks in her lunch bag. "What do you plan to do today?"

"I have more revisions to make. I may go over to Marie's house as well."

She nodded. "Ok. I plan to be on campus most of the day."

"If you need me, call, and I will come to the school."

"Have a good day." She picked up her lunch bag, computer bag, and purse, and she left the house. I stood in the front room and watched as she backed out of the driveway and drove down the street.

I picked up my keys and got in my car. I needed to pick up some things, but first, I needed to make sure Arianna was safe. I drove to the college and spotted her car pulling into a faculty lot. I circled around and saw her walking up the stairs into the building where her office was located. I felt foolish. No one would attack her in broad daylight on a city street, but I could not help myself. I had to know she was safe. I drove off campus and went downtown to the florist. My first stop.

I texted Arianna several times during the day, and she replied, so I was hopeful that she was not as mad at me. I greeted her at the door when she arrived home late that afternoon. "Hi. How was your day?"

"Busy, but good," she replied. Her voice was pleasant, and that gave me more hope that things were back to normal. She came inside and put her computer bag on the table in the hallway. I took her coat and hung it up while she went in the kitchen.

"Thank you," she said when I walked into the kitchen. She smiled at me. On the table was a rotisserie chicken and potato salad for her dinner.

"Sit and eat. I will pour the wine." She nodded and sat down. "I didn't think you would want to cook after working all day."

"Thank you." She smiled again. "You always take care of me, James."

I set down a glass of wine for her. She put chicken and a large dollop of potato salad on her plate and began to eat.

I sat down and took a big swallow of wine. "What did you do on campus today?" I asked.

"I worked at the welcome desk a good part of the day. They were short staffed because classes began today. I went to a meeting, and I also met several other faculty members. Everyone is very friendly."

"That's great," I replied.

She finished most of the chicken and all the potato salad. I stood up, went to the freezer, and took out a tub of chocolate ice cream. "Dessert?"

"Yes, please," she said with a smile.

After dinner, Arianna went into her office to check her email. On her desk was a bouquet of pink and white roses. I propped a card up against the vase. It had two words. 'I'm sorry,' and I drew a sad face. She worked in her office for about an hour. I sat in my den and read. "I'm going to shower," she said as she walked by and then went upstairs. I wasn't sure if that was an invitation to join her. I hoped it was, but I was not sure.

On her dresser in our bedroom was a bouquet of red roses. There were three words on this card. 'I Love You' and I drew a happy face. Once I heard her in the shower, I took a bottle of wine out of the chiller, grabbed two glasses, and went upstairs. I turned on the fireplace in our bedroom. I opened the bottle of wine when Arianna was drying her hair.

"Wine?" I asked when she came out of the bathroom.

"Please." She sat down next to me on the sofa. "The roses are beautiful. Thank you."

"I am glad you like them." I handed her a glass. "Arianna." She turned her head toward me. "I am so sorry. I did not mean what I said. I hurt you, and I have no excuse. The only explanation I have for what I said is jealousy." I shook my head and sighed.

She took a deep breath. "You have no reason to be jealous." She leaned over and kissed me gently. "I love you. Please never doubt that."

I kissed her eagerly. "I cannot say it enough. I am so sorry."

She took my glass and set both glasses on the table. She sat back and opened her robe. She wore nothing underneath it. I took in her exquisite beauty. I loved her so much it hurt. I could not bear living without her, and lately it seemed there was always someone trying to separate us. I longed to take her someplace far away where we could be alone. She leaned over and whispered mischievously in my ear. "You know, people say make up sex is the best kind of sex."

I smiled and kissed her. "Well, I need to start making up to you." I slipped the robe off her shoulders. Ever so lightly I ran my fingers over her skin as I kissed my way down her body. A soft sigh escaped her lips. I ran my hands over her hips and up to her breasts, and she let out a small moan. She ran her fingers through my hair and then guided my head up.

"I want to bond with you, Arianna." I gently moved her hair to the side. I laid tiny kisses up her neck and over to her ear. I kissed her forehead, then her nose, and then I kissed her lips. I looked into her eyes.

She nodded. "I am yours. Never forget it." She tilted her head back exposing her neck to me.

I lowered my head and kissed her very gently. I breathed in her scent imprinting it in my mind. "I love you," I whispered. I moved my lips over her soft skin. I took another breath and then bit her. I tasted her warm blood as it pooled in my mouth and flowed into me. She moaned and ran her hands over my shoulders, and then she tangled her fingers in my hair pressing my head closer to her. I withdrew my fangs and ran my tongue over the bite to seal it.

In a quick move, Arianna reversed our positions. I felt her breath and her lips on my skin, and without any hesitation at all, she bit me. Her hand went behind my head to hold me close.

I let out a deep sigh. "We are one, Arianna."

Chapter XXVIII
Inheritance Accepted

Arianna

I leaned back and looked into James' eyes. We truly were one again. He slid off the sofa and onto the soft fur rug in front of the fireplace. He reached up and ran his hands up my thighs. I could not stop the moan that escaped me. I loved him so much. He pulled me down to him, and I slid my hands inside his shirt and took it off.

"Let me make up to you by making love to you." He took a pillow off the sofa then very gently eased me back and put it under my head.

"I don't like when we fight, James."

"I don't either. I am deeply sorry, Arianna."

If he said anything else, I didn't hear it. I was lost in the sensations coursing through my body at his feather light touch.

When James said he was going to make it up to me, he meant it. For several hours, we kissed and caressed one another. Over and over again he pleasured me, and I pleasured him.

Content in the love we shared, we laid on the rug, and watched the fire. It crackled and burned and cast a red glow over us. I rested my head on James' chest, and he had his arms wrapped around my body. He softly kissed my head. "I love you."

I sat up and placed my hands on his chest. I looked into his eyes. "I love you too." I leaned forward and kissed him then rested my head back on his shoulder.

His fingers slid up and down my back igniting my body everywhere he touched. "Should we move to the bed? Do you want to sleep?"

"Soon. I like laying here in front of the fire with you."

James pulled me in tighter.

I took a deep breath. It was so peaceful here. Why couldn't life always be like this?

"I have been thinking about the wolves, about being a hunter…" I said softly trailing off when I was not certain how to proceed.

James tilted my head up a bit and looked at me. He quietly waited.

"I can't deny what I am." I took a deep breath and continued. "I want to stay out of the politics of everything, but I can't. Can I?"

James gave me a sad look and let out a sigh. He reached up and tucked a strand of hair behind my ear. "I'm sorry, but no. It doesn't matter if you want to be involved or not, Arianna. You are a vampire hunter. No matter what you do, you cannot change it."

"Jason told me to go home, but I didn't want to just sit and wait for one of them to attack me. I didn't want to stay inside while others protected me." I closed my eyes. "I would feel guilty if I was safe and someone got hurt. That's why I went with Jason and Trey into the forest."

"It's a good thing you didn't go home. I have a feeling there might have been other vampires waiting and hoping to get you alone."

"You think so?"

"I do. Obviously, someone compelled a neighbor. Jacob or Tony or whoever it was simply waited for a neighbor to leave town." James looked at me. "I think Jacob used the time we were away to set up his plan."

I sat up and reached over for my glass of wine. I took a large swallow. "You think that is why they had Albert call me and ask me to come to the wedding."

"You did say it was unusual."

I nodded my head. "It definitely was, but I guess I hoped it was because of Patty's influence."

"We don't know anything for certain." James picked up his wine glass and drank the contents down.

"I am going to start taking a more active role with the wolves," I informed James.

He sat up and poured each of us more wine. "If that is what you want, then that is what you should do."

I smiled at him. "Thank you." James was always incredibly supportive. He was not one of those men who had to be in charge all the time. He might be a bit overprotective at times, and I knew it was his overprotectiveness that brought out jealousy and doubt, but so what? Everyone had faults. It was James' other qualities that were important. I knew he respected me and supported my decisions. I knew he loved me as much as I loved him, and I knew he would put his life on the line to protect me as I would to protect him.

I reached up and ran my fingers through his hair. I needed the physical contact. He took my hand and kissed my palm and then kissed each finger.

"James, I would like you to come with me to talk to Marie tomorrow. I need and want your support."

"And you have it, love."

"I know I do. I'm sorry I was so angry."

"I'm sorry I was so jealous."

"I was angry, but now that I think about it."

"What?" he asked. "Tell me."

"Not that I am condoning jealousy or violence." I gave him a stern look. "But it was kind of exciting to see you throw Jason and act all macho protecting me."

James smiled and ran his finger up my arm, across my collarbone, and up my neck. "You like macho?"

"Maybe a little, and only at certain times."

James laughed. "Ok. You tell me when, and I will beat my chest and protect my woman."

I cupped his chin in my hand. "You are always protecting me because you love me. I will protect you because I love you."

"We are a team," James replied softly.

I picked up my glass of wine and so did James. I clinked my glass to his and we drank. I felt we came to an understanding tonight. Relationship growing pains. That was normal.

"James, do you think Marie will be offended because I want to assume my role within the society?"

"No. Arianna, I assure you, Marie will not be offended in the least."

"The three of us can go see John and tell him that I want to be updated directly."

"Well, John will be happy. He doesn't like reporting to a vampire," James laughed.

"Well, I have news for him. He is going to continue to report to a vampire. I still want Marie to be in charge. This is her territory, and I will defer to her judgement. I will tell John to report to Marie, and he is also to report to either you or me depending on which of us is available."

James laughed. "That won't make him happy."

"I'm not the one who set up the rules in this society. As per the treaty, he is supposed to defer to my authority and carry out my wishes."

James looked at me. "Maybe Redman's example of leadership has rubbed off on you," he said seriously, but I saw he held back a smile. "You can be scary sometimes." He leaned over and kissed me.

"Maybe I like the power."

"It looks good on you. I will follow you anywhere, Arianna, my love." He kissed me again.

"After we get everything settled with the wolves, I will call Giovanni and tell him what is going on."

"Giovanni will be very happy with your decision."

"I know." I shifted and sat up straighter. James pulled me to him and kissed me long and hard. When I recovered, I smiled at him. "What was that for?"

"For your strength and wisdom. And your diplomacy. You, Arianna, are an incredibly wise and compassionate woman."

"Thank you." I finished my wine and set my glass down. James did the same.

Something else bothered me. "James, when that vampire bit me, is it possible he also ingested some of my blood?"

James nodded. "I thought the same thing. It is possible. And I am worried."

I let out a sigh. "I am too. Giovanni said hunters have the ability to block vampires."

"Yes, remember you blocked Marie at the ball when she tried to compel Mrs. Ballard."

"But I don't know how I did it, and I need to learn how to consciously block someone. I need to speak with Giovanni, and I need you to help me."

"Of course. I will help you any way I can."

James stood up, reached a hand down to me, and pulled me up. "Tomorrow looks to be another busy day, love. You should rest." He picked me up, walked to the bed, and moved the covers down. He kissed me, placed me very gently on our bed, and then laid down by my side.

I rolled on my side and looked at James. He pulled the sheet and the comforter up to cover us. I slowly traced my fingers lightly over his bare chest. "Tomorrow is hours away, James," I whispered as my fingers continued to travel up and down his body.

He pulled me up on top of him and wrapped me in his arms. "Arianna," he breathed as his lips met mine. "Let me make love to you all night."

"Oh, I like that idea." We continued to kiss. "James," I paused, "I love you."

He rolled us over. He framed my face with his hands and stared into my eyes. "And I love you, Forever."

Chapter XXIX
Something to Celebrate – Epilogue I

James

The next few weeks were remarkably calm. Arianna and I settled into our routines. She practiced blocking Jason, so he could not see her visions. I hated to admit that Jason bonding with Arianna might be beneficial, but he would be able to find her quickly if she were in danger. I pushed thoughts of Jason away and got to work.

Several hours later, I typed The End. I stretched and looked at the satisfying words on the page. This was the second revision, and I believed the novel was ready for final edits. I stood up and went downstairs. Arianna was working in her office.

She looked up as I entered the room. "Finished?"

"I think so."

"Oh, congratulations!" She stood up and hugged me. "We should celebrate."

I kissed her deeply. She was all I ever needed to celebrate.

"I'm serious." She leaned back. Her lips were red from kissing and her eyes were hazy. "I am going to call Marie, and we are going to take you out on the town tonight." She gave me a peck on the lips and picked up her phone.

While Arianna called Marie, I looked at her computer screen. The chapter title *Wolves and Shifters* stared back at me.

"It's settled. Marie is coming over in a couple of hours so you two can hunt, and we are going into Boston tonight to celebrate." She looked from me to her screen and back. "Read it and tell me what you think?"

The chapter on wolves was funny. She used her own story of thinking she found a puppy when in reality it was a shifter in wolf form.

"I like it," I laughed. "Are you making the book autobiographical?"

"No," she chuckled, "but you have to admit it was a funny story."

I wrapped my arms around her and kissed her again. "Will you come with Marie and I when we hunt?"

"Hum, yes," she broke off as I kissed my way down her neck to her shoulder. I flicked open the buttons of her shirt and continued to kiss my way down her body.

"I want you," I whispered. She tangled her hands in my hair and moaned as I sucked on her breast. "Can I?" I kissed my way up to her mouth again.

"Yes," she sighed.

I lifted her up and carried her to the sofa in my den. I gently set her down. Her shirt fell open, and I took in her beautiful body. She watched me intensely as I quickly undressed. I leaned over her and took her mouth in a possessive kiss. She groaned when I leaned back. I kept eye contact with her as I grabbed her leggings at both sides of her waist and pulled them and her panties off in one swift motion.

She gasped in surprise, and her eyes opened wide. "James," she murmured as I claimed her body and mouth. Her arms wrapped around me and held me tight as we began to move together.

*****

Arianna brushed her hair and put it in a ponytail.

The doorbell rang. "Marie, come in," I called.

"Arianna, I am glad you are hunting with us." Marie watched Arianna put on her hiking boots.

I zipped up my fleece jacket and the three of us got in the car.

Most of the snow melted, but there were still small piles in the deeply shaded areas. The hawks were active, and Arianna picked one up quickly. It flew ahead and found a small herd of deer.

"Your abilities are convenient, Arianna," Marie laughed. "I think you should try to get your own deer today. There are several smaller animals."

"Ok." Her voice was shaky.

I saw Marie's shocked expression, but she did not comment.

I surveyed the herd. "That small animal." I pointed to an older doe.

She nodded and concentrated. I knew Arianna was mentally reviewing the steps I taught her. I was glad she finally agreed that she needed to learn to hunt on her own just in case she was ever in a situation when she needed food.

I signaled to Marie and looked at Arianna. "Ready?"

She wiped her palms on the front of her jeans and nodded but kept her focus on the animal.

"Go." The three of us jumped at once. I was watching Arianna, and I nearly missed my target.

She felled the animal easily. She stood up and just beamed with pride. "I did it!"

"You did," I replied happily.

Later, as we walked back to the car, Jason appeared. "Arianna," he called as he approached. He nodded to me and Marie but did not address us. Two others showed up in wolf form. "I planned to stop at your house on my way home and give you a report, but we picked up your scent before we left the forest."

"Is everything ok?" Arianna asked.

"No sign of anyone in the area," Jason informed her.

"Great," she replied. "Oh, Jason, we are going into Boston to celebrate James finishing his novel. I don't expect to be home until very early in the morning."

Jason looked at me and then at Marie. "The three of you are going?"

"Yes." Arianna nodded.

"Be careful Arianna," he warned. "I will have the night patrol expand out further tonight." Jason walked right up to me and looked me in the eye. "Take care of her."

I stared back at him. His attitude angered me, but I was not going to show him anger. I smiled. "Of course."

Jason walked backward, then he turned, and the three of them left the area.

Arianna stood with her hands on her hips. "Men." She shook her head then looked at Marie. "Too much testosterone."

Marie burst out laughing.

Epilogue II

Arianna

Marie went home, dressed, and arrived at our house exactly at eight o'clock. I heard James open the door. "I haven't been out at night in Boston in many years," I overheard Marie say. She sounded excited which for Marie was unusual.

I walked out of the bedroom. "Hi, Marie," I called from the top of the stairs. "Would you come up? I want you to look at the jewelry from my Great Grandfather."

Marie came upstairs and followed me into the bedroom. She looked at my locket but did not touch it. "That really is a beautiful piece of jewelry, Arianna."

"Thank you. I like to wear it for special occasions. The Fall really got away from me. My mother brought these items when she visited in October. I only started to go through them this week."

Marie looked over the pieces I laid out on the dresser. "None of them are enchanted."

"That's good. I guess."

She glanced at the small box on the dresser. "That is an unusual piece."

"It is. My great grandfather gave it to me when I was young to keep my coins."

"May I?"

I nodded yes. She lifted the top which had an ornate wood inlay in a diamond design. Inside were a few half dollars and an assortment of coins. She lifted off the tray full of coins. "What is that?"

"Oh, that's an old key. I have no idea what it is to. It has always been in there. Why?"

"The key. It glows blue. It is enchanted." She pointed to it but did not touch it.

I reached in and took out the key. "So, I have two enchanted objects." It was more statement than question.

"It appears so. Like your locket, there is a protection spell on it." She paused, reached out her hand, and held it over the key, but she did not touch it.

"Your great grandfather certainly was an interesting man," James muttered. He looked at Marie. "Is something wrong?"

She lowered her hand. "No." She shook her head. She looked perplexed, but she stepped back.

I closed the box with the coins. "Well, let's not let this new revelation keep us from having a good time."

We went downstairs and got in the car. At first, we were quiet, but gradually we started chatting while James sped into Boston. He parked the car, and we walked over to Hanover Street. There was a line at the door of our first destination, but Marie walked up to the bouncer, and we were admitted right away.

"Better not try that when Giovanni is around," I laughed.

Marie and I took off our coats while James flagged a waiter. A few minutes later, the waiter returned to our table with a bottle of champagne. We waited while he poured us each a glass.

I lifted my glass. "Congratulations on the publication of your first novel, James."

"And much success," Marie added.

"Thank you both."

We touched our glasses together and drank.

The End

Thank you for reading *Inheritance Accepted*. If you enjoyed the story, please leave a review on Amazon or Goodreads. A review is the best way to thank and author for a story you loved.

Arianna's story continues in *Inheritance Quest*. Her and James' relationship continues to grow, and Arianna moves closer to discovering the secrets surrounding her great grandfather and her family's past.

Cheryl A. Hunter writes in several genres including Contemporary Fiction, Historical Fiction, and Paranormal Fiction.

Visit her Amazon Author's Page for a list of books available and to read excerpts. https://www.amazon.com/Cheryl-A-Hunter/e/B07K657RKJ/ref=aufs_dp_fta_dsk

Sign up for Cheryl's newsletter and receive a free bonus chapter to *Inheritance Accepted* as well as other bonus chapters. When you sign up, you will also be the first to learn about new releases, bonus chapters, and special promotions.

Visit Cheryl's website: http://www.cherylahunter.com/

Follow her on Facebook: CherylAHunter

Follow her on Twitter: @CherylAHunter4